BREAKTHROUGH

One Cop, Two Pasts, Three Murders.

SHANE MCCABE

ISBN: 978-1-949570-97-7 (Paperback)

Z COMM MEDIA
www.zcommedia.com

PREFACE

A NUMBER OF YEARS AGO, I was watching a crime thriller on television when a line of dialogue jumped out at me. That line went something like "The DNA is back...perfect match." I cannot remember exactly which show it was or which character delivered the line, but I do remember thinking at the time, *How convenient* . I thought how much more interesting it would have been had the DNA been compromised or failed to match.

Then an unusual thought struck me. What if the DNA of the victim turned out to be an exact match to that of the perpetrator? Now that would be interesting. At that time, I had written two feature screenplays and had just received funding to produce my first short movie, *Never Judge a Book* . All throughout preproduction on *Never Judge a Book*, this DNA conundrum kept niggling at me. I had begun to flesh out a new feature script based on this one line of dialogue, but the question was still there. How can I make this work? How could the DNA of the perpetrator possibly match that of the victim?

Suddenly the answer hit me, and after shooting *Never Judge a Book*, I wrote *Breakthrough*, a 125-page screenplay. For those of you familiar with writing scripts, you will all be aware of the often-dreaded Treatment phase of screenwriting. Personally, I love this particular exercise. In writing my script *Breakthrough*, I wrote, by my own standards, an unusually long treatment. I remember thinking at the time, *Hey, this could make a good novel*.

But I ploughed on, eager to finish my script. My short film, *Never Judge a Book*, was directed by my good friend Jason Forde and employs an unusual structure in that I wrote it in reverse chronological flashback and book-ended it in the present. Basically, the movie starts, and we are 80 percent into the story. The audience is presented with an event and made to believe one thing. Through a series of five flashbacks, we rewind the clock so that we end up at the beginning. We then return to where we started, only this time, the audience has a completely different perspective on things. My screenplay, *Breakthrough*, employs the same structural format.

I have, to date, written ten feature movies, one of which will hopefully begin production in 2022 . Screenwriting is an all-consuming passion for me. From getting the first spark of a new idea to fleshing out characters, developing the backstory, locking off my ending, mapping out my scene heading, to deciding who will live and who will die, I find the whole process totally captivating.

So in writing this, my first novel, I have attempted to bring this passion and experience of screenwriting and apply it to the modern novel. This book was written in a manner that will enable the reader to explore the story at a cinematic level over three acts, employing the functions of screenplay dialogue to explore the backstory while moving the plot ahead and foreshadowing what is to come. The only major change I have made is to structure it in a linear manner.

I did not do this to try and be clever. I did it because I wanted to give the reader an altogether different experience. In addition, I have set this story in 2004, before the advent of social media and smartphones. Thank you for having purchased my book. I hope you are not disappointed.

Shane McCabe

BREAKTHROUGH

CHAPTER 1

JOE MASON NEVER HEARD THE shot. It was as though some kind of invisible force had simply picked him up and thrown him across the room, knocking the breath out of his body and temporarily blinding him. But what had hit him was not invisible. It was a small-grain hollow-point nine-millimeter bullet. The piece of lead had exited the barrel of the Glock automatic, expanding the air as it travelled at a velocity of over fifteen hundred feet per second, striking him high on the chest, lifting him off his feet, and sending him crashing down on the living room coffee table, splintering the wood and shattering the glass. In a fraction of a second, the bullet had ripped through cloth, flesh, and bone, fragmenting into three pieces, the largest of which now rested beside his heart. Joe knew, in that instant, what it would be like to have a heart attack.

Was he having a heart attack? His breath was gone, and he couldn't see. The entire left side of his body felt numb. It was as though he had been hit with a sledgehammer.

He tried to take short shallow breaths. Nothing. His lungs now screamed for oxygen. He moved his right hand to his chest—the slight movement somehow enabling his breath to return. He gasped as air rushed into his lungs. He felt something strange. A thick oily substance oozed through his fingers. The substance continued to pour, soaking his shirt. It puzzled him for a moment, this warm, sticky liquid.

Blood, he thought.

Then he heard it. A scream! A high-pitched, terrifying scream that seemed to go on forever as it penetrated every fiber of his being, shocking his system. Then it stopped, only to be repeated, this time

1

the pitch even higher. Joe Mason's body went cold. It was a kid's scream. A kid! Oh god, his kid. His little girl, Kell!

At once, a thousand thoughts flooded his mind, racing, merging, each thought pushing itself to the surface, seeking supremacy. Where was she? Why was he on the floor? Why could he not move? What was she afraid of? Was she hurt?

The realization struck him. Suddenly it became clear. Suddenly he remembered.

He remembered Kell opening the door. He had heard a noise, like the scuffling of feet, and had walked through from the kitchen to the living room. A man had stood there, a gloved hand wrapped around Kell's mouth. Joe felt his chest again. Blood! His life's blood. The same blood that coursed through Kell's veins. The same blood that would now be spilt. Why had he not sent her home yesterday? She was supposed to have gone yesterday. She had begged him to let her stay. God, he saw so little of her these days, and she was growing up so fast.

"Okay, one more day, but you had better clear it with your mom," he had said.

She had smiled, her dark eyes dazzling him. Kell had thrown her arms around him and hugged him. "Take the day off, Daddy, take the day off work," she had urged as she lifted her jet-black hair out of her face. How could he have refused such a pretty face? His baby! He loved her so much, he felt his heart would burst.

But now he was lying on his living room floor—dying. Yes, he knew now his time was short. But where was Kell?

Some of his sight had returned. It was no twenty-twenty vision, but he could discern shapes. He was vaguely aware of a figure standing close to him. Then the scream came again. Kell! *No!* he thought. *God, no, don't let this happen!* His mind screamed. He tried to move. The muscles in his legs simply would not obey the nerve impulses being sent by his brain.

Then he saw him. A figure, dressed in black, had turned to follow Kell. Follow her? She was running. *Yes*, he thought. She had the sense to run. She was young and fast. Her tennis coach had said that it was her main weapon, her speed. Kell was relentless on the courts. Nothing was a lost cause. She could run down any ball.

God, please let her get to the door, he prayed. *Let her get outside. There would be people out there. People walking, people shopping, people coming and going to work. Children going to school, as she should have been. Why did I not send her home yesterday? Please let her get to the door, to the busy world of early morning.*

But Kell Mason never made it outside. She had bitten down hard on the hand that had covered her mouth. She had first tasted leather and then blood as her teeth sank deep into flesh, puncturing the skin. The gunman had simply slapped her aside, splitting her lip with the butt of his automatic. As Kell hit the floor, she heard the shot. It was a low, muffled noise—more like a spit—the silencer attached to the end of the Glock having its desired effect.

Kell Mason froze as her father flew through the air. Horrified, she watched as her father lay motionless about ten to fifteen feet away. The gunman started to walk over toward him. Kell knew instantly that he would fire again. She had screamed as she struggled to her feet, desperate to attract his attention. She needed to get him away from her father. But in her panic and confusion, she had run upstairs. Reaching the small landing, Kell realized that she'd made a mistake. The gunman was much stronger and quicker than the sixteen-year-old . Taking the stairs three at a time, he'd caught up to her as she'd tried to push her bedroom door closed, her hands eager to slide across the small brass bolt. Kell had screamed again as he'd kicked the door, breaking it from its hinges, catching her full force in the face, sending her backward.

Lying on the floor with tear-streaked cheeks, her head numb from the pain, Kell looked up at her powerful assailant. The gunman walked briskly over to her. He caught her by the throat, picking her up and flinging her down on her bed. *Yeah*, thought the gunman, his hand still stinging from the bite. He'd have some fun with this little bitch.

Down below, Joe Mason lay motionless as blood continued to pour from his wound. The paralysis he'd felt moments earlier was now spreading over his entire body. Straining his head, he could just about hear the sound of footsteps above him.

His heart sank.

Kell's scream was ear-piercing as it filled the house, echoing around the rooms. And then...the strangest thing...a light! It was as though someone had shone a powerful strobe light directly into his eyes—a blinding bright yellow flash that lasted only a second or so.

Upstairs, another gunshot.

A dark world closed in on Joe Mason...

CHAPTER 2

THE EARLY MORNING SUN WAS a fluorescent orange fireball, its rays bouncing off the glass windows of some of the world's tallest buildings, its arc not yet high enough to cast a shadow on the streets below, but the temperature was already on the rise. Early September was a beautiful time in New York. Fall had always been her favorite season, and now, as she drove down through the busy streets of Midtown Manhattan, heading east on Fifty-Ninth Street toward Columbus Circle and Central Park, Rache Fischer's mind wandered back to another September morning. *Had it really been three years?* Rache thought to herself. She looked at the sun and thought back to the morning when another fireball had lit up the Manhattan skyline. Rache shook her head in an effort to dispel these thoughts.

Never good to dwell too long on the past, she figured.

The past. Funny how we can never get away from it. It forms us, shapes us, and molds us. How strange that a single moment in time can change everything we are and everything we can become.

As she pulled up behind a yellow cab, Rache reflected on the past for a moment. We are who we are today because of decisions made in the past. One cannot exist without the other. The past is like the foundations on which we build the pillars of our future. Yet our present becomes our past in the moment it takes us to comprehend it. Our future becomes a projection, based on past experiences, which in themselves are transitions from our present. So all we really have is our present. *Enjoy the frigging morning without becoming a bloody philosopher, Fischer,* Rache told herself as she gambled on a red light.

But she found this easier said than done. She thought back again. Not to three years back, when terrorists had flown two hijacked commercial airliners into the Twin Towers of the World Trade Center, but to fourteen years before that. It had been seventeen years ago this very month that one single decision had swept away her old life and introduced her to a new one. A life so at odds with all she had experienced before—a new, harsh, brutal, unfair, and totally unjust life. One decision, reflected Rache, and the world becomes divided in two. Time before and time after! As a young fifteen-year-old, it had taken her months to realize she could do nothing about time before, but she would burn in hell if she did not at least try to make a difference about time after. And here she was, seventeen years on, a New York City homicide detective.

At thirty-two, Rache Fischer was well above average-looking. Long blonde hair framed a sallow complexion that belied her age. She had the body and the looks that could stop a conversation at twenty paces and had done so on many an occasion. In her early twenties, Rache had been approached more than once by various talent scouts from some of New York's top model agencies. Her answer had always been polite but firm. Thanks, but no thanks. There was one occasion when a scout had become so insistent that she actually had to pull out her badge. But Rache Fischer was not vain. In fact, she never gave her appearance too much thought. She was athletic and made sure she worked out to keep in shape. For Rache, it was simple; she stayed in shape because of her job.

Rache had left home straight out of high school, not waiting to hear her results, and had graduated in absentia. She had applied to most of the top colleges. But it had only been a ruse. She had never intended to take any offer and had entered the New York Police Academy one month after her eighteenth birthday. The previous day, her brother David had called with the news that Rache had graduated top of her class.

"For the love of God, Rachel, you can pick any college you want!" David had shouted down the phone.

Four years her senior, David Fischer had graduated with honors from Princeton and had secured a place with the firm of Fleischmann-Bennett and Associates. David had been a good student, but had needed to work night and day just to keep pace with his peers. Even now, just out of high school, his little sister could hold her own with him in any legal argument. She could quote laws and precedents he'd never heard of. That was why it had come as a huge blow to the family to discover Rache had joined the New York Police Academy. Her father, Ira, couldn't bring himself to talk to her. Her mother was in deep shock.

"Please, Rachel, just consider it," David had pleaded.

But Rache was never going to budge. Too much had happened. And now, fourteen years on, she was a homicide detective with six years' experience and a 100 percent conviction rate. Word had gotten around fast. If Rache Fischer had you in her sights, no lawyer wanted to tangle with her.

Rache had spent her first four years at the Seventh Precinct on the Lower East Side, with its historic Jewish neighborhood. It was a shock to many of the community to find "a young Jewish girl" wearing the uniform of the New York Police Department. But Rache had not worn the uniform long. By the age of twenty-three, she had headed up her own unit within the vice squad and, three years later, had become the youngest female homicide detective in Manhattan.

"Look, over there!" The distinctive Irish brogue woke her from her reverie. The voice belonged to her passenger, Danny O'Connor. A shade over six feet with graying hair, Danny carried a few pounds too many, something he was reluctant to admit. His family had immigrated to New York over forty years ago, but Danny had never lost his Irish brogue. It was one of the many things Rache liked about him. That and the fact he never bullshitted people. Danny would always call it as it was. The world had gone mad with political correctness, but Danny "never went in for dat bollix." Rache had spent many years trying to get him to explain the origin of the word. Danny never did. But she knew she could trust him. She knew if she were in a tight corner, she would rather have Danny at her back than anyone else on the force, no question. She supposed that that was the reason they had been paired together for over five years now.

"You'll miss it," he said, teasing her.

Rache gunned the sedan, tires screeching, across traffic, and then she stopped and reversed into a parking space.

Danny glanced out the window at a big church that loomed large and whose grounds seemed to stretch forever.

Rache laughed. "You were saying?"

"Lawbreaker," said Danny as he looked at her.

Rache laughed even more. "Lawbreaker, me?" she scoffed. "What is that stuff anyway?" She glanced at Danny's knee.

Danny looked down at a small neatly wrapped package. "Black-and-white pudding from Clonakilty, County Cork."

Rache shook her head.

"Look," Danny said, pointing to the church, "Fr. John is my uncle on my mother's side. She was back home in Ireland for a wee vacation, and she brought him back the pudding. He loves the stuff."

"It's contraband, Danny. FDA could arrest her, and you'd have to answer to the Captain," retorted Rache as Danny began to open his door.

"Yeah, yeah," he mumbled. He turned to her. "You coming?"

"To a church?"

Danny shook his head and climbed out of the car.

Rache watched as Danny opened the huge iron gates, taking care not to drop his package. Settling back in her seat, she stared up at the church. Saint Killian's, on Fifty-Eighth and Eight, was indeed huge. Consecrated on Easter Sunday 1856, its massive neo-Gothic spire had once dominated the skyline of Midtown Manhattan. It had taken over seventeen years to build, each stone being hand-cut, and it contained one of the oldest cemeteries in Manhattan. But it all meant nothing to Rache. Sure, as a building it was impressive, but that's all it was. A building.

Rache watched as one or two people walked down the worn granite steps. *Lost souls*, she thought, *praying to a god who, if he were listening, didn't care or had wax in his ears*. What possessed people to place their trust in something so devoid of logic, Rache could never understand.

Rache closed her eyes a moment. She felt a fleeting pang of guilt. She knew it had not always been this way. As a young girl, she had always looked forward to school on the Shabbat. Although not strictly orthodox, Ira Fischer had accepted no excuses. His children would not become like the others, people who only paid lip service to a belief that meant something. His own mother had survived the death camps in Poland. God had spared her; she had always told Rache. But God hadn't spared Rache. Seventeen years ago, God hadn't spared her or her sister, Ruth. Since that day, she had refused to set foot inside a synagogue, church, or temple. This had caused untold hardship at home. Looking back, she wondered how her parents ever stayed together. It was, in some ways, a minor miracle. Rache smiled at the irony of her thoughts.

"Two-niner, what's your twenty, over?"

She opened her eyes. The police radio had made her jump. *What is it with me today? Stop the damn daydreaming, will ya?* she told herself.

Picking up the radio, Rache cleared her throat. "Two-niner, we're outside St. Killian's on Fifty-Eighth and—"

"Danny gone for absolution again, Rache?" the dispatch voice of Martha Banks boomed at her.

Rache began to smile. "Yeah, something like…"

Then she saw it. It was brief but unmistakable. It had only been a quick glimpse in the side mirror, but Rache's eye was not that of the average person. Years working in vice had seen to that. No way she'd confuse a slap across the face for anything but what it was.

"Rache, you still there?" Martha asked.

"Yeah, yeah. Martha, I gotta take a look at something…" Rache's voice trailed off.

Martha giggled. "Don't get too close to that church, d'ya hear. We don't want ya burning up on us."

But Rache didn't hear. She was already out of the car.

Jason Patrick Summerville, or Mr. Jakes, as he liked to be called by his bitches, was a nasty pimp. At five feet two inches, what he lacked in height, he more than made up for in viciousness. He'd beat a girl for no reason. "Gotta let dem bitches know who's boss, know I'm sayin'," was his catchphrase. Today, it was the turn of Jessie Adams. Jessie had been working for Mr. Jakes for six weeks. Originally from Kentucky, she had met Mr. Jakes at a club. He had liked her accent, and although she was eighteen, she looked much younger—something that held a certain appeal for Mr. Jakes. Jessie had had little money when she'd arrived, and what she did have was soon gone. That's when she'd met Mr. Jakes. He had been so sweet, finding her a place to stay and then loaning her money. But it had all come at a price, and before long, she had paid that price. Overnight he'd changed. From this sweet guy, he'd turned into the Antichrist. She couldn't believe it. But the cold reality of her situation had bitten her quickly. He had repeatedly raped and beaten her, forcing her to engage in a multitude of seriously depraved sex acts, often with three or four men. Now her spirit was broken. She had begun to feel the life ebb from her body as the realization had set in that Mr. Jakes now owned her. For the past two days she'd been ill. She hadn't been able to get out of bed. Just this morning she had passed blood.

The alley at the back of the church was rarely used. It ran the entire length of the church grounds. Years ago, the church had taken deliveries via the alley, but when the priests moved into a new parish residence, no one had bothered to use it. It had been blocked off at one end due to ongoing construction work. So it now had only one way in and one way out. It had become a haunt for junkies looking to score. The homeless and destitute frequented it when there were no beds at the Mission. Now, halfway down, among overgrown weeds and discarded junk, Jessie Adams lay on her side, her pretty young face contorted in agony. Mr. Jakes stood above her, kicking her viciously in the ribs. Each kick followed a word in his sentence as he showed her no mercy.

"You ain't"—*kick*—"been"—*kick*—"working"—*kick*—"bitch!" he screamed. Each blow rained down harder than the last. Mr. Jakes paused, more to catch his breath than any desire to show Jessie mercy.

Jessie cried at his feet as he stood above her, his chest heaving from his recent display of unadulterated viciousness.

He pulled her violently to her feet, punching her in the stomach, knocking the last of the breath out of her frail body. Jessie doubled over in agony. "Please, please," she begged, tears streaming down her cheeks. She didn't think she could take anymore. "I've been ill!" she cried, coughing blood onto her clothes.

Realizing he had made his point, Mr. Jakes went to wipe her eyes. "See, it's a question of e-co-nom-ics." He said the word slowly, pronouncing each syllable, as though he were some kind of authority. "No need to be crying. Customers don't want to be seeing no tears, girl."

Jessie tried to back away, not knowing what was coming next.

"Where you going, girl?"

Rache had caught the last few moments of the beating, and it had utterly repulsed her. She slinked, catlike, down the alley, hugging the wall, her gun drawn, almost daring not to breathe. She had wanted the element of surprise.

The cold barrel of Rache's Beretta 92F nine-millimeter police special pressed against the back of his head, digging into his scalp. Rache pushed it so hard that it caused Mr. Jakes to bend forward. At the same time, she flashed her badge in his face.

"You touch her again, and you're a fucking organ donor," she said, shoving him to the ground. Flipping her cop's ID closed, she pushed it into the back pocket of her pants.

Mr. Jakes struggled on all fours.

Jessie backed up a little to get out of his way, her eyes fixed on Rache, who never took her gun off Mr. Jakes. This was the first time in her life a cop had done anything for her.

Rache turned to Jessie. "You okay?" Rache asked.

Jessie could only stare back at Rache, her mind a swirl of confusion. Christ, Mr. Jakes would be pissed. But looking at this cop now almost made the beating worthwhile. Her ribs had begun to ache. She was sure he'd broken some. Mr. Jakes was still on all fours. If she had the gun, there was no doubt she'd have already emptied the clip. Jessie began to fantasize about killing him.

"Got a name?" Rache shouted over.

Jessie was still in shock. "J...Jessie," she stuttered.

Mr. Jakes scrambled to his feet. He couldn't let this bitch away with it. Jesus, if word got back that he was taken by a bitch... He rose to his full height, which was a good couple of inches shorter than Rache. Mr. Jakes looked ridiculous as he tried to square up to her. Even though the pain in her ribs had become more acute now,

Jessie allowed herself a giggle. She winced. Her discomfort was not lost on Rache.

"You crazy bitch. I know my rights. This is police harassment," he babbled, shifting his weight from one foot to the next.

Rache wasn't sure if it was the way he had looked at her or if it was just his attitude, but when she smelled the liquor on his breath, it seemed to act as a catalyst.

Oh, she had seen his kind before. Scum! Scum that preyed on young kids. Scum who thought another life was theirs to use and toss aside like a piece of garbage.

A dark anger descended on her, anger so primeval that it actually frightened her. The professional in her now battled with whatever demon had control of her. But the professional was losing. The world suddenly slowed down for Rache. She was aware that Mr. Jakes was in front of her, talking. His mouth was moving, and he was babbling incessantly. She knew the gun was pointed at him. But it all felt so far away. It was as if she had read about it somewhere, and it was not actually happening to her. But it was happening!

Her finger began to tighten around the trigger. The professional desperately tried to gain the ascendancy.

"You still here?" It was all she could think of saying to stop herself from pulling the trigger. Rache looked him in the eye now. Slowly, she felt her arm drift upward. It was as though it were no longer part of her. The Beretta was now pointed at his head.

She swallowed hard. She found an almost passive participant in the unfolding chain of events.

As Mr. Jakes looked into Rache's eyes, he knew. He knew his death was only seconds away.

She was struggling to breathe. Once again, the demon had pushed the professional aside. Once again, her finger began to squeeze the trigger. She knew she would kill him.

Mr. Jakes's eyes were wide with terror. *Christ,* he thought. *This crazy cop is going to shoot me.*

"I'm out of here," Rache heard him say, her mind still in a haze. He turned his back and walked off in a hurried manner. Rache blinked, gaining control.

The moment had passed. The professional had won. But only just.

"Got a second name there, Jessie?" Rache said, holstering her gun and reaching for a pen and paper.

For the first time in a long time, Jessie smiled a genuine smile.

As Rache and Jessie rounded the corner, they found Danny sitting, half in, half out, of the car. In one hand he held a police radio. Upon seeing Rache, he beckoned her with his free hand. His manner was a mixture of annoyance and frustration. Rache was normally reliable. What had possessed her to go off and leave the car unlocked, he didn't know. What he did know was that it would be best if he didn't push her on it.

Five years his partner, Rache was still an enigma to him. He trusted her. God, he trusted her. She had saved his life on one occasion. She had never talked about that. Never once mentioned it. Rache was unlike anyone he had ever met. How can you work with someone and not know them? he had often wondered. But he didn't know Rache. No one did. Rache always held something back. There had been one occasion, shortly after the incident, as he called it, when she had called by to see him at the hospital. They had talked a long time. Not just talked, but communicated, and for the briefest of moments, he thought she would open up. But she never did. Rache had secrets, secrets no living person would ever find out. But he trusted her with his life. So when she turned the corner with a young kid in tow, Danny thought, *Best to leave this one.*

"Ten-four, over and out," Danny spoke into the radio. "Come on, we got a shooting in progress!" he shouted at Rache as she approached.

Rache was only three car lengths away, but she started to run. She looked back at Jessie to find that Jessie had already begun to walk away. *Shit*, thought Rache. She had wanted to bring this kid in.

CHAPTER 3

RACHE WASTED NO TIME. SHE was in the seat and had started the car before Danny had a chance to fasten his safety belt.

"It's around the block, just off Fifty-Seventh and Ninth," Danny told her as he watched for passing traffic.

Rache swung the car around. The sedan took the first right, hugging the corner as it headed west on Fifty-Seventh Street.

West of Times Square to the Hudson River and sandwiched between Thirtieth and Fifty-Ninth streets lay Clinton, or Hell's Kitchen, to give it its more famous moniker. At one time Hell's Kitchen was New York's most crime-ridden neighborhood. The Westies, a notoriously violent gang, had claimed the streets in the seventies and eighties, but the dawn of the nineteen nineties saw the area witness a steady decline in crime. By the beginning of the first decade of the twenty-first century, Hell's Kitchen had begun to attract a new population. Musicians as well as professionals and other artists had started to take up residence.

Passing through the junction at Ninth Avenue, Rache took the first right. She was puzzled by the fact that someone had reported a shooting. She hadn't heard of any violent crime in the area in well over two years. But as her car banked around the corner, an almost surreal sight greeted them.

The street was awash with cops.

Danny blinked, not trusting his eyes. "Jesus," he muttered under his breath. He'd thought he'd heard sirens while back at the church, but with the thickness of the walls, he hadn't been sure. Back in the alley, Rache had heard nothing, her attention riveted on Mr. Jakes.

Danny looked over at Rache. He glanced back out through the windshield. Two marked blue-and-white patrol cars were parked out

14

front of a small house, set well in off the street. It was the kind of house you'd drive by three or four times and never spot. An ambulance, siren blaring, sped past them, momentarily causing Danny to jar his neck as he looked back over his shoulder. Danny's eyes followed another car, the letters NYPD embossed on the sides, as it chased after the ambulance.

Rache drove straight in behind the two cop cars. Another police car sat squarely across from the house. Four or five officers milled around it. As she stepped out of the car, she noticed two more cops standing in a doorway. Danny watched as the ambulance turned the corner, disappearing out of sight. "Jesus!" Danny muttered again.

Officer Cole Marks, a young cop with just two years on the force, met them.

Rache flashed her badge. "Detective Fischer, this is Detective O'Connor," she said, indicating Danny, who nodded an acknowledgment.

Two years on the force, but Officer Cole Marks had already heard of Rache Fischer. Jesus, she was good-looking, he thought.

"So what have we got?" Rache inquired.

"We—my partner and me—we got a call on what appeared to be some kind of domestic. Neighbors heard screaming, like a kid screaming, then a gunshot."

Rache took it all in as she and Danny moved toward the house. Officer Marks kept pace with her as he continued with his report.

"We were almost at the corner there," he said, stopping abruptly as he pointed to where the ambulance had just passed. "It only took us fifteen, twenty seconds tops, to get here." The young cop struggled now to find the words to describe what he had just witnessed. Officer Marks's sudden pause caused Rache to check her stride.

She threw him an "I'm waiting" stare.

Officer Marks looked at Rache, looking away almost immediately. He steadied himself before answering. The memory of what he had just seen was forever burned into his brain. It was an image he knew he'd never purge. Two years on the force, and he'd seen some shit, but never had he experienced what he could only describe as a scene from hell. It was a demonic sight that would stay with him to his grave.

"We found one guy inside the door," he began, his mouth parched, his saliva drying. "He'd been shot once in the chest. It was a mess—blood everywhere. My partner gave him CPR, and I radioed for back up. The guy was already unconscious." Officer Marks looked at Danny, his discomfort clearly evident.

Rache went to press him again, but Danny caught her arm. "It's okay, son. Take your time," Danny said.

Officer Marks took a breath. His palms were sweaty now. He wiped them on his pants, but it didn't help. It was as though his skin was leaking.

Rache noticed the stains. "You okay?" she asked, wondering what had upset him so much.

He nodded. His voice, however, belied his composure. He choked as he explained. "I go upstairs, and I hear it...very faint...like a whisper. I couldn't make out the words, but it's constant, ya know, like wind blowing. So I draw my weapon. And there's this door. It's broken, ya know, half hanging off. But that's where the voice is coming from." Officer Marks took a deep breath. Rache could see tears in his eyes now, and she braced herself. "I go in this room," he started. "It's a kid's room. Man, it was trashed, and...it had the weirdest smell, like burning, and there's this girl. She's like fifteen or so, just lying on the bed. Her clothes are all torn. Not like...ripped, but...shredded. It was awful. Her face is all blue, and she's got blood coming out of her nose and ears. Jesus, man, her eyes were bleeding. She had blood coming from her eyes."

Rache turned white. She felt sick. She had to draw on all her training and experience to stop herself from retching. She glanced at Danny. He too looked shocked.

Officer Marks continued to talk. At first, she thought she'd misunderstood. So she asked him to repeat himself.

"Then I saw him," he repeated. Four simple words, but Rache couldn't believe her ears. "The sick fuck was leaning over her, whispering to her."

Rache's mind was in a spin. "What? You have him?" she asked incredulously.

"Yeah, we got him. Kid's on the way to the hospital now," replied Officer Marks, nodding his head.

"I want to talk to this son of a bitch. I want this entire area sealed off. And I want to see this scumbag!"

Danny picked up on the anger in her. He decided to step in and try and calm the situation.

The rage that had almost overtaken her in the alley had returned. Rache could feel eyes on her. She had to gain control—control of the demon that manifested itself as wild anger.

"We'll do it down at the precinct, Rache, okay?"

Officer Marks nodded his head, indicating the marked car opposite the house. Rache followed his stare. Behind foggy windows, she could only just make out a hunched figure.

"Never even put up a struggle. Just let us cuff him and lead him off. Weirdest thing was…he seemed to know her," the young officer said. With that, the figure in the car turned. For the briefest of seconds, Rache caught his eye. His stare was intense. It was unlike anything she had ever experienced. It was the cold stare of a madman, a dark, penetrating stare, with an intensity that frightened her.

Animal, she thought.

It was only fleeting. A small turn of the head. But in that instant, she saw it. Was it a hint of recognition? Did he know her? Was he some lowlife she had once let go, to catch a bigger fish? So many questions. But one thing was sure. She'd break this bastard. What could have happened to cause a child's eyes to bleed? Rache stared at him.

Animal!

The patrol car carrying the perp eased down the street. Rache felt a chill run through her as she watched the silhouette figure through the rear window. Even after the blue-and-white rounded the corner, Rache continued to stare, her mind lost in thought.

She felt Danny touch her lightly on the arm. "You alright?" Danny asked.

She didn't respond.

"You alright, Rache?" Danny repeated.

"Yeah, Danny, yeah, sure…I'm good…sorry," she said, forcing a smile. She looked over at Officer Marks. "What's the ETA on forensics?" she asked.

"About five minutes," the officer replied.

"Okay, everybody listen up. Forensics are on their way," she said, turning and addressing the remainder of the officers.

Small conversations died out as everyone gave their full attention to Rache and Danny.

"As you all know, we got an unidentified male, GSW to the chest, and a little girl en route to hospital. Her condition is not known, and we got what looks to be the perpetrator in custody. I want everyone out of here and the entire area sealed off. I want it locked down now. No one goes in or out without my say so."

Rache took Officer Marks to one side. "What did you say your name was?"

"Cole, Cole Marks."

"Okay, Cole, you're in charge. It's your baby, least till forensics arrive, okay?" Rache said, throwing her eyes over the scene. "Think you can handle that? I don't want this son-of-a-bitch sliding out through some fucking loophole."

"No problem!"

"Good."

Rache nodded at Danny and walked to her car. She threw him the keys.

"Will you drive?"

"Sure," he said as he deftly caught the key chain.

Rache spent the short journey back to the precinct lost in stony silence. Danny was only a block away when he spoke for the first time. Shifting his weight in the seat, he cleared his throat.

"Okay, Rache, spill it!"

The question caught her off guard.

"Spill what?"

"Come on, Rache, you've been distant all week, and now this," Danny said.

Rache smiled at him. "I'm okay, really."

Danny just kept staring at her. He wasn't going to accept this.

"Okay, okay, I had a lousy night, and the thought of some poor kid being attacked in her own home has me a little freaked. You heard what that cop said."

"You want me to question him?" he asked, seeing that she was upset.

"No, Danny, we do it together, the usual way." Rache smiled back at him.

"Okay."

Danny swung the car into the precinct parking lot.

I've got to get a grip, Rache thought. She knew she was far from okay, and it was beginning to show. Danny was not the only one who had noticed this over the last few days. Another detective, Susan Jay, had worked at the Midtown Precinct for a year and a half now, and they had become close. But even Susan had begun to notice. Rache had always taken her vacation in September, the memories too vivid to bear. Her sister, Ruth, would be thirty-four now, had she lived.

But Ruth was dead, and every September, around the time of her sister's anniversary, Rache had gotten away for two weeks. She had always used the time to think about the positive aspects of her sister's short life. She would banish all thoughts of Ruth's brutal death to a part of her brain she would never access. But this year had been different. Too many unsolved cases and terror alerts had found Rache skipping her vacation to concentrate on work. It had been a mistake, and Rache was only beginning to see that now. The two weeks away had always left her refreshed, if a little sad. Ruth had been dead for seventeen years now, two years longer than Rache had known her.

Turning, she smiled at Danny. How could she tell him? How could she tell anyone? Ruth had not only been her sister, but she had been her best friend. Two years had separated them, but they were like twins. They had shared everything. Rache cursed herself for not having taken the holidays.

Danny pulled the car to a stop, and they climbed out. Rache stretched and took a few deep breaths. *Got to pull it together. At least this case looked cut and dry. Yeah, yeah, it was a no-brainer*, she thought. She'd book this guy; check in on the kid and her father. Was he the father? Shit, she'd have to find out how the kid was doing. What was it Officer Marks had said? He saw a kid, fifteen or sixteen, with her clothes shredded and blood coming from her eyes. Rache shivered. Already more questions than answers. But they had him. She'd finish this case and get away. She was due some vacation time. This case would only take a few days.

Midtown Precinct North, situated on West Fifty-Fourth Street, was an imposing building. Four storeys of red brick looked down on one of the busiest streets in Midtown Manhattan. It had been Rache's home for the last four years. The precinct had seen many unusual cases in its lifetime, but as she walked up the steps now, Rache Fischer was completely oblivious to the fact that she was about to undertake the most bizarre and positively frightening case of her career to date. It would be a case that would change her life forever.

The first and second floors took care of the usual administration and cells. All suspects were processed here. Depending on the nature and severity of the charge, suspects were either held here or below in the cellars. The top two storeys housed the detectives' offices. Rache shared hers with Danny. Located on the corner of the building, it faced both north and west . She had often spent a summer's evening working on a case while watching the sunset over the skyline.

Rache and Danny walked up the last few steps to reach the third floor. Theo Wald greeted them. Of Polish-German descent, Theo was a bear of a man—one summer he had single-handedly carried a refrigerator up two flights as the elevator was bust, prompting both Rache and Danny to speculate that Theo came from a race of trappers from the Bavarian Forest. All three had often joked about it. Theo's strength was not only physical, but he was often a willing ear to many of the younger detectives. Thirty years on the force, Theo had seen it all. If you had troubles at the Midtown Precinct, you didn't talk to a counselor—you went to Theo.

Theo's smile was broad as usual as he thrust a dark green folder in Rache's hand, but there was a sadness behind his eyes. "Hey, Rache, this is what we got so far."

"Thanks. How's the kid doing?"

"No word yet."

Danny and Rache walked on toward their office. Theo followed a little behind.

"Rache," a familiar voice called after her. As Rache reached her office, Susan Jay, approached, her mood similar to Theo's.

"Hey, Susan," Rache greeted her.

"Little girl is a Kell Mason, sixteen. Father is a Joe Mason, works as a store manager," Susan told her. At twenty-nine, Susan had strong if not unattractive features. She had been through a messy divorce over the past year, but as Rache remembered, she'd had kept her dignity when a lot of false accusations had been thrown about. It was something that had impressed Rache.

"How're they doin'?"

"The kid, Kell, she's in some kind of coma, and the father's undergoing surgery now."

"Coma...what do ya mean coma?" Rache asked, puzzled by this revelation.

Susan shrugged. "That's all we got."

Rache looked down at the ground. She seemed to pause. She could feel her pulse race as she thought about the next question. "Was...was she raped?" she asked finally as she looked up at Susan.

"Don't know yet," Susan said. "But she's in a bad way. They got two docs looking at her now."

Rache turned the folder over in her hands. She looked at Theo. "This is everything?"

"On the perp, yeah," Theo said.

Rache pushed the door to her office. She turned to Danny and Theo. "Can you give us a moment?" she asked, nodding to Susan.

"Sure," was the word out of both their mouths.

Susan and Rache walked into the office.

"Coffee?"

Susan shook her head as Rache poured herself a large mug from a piping-hot coffeepot.

She sipped it as she spoke to Susan. "Is it true...about the bleeding?"

Susan nodded.

The precinct had received a preliminary report from the hospital. Kell Mason had suffered severe blood loss. Almost three pints had been vented from her eyes, nose, and mouth, a dangerous amount in a sixteen-year-old, as the average adult carries only eight pints in their bloodstream. It was Kell's young face, contorted and streaming blood, and her clothes shredded and stained crimson red that had greeted Officer Cole Marks, shocking him beyond words.

Susan had been profoundly disturbed when she'd studied the preliminary report. She looked at Rache now. "Yeah, she seems to have ruptured her ears, and there was extensive bleeding from her nose, mouth, and...eyes." As she said the last word, she had to clear her throat.

Rache shook her head in disbelief. "You did that forensics course. Ever hear of anything like this?"

"No," said Susan. "I mean...it is usually blunt force trauma to the head that would cause the ears to bleed, but...man...I've never heard of anyone bleeding from their eyes. What the fuck did he do to her?" Susan couldn't contain herself. "Jesus, I've met a few sickos in my time, but I've never seen this. I know what I'd like to do."

Rache put her coffee down. "I know. But let's concentrate on what we have. We've got the bastard, and the kid's in good hands."

Susan nodded. "You got another coffee there?"

"Sure." She poured Susan a mug.

Susan took the coffee gratefully. She was glad Rache was on this one. The guy they'd brought in was a total weirdo. He'd really creeped her out. She had stolen a quick glimpse of him while he was being printed. Susan was shocked at just how handsome he was. *Just shows, you never can tell,* she'd thought. But he'd never even acknowledged her. In fact, this was one of the strangest aspects about him, she'd remarked to Theo—his inability to focus his eyes on anything for longer than a few seconds. She knew he'd been caught at the scene and that he'd shot and attacked a young girl, but it was not until she'd read the preliminary on Kell's injuries that he'd truly frightened her. What kind of monster was he?

Susan drank some of her coffee. "So, how do you want to work this?" she asked.

"Two teams. Danny and I'll go first," said Rache.

"Want me to call the guys in?" Susan offered.

"Yeah."

Susan strode over to the door as Rache flipped opened the file. A single typed page sat inside the green folder.

Danny and Theo walked in.

"Is this it?" Rache asked as Theo's large frame settled itself into a chair opposite her.

"That's it, Rache!"

Rache took a seat. She looked at the sheet of paper. "Okay, let me get this straight," she said, reading from the report. "He's got no ID, no priors, no convictions, prints are being run now, and we found no weapon."

"Rache, it's a strange one, no doubt," said Theo.

Rache glanced down at the page. "We got gunshot residue on his hands! Do we have the slug from Mr. Mason?" she inquired.

"Not yet," said Susan. "He's undergoing extensive surgery right now. He could be in there for hours."

"How soon can we get a preliminary from forensics on the crime scene?"

"Two maybe three hours is usual in these cases."

"Any idea of the motive?" asked Danny.

Susan looked over at Theo. Theo just shrugged.

"What about the kid? The cop said he smelt burning. What's that about?" asked Rache.

"Again we have to wait on forensics, Rache," Theo told her.

Rache looked around at all three. "Guys, we really got nothing here, and I don't want to question that SOB unless I got some of the facts."

Theo threw a quick glance at Susan. It was not lost on Rache.

"Okay, want to tell us what's going on?"

"He won't talk!" Theo said, shrugging his broad shoulders. "Got him in here a little while ago, and he hasn't said as much as boo!"

"He'll talk to me!"

Rache stood, and picking up the folder, she headed straight for the door.

The interview room was on the third floor. It was spacious but functional. A small cell, built into the corner, the usual 10×8, held the suspect directly after and sometimes before. Rache and Danny had between them questioned hundreds of suspects and always worked the same routine. If they had little or no information, they would get a couple of cops to "soften up" a suspect. This sounded more sinister than what it was. The cops in question would put the suspect through a series of questions, not really paying too much attention to the answers. It was simply to bombard him, to get him to say more than he should. Rache and Danny would look on through a two-way mirror system and gain as much information about a suspect as possible. The more violent suspects were often cuffed during questioning. This had been a tried-and-tested method over many years, and although their captain frowned on it, he would agree that it was a necessary method in cases where the suspects were nonresponsive.

The two cops today were Joe Spandau and Pete Wall. At six feet and sporting a marine crew cut, Joe was an imposing figure. He'd served in the first Gulf War and had joined the NYPD shortly after. A native New Yorker, he considered it a privilege to serve. His marine record was impeccable. The only blemish was that on two occasions, he had been found guilty of violent conduct against his fellow marines. Joe had never offered an excuse. He had simply taken whatever punishment was dished out.

Pete was the same height as Joe but had just made detective grade. In most of these cases, Pete was a casual observer, allowed only limited participation. Pete knew his place in the hierarchy of the game. "Listen and learn" had been Rache's advice to him on his first job in the room. Pete had taken her advice.

But today's interview was different for many reasons. Word had gotten round that the suspect, or perp as he was already been labelled, was some kind of kiddie rapist. He had been found at the scene and had the kid's blood all over him. The fact that Kell Mason had been badly beaten, suffering severe facial injuries, and now remained in a coma made it all the harder for the detectives as many had children of their own. The precinct had always prided itself on being professional no matter what the crime—but today that professionalism was under strain.

Aside from Officer Cole Marks, Pete and Joe were the first two cops to have had any real dealings with the perp. They had booked him, fingerprinted, and taken his mug shots. But he hadn't uttered a word. A twenty-minute ride in a cop car, another twenty in the precinct, and another hour in the interview room and not a word. Joe's patience had begun to wear a little thin. The word *guilty* was written all over his face, as far as Joe was concerned, but his efforts had begun to frustrate him. He knew Rache was in the next room looking on.

He had always liked her, and if truth be known, he had often fantasized they might go out together. A number of years back, he had tentatively broached the subject while at a party. The answer wasn't what he had wanted to hear, so he had laughed it off as a joke. He was angry that he had embarrassed himself. But Rache had never brought it up again, and he respected her for that. You could always rely on Rache, even if she were a little distant. He supposed that three years on, he might have a shot at it again, so he desperately wanted this fucker to break. He was sure it would improve his chances with her—that and the fact that she had been single over four months now. But Rache had never dated a cop, and this fact discouraged Joe a little.

All his experience and knowledge were not working today. The perp—in everyone's mind he had become the perp, the word *suspect* never mentioned—was totally unresponsive. He had tried the hard approach, the soft approach. He had even tried to plead with him.

Nothing!

Not one single word.

At one stage, Pete had intervened to say something. One look from Joe put paid to that.

Joe looked at his watch. *An hour and ten minutes*, he thought. *This fucker's gotta say something.* Joe picked up a chair and sat directly opposite him, staring at him for a full minute, saying nothing.

"Look, buddy…"

Joe stopped. He stared into the perp's eyes. They darted about, not focusing on anything. They looked briefly at Joe, quickly jumping past him, stopping momentarily to stare at the door, at the ceiling, at the pictures on the wall, back to Joe's shirt.

Joe patted him lightly on the cheeks. "You high, buddy?" he said.

Nothing.

Joe looked up at the two-way mirror. It was a signal to Rache and Danny. He needed help.

Behind the mirror, Rache had watched the entire process with mixed emotions. She knew Joe was good, but this was the first time he had failed miserably. Part of her wanted to go in and slap the truth out of him. Shit, they hadn't even gotten his name.

Rache studied him more closely now. He was handsome, no doubt. Aged between twenty-five and thirty, he was just less than six feet with rugged good looks. Black shoulder-length hair was pushed back off a dark chiseled face. But it was the eyes that caught Rache's attention the most. They were like two orbs of chestnut brown that darted in every direction.

But she felt no empathy toward him.

The dark anger that had possessed her earlier in the day had lifted somewhat. And she felt nothing.

Yeah, she held him in contempt, but the desire to get the case over with was stronger now. She just wanted to get it done and dusted. Hell, it was Friday evening, and she had the whole weekend free. She needed time alone.

Rache watched as Joe looked at the glass mirror. She turned to Danny. "Anything on the prints?"

"Nothing."

"Okay," said Rache, closing the folder. "Let's see if we can find out who this mystery man is."

Joe was still trying to catch the perp's eye as the door behind him opened, letting Rache and Danny in. Joe's head bobbed and weaved as he tried to catch the perp's eye. Pete touched Joe on the shoulder as he leaned in and whispered in his ear.

"Here's Rache," Joe heard him say.

The perp's eyes stopped moving about. They focused in on Rache as she walked through, closely followed by Danny. Rache had removed her jacket, and her breasts pushed against the tight blouse she wore. The perp's stare was intense. His eyes followed her as she walked into the center of the room. He was captivated by her. Joe and Pete caught it too. The perp began to breathe a little heavier. His chest rose as he expelled air through his nostrils. A pink tongue peered out of his mouth, snakelike, as he wet his lips. He uttered his first word.

"Rachel!"

Joe's patience was at an end, and when he heard the perp say Rache's name, he snapped. Hitting him full in the face, Joe sent him spinning backward off the chair. Joe's fist connected with the perp's jaw, crushing his lower lip against his teeth. His whole lower lip seemed to open up. A spray of blood shot across the desk.

As the perp lay on his back, blood continued to pump from his mouth. He tried to sit up but fell back down.

"Jesus Christ, Joe!" Danny shouted, running over and grabbing hold of him.

Pete tried to help the perp sit up, but he fell back again, his eye blinking rapidly.

"Get him out of here!" Rache shouted at Danny. "Get him out of here!"

Danny put his hands on Joe's shoulders, pushing him toward the door.

Realizing he was in big trouble, Joe offered no resistance. He turned to Rache. "Sick son of a bitch was getting off looking at you, Rache."

"Get him out of here."

Pete struggled but managed to get the perp onto the chair. He took a handkerchief out of his pocket and placed it against the perp's lip. He looked up as Danny led Joe out of the room.

The perp held the handkerchief against his mouth. He took it away slowly and stared at the blood.

"I'm Detective Fischer," Rache said as she sat opposite him, where Joe had been, only moments earlier.

He dabbed the handkerchief against his lip, staring as the blood flow slowed.

Rache watched him, Kell's medical report, citing serious blood loss, intruding on her thoughts now. This wasn't how she'd wanted to play it. What the fuck was Joe up to?

"Do you know where you are?" she asked him, more to help ground herself and get the interview back on track.

The perp looked at her now, holding her eyes. But within seconds, they had begun to flit about, unfocused as before.

Rache watched as his eyes started to roll back in his head.

Danny walked softly back into the room, closing the door quietly behind him.

"Do you know why you are here?" Rache continued, raising her voice slightly. She didn't want him passing out.

No response.

Rache looked back over her shoulder at Danny.

"Water."

It was a simple word, but it was the simplicity of the request that startled her. Here was this guy looking for one of the most fundamental elements needed for survival.

Could she get somewhere with this scumbag? she wondered.

Rache nodded at Pete, as if to say, "Can you do it?"

Pete made his way to the door.

Rache stood up and walked over to the corner of the room. Picking up a trash can lined with a plastic sack, she walked over to the perp. She nodded, indicating the handkerchief. The bleeding had stopped now.

The perp dropped the blood-soaked rag into the trash can.

Pete came back in with a pint glass of water. He handed it to the perp.

Danny started, "Okay, pal, let's have a name..."

The perp opened his mouth and downed the water in one go, placing the empty glass on the table in front of him.

Rache threw a quick glance to Danny. She didn't need to ask the question.

Danny was on the same wavelength. He raised his eyebrows, confirming Rache's unspoken suspicions that the perp was possibly strung out on some kind of narcotic.

Rache stared at the glass. She watched closely as the perp's saliva slowly slid down the inside of the glass. A thin smile spread over her lips, her eyes fixed on the glass. "Would you like some more?"

The perp nodded.

"Pete, think you could get our friend here a pitcher of water and a clean glass?"

Pete glanced over at Rache. "Sure."

As Pete left the room, Rache walked over to Danny. She spoke in a whisper. "What do you think?" she asked, her voice barely audible. "Think he's strung out?"

"He's revved up, no doubt."

"Speed?" she suggested.

"Speed, meth, crack…God knows what."

"Then we won't get much sense out of him, will we?"

The door opened. Pete walked in, carrying a pitcher of water and a glass. He placed the pitcher on the table in front of the perp. He spoke as he put the glass down. "Captain wants—" But Pete didn't finish.

All eyes had turned to the perp as he downed the entire pitcher.

Pete simply stared at him. He looked over at Rache and Danny. "Captain wants to see us all," he said. "It's about Joe."

Rache sniffed. "Pete, why don't you get our friend here another pitcher of water and make him comfortable." She nodded toward the cell.

Pete took the hint.

Danny walked over to the table. He lifted the glass, using his thumb and forefinger. Rache tied up the plastic sack in the trash can. She lifted it out, staring at the bloodied handkerchief inside. Rache handed it to Danny as Pete turned the key, locking the perp into the cell in the corner of the room.

Rache left the room.

"Pete, can you get me an evidence bag?"

Pete turned to Danny.

"Huh?"

"An evidence bag," replied Danny, holding up the glass.

"Sure."

Pete followed Danny to the door. Danny stopped, allowing Pete to hold the door open for him.

Once outside in the corridor, Pete locked the door and hurried off.

Never underestimate Rache, Danny thought. Jesus, she was a clever girl. She had taken advantage of Joe hitting the perp. They had his blood now and could do a DNA analysis with the crime scene and test for any drugs he was on.

Pete arrived back with the bag. Danny got Pete to hold the bag open. "Why test for drugs? We know he's dusted to the eyeballs," Pete asked after Danny had explained what they were up to.

"Prescription drugs. Find out what he's on, maybe we can find out who dispensed it. Could be we get a name."

Pete nodded his head. "Yeah."

Rache passed by, glancing quickly at Danny. They both watched her disappear into the captain's office.

"Whatcha think?" Pete asked, staring at the captain's door.

"Come on, let's leave it for the moment," Danny said, walking off in the opposite direction.

Captain Don Woods lived his life by the book, and the thought of one of his officers hitting a suspect horrified him. So when Rache entered his office and saw Joe sitting on a chair looking like a lost schoolboy, she knew, straight up, they were in big trouble.

She liked the captain, even if he was a little straight. Sometimes you had to bend the rules a little to get results. *Hey, if Joe hadn't hit the scumbag, they wouldn't have the blood sample now*, she thought. They had nothing on this guy. Nothing. Yeah, Joe could take a little heat. But it was worth it.

Captain Woods had looked in on the room adjacent the interview room right after Danny had pushed Joe out. Theo and Susan had been following the interview through the two-way system as they would question the perp after Danny and Rache.

Joe smacking him had messed everything up.

"Did you see what happened here, Theo?" Woods had demanded.

"Er…I…was chatting with Susan, and the next thing I know—"

Woods didn't let him finish. "Susan?"

"I was talking to Theo about—"

"You're both supposed to be observing, so observe," he had said as he stormed out.

"Fuck," said Theo.

They had watched the remainder of the interview with annoyance. Everyone wanted this scumbag, and he had clammed up.

"Think he's running a game?" Susan had asked Theo as the perp had downed the pitcher of water.

"Insanity plea?"

"Maybe."

"Hasn't asked for a lawyer yet," Theo had said.

"Could be part of his strategy," Susan had replied.

"This is our guy, Captain. We caught him at the crime scene for Christ sakes!" Rache said, her voice rising as she spoke. Damn, she was frustrated. The captain seemed more interested in Joe smacking him than getting him to fess up. Rache stood in front of captain, uncomfortable at being summoned to his office. She wanted to be back in the room. The answers were there, not here.

"I will not tolerate that tone in my office, Detective, understood?"

Rache nodded. "Yes, Captain," she replied, her voice softening.

"This is not about guilt. It is about one of my officers hitting a suspect—"

"But—"

"Suspect, Detective, not perpetrator. Yes, I hear the gossip too." Captain Woods stared at Rache. "So please answer my question."

"Look, we got his DNA, and we got his blood."

"Yes, and how did we obtain that?" Woods demanded.

"We can run a tox-screen for drugs, and we can tie him in at the scene—"

"That was not my question—"

"No, I didn't see anything," she said, interrupting him.

Captain Woods leaned back in his chair. He studied Rache a moment. "Rache, I'm just trying to get to the truth here."

"The truth? The truth, Captain. I'll give you the truth. There's a little girl lying in a coma...probably raped. Her father is fighting

31

for his life, and that scumbag did it. That's the truth," Rache said, her voice low and even as she tried to contain her frustration now.

Woods nodded.

Neither spoke for a full minute. Captain Woods tried to take it all in. This particular case had got everybody jittery. He didn't need the added problem of having to rein in his detectives. Joe hitting the suspect was cause enough for alarm, but Rache's defense of it puzzled him.

Rache stared at him. "Are we done here?" she asked finally.

Joe couldn't believe his ears. The whole conversation, he had kept his eyes fixed on the ground, not daring to speak. But to hear Rache talk to the captain like that…

Jesus… he thought.

Captain Woods stood up. "For now," he said to Rache. "For now."

Rache turned and walked out.

Woods stared at Joe. "Get out."

Joe didn't need a second invitation. He bolted for the door. Catching up to Rache a little way down the corridor, he tapped her on the shoulder. "Thanks, Rache, I owe you one."

Rache stopped dead. She smiled as she looked at Joe. "If that scumbag walks coz of some stupid technicality, it's not the captain you'll need to worry about." Rache turned her back on him and walked off to her office, closing the door behind her.

She poured herself a coffee. She drank it slowly. *So much for cut and dry*, she thought. Pulling out a scratch pad from her drawer, she started to scribble down some notes. After a moment, she looked at her work.

Suspect/Perp – No name, no ID, no priors, no convictions.
DNA – Yet to be analysed.
Fingerprints – No match.
Motive – None. No sign of robbery. No forced entry.
Did they know him?
Kell Mason - Age 16. Current Status. Raped? Coma?
Joe Mason - Age 42. Current Status. Shot! Critical!
No Weapon found.

It was the last piece of the puzzle that disturbed her. If uniform had found the perp at the scene, how come they had failed to find the weapon used to shoot Joe Mason? Forensics had been on the scene over two hours and still no weapon. Rache had spoken with Dion Chavez, the lead forensic scientist at the scene, and even Dion was puzzled. He had assured Rache that if the weapon was there, he'd find it. She had thanked him and hung up.

Rache tried to piece them all together. But she had more questions than answers. She looked at her watch. Suddenly, she felt very hungry. She'd get some lunch and then question the perp. *The suspect*, she corrected herself. Maybe she could get Danny to go with her. The more she looked at the case, the less she liked it. But she and Danny were primaries. It was up to them.

CHAPTER 4

THE PHONE ON HER DESK rang, the hollow-sounding noise diverting attention away from the file in front of her. Rache looked at it a moment. Closing the file she'd been reading, she answered it. "Yeah."

"Hi, Rache, I've got your mom on line 2!" Martha Banks's distinctive voice boomed out from the earpiece.

Rache made no reply, her mind focused on the person waiting on the other end.

Her mother.

"Rache?"

"Yeah, Martha, I'll take it. Thanks."

She watched the little red light flash above line 2. Holding her finger above it a moment, she pressed it.

"Hi, Mom."

"Rachel."

They hadn't spoken in over a month. Rache's love for her mother, for both her parents, was as strong as it had always been. But they had all grown apart. They had never fully accepted her as a cop. Neither had attended her graduation, and when she'd made detective grade, only her brother, David, had shown up. She knew they were, in their own way, proud of her, but if truth were known, it was Rache's total rejection of her faith and her continued insistence to take no part in any religious ceremony that had really driven a wedge between them.

Rache didn't believe in any of it. She had made those feelings known from an early age. She had fought many battles at home in the years following Ruth's death. Her father had become impossible to talk to. Rache had tried to argue her own points, but Ira Fischer

34

believed that Ruth's death had a meaning, a purpose. A sentiment not shared by Rache. Caught between the warring factions was her mom, Miriam. She knew she had caused her mom pain, and it ate her up at times. She had never wanted her mother to choose—it had been one of the reasons she had left home at a young age. When she'd joined the NYPD, she felt relieved.

"Mom, you shouldn't call me at work. Use the cell number I gave you," Rache began.

"Oh, I hate those things."

"Mom, really…"

"Your brother made senior partner. We're having a celebration next weekend, and you have to come," interrupted Miriam Fischer. "There, I've said it."

Rache smiled to herself. She knew where she got her feisty nature. "I'm happy for him, Mom, really I am. I'll call him later, but you know me and family celebrations," Rache said.

"Your father would love you to come."

"My father who doesn't talk to me!"

"He loves you, and he misses you."

"Ah, you know me and lawyers, Mom."

"Please say you'll come."

There was a desperation in her mother's voice now that pained Rache.

"Okay, I'll see what I can do. Let me get back to you on it, okay?"

"I love you, Rachel."

"Yeah, I love you too, Mom, but I'm kinda in the middle of something. I'll call you later, huh?"

"Okay."

"Thanks, Mom." Rache hung up.

She'd have to get out. She stood up from her desk. Pulling on her jacket, she walked to the office door. Danny opened it just as she was about to grab the handle. She gave him a disarming smile as he stood there in the doorway.

"Danny, lunch?" she asked.

"Sure, Rache," he said.

"I thought we'd go over to Flaherty's," Rache suggested.

"Hey, it's your turn," Danny goaded her.

Rache grabbed him by the arm. "Come on. Anything you want!"

Flaherty's Restaurant, directly across the street from the precinct, made the best Irish stew in all of Manhattan. Danny had introduced her to it four years ago during one of the coldest winters on record. John Flaherty had opened his first restaurant a month before, and Danny had spent every lunch hour possible eating there.

Curiosity had gotten the better of Rache. What was so special? she had asked Danny out straight one ice-cold December morning. Danny had taken her by the arm and walked her over to the restaurant, introduced her to John Flaherty, and ordered two bowls of Irish stew. Rache became hooked immediately. She had ordered a second bowl, which impressed John. Flaherty sold only traditional Irish food. No burgers and fries on his menu.

Rache finished the last of her stew, slowly mopping the remainder up with some soda bread. Although it was September and winter was a little way off, the warm stew always gave Rache a sense of well-being. She wiped her hands on her napkin.

"So, whatcha think?"

They had been mulling over the more salient aspects of the case on and off during their meal. Rache had been puzzled by the fact that they still had no weapon. That and the fact that the suspect had offered no resistance when he'd been arrested at the scene really had her mind working overtime.

Danny wiped his mouth and took a sip of water. Watching him drink brought Rache back to the interview room. *Man, he'd downed it like no tomorrow*, she thought. She made a mental note to check the toxicology report as soon as she got back. But one thing still bothered her. Motive!

Danny put his glass down. He shrugged his shoulders. "Could be he went after the kid, and the father disturbed him."

"But why stay after?"

"Well, maybe he shot the father and then attacked the kid."

Rache shook her head. "Doesn't add up."

"Uniform found him at the scene, Rache."

"Don't get me wrong. I think he's guilty. I just can't figure out him not trying to get away, plus we got no weapon."

"Sometimes it's best not to figure out the crazies!" Danny said. "Otherwise you could end up there with them."

Rache laughed. Danny looked at her with an expression of hurt. This only made her laugh a little harder.

A waitress approached them, asking if they would like some coffee. They both nodded.

The waitress filled both their cups, and as Rache watched her walk off toward another table, she turned to Danny. She started to speak but hesitated.

"Come on, Rache, what is it?" Danny asked.

"Maybe it's nothing, maybe it's…" Rache trailed off, holding her hands up.

"What?"

"Back at the house…the kid's house, when he was led away… he kind of gave me a look."

"A look?"

"Yeah, like he knew me or something. And then in the interview room. Fuck, he stared right through me. He called me Rache."

"Yeah, but Pete blurted out your name. And I'll have words with him about that," said Danny.

"I know, but it just freaked me a little."

"Rache, you should know better than to let looks deceive you. This guy hears your name, and he uses that. Maybe he's brighter than we think," Danny said, putting his two hands on hers. The gesture was one of reassurance, and Rache was grateful for it.

She smiled at Danny. But the perp's look had troubled her. Did she know him? Did he know her? She knew she had something of a profile. Three years ago, they had stumbled across a heroin deal gone sour. Danny was shot, and it was only Rache's quick thinking that had saved both their skins. She had shot and wounded two felons, later testifying at their trial. Her solo action was hailed as courageous. The media had been quick to pounce on it, with both *The Herald* and *The Tribune* running follow-up stories. Rache had tried her best to play down the attention. But her model good looks were something the papers could not ignore. One broadsheet in particular had dubbed her the "Angelic Savior." Rache found this attention somewhat amusing. But as far as she was concerned, she'd only done her job. It had all happened in late summer, but in the aftermath of 9/11, it quickly became old news. *Maybe this guy read about it back then and recognized me,* she thought.

She now mentioned this to Danny, playing down her so-called heroism.

"So you think he could know you from the papers?"

"Maybe!"

"Like a fan or something?"

"Who knows. It's got me a little freaked."

"Rache, this city's full of weirdos. Just cos he stared at you, doesn't mean he knows you," Danny said, trying to reassure her.

He threw a few bills on the table and stood up.

"Come on, let's sort this before we go home, what do you say?"

Rache smiled and nodded. She stood up and slipped on her jacket.

CHAPTER 5

E SAT ON A BUNK, staring silently at the floor, a million questions clouding his mind. He could still taste the blood in his mouth. He had managed to stop the bleeding almost immediately. The taste of blood was unique to him. The water had quenched some of his thirst, but he needed more. Hearing his voice in the interview room had frightened him. It sounded strange, far off. Everything around him seemed magnified. One question took center stage now. Was it really her? Was it? How could this be, and why now?

The world began to blur again. He needed more water. The thirst, the thirst was unquenchable. What was it she had said? *I'm Detective Fischer.* Surely it was her? She would help him. He marvelled at his hands, his attention drawn to the tiny creases on his palms and the length of his fingernails. He closed his fists and opened them again. He smiled at the simplicity of the action. His head was itchy now. Scratching it, he felt his long dark hair. It was strange to the touch. He pushed it back off his face. He went to speak again, but the words wouldn't come. They were there, at the front of his mind, but he struggled to organize them. Everything went beyond his wildest expectation. He felt his face now, his fingers exploring every inch of skin, as they gently moved over his features. He held his nose. After a moment, he had to draw breath through his mouth, the sensation of air rushing into his lungs both shocking and exciting him.

He looked around. Where was he? Standing, he walked to the small cell door. He looked at the lock. He tried to open the door. It wouldn't budge. This puzzled him.

He desperately needed water.

Theo and Susan had been following his action with interest as they looked on in the adjacent room. Both had reached the same conclusion. Insanity plea!

They knew insanity was a hard one to pull off. It was usually smart-ass lawyers who suggested it to their clients, but it appeared that this guy was well ahead of the posse.

They had discussed as much when Rache and Danny walked in.

"Want to bring us up to speed?" Rache asked, looking through to the next room.

"Guy's been acting weird for the past while," Susan told her. Theo helped fill them in on what had been happening.

"We recording this?" asked Rache.

Susan nodded.

"So what's his game?"

"Insanity plea?" inquired Danny.

Both Susan and Theo agreed.

"I'm not having that," said Rache.

"Tox is negative for drugs," Susan told her.

Rache spun around on her heels. "Negative?" This surprised her. She'd been sure he was dusted up on some chemical stimulant. Both she and Danny had even speculated on what. She hadn't expected this. Theo told her that the lab had tested for all the usual suspects. Everything had come back negative. "This guy hasn't even taken an aspirin in the last two weeks," he finished off.

"Shit! So you think he's just acting crazy?" Rache asked.

"Could be. How do you want to play this? It's your case, Rache. Your call," Theo said.

"Okay, we'll leave him another half hour, and maybe you and Susan talk to him. He spoke a few words to me, but we've got to get his name. Danny and I will watch him a little longer," Rache suggested.

"What's the word on Joe?" Danny asked.

"Looks like he might ride it out," Theo said.

"Yeah, Theo, no smacking," Rache said dryly as she watched the perp through the window. He was quiet now as he sat toward the edge of the small bunk.

They decided that Susan and Theo question him. Rache and Danny would look on. Something had to give. Joe had been sent home early. The captain was still pissed. But he gave the go-ahead to run the routine on the suspect one more time.

Theo and Susan spent the best part of an hour but got nowhere. He had clammed up and would not talk. Danny suggested to Rache that she go in one more time. But Rache shook her head. He had unnerved her the first time, and she was tired now. No, let him stew overnight. To hell with it, she'd come in tomorrow and grill him till she got something. She'd said as much to Danny.

It was at this precise moment that the perp had jerked his head up. He had spent the entire time staring at the table. Susan and Theo had questioned him relentlessly. But he had said nothing. He hadn't given either of them a second glance. Rache and Danny had watched in silence as both their colleagues had become more and more frustrated. Danny had only left the room once. He had asked Rache if she had wanted a coffee. Rache had simply nodded. But when Rache spoke for the first time in the adjacent room to tell Danny her plan, the perp had jerked his head up. He looked around the room, fixing his gaze on the mirror. He seemed to look right through it. Rache could feel the intensity of his stare in the next room. It completely freaked her.

"Did you see that?" The words jumped out of Danny's mouth. If he had not witnessed the reaction to Rache's voice, he would not have believed it.

But Rache was already out of the room. A cold shiver ran down her spine. Her heart rate was up now, the adrenaline surge pumping her legs forward. She threw open the door into the interview room, startling both Theo and Susan.

"I don't know what fucking game you're playing here, sonny, but you're on thin ice. Do ya hear me? You're on thin ice. Now spill! Name, rank, and fucking serial number!" she shouted at him.

But he just stared at her, his gaze causing her more than quiet discomfort. It was not the gaze of a madman. It was the slight hint of recognition that had begun to frighten her.

Where did she know him from? she wondered.

41

He was too young to have been in school with her. She could recall nearly all the guys she had put away. So who was this guy who wouldn't speak? She racked her brain, but she didn't know him.

He continued to stare at her. Theo threw Susan a glance that said it all. They'd best get Rache out of there. Joe hitting him was bad enough, but Rache looked fit to kill him.

"Water!" he gasped.

It broke the spell.

Rache dropped her shoulders. She looked over at Theo. "Drown the fucker," she said, turning on her heels and walking out past them.

Susan followed her. Catching up to Rache, she asked if everything was all right.

"I just need a moment," said Rache, walking off to her office.

Susan watched her close the door. She went into the kitchen and filled a pitcher. Returning to the interview room, she placed it in front of him. Susan and Theo watched as he drank it all. Not in one go, but he still emptied the pitcher. Theo escorted him to the holding cell.

"Come on, buddy, let's go," he said, leading the perp.

The perp walked over unaided and sat on the bunk. Theo locked the door, rattling it as if to make double sure. He looked through the bars that separated them. "You know, the longer you leave it, the worse it gets. You've got to talk sometime, so you may as well do it now."

But the perp said nothing. He just sat there, his head bowed, eyes fixed on the floor, lost to the world around him.

"Okay, buddy, it's your funeral."

The perp didn't respond to Theo. Slowly, he began to rock himself back and forth. Theo turned around and, shrugging his shoulders at Susan, walked out with her, turning the key and locking the door to the room behind him.

As Theo dropped the keys into his pocket, Danny passed by. "Got a moment?" he asked them.

All three stood in the small kitchen.

Danny filled them in on what had happened earlier.

Theo looked at Danny and then back at Susan. "Sounds freaky to me," he said.

"Maybe it's just coincidental," remarked Susan.

But Danny shook his head. He wanted their input. He had seen the perp's reaction to Rache's voice. And it puzzled him. No way could he have heard through the wall. It was soundproofed.

"No, he seemed to come alive when Rache spoke. We watched the whole interview without saying a word, but when Rache spoke, he lit up. I wouldn't have believe it, only I'd seen it myself," Danny said.

Theo took a deep breath. "Susan, you talk to Rache. Sound out her feelings on it. None of us say anything to the captain. Agreed?"

Danny and Susan nodded.

"Don't want to end up in a cell myself," Theo finished off.

Danny smiled. "Don't worry. They haven't made a straitjacket big enough for you yet."

Susan left the two guys, walking off to Rache's office. Approaching Rache's door, she wondered what the hell she was going to say. She knocked on the door.

"Yeah," came the reply within.

Susan walked in and closed the door. *Best be up-front with Rache,* she figured. "Danny told us," she blurted out.

Rache looked up from her desk. She knew what Susan meant. "Kinda freaky, don't ya think?" Rache said, not really wanting to get too into it. But if she were honest with herself, it had upset her more than she cared to let on.

Susan shrugged in a noncommittal fashion.

Rache flipped open the perp's file that sat in front of her. "Yeah, you're right, probably just a coincidence," she said, looking at the file.

"Hey, Rache, we get lots of crazies in here," Susan said, sitting down opposite Rache.

Rache looked over at her. "Yeah, but this guy is a little more on the disturbing side."

Susan checked her watch. "Let's look at this fresh in the morning. We're all upset about the kid, and sometimes it can cloud our judgment. What do you say we get a couple of drinks down at Sally's? My nickel."

Rache smiled. "Okay, but I'm talking to this guy in the morning."

"You and me both, girl," Susan told her.

***

Get out for a few hours and have a couple of drinks. Yeah, sounds like a plan, Rache thought as she shook the excess water from her hands before holding them under the automatic hand dryer. She had been wound up the last week, and today had been a whirlwind.

She had spoken to the doctors at the hospital. Joe Mason was out of surgery but was critical. The bullet had caused extensive damage, with the doctors telling her the next twenty-four hours would be crucial, but it didn't look good. Kell was a different story. The hospital had run an MRI and CAT scan, but everything looked fine. They had found no sign of head trauma, and the bleeding from her eyes and ears was a complete mystery to them. Kell was in some sort of coma. She was not catatonic, but they had called in some specialist, and he would examine her in the morning. Her clothes had been sent to forensics for testing. It would be tomorrow before they could have anything back.

The hot air flow stopped abruptly, and Rache turned back to the mirror. She smiles as she watched Susan generously apply flame-red lipstick. Rache knew she could do nothing else tonight. What the hell, she'd have that drink, maybe even more.

CHAPTER 6

"SO, WHEN'S THE LAST TIME you got laid?"

Rache turned to Susan with a look of mock indignation.

Susan smiled back, arms folded, her head set to one side. She wanted an answer. "Come on, tell me!"

"Have you no shame, woman?" Rache said, a small smile creeping over her lips.

Susan laughed. "No! Now answer the question, Detective."

Rache could not. Yeah, she knew the last time, of course she knew. But she was embarrassed. Must be a Jewish thing. *Four months*, she thought. It had been over four months since she'd shared her bed with a guy. Only, he wasn't just any guy. His name was Jensen Wright, and he worked for the international charity, Concern. Jansen was from Southern California, but had a strongly pronounced English accent. He'd spent his formative years at a very upmarket English boarding school. At five ten, he was a little taller than Rache, but at forty-three, he was a good ten years her senior.

Jensen had spent most of his adult life working in sub-Saharan Africa, the harsh lifestyle contributing to a wiry frame and skin burnt almost black by the relentless African sun. Bluntly put, Jensen Wright was no oil painting. But that hadn't bothered her in the slightest. Straight off, she'd felt a real connection with him. They'd met at a fundraiser she'd attended. The instant attraction had been mutual. Rache had been aware from the start that he was only going to be in New York for a couple of months before returning to Mozambique where he was to coordinate a new schools initiative. She had really enjoyed his company, and the sex had been great. Rache had done her level best to keep him as far away from the precinct as possible.

Susan had been so anxious to meet him, constantly teasing Rache about his name. Rache had always laughed it off. Rache had always been too painfully aware of the difficulty she'd experienced in forming close personal relationships. That was why it had surprised her when she and Jensen had hit it off so well. Maybe it was because he did charity work and was not obsessed in leaving his mark on the world. But deep down, she was knew it was more than that. She had genuinely liked the person who was Jensen Wright. She almost dared to call it love.

One thing about Jensen, he never questioned her about her job—never told her that it was too dangerous. Yeah, Jensen had never felt intimidated by her. He was comfortable in his own skin. Sometimes at night she'd just lie in his arms after they'd made love, and he'd listen to her as she'd sketch out her day. In all that time, he never once judged her.

Opening her purse now, she thought of Jensen. She missed him, plain and simple. But Susan's question was still ringing in her ears. Four months, she figured, but she certainly wasn't telling Susan, especially standing in front of a mirror in the precinct's ladies' room.

"Not all of us flit from one relationship to another," she said, almost defiantly.

"You're stalling, Fischer. And hey, I don't flit."

Rache closed her purse. She was about to give Susan another jibe, but it would be the last time she'd laugh that night.

"Susan…" It was as far as she got.

The internal alarm sounded.

Rache looked at Susan in horror. Only when a precinct came under direct attack was the alarm triggered. Rache and Susan stood looking at each other in total disbelief, the dull thudding *wah-wah* sound ringing in their ears. A red light in the corner of the room flashed on and off in unison with the alarm.

Rache was the first to react. She unholstered her gun, Susan only moments behind her in the same action. Rache pulled open the washroom door. Three uniformed officers ran by. Rache and Susan stepped out. The world had gone mad. Cops were screaming, shouting orders. Rache looked down the corridor toward her office.

Unanswered phones rang on desks. Officers, who moments earlier would have picked up the calls, ignored them now, their attention focused on checking the weapons. Was it a terrorist attack? Shit, no, not now. She'd heard nothing, been given no indication that they'd been attacked. Why all the madness?

Danny ran up to them. He was out of breath and huffing. Rache thought he was going to keel over. He panted between words. "He's escaped… He's… he's fucking out…"

Rache grabbed hold of Danny. "What?"

"The fucking perp. He's got out!"

Rache was stunned. She looked at Susan. Susan was white.

"Someone saw…someone saw him go up on the roof," he panted, holding his chest.

Rache didn't need a second invitation. The information was enough to compel her into action. She took the stairs to the roof in seconds. Goddamit, how could this happen? How could he get out of a locked cell? Had his docile act been just that? An act?

There would be hell to pay if they didn't get him. Reaching the top of the stairs, she could make out a voice behind her. It sounded like Danny. Rache was at the door that led onto the roof. It was wide open. She had been up to the roof on only one occasion. She pushed her brain to remember its geography. Yeah, there had been a party a few years back when one of her colleagues had retired. Joe had attempted a pass at her. He had drunk too much and had embarrassed himself. Rache had laughed it off with him to help him save face. Guys, they were so insecure!

But Rache wasn't laughing now. The perp was up here, no doubt. She cursed herself for falling for his routine, his so-called insanity plea. He had fooled them all. How had they been so stupid? Rache was annoyed with herself now. Annoyed that she had allowed this scumbag to lull her into a trap. That look he had given her in the mirror had sent shivers down her back, but it was a calculated risk he had taken. She was certain of that now. Yeah, there was a two-way mirror. He knew they were watching him. He had banked on it.

Clever son of a bitch, she thought. *Watch those questioning you, then turn it to your advantage.* Divide and conquer? Was that his agenda? He had kept it up for hours. This confused game he'd played. *Clever bastard. But how the fuck had he gotten out?*

There was no doubt in her mind of his guilt. Some of the officers had begun to feel sorry for him. Fools!

Rache had never felt sorry for him. Anyone who would hurt a little girl so much that her eyes bled was capable of anything. No, she had not felt sorry for him. But she had fallen for his game.

A warm breeze blew the door to the roof closed. The sudden noise made her jump. Rache cocked her gun. If need be, she'd shoot him.

She gently pushed the door open. She stepped out onto the roof just as Danny caught up to her at the door. Rache beckoned him out with her free hand. She put her fingers to her lips.

The precinct roof was flat. On either side, walls rose high above it. No way anyone could climb them. There was an electrical junction box half way across it. It was the only place to hide. Steadily, Rache and Danny inched their way across the roof to the box. She glanced over at him. Danny had his gun drawn. He nodded at Rache. She knew she could rely on him.

They pulled around the side of the junction box.

Nothing!

Rache looked around.

"Maybe he didn't get this far," Danny suggested.

"The fire escape!" she exclaimed. Rache ran the ten or so yards to the south wall. She looked down the fire escape. It was easily a twenty-foot drop to the ground from the last rung of the ladder. Had he jumped? She had no way of knowing.

She'd print the fire escape. That way they could tell.

Danny's walkie-talkie crackled to life. It was Theo!

"You see him, Danny? Over?" Theo's voice asked.

Danny held it to his mouth. "No, we got nothing, over."

Theo's reply sent a bolt through both of them. "We're completely locked down. He's gone, man, he's gone!"

Rache beckoned to Danny for the walkie-talkie. Danny passed it to her.

"Theo, it's Rache. Say again, say again."

"He's vanished, Rache. No sign of him anywhere!"

Theo's words bit into her. Rache held the radio to her chest. Holding the radio to her lips, she spoke again.

"Theo, get a print team up here, ASAP! He may have used the fire escape to get to the street. If he did, he's hurt. It must be a twenty- or thirty-foot drop . It's our only chance," Rache said into the walkie-talkie.

"On it," came the reply.

Rache looked out over the Manhattan skyline. The sun had disappeared behind the buildings, and suddenly, Rache felt cold. It wasn't from the lack of sunshine. All day she felt a little weird.

Danny put a hand on her shoulder.

"Goddammit, Danny, goddammit! How could this happen?" she asked, her frustration evident.

"Come on," he said.

They both walked down.

CHAPTER 7

T HE PRINT TEAM DIDN'T TAKE long. As they had only to check one set of prints against a few on the fire escape, it had taken them a little time to pull up a match. The perp had used the fire escape to gain access to the street. An all-points bulletin had been sent out immediately, but Manhattan was one large haystack in which to find a human needle. Captain Woods had set up a center of operations in his own office. Working out a timeline, he had summoned the main protagonists in the unfolding drama to his office. Forty-five minutes from the time of escape to now. Already he had a sinking feeling that it was too late. But he had to act. He had to be seen to take action. He knew now how the suspect had used the fire escape to gain access to the street. He didn't yet know how he had managed to escape from a locked cell. That could come later. *Focus on the here and now*, Woods urged himself.

Those who worked the night shift had already been called and asked to come in early. They answered to a person. Most had already arrived.

Sitting in the office, Rache felt a little sad for the captain. It was ultimately his responsibility. It had happened on his watch, and he would carry the can. But more worrying than responsibility or blame was that the sick bastard was out there, and they had no clue where.

Rache glanced about. The faces of her colleagues said it all. Rache's eyes wandered over the room. She found herself being drawn to a large map of the New York subway. *The subway*, she thought. Looking at the map now, her heart began to sink. The New York City subway was a giant living, breathing organism with its seemingly endless network of tunnels and tracks that served as the veins and arteries that feed the creature, carrying in excess of seven million people daily. With over four thousand skyscrapers crammed onto the island of Manhattan and literally thousands of cabs choking the city's congested streets, the subway offered a more efficient alternative mode of transport.

Rache's eyes quickly glanced over the multitude of separate lines that crisscrossed the city, weaving through the hundreds of square kilometers that stretched from the Hudson River across the island and into Brooklyn, Queens, and the Bronx. The perp could easily take a tube off the island, over to Queens, and be gone, Rache figured. In all, the subway had over four hundred stops. The enormity of the task facing them began to hit home for Rache. They couldn't police every stop. Plus the New York system was unique in that it never shut down, never stopped running. Forty-five minutes—he's gone.

Rache shifted her attention back to the captain. Woods had decided that there was nothing more to do but search the immediate area. After that, they were to go home. Susan, Danny, and many others protested. They would stay all night. Everyone knew they had been duped, and their pride was a little hurt. But the captain made sense. The guys working nights would work nights. He needed his people fresh. "If you have no sleep, you're no use to me," he said, addressing them from the top of the room. "Running around the city looking for this guy will get us nowhere. We need to be focused, people. We need to be focused."

Everyone agreed.

"Now, I need these people brought up to speed. We've got every patrol car with a picture of this guy, and if he pops his head up, we'll get him. Your shift starts at eight. I'd like you all here by six thirty. Now finish up and go home."

A slow murmur started up.

Captain Woods raised his hands. "Enough already. Pair off and get on with it."

Rache and Danny sat in their office. It was almost ten when they finished briefing their colleagues on the day's events. There was a knock on the door.

Matt Brook, one of the top fingerprint experts in the city, stuck his head around the door. "Got an interesting result for you guys on the fire escape," Matt said, closing the door behind him. Matt and Rache had worked many cases before, and she knew him to be reliable.

All four officers gave him their full attention.

"As you know we picked up his prints at the top, which pretty much identified him straight away. Well, I'm a thorough guy, so we dusted it the whole way down…"

"And?" Rache asked, wondering why Matt felt this was important.

"Prints stopped halfway, Rache. Looks like your mystery boy thought he could fly."

"What?"

"Prints only go halfway. We got a couple of people on the ground now."

"I gotta see this," Rache said, standing up and walking to the door. "Danny, can you finish up with the guys here?" She nodded to the two detectives who would take over from there.

"Sure."

Matt held his hand out, as if to stop her. "Rache, there's nothing to see."

"Come on," she insisted, heading for the stairs.

Rache stood directly below the precinct fire escape, looking up at the building. *No way he could have jumped from the second floor. It must be fifty feet*, she thought. *No way he'd have made it without shattering his legs. No way.*

She peered down the street. He could be anywhere by now.

Matt spoke to her. "Rache, the captain's right. Go home and get some sleep. We got a lot of people working on it."

Rache nodded. "Yeah, maybe you're right, Matt." She stared down the street, watching as fluorescent streetlights illuminated those passing beneath. Friday evening, and the city was alive. *He could be any one of those people*, she thought.

The short drive home gave Rache some time to reflect on the day's events. It all seemed surreal. In a little over twelve hours, the world had changed. The sick son of a bitch who'd attacked this poor kid and shot her father was free. He'd escaped police custody. But how had he managed to get out of a secure cell? If she'd buy Matt's theory, he'd jumped at least fifty feet to the sidewalk. Sure, if he'd been on PCP or something more exotic, he might have done so in the chaos of the escape. But he'd tested negative for all the usual suspects. What was it Theo had said? He hadn't taken as much as an aspirin. Anyway, if he'd jumped, drugged or not, he'd never have survived the fall. There had to be some other explanation.

Rache lived in a small two-bedroom apartment off Fifty-Sixth and Broadway. She had rented the apartment on a short-term basis when she was first stationed at Midtown North, but five years on, she was still a resident. The rent had been reasonable, and the landlady had never asked for an increase. In fact, her landlady had never asked for anything, which suited Rache. She hated rehashing the past. She barely knew her neighbors. She preferred it that way. Solitude was a comfort for her. In the five years she'd lived there, only three men had been to her pad, and one of those was her brother. Rache Fischer was not big on socializing.

Rache had converted the smaller bedroom into an office, installing a PC, printer, and scanner. If the occasion merited it, she would often take a particular case home. It was sometimes easier to work away from the station. There were times when a case would get to be too much. Rache had developed a habit of taking the case with her. She had a big whiteboard, and she would often jot down the more salient aspects in the case and then sleep on it. In the morning, over coffee, she would look at what she had written, and things were often clearer.

Tonight, however, there would be no whiteboard. She just wanted a hot shower and to go to bed. Rache knew that tomorrow would be insane, with accusations flying about. Yeah, tomorrow would be a day of finger pointing. Personally, she felt that achieved nothing. Better to concentrate on the task at hand. Two questions weighed on Rache's mind as she got into bed.

How did he get out?

And more importantly, where was he now?

She removed her bathrobe, tossing it on the chair that sat at the end of her bed. As she climbed under her duvet, she bunched it up around her. Hugging it close, she thought of Jensen—of how she missed him. In times like these, she felt she could always talk to him, confide in him.

Rache lay still a moment, deep in her thoughts. Yeah, she thought, it had been one fucked-up day. Asides from the perp talking a walk, chatting to her mom had brought up memories of her sister. Soon it would be her sister's anniversary—and she didn't even want to think about that.

Reaching over to turn off her bedside lamp, she glanced at the clock. Eleven thirty. Six hours. It ought to be enough.

CHAPTER 8

CONSIDERING THE DAY SHE'D ENCOUNTERED, Rache's sleep remained almost undisturbed. But just before she woke, at the time when the subconscious hands the baton over to the conscious mind, one thought, above all, slipped through the net, the net that seems to filter out our dreams.

Most people remember little of what they dream. Rache was not such a person. As dawn broke over Midtown Manhattan, Rache found herself back in the interview room with the perp staring intensely at her. For some reason, he was refusing to allow Matt to print him. Danny and Susan were there, but they seemed to be passive participants in the unfolding drama. The perp aimed a very disarming smile at Rache. He looked over at Danny and Susan. Suddenly Joe was in the room, wielding a large wooden baton as he started to beat the perp. The perp cried out. Danny and Susan's gaze was fixed on Rache, who was too paralyzed to move.

The perp screamed as Joe turned his face into bloody pulp.

"Help me, Rachel, help me!" he begged her.

Rache woke with a jump. Her hair was soaked, sticking to her face in a wet lather. Brushing it aside, she realized her hands were shaking. *Gotta lay off the coffee*, she thought. But she knew it wasn't the coffee. It was the name. He had called her Rachel. In the dream, he had begged for help, and he had used the name Rachel. No one called her that. No one but family!

It had all started with a small typo on her application form, back when she had first joined the academy. Someone had put her down as Rache Fischer, and somehow, she had kept it. It seemed fitting. As a young eighteen-year-old, she was starting a new life, a life that would have some purpose other than getting rich, so it seemed fitting she would have a new name.

Rache walked into her bathroom, yesterday's images flooding her mind. She remembered Joe hitting the perp. "The sick son of a bitch was getting off looking at you, Rache," Joe had said. Yeah, that was it. She remembered Pete saying her name. "Here's Rache." Or had he said, "Here's Rachel"? Pete was relatively new to the precinct. Could have been a genuine mistake, she figured. But what had the perp said? Rachel, it was definitely Rachel. Or was it?

Why this detail bothered her, she did not know. She would not have given it any thought had she not had that dream. The dream was still fresh in her mind.

Rache stood under a hot shower for a long time.

Arriving at the precinct a little after six, she found the place was a manic buzz of activity. Rache looked about, quickly scanning the parking lot. No camera or news crews yet. Something to be thankful for.

Susan met her as she made her way upstairs. "Captain's got a briefing room all set up on the fourth floor. He wants everyone there by six thirty," Susan told her.

Rache nodded. "Gotta get a coffee," Rache said, forgetting her earlier advice.

"Yeah, me too," Susan added.

They both made their way to Rache's office. Brett Becker, one of the detectives who had taken over from her last night, was sorting through some files. Rache barged in on him. "Oh, sorry, Brett!"

"No, Rache, it's fine," he said, shuffling some papers together.

"Got anything?" she inquired.

"Nada! No one's seen sight nor sound of him since he walked out." Brett looked away, embarrassed at what he'd just said.

Rache nodded. "You're right, Brett, he walked out of here, no question. What bothers me is how?"

Brett smiled. "We've had cops from all over looking for this guy. Even had some from the Nineteenth, Seventeenth, and the Thirteenth Precincts looking for him."

"So word's got out, huh?"

"Yeah, but look, Rache, everyone is pulling on this one. No one wants a rapist on the streets, least of all a child rapist."

"Any word from the hospital?" Rache asked.

"Father's out of surgery, but it's touch and go. Kid's still out cold."

"That's weird, isn't it?"

Brett nodded. "Doc...or some specialist guy saw her late last night. Figures she may have internal organ damage."

Rache looked at Susan.

"Damage? What kind of damage?"

"They don't know, Rache. But this doc said it was as though someone had squeezed the life out of her," Brett added.

"Thanks, Brett," Rache replied as she poured two mugs of coffee.

"Sure."

Brett pulled on his jacket. "Can you place his accent?" he asked as he walked to the door.

Rache shrugged. "He only spoke once or twice. That was the problem. We couldn't get a word out of him."

"Try and think back, Rache. It could be a clue."

Brett was right. His accent. It was different, foreign, and yet somehow familiar.

"Well, I'm sure we're going to review the tapes anyway, so—"

"Didn't you hear?"

"Hear what?"

"The tapes. We looked at them last night. They're all blank!"

"I don't believe this," Rache said, spinning around.

"The whole precinct?" she inquired.

"No, just the interview room," Susan told her.

Danny opened the door. "Hey, Brett," he said, greeting the night shift officer.

Brett nodded back.

"Captain's ready for us now, guys," Danny informed them.

"Good luck," Brett said, looking at Rache.

Brett walked out, leaving Rache dumbfounded.

"Did you hear about the tapes, Danny?"

"Just now. Strange, don't you think?"

"What happened?" she asked.

Danny shrugged.

Susan took Rache by the arm. "Let's see what Woods has to say."

Captain Don Woods was a man under severe pressure. He knew his job was on the line. Job, pension, credibility. The whole nine yards. A suspected felon had escaped from a locked police cell in broad daylight. To compound matters, the suspect was wanted on attempted murder and attempted rape. He hadn't got that far, thank god. Kell Mason was still in a coma, but the rape kit had come back negative. *One small mercy*, thought Woods. He knew he needed a result, and he needed it fast. The video had broken down for a couple of hours, so all they had was snow. From what the detectives had said, it wouldn't have been much use anyway as the suspect had refused point-blank to talk. But that wouldn't carry any weight. The suspect had disappeared on his watch, and ultimately, he was responsible. *Disappeared* seemed the only word to use in this case. There was no sign of him anywhere. Jesus Christ, Matt almost had him believing he'd jumped the last two storeys. They had done a thorough search of all the neighboring hospitals. Nothing.

Woods was glad of his experience. He was glad he had sent them home last night. He had only managed a couple of hours tossing and turning on the couch, but at least the guys would be fresh. Everyone would look to him now. He had to step up, as the saying goes.

A loud noise greeted him on entering the briefing room. Danny, Theo, Susan, and Rache sat at the front. Pete, Joe, and two other detectives sat behind them. He had requested some uniform and traffic cops. And they were there too. He even had a couple of guys from another station house. The usual inter-precinct rivalry was gone here. The case was too serious. A madman was out there, attacking kids and shooting people in their own homes.

The chat died down almost immediately. Everyone looked at the captain. They expected leadership. He looked at Rache, Danny, Theo, and Susan. If anyone could crack this, they could. But they needed leadership. No time for half measures. This was it.

"Okay, people, here's what we got," he started. He stopped. Honesty. That was the one word that jumped to mind. Honesty. He nodded, almost to himself.

When he spoke, he spoke rapidly. "We got nothing. No name, no ID, no priors, and we got an empty cell. Elvis has left the building. Tox-screen came back negative. So he wasn't revved up. We're running his DNA now, but it's going to take a bit of time."

Everyone looked shocked. But Captain Woods didn't stop.

"Did I say what we had? Well, that's not what we have—it's what we don't have. We don't have him, and we don't have a history. What we do have is a crime scene," he continued. "Forensics..." Woods paused, looking at his watch. "Forensics are working it now!"

He turned to two of his people.

"Danny, I want you and Rache to start there, this morning. Find out what you can."

Rache and Danny nodded.

"Theo, when you're done distributing photos, you and Susan look at those tapes again." Woods held his hand up before Theo could say anything.

"I know, I know, the tapes are a bust. But let's be sure. Are the tapes faulty? Is it our equipment? Did they record something, and we can't make it out? I want to know! If you have to get someone from NASA over in a space-hopper suit to run a quantum scan on them, then do it. Rule nothing out, understand?"

Theo stared to pass among the desks with photos of the suspect, nodding at everyone as he did.

Woods spoke again. "Joe, Pete, I want you guys to head over to the kid's school. Talk to the students, to the principal, to the fucking janitor. Any suspicious activity lately, and I want to know. This guy didn't happen on his victim by accident. She was carefully chosen. He brought a gun with him and was prepared to use it. If there was some old lady walking butt-ugly pugs near the schoolyard, I want to know."

Woods nodded at the two detectives at the back of the room.

As they approached, Woods said, "Officers Smyth and Brooks are on loan from the Seventeenth Precinct. Any work you cannot do yourself, you are to ask them. That is why they are here, and we appreciate it."

All the other cops nodded their approval.

Woods took a deep breath. But before he could say another word, there was a knock on the door, and the young officer from the previous day, Cole Marks, entered. He smiled at Rache, but didn't hold her eye. She knew immediately it was bad news.

Officer Marks spoke into the captain's ear. She could see the physical reaction of the captain. He was a good man trying to hide bad news. Officer Cole Marks left the room as quickly as he'd entered.

Someone was dead, that was for sure, thought Rache. God, was it the little kid? She was in a coma, yeah, but had she deteriorated? Was it the organ damage?

"This has officially become a murder hunt."

His words stung her and the others. There were one or two gasps.

"Joe Mason didn't make it. He died from complications ten minutes ago."

The room erupted in a hum of noise. Everyone started to talk at once.

Woods raised his hands in an attempt to quiet the din. "Everyone...everyone...please, people."

The noise died down.

Woods composed himself a moment. "We all want this scumbag. He led us up the river with some looney act and made a mockery of this precinct. That happens only once, understood!"

There was stony silence.

"Good."

Rache cleared her throat. "Maybe I should swing by the hospital. Check on the kid?"

"No, go to the crime scene. We have no weapon. We need that, Rache. You can swing by the hospital later," Woods replied.

"Okay," said Rache.

"Theo, as soon as you and Susan are done on the videotapes, I want you to check into this kid's mother. By the looks of things, parents were separated. We need to find her mother, okay?"

"Rache Fischer and Danny O'Connor are primaries on this case. You keep them as up to date as you do me. You all have your assignments. I want results."

As everyone began to file out, Woods asked Rache to hang back. She turned to Danny. "See you downstairs."

Danny nodded. He looked over at the Captain and smiled.

When everyone was out, Captain Woods walked over to the door. He checked it, making sure it was closed. He turned to Rache. "I don't know how to say this, Rache…some of the—"

"Say what?" Rache asked.

"Okay, Danny and Susan thought he recognized you. I know that sounds crazy—"

"No, no, it doesn't," she replied, sitting down.

Woods sat beside her.

"It's been troubling me too," she continued. "I mean, I've never met the guy, but he has this way of looking at you." She lowered her tone. "It kinda scares me, ya know!"

"But you don't know who he is?"

"Honest, Captain, before yesterday, I never set eyes on him."

"Rache, Internal Affairs is all over this one. I gotta meet the mayor after lunch. I need something to feed him, or you'll be reporting to someone else tomorrow."

Rache studied him a moment. It wasn't the captain's fault. But he would carry the can. But it wasn't just the captain who needed a result. She needed one. She needed to put this one to bed.

"I'm on it, Captain."

"Thanks, Rache. I made you primary 'cos I know you, and I know your commitment."

"Look, after I check out the kid's place, I'll look into some old cases. Maybe I know him, I can't say," she said, standing up from the desk.

"It's a place to start," Woods said, nodding.

"I'd best be going." Rache walked out past Captain Woods and closed the door.

CHAPTER 9

D RIVING BACK TO KELL MASON's house, with Danny looking over a file in the passenger seat beside her, Rache tried to come to terms with the gravity of the situation. It was less than twenty-four hours, but everything had changed. Kell Mason's father had died. The kid was in some sort of vegetative state. The guy they had in custody—the bastard responsible—had escaped.

Shit, there'd be hell to pay on that one!

The captain's speech was inspiring, but Rache knew he was reaching. They had nothing. The one person they did have had disappeared into a September dusk and was probably miles away at this stage.

They were, all of them, clutching at straws. No matter what they found at the house, it would be futile. Rache felt a sense of helplessness overwhelm her. *Get it together, girl*, she told herself. *Look at the positive side. The kid hadn't been raped. Something to be thankful for. If she came—no*. Rache corrected her thoughts. When *she comes out of it, she'd be able to ID the perp and wouldn't have to deal with the torment of rape. Yeah, Kell must be able to ID him. So, Rache*, she told herself, *concentrate on catching this bastard*. Maybe he hadn't strayed too far. *I have to believe that*, she thought. Otherwise, why go on with the investigation?

Yes, but where to start? Rache didn't think she could help by going to the house. As soon as forensics got anything, they'd let them know, she figured. So when a uniformed officer lifted the yellow plastic tape to let herself and Danny in, she thought she'd spend a few minutes, let Danny talk to them, and she'd swing by the hospital and look in on the kid.

Shit, she's just lost her dad and was unaware of it. It hit home for Rache. As much as she disagreed with her father over things, she'd go and see them. What if she got a call to say her father was dead? How would she react? she wondered. Yeah, she'd go to the dinner. David's wife, Sarah, would be there. But she'd go. Even if she didn't say too much, she'd go. It might be that Sarah had mellowed a little. What was it with lawyers and this presumption of innocence, when even their own clients told them they were guilty? It frustrated her at times. She had seen too many scumbags walk when she had worked vice. Seen too many victims too frightened to testify. It was where she'd built her reputation. Well, started to build it anyway. She knew how some of the other cops spoke about her. But she didn't care. She had often used that reputation to coerce another officer into helping her get a result. But she had always acted within the law. That was why she had a 100 percent conviction rate as a homicide detective.

Until now.

Kell Mason's house was nothing out of the ordinary. A three-bedroom detached structure, set in a little in off the street. Rache threw a cursory glance at the front door. No sign of forced entry. Maybe he got in some other way. As Rache and Danny walked slowly past the officer, they heard voices upstairs. Rache went to walk upstairs. Danny touched her lightly on her arm. He nodded. Rache looked into the living room. A large pool of congealed blood stained the wooden floor, where Joe Mason had fallen. The glass from the coffee table had been cleared away. The scene had been thoroughly worked the day before. The downstairs work complete, the forensic scientists had moved upstairs.

Rache looked into the living room. The dark stain was the blood of a dead man. *How simple*, she thought. *How simple to categorize things.*

"Let's see what the guys have to say," she said to Danny as she began to climb the stairs.

"Yeah."

His reply puzzled her. She looked back at him as he just stared into the lounge.

"You okay?" she asked, pausing on the first step.

63

"Doesn't it seem too sad?" Danny said. "I mean…the kid's in a coma, and her dad is dead. That's his blood on the floor. We can't find her mother, and the poor kid has no idea her father's gone. Doesn't it all just seem too sad?"

Rache nodded. Danny had just articulated her own thoughts.

"Come on, Danny, don't go soft on me," she said, punching him lightly on the shoulder.

But Danny just shrugged.

They stood at the door to Kell's bedroom. The door had been literally kicked off its hinges. Rache stared into the room. Her heart skipped a beat. She had never seen anything like it. The bedroom was trashed!

Her eyes were immediately drawn to Kell's bed. A deep mahogany brown headboard exhibiting a large fissure down the middle first caught her attention. The wood had splintered in all directions. *Must have thrown her against the headboard*, Rache thought. The idea of Kell's head crashing against the wood freaked her. Rache steadied herself. *Come on, Rache, this is just speculation*, she told herself.

Her eyes checked out the bedclothes now. They were shredded. It was as though someone had taken a scythe or some other sharp instrument and had carefully sliced up the linen. But it was the amount of dried blood in particular that really upset her. One pillow was almost covered by a large crimson stain. Rache recalled some of the photos taken of the perp, before he'd been cleaned up, his face and hair covered in Kell Mason's blood. Rache shuddered, a cold tingling running from the base of her neck to the bottom of her spine, causing the muscles in her back to twitch slightly.

She looked over at what she could only guess had been a small dresser. It was smashed beyond recognition. A large chest of drawers opposite Kell's bed looked as though someone had taken a baseball bat to it. Framed photographs that had once adorned it lay broken on the ground now, the glass shattered, forming small spiderweb patterns over the pictures within. Many of them had Kell posing with a tennis racket. One in particular had her standing between two adults, her young smile bright as she held a silver cup that seemed too big for her. Rache recognized the man as Joe Mason. The woman had to be her mother. They were so alike. Rache made a mental note to take the photo before she left.

Two detectives, Dion Chavez and Raul Ramirez, worked the scene. With any crime scene, those processing it always started at the extremities, working inward in ever-decreasing circles. The process was painstaking and time consuming. Leaving no stone unturned literally meant that. Everything was potential evidence. Rache was glad it was Dion Chavez on this one. Dion was the best. They had worked together on dozens of cases, and Rache found she had always got the quickest results with Dion. She smiled over at him.

Rache Fischer, now there was a strange one, thought Dion. Twenty years working crime scenes, he'd come across Rache on a number of occasions. She was like a bloodhound—relentless! He'd tried, on more than one occasion, to convince her to move to the forensics unit. But she'd always declined. Yeah, Rache Fischer, he liked her. Couldn't figure her, but he liked her.

He smiled back. "Hey, Rache, Danny," he said, looking up.

"Dion."

"Anything?" Danny asked.

"Nothing and everything."

"Whatya mean?" asked Rache, puzzled by this remark.

"I gottta say this is by far the strangest one to date."

"Strange how?" she replied.

Dion stood up and walked over to them. "Normally you have to look really hard. I mean down and dirty on the floor, under the beds, down the toilets…" he said.

Rache and Danny were nodding.

"So you look at everything. Semen on the sheets, lipstick on cigarettes, fibers, dog hairs, urine splashes on the floor, etc., etc.," he continued. "Then you usually get a break, not always, but usually. We nailed this one guy 'cos he'd blown his nose on a curtain, but this is different. This is the opposite. All the evidence is presented to you on a platter."

"So why is that a problem?" inquired Danny, unsure exactly what Dion was driving at.

"Because the more you examine it, the less it makes sense," Dion said. "You remember after the Oklahoma bombing how the government became suspicious of anyone buying fertilizer?"

"Yeah, but what has that got to do—"

Dion held up his hand.

Rache fell silent.

"Well, we were all given advanced training on how to detect the presence of explosives."

"I'm still not with you," Rache said.

So he told her.

The bombing of the federal building in Oklahoma had, until September 11, been the single largest terrorist attack in the United States. Dion explained that the forensics scientists had, with the help of the military, been given extensive training in the detection of the minutest particles of fertilizer, ammonia, and other ingredients that could be bought over the counter. Dion was educated in how to distinguish explosive patterns. He could tell at a glance from the pattern if the explosive was homemade or professional, if it were a grenade or C4 that had been used. Rache told him she was impressed but did not see the connection.

"I can't join the dots, Rache," Dion said.

"What dots?"

"Look, if I didn't know better, I'd say someone lobbed a Russian-made RPG scatter fragmentation hand grenade into the kid's bed."

Rache was dumbfounded.

Dion continued. "Yeah, it sounds like I've lost my marbles. But take a look around, Rache. What do you see?"

Rache studied the room. "A mess!"

"Yeah. Were you a messy teenager?"

"No, why?"

"Neither was this kid. Everything folded away neatly, yet the place is a-shambles. The sheets and bedclothes are shredded..."

Rache went to interject, but Dion wouldn't let her.

"And when we examined Kell's clothes, they were shredded also. Both are consistent with some sort of explosion."

Danny cut in. "How is that possible?"

"It's not," Dion told him. "But the kid's wounds are also consistent with the same sort of trauma. She was haemorrhaging from the eyes, ears, and nose. She'd lost an inordinate amount of blood. All these wounds are typical of blast victims. Only we got no blast."

Rache looked at Danny.

He shrugged. "I don't get it."

"If you are close to the center of a bomb, the air is pushed at you at about four thousand feet per second. It will liquefy your organs and remove clothes, skin, and limbs. People farther away will suffer soft tissue damage, sight loss, and ear damage," Dion said.

"The doctors said that Kell could have some kind of organ damage. Would explain it," Rache told him.

"You may think…but there was no explosion."

"But you said—"

"Yes, that is how the evidence presents itself. Like I said, Rache, the more I dig into this, the weirder it becomes."

Danny looked perplexed. "Let me get this straight. You're saying the kid's injuries are because of an explosion, but none took place, is that right, Dion?"

"Yeah, but I said her injuries are consistent with an explosion."

"This is madness," Rache said. "How is the perp—"

She caught herself, but Dion smiled.

"What I mean is how is our mystery man tied in?"

"Did that guy actually walk out of a police station?"

The question shocked her. It was the starkness of it. Also, it was the honesty of it. All three looked over at who directed it.

Raul!

"Raul," said Dion, staring him down now.

Raul looked away. "Yeah, sorry. I just thought it was strange…"

"It's okay," said Rache. "You're right, it's weird."

"Tell her about the bullet, Dion!" Raul piped up.

Dion gave him another icy stare. Raul was good, but he had never learned when to shut up. Dion told him to head downstairs and start the preliminary work on the kitchen. Raul looked like a scolded schoolboy. He literally sulked as he walked out past Rache and Danny, both of whom stood at the door.

"So what's with the bullet?" Rache asked when Raul was downstairs.

"We found a bullet in the ceiling," he told her.

"And?"

"It was fired at an angle, indicating that someone must have caused the shooter's arm to be pushed upward."

"She fought back. Good for her."

"I don't think so. This place is trashed. No way a kid could put up that kind of a struggle."

The words echoed in her head. Rache's heart began to pound. The memories began to flood back. They were painful and sharp. Her breathing became labored.

Dion was looking at her now.

"It's okay, Rache, it's okay," he said.

Rache had to fight down the nausea. She swallowed hard. The bile tasted awful. But she couldn't let them see her like this.

She looked over at Danny. He gave her that same questioning look from yesterday.

"I'm fine. It's just a little upsetting, that's all. The bullet, you get a match?" she asked, recovering some of her composure.

Dion nodded. "The slug taken from Joe Mason had fragmented, but we were able to match it to the bullet taken from the ceiling."

"So he fired twice."

"Yeah, but why not just shoot the kid?" Danny asked. "I mean, he shoots Mr. Mason, comes upstairs, and doesn't shoot the kid." Danny looked about. He had to agree with Dion. "Dion's right. No way Kell Mason put up a struggle like this. No way."

"He had an accomplice."

Dion and Danny stared at Rache.

Shit, thought Danny. He hadn't considered that.

"No!" said Dion. "That's not possible."

"God damn it, why not?" Rache demanded, exasperated.

Dion stood in front of the bed, just below the bullet hole. He explained that Kell was found on the bed in front of where he was standing. He held his hand out as if to fire a gun.

"Now if you were my accomplice, and you wanted to prevent me from firing," he explained, "the only way possible, from the trajectory of the bullet, would be if you were straight in front of me. You would have to have been in front and grabbed my hands for the bullet to end up in the ceiling. If I were knocked from the side, the bullet would end up in the wall."

He beckoned Rache to come over to him. Positioning her at the end of the bed, he asked her to point at the bed as if to fire her gun. Rache stood too far back, so Dion edged her closer. She now stood with her legs pushed right against the bed.

"Now," he said, "move your hands up slowly in an arc."

Rache did as he asked, following her arm movement with her eyes. She stopped when her hands were directly above her head. She stared at the hole the bullet had drilled in the ceiling. Dion told her to hold the position.

"So for someone to have prevented that shot, he or she would have had to been lying on the bed."

Rache lowered her hands. She looked deflated. "How do you explain it then?"

"At this moment in time...I have no idea..."

Danny sniffed, scratching his nose. "I got a question for you! Where'd he stash the gun he used to kill Joe Mason?"

Dion and Rache looked at him.

"I don't know, Danny. I just don't know," Dion said.

CHAPTER 10

Rache drove away from Kell's house toward the hospital. She felt the need to see this kid. She didn't care what the captain said. She just wanted to see the kid. Rache really felt for her. Her father had been murdered, and her mom was missing. Kell was in some kind of comatose state, and they had no leads.

"Look, maybe the doctors can shed some light on her condition. Maybe he forced her to swallow something," Rache had said to Danny. "If so, could be something we can use."

Danny had reluctantly agreed.

She had asked him to check with the neighbors. Rache would swing by the hospital, look in on Kell, and pick Danny up later.

She hadn't said it to Danny, but she really needed to get away. No matter where they looked, they were drawing blanks! The perp was AWOL, and forensics were tying themselves up in knots. They had explosive theories without explosions and bullets in the roof that couldn't be explained. *Best to get out of here*, Rache had thought. She could always think better when she was alone. And she needed to think.

Dion had found some hairs on the bed that could belong to the perp. But even if they did, what good was it? He was more than likely long gone. Nevertheless, Dion had said he would run them in the DNA lab along with the blood and saliva from yesterday.

Rache had thanked him and told Danny she was going to check in on the kid.

She tried to sum up the last twenty-four hours. It was weird, no question.

She was at the entrance to the hospital car park when her cell phone rang. It was Susan.

"Hey," Rache said into the phone, pulling the car over, allowing her to give the call her full attention.

"Hi, Rache. Nothing on the precinct video," Susan said. "We got a couple of guys coming in this afternoon from outta town. Experts on rubbed-out tape or something. You get anything at the house?"

"Nothing but more questions. The house and grounds have been thoroughly searched. Still no weapon," Rache said.

She told Susan about Dion's theory on the explosion.

"Rache, this is too weird."

"Tell me about it. Any word on the kid's mother?"

"No."

"Susan, I'm on my way over to the hospital now. Maybe the doctors can help us."

"Yeah, I mean, if the kid wakes up, ya know…"

"Yeah, but I get this sinking feeling the poor kid's not gonna wake up."

"Come on, Rache, you gotta be positive," Susan encouraged her.

"Look, I'm at the hospital now. I'll call ya later, okay?"

"Okay, see ya."

Built at the beginning of the 1990s, Washington General had been named after the first president of the United States of America. George Washington had presided over a newly formed country, so when city officials had built a state-of-the-art hospital with a cancer research unit attached, they had described it as only fitting to name it after the great president. In a way, Washington General was a new beginning for many.

Rache parked her car in the small parking lot out front. Making her way to reception, Rache flashed her badge at a young nurse standing beside a conservative-looking receptionist.

"I'm Detective Fischer. I'm here to see Kell Mason."

The nurse took Rache aside. She told her that her name was Jenny, and she had been attending Kell since she was brought in the previous day.

"She's on the fourth floor. We moved her out of intensive care, and we have her in a room near the nurse's station."

Rache and Jenny took the elevator to the fourth floor. As the doors opened, Rache asked if she could see the kid alone. Jenny nodded. She told Rache that Kell was stable, and they were doing everything to make her comfortable. Rache asked her if there had been any improvement. Jenny told her that Kell's condition remained stable, but unchanged. She was in some sort of coma, and to be honest, it had the doctors baffled. They had brought in two specialists from upstate—experts in the field. But after a series of tests, they seemed to concur. Nobody could figure out what was wrong with Kell Mason.

Rache thanked the nurse.

Kell's room was directly opposite a small nurse's station. A uniformed officer stood guard by the door. It was the first thing Rache had done after the perp had escaped.

She greeted the cop as she prepared herself.

Rache wasn't sure what to expect when she opened the door. She recalled the photos of Kell she'd seen back at the house. But they were photos of happier times, photos of a happy family—a family that was no more because some lunatic had shot a family man with a hollow-point bullet, making a young kid fatherless.

Why? It was the question that troubled her the most. Of course, there were all the associated problems with the escape. But the question that took center stage was why? The perp being totally unresponsive hadn't helped. He had only uttered a couple of words, and even those troubled her. But above all, she could find no motive. Why kill Joe Mason? What had he done to deserve it? Was it random or planned? Was Kell the intended victim? And if so, why stay afterward? Man, he was strung out when they had him. Straight up whacked. Yet the toxicology report had come back negative—which only added to the mystery. Explosive theories, a vanishing suspect who'd tested negative for every substance known to man.

The whole case was straight up whacked.

Rache also knew that she would have to look over old arrests. This guy seemed to know her. But she couldn't figure it.

She took a deep breath and pushed open the door.

CHAPTER 11

E WALKED DOWN PAST THE church. It seemed oddly familiar; its huge spire thrust skyward served like some kind of homing beacon. He did not know why he had found his way to this place. He knew he should not have been in that cage, and he had left there, gone up on the roof, and down the ladder to the street. The warm September night had turned cool as he walked the street in the early hours. The cold had been a strange sensation for him. Goose bumps ran up his arm. He had walked on nonstop and was now outside the church. The huge edifice dwarfed him as he stared up at it from beneath darkened shadows.

Why was he here? What had brought him here? He did not know the city, yet he had been here before. Why?

He stood there for a long time, unsure of what to do. But most of all, he was puzzled by its familiarity. Yes, he had been here before. He felt comfort in that. The comfort gave him purpose. Purpose! It all came down to purpose. What was his purpose? He wasn't sure, but he knew the answer must be behind the door.

He pushed the door open…

CHAPTER 12

KELL MASON LAY SUPPORTED BY three pillows. Some of the nurses had placed flowers in vases that now sat in the window near her bed. News that her father had died had swept through the hospital wing. The fact that this sleeping beauty had not had a single visitor only fueled the nurses' desire to do all they could for Kell Mason. A small white rabbit looked up at Rache from Kell's pillow. Kell's jet-black hair flowed over her shoulders. Thick black lashes jutted from peaceful eyelids, closed now to the horrors they had witnessed. She looked peaceful, almost serene—all traces of the tortuous ordeal washed clean.

As she watched her, Rache thought she could almost be sleeping, and if she made a loud noise, Kell would wake up. A cardio monitor displayed the slow methodical beat of Kell's heart. Rache looked at the little bleeps on the screen—58 beats a minute. *Low but not dangerous*, thought Rache. Rache pulled a chair over to the bed and sat beside her. Pausing at first, she slowly took Kell's small hand. It felt cold to the touch. Instinctively, she held it with her other hand as if to warm it.

"Where's your mommy, baby, huh? Where's your mommy?" Rache whispered softly. She brushed some of Kell's dark hair off her face. She could feel a lump in her throat. A small tear ran down Rache's left cheek. She sniffed, brushing it away.

A deep sense of sadness and helplessness descended on her.

Rache recognized it immediately.

Another demon had begun to take hold of Rache. It was not like the one in the alley at the back of St. Killian's. No, that particular one had almost wrestled control of her, forcing her to shoot Mr. Jakes. That demon was born out of anger and a near pathological hatred of injustice. This demon was different. Although it still toyed and taunted her, it was fundamentally different. The demon of helplessness had come to visit.

Years ago, Rache had found it easier to compartmentalize her darker feelings into categories. These she called demons. Rache had a demon for all the worst feelings. She couldn't put a finger on when it had all began, but deep down, she was sure it was around the time of her sister's death.

She had always being able to fight these feelings—or demons, as she'd labeled them—but lately they had begun to grow stronger.

As a homicide detective, Rache's work had brought her into contact with some of New York's vilest and most depraved individuals. Shadows who passed themselves off as human beings. To Rache, they appeared as human, but when presented with the evidence of many of their horrendous crimes, Rache found it impossible to feel any empathy toward them. It was as though their humanity had been snuffed out, extinguished like a candle, and all that remained was a charred wick.

In Rache's experience, the majority of murders were committed in the heat of the moment. It was the premeditated ones that got to her the most. These were the times when the demons would come to visit. They appeared wearing many faces—apathy, hate, anger, and helplessness, to name but a few.

Rache was strong both mentally and physically. She had always been able to vanquish her demons. But this case was stranger than any other, and now the demons had begun to push the door open. Once inside, she knew she might never chase them out.

She looked down at Kell Mason. Another tear ran down her cheek. More followed, and soon she couldn't stop. She wiped them away. She stared at Kell again. Who could do this to a child? Who would want to? Rache wiped the last tear away. She shook herself. As she looked at Kell, a strange feeling came over her. It was no longer a case of being helpless but more of grim determination. Yes, her mind was made up. She'd nail this bastard.

In her mind, the demon of helplessness had been shut out.

Whatever it took, however long, or whatever methods needed to be employed, she'd catch this guy, this perp. She thought about the word. Perp! Short for perpetrator. A perpetrator of unspeakable evil against a young defenseless kid. Yes, thought Rache, it was clear now. She'd catch him. Dion could espouse all the scatter pattern theories he wanted. They had found the guy at the scene, and that was enough for her. Sure, he had run some number over them all with his antics, but in her gut, she knew he was tied in.

"I promise I'll get him, baby. I promise," Rache spoke quietly in Kell's ear. She leaned over and kissed Kell on the forehead. Noticing a small two-inch scar running just along her dark eyebrow above her left eye, Rache had a strange sensation of dejá vù. Where had she seen that before? *Weird*, she thought.

Her thoughts were interrupted by the sound of the door opening.

As she stood up, the door was pushed in by a man dressed in black, carrying what Rache instantly recognized as a Bible. "Hello, I'm Fr. John," the priest said, offering his right hand to Rache. In his other hand he held the Bible.

"Detective Fischer," replied Rache, shaking his hand. "And you are here because…?" She eyed him up and down.

"I've come to pray for her." Fr. John smiled back.

"Whatever," Rache said, walking straight past him.

She closed the door behind her. *Priests, strange bunch*, she thought as she turned to the cop outside the door. "No one else goes in there, understand?"

The cop nodded.

"And keep an eye on him," she said, indicating the door with a gesture.

Rache headed off down the corridor. The poor kid needed more than prayers, she figured. What did this guy hope to accomplish? Some Latin mumbo jumbo, and hey, presto, Kell Mason would snap out of her coma, and life would be rosy again. No, she needed more than prayer. If Rache couldn't help her get better, she'd sure as hell find the bastard who did this to her.

She reached the elevator, jabbing the down button a couple of times. The doors opened with their customary ding. The young nurse she'd met earlier greeted Rache. Behind her stood Dr. Sam Weir. Jenny introduced them, explaining that Dr. Weir had been treating Kell since her arrival yesterday.

"Got a moment?" Rache inquired.

Dr. Weir looked at Rache. *Jesus, she's a beauty.* He stared at her.

"Well, Doc?" she said, looking into his eyes.

Sam Weir managed to compose himself. "A moment, yes, of course. How can I help you, Detective?"

"Dr. Weir—"

"Sam, please." He smiled at her.

Years of questioning suspects had given Rache a type of sixth sense. She could tell, in almost 90 percent of the cases, who was lying immediately. It was uncanny. There seemed to be some external force guiding her, and her judgment was nearly always right. So when Dr. Sam Weir smiled at her, she knew straight off he was genuine. She had seen plastic smiles all too often.

In his midthirties and a shade under six feet, Sam Weir cut a handsome figure with his white coat and deep tan. What was it Susan had said to her again? "How long since you got laid?"

Rache felt her eyes wander over his face and body. It was only for a second, but he noticed it too. She felt herself blush.

"Let's get a coffee," Sam suggested.

They sat for well over half an hour discussing Kell and her condition. Sam told Rache that he was in the ER when both Joe and Kell Mason were brought in. As a doctor working in the emergency room, he had dealt with many types of trauma. He had, at first, treated Joe and had prepped him for surgery. Sam explained to Rache that due to the nature of the wound, he had given Joe less than 20 percent chance of survival. His aorta had been ruptured, and his left ventricle had all but collapsed. The bullet had fragmented, and part of it had penetrated his lung.

"You were right," Rache said.

"Wish I was wrong." Sam shook his head. "You know, ten years ago I worked in Bosnia. Saw some shit over there, but when they brought that kid in, I nearly vomited. She was in such a mess."

Rache looked away.

"Hey, I'm sorry."

Rache cleared her throat. "Don't be," she said. "You didn't do it."

"Ya know, that's part of it."

"Part of what?" Rache inquired.

"We don't really know what happened to her."

"What do you mean?"

"To be honest, this case is unlike anything I've ever seen. Kell has no physical wounds, bar some normal cuts and scrapes. She has good muscle definition. I'd say she is athletic, probably plays a sport competitively," Sam said.

Rache was impressed. No way he could have known that Kell was a tennis player.

"It was the bleeding that had us all confused," he continued.

"Confused?" Rache said, frowning.

"Well, there was no evidence of trauma. In cases like this, we usually see some kind of blow to the head. When I worked in Bosnia, I saw people who lost eyes and had their eardrum perforated, but that was due to explosives."

At the mentioned of the word explosives, Rache snapped her head up, startling him. "Explosives?"

"Yeah, but this kid was not involved in any kind of explosion. There'd be burns, for one thing. And she hasn't got a mark on her."

"This is madness. Why is she in a coma then?"

Sam shook his head. "She's been through a lot. Probably saw her father shot. She was attacked—"

"Thought you said she wasn't harmed."

"I said we had no evidence of trauma, I didn't say she wasn't attacked. Look, this guy, the one that escaped. He more than likely shot the father and then attacked her. She's only...what...sixteen?"

Rache nodded. She was silent now. Thoughts of another attack were intruding on her mind. *This won't help me*, she thought. She pushed them away, far away into a small part of her subconscious where she dared never go.

"You still haven't answered my question."

"Why is she in a coma?" Sam asked.

"Yeah."

"Like I said, she saw her father shot. When faced with an intense trauma, a person's mind may fracture, leading to partial or, in some cases, total shutdown. I think this is what happened to Kell."

"That's it? That's your professional opinion?"

Rache wanted to shake him. But in some ways, she knew he was right. She had seen it before. A person's best defense, when faced with an unthinkable situation, was to block it out. And in blocking it out, Kell had blocked out everything else. The poor child's mind had been so traumatized, it had closed down.

"But could you help her open it again?" she asked Sam.

He was noncommittal. "Maybe, if she heard a familiar voice, a friendly voice. Someone she knew. Someone she could identify."

"What about her mother?" asked Rache.

"Yeah, maybe, but this is not an exact science. Kell won't just wake up if her mother talks to her."

"But you—"

"It'll help, of course."

Rache's shoulders dropped. Everywhere she turned, there were dead ends. She needed a break. They had turned up nothing, and they needed a break.

Rache thanked Sam and gave him her card. She told him to call her if there was any change in Kell's condition, no matter how small. She checked her watch. Half an hour had passed in what seemed like a few minutes. She liked Sam. But that didn't help Kell. She'd swing by the house, pick up Danny, and head back to the precinct. They had a briefing there later this afternoon. Maybe Danny had learned something from the neighbors.

CHAPTER 13

D ANNY, SUSAN, THEO, JOE, AND Pete had all drawn blanks. Video from the room was a total bust. Susan and Theo had spent hours trying to work through it, with no results. Theo had used the remainder of the time trying to track down Kell's mother. Kell's school had been unaware that she was missing. They knew nothing about any kind of separation. Kell's mother was out of the picture, and the school knew nothing. Both Pete and Joe had canvassed the entire student body between them, and everyone had said the same thing. Kell was popular. She was captain of her tennis and hockey team and a popular straight A student. Who would want to hurt her? Pete had asked a few close friends about any romantic interests. Kell had dated a boy last summer, but he had moved with his family to the West Coast, and as far as anyone knew, she didn't have a current boyfriend.

Rache now stood in a room full of uniformed officers, and she had no leads. All the officers present looked up to Rache, especially the female officers. She had achieved everything they strived for. Rache Fischer was known not only in Midtown Manhattan, but also throughout the whole island. As the youngest woman ever to receive the Medal of Honor, Rache was held in an almost iconic status.

With that came responsibility. It was something she had no difficulty in bearing. Rache enjoyed her job and her status. But today she didn't feel iconic. She felt lost. They, all of them, had failed Kell Mason and her father. They had allowed the prime suspect to escape. Not only did the precinct feel foolish, she did also.

When the captain had asked her "to brief the troops," she had agreed. Internal Affairs were all over Captain Woods, and he was hanging on by a thread. To date, no one had been able to work out exactly how the perp had escaped. Theo had secured him in the holding cell, locking it, and then locked the door to the room. Yet both were found open. Video footage from the precinct corridor had simply shown the perp exiting the door and walking out. Since they had no footage from inside the room, nobody could determine how he had managed to open both doors.

Captain Woods had managed to fend off some spurious accusations. Bottom line though was that a homicide suspect had simply walked out of the precinct.

Rache tried to put this to the back of her mind as she looked into the faces of the officers gathered before her. Trouble was, she didn't know where to start.

Start with what you know, Rache. Start with what you know.

She stood in front of the top of the long briefing room. Danny had parked his butt on a desk next to her. She knew he'd back her and found some comfort in that.

She felt all eyes on her.

"Okay, listen up everyone. Here's what we know. He's a white male, approximately six feet tall, between twenty-five and thirty. This guy is a loner. He is a prime example of a predatory-type offender who doesn't care about the victims he comes in contact with. Make no mistake, this is one clever bastard. We have nothing on his prints, no priors, no convictions, and the lab tested negative for all the usual substances. Murder weapon, a Glock, nine millimeter, is also missing. Could be he's stashed it. This is one dangerous SOB. He took a gun with him and was willing to use it. You do not approach him alone."

The room was deadly silent now, the cops' attention riveted on Rache. Danny walked down the rows of tables handing out photos of the perp. Everyone watched Rache. One of the female officers at the front looked over at a colleague.

"Don't let his good looks fool you. This guy is a killer," Rache said, staring at the young officer, making her blush.

"I want him top of everyone's list. Anything you discover, no matter how trivial, you report back to me or Detective Fischer here.

Take no chances with this individual," Danny said as he walked back to Rache.

"Before you go, I want you all to know something. I will not stop until he is back in custody, and I expect no less from all of you," Rache said. She opened a folder and started to pass out some more photos. They were pictures of Kell, taken when she was admitted to the hospital. As the officers viewed the photos, small gasps and slight coughing sounds could be heard. Rache gave them all a moment or two before she continued.

"It's okay to feel emotional. This is what he did to the kid. I want everyone to be aware of what we are dealing with here. Let me make it clear one last time. This guy is one clever piece of work. He is cold, calculating, and feels no empathy toward any human being. Do not approach him alone. You have your assignment. Let's see some results."

The officers all filed out while Rache and Danny waited. Danny wondered about this change in Rache. It was a hardening, he thought. He challenged her on it.

"Look, we have a lot of conflicting evidence, Rache," he said.

"Conflicting bullshit, you mean."

"Why this change? This isn't you. You heard what Dion said."

"No, Danny, I heard what Dion thought. I don't buy it. Explosions—yeah, I know Dion is good. He's helped me put away some real scum. But you want the truth. He's reaching. He doesn't know. I spoke with Kell's doctor, and guess what?"

Danny shrugged his shoulders.

"He doesn't know either." Rache picked up a photo of Kell and showed it to Danny. "Take a good luck, Danny. It's all the evidence you need. He did that to the kid, and we let him fucking escape. We can talk about scatter patterns all day, but the fact is that he shot and killed Joe Mason and did that to a helpless child." Rache found herself out of breath. "I need a coffee." She dropped the photo on the desk and walked out.

***

Rache sat at her desk, looking over Kell's file. She picked up the photo of Kell with her parents. *Happier times*, she thought. She examined it closely. Something disturbed her. She couldn't put her finger on it. It was something about Kell's face. She couldn't quite figure it out. She sat back in her chair and looked at all the material spread out over the desk. What was it? *Come on, Rache*, she urged herself. *You're good at this sort of thing.* She knew in her gut there was something up, but couldn't figure it.

Joe's head appeared around the door, breaking her concentration. "Hey, Rache, lab guys got the results back on the…suspect. Matched his DNA to hairs found at the scene."

"That's great, Joe, if we still had him," she snapped back at him.

"Yeah," replied Joe as he began to slink out the door.

"Look, come in a second?" she asked.

Joe's whole demeanor changed. His eyes lit up. He was almost like a bold puppy whose master had forgiven him and was now ready for a tummy rub. Joe sat beside her. He could smell her hair, and he struggled to compose himself. *Better not say anything*, he thought. *Just play it cool.*

But Rache had already asked him a question, and of course he had missed it. *Great fucking start, Joe*, he told himself.

"Say it again, Rache. I'm not with you." It was all he could think of, and hopefully she wouldn't cop it.

"Anything from the school? Anything out of the ordinary?"

"No, Rache, nothing."

"There must be, what, four hundred in the school."

"What are you getting at?"

"I'm not sure, but I don't think this was random. There was no forced entry. He knew where she lived, and more importantly, he knew her."

She had said it. It was the one thing that they had skipped around. The perp knew her. How could she have missed it?

"The officer first on the scene, Marks, was it?"

Joe nodded.

"Think you could get a hold of him for me?" she asked.

"Sure, Rache," he replied, only too happy to oblige. "I'll get him right away." Joe was up and gone before she could thank him.

Rache started to put the file together. She shuffled the papers together, but one in particular wouldn't fit in the bundle. It was a mug shot of the perp. Rache fished it out of the pile. She put it at the front and was about to close the file when it struck her. She picked it up again. The perp looked to the left of the page, in profile. It was the way he held his chin that caught her eye. She picked up a picture of Kell Mason with her family. Kell had her arms around her mother, giving her a kiss on the cheek. Right profile!

They had the same chin!

Searching quickly through the file, Rache compared two different photos, face on this time. *No*, she thought. *This cannot be.*

But the resemblance was too great. They had to be related. The hair color and eye color were almost identical. Kell Mason knew her father's killer because they were related. Dammit! How could she have been so stupid?

Her phone rang. Rache picked it up. It was Officer Marks. She asked him if he could remember the perp saying Kell's name. He told her no, that he couldn't make out what the perp had said. "Must be some kind of foreign lingo, Detective Fischer. Do you think it is important?" he asked.

"I'm not sure yet, but I got to try all avenues." She thanked him and hung up. She was sure he'd said he'd heard the perp whisper Kell's name. But she must have been mistaken. She looked at the photos again. *Maybe I'm the one reaching now*, she thought.

Danny walked in, and she pushed the photos back into the file. She'd say nothing on this until she was sure. Best not to appear foolish.

"Rache, let's take a drive," Danny said as he took his jacket off the chair.

"Where?" she asked.

"Come on, I've got an idea."

"Danny…"

"It's related."

Related. That word again. Should she tell Danny her suspicions? No. She'd look into this herself. No point going off half-cocked.

CHAPTER 14

DANNY GUIDED THE SEDAN UP to the curb outside the gates of St. Killian's.

Rache stared at him. "You're kidding, right?"

"No."

"And how is this going to help?"

"Rache, we need all the—"

Her cell phone interrupted him. "Hold on," she said, reaching into her pocket. Rache checked the caller display.

"You going to take that?"

It was her mother. She couldn't fight on two fronts right now. She'd let it ring out. Rache pressed the cancel button. She stared out the window at the church. "Okay, okay, let's get this over with."

As Danny killed the ignition, he too wondered how his uncle could help. But anything was worth a try at this point. His uncle was well known in the parish and was actively involved with many of its youth programs. The Catholic Church had suffered with a multitude of abuse cases being taken against it, but Fr. John had been at the forefront of urging the clergy to accept greater responsibility and show more openness. He had been reprimanded in many quarters but praised by his congregation. If anything strange was going on, Danny was sure he'd know.

Fr. John was no shrinking violet. If something needed to be said or done, he was the one to do it. Yeah, thought Danny, if anything was up, his uncle would know about it.

Rache opened the file on her knee, settling herself in the seat until Danny returned. "You coming?" he asked.

Rache glanced up at him. The look on his face told her he was not going to take no for an answer.

Rache smiled to herself. "Why not?" she replied, closing the file. *This could be interesting*, she thought.

They both got out of the car and walked up the steps to the church. Danny held the huge oak doors open for Rache. She entered the church.

St. Killian's was massive. It could comfortably seat five hundred souls. Long teak pews ran up either side of a central aisle from double doors to a magnificent marble altar. Rache was taken by the vastness of the building. She had never been inside a church. Sure she had seen them in the movies and such, but until today, she had never set foot in one. She looked about. Huge hand-carved arches, rising fifty feet to a beautiful gold flake ceiling, framed the central aisle with its pews. The arches ran all the way to the back of the altar. Behind them were even more pews.

Rache and Danny walked up the aisle toward the altar. Behind the altar lay the vestry, where the priests changed before celebrating mass. Rache was not ignorant of Catholicism. It was important to have a knowledge of the various faiths. But that was all it was. Knowledge! She didn't believe it any more than she thought the world was flat.

A middle-aged priest walked out from behind the altar. He stopped on seeing Rache. He smiled. It was the same priest she'd met at the hospital. Rache bit her lip, feeling her face flush with embarrassment. She knew she had been somewhat rude to him.

Danny made the introductions. "Rache, this is my uncle, Fr. John. Fr. John, Rache Fischer."

Fr. John held out his hand. She shook it.

"We've met," he said.

Danny looked at Rache.

"At the hospital," she told him.

"Oh."

Rache nodded. Shit, she felt foolish. She stood there for a moment, lost for words.

She looked up at one of the Stations of the Cross. It was a painting of the Ascension. She walked over and stood under it. Fr. John and Danny joined her.

"Pretty picture," she said.

"Yes," replied Fr. John.

"Why all the light?"

All three of them gazed at the painting. The figure of Jesus rose high above the apostles. Jesus was painted bathed in light. Blues and yellows surrounded and infused his body. His disciples, or followers, stood below him with their hands outstretched. Their heads shone with halos.

"It's a nimbus or luminous energy field," Fr. John answered.

The answer took Rache by surprise. "A what?" she asked.

"A nimbus. We all have them. See how the disciples are depicted with just halos and Our Lord is surrounded by light? The light represents the luminous energy field that surrounds us all. Only in His case, it is brighter than our own," he told her.

Rache was truly puzzled. "A luminous energy field?" she enquired.

"You, Detective. Your spirit, your being, your soul!"

"Father, have you been sniffing the incense?"

"Rache!" Danny interjected, angry at Rache's taunt.

"I'm sorry, Father...I don't...I didn't mean to cause offense."

Fr. John smiled. He looked over at Danny.

Rache walked away, looking at a few more paintings.

As Rache walked down the aisle taking in the various Stations of the Cross, Danny explained the reason for their visit. He briefly told Fr. John about the case. The priest nodded and said he would do what he could. Rache walked back towards them as Danny was finishing up.

"Hey, Rache, give him one of those photos, will you?"

Rache began to open the folder. She closed it. "How well do you know her?" she asked, folding her arms.

"Kell sings in the choir. Tuesday and Thursday practice and Sunday mass. She loves it," he told her.

"We can't locate her mother. Know anything about that?" she asked.

Fr. John shook his head.

"Give him a photo, Rache," Danny said, indicating the folder.

Rache opened the folder and handed a picture of the perp to the priest. "If you see or hear anything, call me. I don't care how trivial you might think it is!"

"Good god!" the priest said, examining the photo. He blinked rapidly, as if not really trusting his own eyes. He turned the black-and-white photograph over in his hands. He was aware of his heart beating slightly faster. He began to sweat, the reaction involuntary. He was also aware that this reaction had startled his nephew and the other detective.

His sudden exclamation had focused their attention on him.

"This...this is him?" Fr. John pointed with one finger at the picture.

"What is it, Father? You recognize him or something?" Rache demanded.

"He...he was here. Earlier. He was here."

Rache's head was in turmoil, her mind turning somersaults. She looked at Danny, who just stood there with his mouth open. She took the photo from the priest's hand. "You're sure? You're sure it was him, Father?"

"Yes, yes. I spoke with him," Fr. John said.

"You're sure?"

"Church attendances are down. Someone spends six hours in your church, you tend to notice, Detective."

"But Danny asked you if anything unusual had happened—"

"Hey, that's not important now, Rache. Just tell us, Father. Tell us what he said," Danny interjected.

"I'm sorry. I thought it were unrelated. Really I did."

"Like he said, it's not important," Rache assured him. "What is important is that you tell us everything."

Fr. John nodded. He looked at the photo again. He walked over to the front pew and sat down. Danny and Rache sat on either side of him.

Fr. John held the photo in front of him, his arms resting on his knees. He studied the picture as he tried to cast his mind back. "There's not much to tell, really. He wasn't very talkative. He seemed very confused. We get that sometimes. People wander in, not sure why they are here," he said, looking up from the photo.

"But this guy isn't just anybody. He is the principal suspect in a brutal homicide," Rache told him. "So anything you know could help us. Earlier today, you told me you had come to pray for Kell. You had come to help her. Please try to remember everything. It could be important."

Fr. John pointed back down the church toward the entrance. He explained that after mass, it was not unusual for a few members of the congregation to stay on and say some of their own private prayers. In fact, he liked to see it. So when the guy in the photo had sat at the back of the church, he had thought nothing of it. He had simply gone about his normal chores and returned some time later. The guy was still there. Mass had finished almost three hours now, but this was a House of God, and if someone wanted to pray...well, who was he to stop them? It was only after a further two hours had elapsed that Fr. John had decided to approach him. He had walked up and sat beside him. The guy had barely glanced up.

The priest explained that he had just sat with him to comfort him, if it was comfort he was seeking.

"To tell you the truth, I didn't know what to say. Here was this guy, clearly lost, and I felt a little foolish. But because he had been there such a long time, I thought he might be...you know..."

"A suicide?" Rache offered.

"It's not uncommon. Well, we talked a bit. He didn't make much sense, really. He seemed to have difficulty articulating himself. He kept saying he didn't know why he had come. That everything was different."

"Different?" Rache asked. "What do think he meant?"

"I don't know. He said he had failed. Yes, that's it," the priest said, remembering now. "He'd failed in his assignment, and he couldn't fail again. He wouldn't fail again."

Rache jumped up. "Kell!" She looked at Danny.

"Jesus!" he said. "Sorry, Father," he added quickly.

"It has to be. He didn't kill her, so it was a failure," Rache said. "It's the only explanation."

"I don't think so, Detective." Fr. John said. "He was very confused. I don't think he—"

"Look, forget that. What happened?"

"He got up and walked out. Like I said, he was very confused, like he was concussed or something."

"So all this took place yesterday, yeah?" Danny asked.

"No, today, just before you arrived."

"Jesus Christ, Kell!" Danny said the words involuntarily.

Rache nodded. "He's going after her again." She gathered the folder and started to run down the aisle. Danny thanked his uncle as he hurried to catch up with her.

They bolted out the church doors and down the steps to the car. Danny gunned the engine and hit the gas. Rache worked the radio, requesting backup at the hospital.

Danny punched through every red light between St. Killian's and Washington Memorial, covering the five city blocks in less than six minutes.

Pulling up to the doors, Rache spotted one or two uniformed officers waiting outside. Stopping the car as close as possible, Rache and Danny scampered out. Rache ordered the officers to stay put and call for more backup. She wanted the hospital sealed tight. No one in, no one out! She also requested they seal off a four-block radius.

As she turned to enter, she saw three more patrol cars arrive. Good, she though, they'd get him this time. But was it already too late for Kell?

Rache scurried up the stairs to Kell's room on the fourth floor. She pushed the door open slowly, desperately trying to control her breathing.

She didn't want to spook him. As she eased her way out through the exit door and onto the corridor, Rache became acutely aware that the nurse's station was abandoned. A police hat sat on an empty chair outside Kell's room. A deep sense of foreboding griped her now. She could feel her heart pounding in her ears.

Slowly, purposely, she drew her weapon. If she saw him, would she shoot? She was aware that this contravened police procedure and ethics. To hell with procedure! If she got a visual, she'd fire, no question. The photographs from the assault flashed before her eyes—Kell's contorted face, blue from the lack of oxygen, her bulging eyes—images that drove Rache on.

The demon she had fought when she'd faced down Mr. Jakes in the alley was back. It cast a dark shadow over her reasoning and began to consume her. *Fuck procedure*, Rache thought. This piece of shit had foregone his rights the moment he'd tortured a helpless child. No, she'd end it now. To hell with the consequences.

Danny had remained downstairs to organize the lockdown. He had wanted to come up with her, but he knew they needed someone with experience down below. She wished she had him with her now. Her hand began to shake a little as she edged her way to Kell's door. She listened. Silence.

Rache tried desperately hard to control her breathing. But she was fighting a losing battle. She was at the door now. Dammit, where was the cop? She gently pushed the door. It slowly creaked inward. Nothing! The room was empty! Where was Kell?

Rache heard voices. She spun around. Two nurses approached. Rache grabbed them. One screamed. Rache holstered her gun.

"I'm a cop. Where the fuck is Kell Mason? Where's the cop?" she shouted at them, panicked now.

They both stared at her. She shook one of them. Julie, the younger of the two, seemed to regain some of her composure. "We... we found some kids smoking weed up on the roof."

"What?"

"Kids, you know...they were on the roof, smoking. The officer brought them to—"

Rache couldn't believe her ears. "Enough! Kell Mason, where is she?"

"She was having breathing problems. She was moved to Intensive Care—"

"ICU! Where is it?" Rache shouted at her.

"Second floor."

Rache was gone, leaving both nurses staring after her in shock. She rushed down the stairs to the second floor, her right shoulder hitting off the wall as she raced down. *No time to wait*, she thought as she followed the signs for intensive care. She drew her gun again and opened the door. She froze.

Standing above Kell was the perp!

"Freeze! she screamed at him.

"Don't shoot!" he replied, blinking rapidly.

She looked him in the eye, cocking the hammer, her finger lightly touching the trigger.

"Don't shoot!" he repeated.

Rache looked at him. He was holding Kell's arm. Why? Was it the IV? Had he put something in it?

"Back away! Do it now!" she ordered him.

But the perp did not move. Then she heard it—a low hissing sound, as though someone had just poured a soda. What was it? she wondered. It was faint but continuous, like a fizzy drink.

Oxygen!

Shit, the tanks were on full. *Clever bastard*, she thought. Muzzle fire would ignite the whole room. They'd all go up. No wonder he didn't want her to shoot. Damn it!

The perp stared at her, holding up both hands as if to say, "I'm clean." He began to back away from Kell. Rache depressed the hammer, but holding the gun on him all the time. She glanced quickly at Kell. The perp continued to look at her as he stepped back. He bumped into a door behind him, momentarily halting his retreat.

Rache felt utterly frustrated. *Kell's safe*, she told herself, the distance between Kell and the perp growing as he retreated. She watched him slide his arm behind his back and turn the door handle. No way she'd let him get away again! She could hear voices now and the sound of running feet. Shit, she felt helpless.

Four cops burst in, briefly causing Rache to look behind her. When she looked back, he was gone. Rache rushed to the door. It was locked.

"Out, out, all of you out!" She pushed the officers out. Taking a radio from one of them, she called Danny. "He's somewhere on the second floor. Tell me you have the place locked down?"

"Tight, Rache. If he comes down, we'll get him."

Sam Weir appeared with some nurses. "What the hell is going on here, Rache?"

"He's here, Doc, he's here."

"What?"

A radio crackled to life, the voice telling them that the perp had been spotted on the first floor. Rache spoke into hers. "Danny, he's heading toward you."

"I'm on it, Rache," he replied.

Rache turned to Sam, but he was already in the ICU. He had pushed the remaining cops out, and the nurses were checking on Kell. Rache caught his eye. He nodded, knowing she had to go. She ordered two cops to stay behind. She needed to be sure in case he came back.

Rache took off toward the stairs, but before she reached it, Danny was on the radio. "There's no sign of him, Rache," he said.

"Damn it, Danny, he has to be heading in your direction," she said. She reached the stairs.

Officer Marks burst through the doors, almost falling forward. He was out of breath. "He's…he's gone up again. Christ, the son of a bitch can run."

"Up?" asked Rache.

"You didn't see him? He was just ahead of me. Took out two of our guys. Didn't even faze him."

Rache radioed Danny. She asked if they had a visual.

"No, Rache, we got nothing."

Rache, Officer Marks, and some other cops ran up the remaining flight of stairs. "I don't like this," Rache said as she thought back to the escape in the precinct. They reached the roof, only to find the door locked. Rache tried it. Nothing! It was shut solid. Officer Marks tried it. It wouldn't budge.

"It's locked," he said.

"Yeah, but look. It's bolted from the inside," Rache said, pointing to two dead bolts.

Again she called Danny.

"Rache, he hasn't come down."

She looked at Officer Marks. "Come on."

The following hour saw the entire hospital searched from top to bottom. Room by room, floor by floor, every inch was meticulously combed. But the perp was gone.

Rache was visibly upset now. She did her best to conceal her annoyance, but she was struggling. She had had him in her sights but had been unable to fire. It was not so much that he had eluded them. It was the feeling of utter helplessness that overwhelmed her now. The sick bastard had come back to finish his assignment, as he called it, and had almost gotten away with it. For the second time in twenty-four hours, he had made them look foolish.

Rache headed back up to ICU to check on Kell. Sam assured her Kell was doing fine and that the perp had not caused her any harm. It was the one thing she could take from the day. She told Sam that she would call by tomorrow.

A four-block radius also proved fruitless. He was gone, and all the looking in the world was not going to find him. Rache was sure he would not return now. He had come back once; it was doubtful he'd try again. Regardless, she'd ordered two uniform officers to remain at the hospital.

As Rache and Danny headed back to the station, she suddenly felt very tired. She needed to recharge. She told Danny she was going to head home and that she would see him early in the morning.

"Tell the captain I've gone back to the hospital or something. I need a break from this, Danny. It's been 24-7, and I need a time-out."

"Sure, Rache. I'll cover you."

"Thanks. I'll drop you at the precinct, okay. And I'll swing by your place in the morning early, see what we can turn up, yeah?"

"No problem, Rache."

She left him at the precinct and headed home. By the time she had taken a hot bath and dried her hair, it was after nine. She decided to get to bed and try and sleep. The events of the last two days were catching up with her, and tomorrow was her sister's anniversary. That was going to be tough. She had never worked on those days, so tomorrow would be a whole new experience. But she needed sleep if she were going to get through it.

As she pulled her duvet around her, she tried to push all thought of the current investigation out of her head. But the image of Kell Mason lying defenseless in her hospital bed as that bastard stood over her simply would not leave her mind. Try as she might to dispel it, she couldn't. It remained with her, indelibly etched in her mind. There were just too many similarities with Ruth...too many.

And as Rache began to drift off to sleep, she thought of Ruth. She thought of their childhood together. Of how Ruth had encouraged her when she had made her breakthrough in the swim team. She smiled as the subconscious began to assert its supremacy, and the conscious mind reluctantly yielded its territory, and the blanket of sleep enveloped her.

But her dreams were not of happier times. Instead, she found herself back in the hospital room, her gun held on the perp. He looked different as he stood over Kell. Rache was drawn to his face. His features were twisted and distorted. His eyes spun in his head.

"You can't help! No one can!" he screamed at Rache, his voice making a hollow sound as though it was almost not human.

"Let her go!" Rache roared back, her thumb cocking the hammer. "You fucking let her go!"

"But she's mine, you know that now, don't you? She's mine."

"Let her go, you sick fuck, or I swear I'll end you!" Rache shouted, her finger depressing the trigger.

The room exploded in a massive fireball. She felt the searing heat as it raced toward her in milliseconds.

Rache jumped up in bed. Waking in a feverish panic, she sat bolt upright. Her throat hurt like hell. *Must have been screaming*, she thought. Rache struggled out of bed, walking barefoot into her kitchen. *Must have been dreaming*. The floating remnants of the nightmare were already beginning to fade. Two nights running, she'd dreamt of him. In both dreams he'd been in pain, almost as though he were the victim. But why? Was it her own subconscious projecting a type of justice? She couldn't tell. But she was disturbed by it. *Two nights. Better figure this bitch out in the morning. No point trying to make sense of it feeling like this*, she figured. Pouring a glass of milk, she cursed herself for not having taken the vacation. She was still half asleep as she plodded her way back to her bedroom. It was 1:15 a.m. She could still get a few hours.

Although Rache's sleep remained undisturbed for the rest of the night, when she woke again in the morning, she felt exhausted.

CHAPTER 15

RACHE TOOK A LIGHT BREAKFAST and collected Danny a little after seven. He quickly filled her in on yesterday's events. The captain had passed no comment on Rache absence; so preoccupied was he by the perp returning to the hospital. She thanked him, telling him she was simply beat and had needed the rest.

"We got a briefing at seven thirty," Danny said as they pulled up to the precinct. *Christ, she looks like shit*, Danny thought.

The whole way in they had discussed the events of yesterday, from meeting Danny's uncle to discovering the perp. Neither Danny nor Rache could figure out how he had managed to get out of the hospital without being seen. They had acquisitioned the CCTV footage from the hospital, and it had been thoroughly detailed last night. But as there were no cameras in the ICU, it had been of little help. Talking about the case now, as they arrived at the station, had once again made Rache feel helpless. She had called the hospital before picking Danny up and had been assured that Kell was in no danger. Her breathing had returned to normal, and she had been moved back to her own room. Rache had placed two cops on her door with strict orders not to allow anyone to see Kell who wasn't attached to the hospital. She didn't want a repeat of yesterday's performance.

Rache climbed the steps to the precinct. Danny held the door open for her. She smiled at him. Danny was one of life's true gentlemen. "Thank you," she said. She told Danny she was going to get a coffee.

"Meet you in the briefing room in ten, Rache," he replied.

Rache made her coffee extra strong, heaping four spoons more than usual into the filter paper. She knew she would need it. She glanced at her watch, and her heart stopped. Seven twenty!

She began to experience a panic attack. It wasn't something that had gradually crept up on her. No, this had hit her full blown. Her legs started to shake, her knees twitching involuntarily now. Rache struggled to the nearest chair, not trusting herself to stand. There was simply no way she could get through today. Suddenly she felt very claustrophobic. She had to get out. She tried to control her breathing. She was beginning to hyperventilate. It was no use.

She should have called in sick. But when she had risen this morning, she had felt unusually calm. Rache looked down at her wrist. She began to fiddle with a beautiful silver identity bracelet that adorned her right wrist, twisting it between her thumb and index finger. It was the only jewelry she wore. She was about to turn it over to look at the inscription when Susan knocked and entered.

"Hey, Rache, morning. Jesus, what's up?" Susan asked, shocked at Rache's appearance.

"Nothing, Susan. Didn't sleep too well," she replied, looking down at her desk in an effort to hide her eyes. She knew she looked like shit.

"Captain's ready for us now. Just wants an update, I think."

"Okay, gimme a moment, will ya?"

"Yeah, sure, Rache."

Susan left and headed to the briefing room, wondering what the hell was the matter with Rache.

Rache steadied herself. She removed a small mirror she kept in a desk drawer. She had taken it from a small-time coke dealer a couple of years back, and it had ended up in her drawer. Staring at her reflection in the small square, she knew she was in trouble. Dark rings circled bloodshot eyes, and her skin looked pasty. She looked like she was coming down with something. But Rache was not sick. Well, not physically anyway. *Go to the briefing and then go home*, she told herself. That's it. She'd go home and get into bed.

Walking into the briefing room, she found Captain Woods standing by an opened flip chart. He nodded, obviously waiting on her arrival. He too noticed that she didn't look too hot. *Jesus, don't let her be sick*, he prayed. She was his best detective, and he was relying on her more than ever now. What with Internal Affairs breathing down his neck and the mayor demanding answers? And now, the suspect showing up again. More than ever in his career, he needed a result. He knew Rache was the best person for this. Yeah, Danny was good. He was a plodder, and he was reliable, but Rache was inventive. She was like a magician. She could conjure something out of nothing. She had a way of looking at things and seeing a different angle. If anyone could shake something lose, it was Rache.

But looking at her now, well… *God, don't let her be sick.*

Joe, Pete, and Theo all looked shocked when they saw her. The look was not lost on Rache. *Damn it, I should have called in sick,* she thought. On any other case she would have, but the thought of the perp returning to complete his assignment had pushed her to get up out of bed. Poor Kell. Her father was dead, and no one could trace her mother. The child was all alone.

Captain Woods had been talking almost a minute, but she had heard nothing, her own world dominating her thoughts. She focused her attention back on the captain.

"So, people, this is what we got."

Captain Woods stopped short. Rache had begun to walk toward him. She was glaring at him now. The demon of contempt had filtered through, ushering others in its wake.

Anger and bitterness coupled with a foreboding sense of helplessness had swiftly followed, and they all seemed to merge, taking control of her.

Rache snapped!

"I'll tell you what we got, Captain," she said, walking to the front of the room, the gesture itself an act of defiance.

All eyes were on Rache now.

Danny and Susan exchanged worried glances.

"We got police incompetence. That's what we got. That scumbag murdered Joe Mason, almost raped and killed Kell, and then came back to finish her off. All the time we're supposed to be looking out for her. That's what we do. We look out for those who are too weak to help themselves. But we didn't do that yesterday now, did we? NO! We failed that little girl. We let a murderer escape, and he almost got to commit a second one. What we have is police failure on a grand fucking scale."

Rache looked at the captain. "You, me, all of us. We failed. Plain and fucking simple." She shook her head and walked out of the room, leaving only stunned silence.

Captain Woods watched with an utter sense of helplessness as Rache closed the door behind her. She was right though, he thought. But he needed her on board. More than ever, he needed her on board. He looked to Susan for help. He didn't ask out straight, but she could see it in his eyes.

Susan nodded and took Danny's arm. "Come on," she said as she escorted Danny from the room.

***

Rache stood in the room, arms folded, her eyes closed to the world outside, her thoughts lost to a different time. Slowly she opened them, looking around. Rache glanced out the window at the building across the street. Walking into the small holding cell, she sat on the bed, as the perp had done. She tried to get a feeling of how he had done it. Theo had locked the cell and the door to the corridor, the one where the surveillance camera had picked him up. She thought back. She had picked up the trash bag—must check out that DNA profile.

Rache walked out of the cell and paced the distance to the door. The door opened, and in walked Danny and Susan. Danny handed her a mug of hot coffee.

"Thanks, Danny," Rache said, accepting the mug. She sipped it but avoided making any eye contact. Danny looked at Susan as Rache walked back over to the holding cell. Susan nodded at him as if to say, "Go on!"

They had both being discussing Rache's physical appearance and her verbal assault on Captain Woods. They knew she was some- what feisty, but the way she'd attacked the captain had been way out of character—almost manic. Danny had confided in Susan that

Rache had been a little reserved, if not distant all week, and that the Mason case had given her a case of the jitters.

"It's got us all upset, Danny, but that's no reason to take it out on Woods," Susan had said. Danny had agreed, and between them, they had decided he should talk to Rache as he'd known her longer.

Danny observed Rache now as she sipped some more coffee.

"Little hard on the captain back there, Rache," he said, clearing his throat. "I mean we're—"

"I know, Danny," Rache whispered, keeping her back to him.

Danny walked over toward her. "We're all pulling on this, Rache. We all want the same thing."

"Yeah!" It was whispered, but again with no conviction.

Danny wasn't sure. There was something in the tone of her voice. He'd never heard Rache unsure of herself before.

Susan noticed it too, but not in the way Danny had. It was resignation, or worse, apathy.

Something had happened to Rache to make her feel this way. It was something bad, no doubt. But what?

"We'll get him, Rache. We'll get him," Danny said.

But Rache was shaking her head. "No, Danny, no, we won't. These guys always get away."

Danny was behind her now. He put a hand on her shoulder to comfort her. "We'll get him," he reassured her.

Rache turned to face him. She looked a mess. Danny had difficulty believing it was the same person. He hardly recognized the woman in front of him. Rache shook her head from side to side, the movement itself labored. Rache tried to articulate her thoughts, but when she went to speak, only her lower lip moved. Rache started to blink rapidly as her bottom lip quivered. He could see she was on the verge of tears. What the hell was wrong?

Danny took her hand in his. "We'll get him, Rache."

But Rache wasn't listening. Her mind was elsewhere. She shook her head again, disengaging her hand from his. "They always get away, Danny." Her words were tinged with a sense of finality, a sense of doom about them. "They always get away. If it's not through some

101

unlocked door, it's through some fancy fucking lawyer. That's a fact, Danny. They always get away," she said, walking away from him.

Danny looked over to Susan for help. He had never seen Rache act like this. It was as though she were possessed.

But Susan knew. In that instant, she knew. It was there, in Rache's her words.

They always get away.

The words had a prophetic ring to them.

"It happened to you, didn't it, Rache?"

Rache looked at her. Slowly, she lowered the cup from her mouth. She nodded. Tears began to well up in her eyes. Try as she might, she couldn't stop them. They spilled down her cheeks. She couldn't stop. Years of torment poured out. She just stood in the center of the room, crying, her shoulders heaving as her whole body shook with anguish.

Danny was shocked. In five years he had never seen her once cry. But he was not so much shocked at the tears, but rather at what had triggered them. Susan's words echoed in his mind: "It happened to you, didn't it, Rache?"

Had she been attacked? As a child, had she been attacked? It would explain so much. He looked at her. Reaching into his pocket, he offered her his handkerchief.

Rache half smiled at him as she dabbed her eyes. She sniffled back the last of her tears.

Danny and Susan stood in the middle of the room, neither knowing what to do or say.

Rache walked over to the table and sat down, placing her coffee in front of her. Her eyes were red and glazed as she stared at the surface of the table, her mind in another world, another time. The past had come to visit.

"When I was fifteen, I was top of my swim class for the one hundred, two hundred, and four meters individual medley," she started.

Danny and Susan slowly moved to the table and sat down opposite her.

"Medley?" Danny asked quietly.

"Freestyle," Rache said, her eyes flickering back to the table.

Danny nodded.

Rache sipped some more coffee. She looked up at them. "We lived about an hour's drive north. We, my parents and I, along with my sister, Ruth…we had all come down for the state championships. I had been swimming since I could remember. Man, I won those events so easily. Set two new records. My coaches wanted to put me forward for the nationals, with the Olympics only a year off."

Rache sipped some more coffee. She stared at the floor. Somewhere in the back of her mind, she'd made a decision, or maybe one had been made for her. Either way, Rache knew, deep down, she had to tell them. She knew she had to purge this awful feeling.

"Everybody was thrilled. I was so excited, I could have floated home. Later that night, we went out to celebrate. Ruth and I…we… we had never had a drink. My dad had a thing about drinking. No way Ira Fischer would ever allow alcohol in his house. But I remember him that night, saying that God had blessed our family and me in particular. So we were each allowed a glass of champagne."

Rache smiled a little, recalling the evening. She looked at Susan.

Susan knew something horrible was coming next.

Rache finished the last of her coffee, and she told them.

Dinner had just finished when two young well-dressed college kids had sauntered over to their table. They had introduced themselves as Paul and Shaun Williams. They were brothers, and their father was the Massachusetts senator. Both guys were very handsome, and they explained to Rache's father that they had come over to offer their congratulations to Rache. They had swum in the four-by-one relay and had failed to qualify. Rache recalled how they had looked like schoolkids as they'd hung their heads in shame. She had giggled, and Ruth had told them there was always another chance. Shaun had made some remark about not swimming ever again unless someone as lovely as Ruth were there to cheer him on.

But Ira Fischer was a shrewd man and would have sent the boys packing had the maître d' not intervened. He had spotted the boys and had asked after the senator, their father. This had added some respectability to the boys as Ira had been a fan ever since the senator had taken an unpopular stance on below-cost selling.

The Williams brothers were asked to join the family and had accepted.

"They were so polished and polite. They had us all fooled. I was fifteen, and Ruth was only two years older," Rache told them as she rose out of the chair and walked to the window. She looked out through the steel bars as she continued her story.

"They ordered a bottle of champagne, and of course the maître d' refused to take any money from my father for the meal. The senator was a friend of his, as were his sons. My father is not a material man, but I think with the champagne and the night, he got a little carried away. He proposed a toast to me. We all drank to it. I was so excited."

Rache walked back to the table. Danny and Susan hadn't budged, their full attention fixed on Rache. Rache felt a little calmer now. She told them that the boys had asked Ira's permission to allow the girls to join them to listen to the jazz club next door. It was only ten, and Ira had told them he expected to see the girls back by midnight. Rache and Ruth had never been on a date together before. In fact, Rache had never been on a proper date. Sure, she had kissed a couple of guys, but never anyone older. Shaun and Paul were eighteen and nineteen respectively.

"They were very good-looking and very charming. We had a couple of drinks at this jazz club. We were both underage, so we hid in a darkened corner, the two guys buying us drinks. We were very impressed, both Ruth and I...it was like tasting forbidden fruit. Ya know how it is when you're a teenager," she said, glancing over at Susan.

Susan nodded. *Who didn't?* she thought.

"Well," continued Rache, "we listened to the jazz. They were so charming, ya know. They had a way of listening that made you feel you were the center of their universe...special. Both Ruth and I fell for it." Rache paused a moment. "They must have been buying us doubles or something cos next thing we know, we're back on their boat, and they're pouring more champagne. I remember looking at my watch, and it was already twelve thirty. I thought we'd be in so much trouble. If only that was all we had to worry about."

Sucking in a deep breath, Rache continued. "We asked them to take us back, but that's when it got nasty. Shaun tried to kiss me. He stank of drink. I pulled away. I told him to take us home. Ruth got angry, and she slapped him in the face. But he just laughed. They started to call us names, saying we were cockteasers. Paul grabbed Ruth. He was very strong, and he easily overpowered her. Shaun was a little drunker, and when he tried to grab me, I kicked him. He fell back. Ruth somehow managed to break free from Paul. She grabbed a bottle of champagne and broke it over Shaun's head. He fell to the deck."

"Run, Rachel, run!" Ruth Fischer had screamed at her younger sister. Rache had taken off as Shaun had stumbled to his feet to chase her. Rache hadn't hesitated. Reaching the stern of the boat, she'd dived overboard. The cold seawater shocked her, but she continued to swim down. At fifteen, Rache was super fit and could hold her breath for over three minutes. She swam under the boat. She knew she had jumped over the stern, and so she swam back along the length of the keel to the bow. She knew they would look over the stern. If she could get to the bow without being seen, she could get to the pier and raise the alarm. She knew she was their only hope.

Up top, Paul had grabbed Ruth by the hair, pulling her back off her feet. He punched her hard in the stomach a couple of times in an effort to subdue her. Shaun arrived beside him. He was out of breath.

"She...she jumped overboard," he said.

"Don't worry, she's a good swimmer." He laughed at his joke.

Ruth moaned. Paul pulled her close to him. He kissed her. She couldn't fight him.

"Come on. We can still party," Paul said.

Rache looked at Danny and Susan now. "They raped her. Both of them. They took turns raping her. They raped my sister, and like a coward, I ran away."

"Rache, you can't blame yourself. You were only fifteen. You can't blame yourself," Susan said, holding Rache's hand.

But Rache could only look down. All three sat silent for a few moments.

"Did…did they get them?" Danny finally asked, his discomfort at having asked the question clearly obvious.

Rache stared blankly at her hands a moment. She began to twist her silver bracelet. Danny watched before glancing over at Susan. Susan quickly shook her head, indicating to Danny not to say anything else.

Rache spoke. "Yeah, they got them," she said, wiping another small tear from her cheek. "But their father was a senator, ya know. He had the best lawyers, and we had some incompetent state prosecutor. Not the type to inspire confidence."

"What happened?" Susan asked. She could tell Rache was hurting, but she knew Rache had never spoken of this to anyone. Susan knew it was essential for Rache to continue.

Rache rubbed her face, the tips of her fingers making little circles as they massaged her eyes. She could feel the tears coming again. She drew in a deep breath. It was to signal what was to come. A conclusion that neither Danny nor Susan could have envisaged. She nodded her head.

"Like I said, the prosecution were idiots. My father didn't want Ruth to take the stand. She was on a lot of medication after the rape. They convinced my father and…and somehow…somehow their lawyers got hold of her diary. She was just a kid who wrote silly fantasies, and they made her out to be such a slut, like it was her fault. But she was raped."

Rache couldn't fight the tears. They came thick and fast. But she desperately wanted to finish.

"We can talk about this again, Rache," Danny told her, but Rache shook her head.

"No, it's okay," she said. "I urged my father to let me take the stand, but after what had happened with Ruth, he wouldn't hear of it. So they walked."

"They walked?" Danny repeated, his voice choking.

Rache nodded.

Danny glanced at Susan. Rache caught it. This was the hardest part. But she told them. She told them about that morning, seventeen years ago to the day, how she had risen early to make herself and Ruth some breakfast. Her parents had gone to see the police. Rache had taken to making her sister breakfast every day after the attack. But Ruth ate little. Rache would try and encourage her to take something. The medication had suppressed much of her appetite. But Rache didn't care. Every morning she rose at the same time to make her sister something to eat. After, she would lie beside Ruth and try and comfort her. But Ruth was inconsolable. She would weep for hours. A low, soft cry that tore a hole in the pit of Rache's stomach. Ruth spoke very little, but every day, Rache would snuggle up beside her and try to assure her things would get better. Rache hated herself for jumping overboard. She had said as much to her mother, but Miriam Fischer would have none of it, telling Rache not to blame herself, but rather the boys who'd attacked Ruth. It seemed to give Rache a focus. She believed in a system that would punish the wrongdoers. But Rache had been naive. She'd found that out quick enough.

Someone had broken into their house and stolen Ruth's diary. It was more of an attempt at a first novel by a young child with no experience of love or sex. It was a small compilation of fantasies. But the defense had used them against Ruth, exposing Ruth as some kind of teenage slut who'd been begging to get laid. They literally destroyed her on the stand. Ira Fischer and his wife had driven to the police the next day to talk to them about the break-in. They would try anything to avoid a repeat performance.

Rache would usually call in to Ruth's bedroom before breakfast, but after the diary incident the previous day, her mother had told Rache to let Ruth sleep. Rache made black coffee for herself and Ruth that morning. She had begun to drink it black and strong just after the attack. She decided just to bring the coffee. Rache placed the small tray outside the door and knocked. Getting no response by the third knock, she pushed the door in. Ruth was gone! Had she gone with their parents? No, the doctor had given Ruth a heavy sedative the previous evening, saying it would keep her out for twelve hours. Where was she?

Rache started to panic. She checked the bathroom. No Ruth. She rushed downstairs. But she had been there, making the coffee.

She searched everywhere. Then she saw it. A light! A light was coming from under the garage door. Why was she in the garage? Rache had wondered. Rache opened the door into the garage, and her whole world came to an abrupt end. Hanging from a crossbeam, Ruth's lifeless body swayed back and forth, her face blue and contorted.

At first, Rache couldn't move, an invisible glue sticking her feet to the garage floor. Her head began to twitch slightly; her eyes blinked rapidly, like the shutter on a camera, as her young mind tried to process it. She saw the overturned chair below Ruth's feet. It was a full ten seconds before the realization hit her.

Ruth had hanged herself.

It spurred Rache into action. In seconds, she had sprinted into the kitchen, grabbing the largest knife she could find, before racing back into the garage. Quickly turning the chair upright, Rache had leapt onto it and, in one motion, had sliced through the rope that had choked the life from her sister. Ruth fell forward, knocking Rache off the chair. As she fell, Ruth landed on top of her. Rache held her dead sister in her arms and screamed. She screamed until she had no breath left.

It was some time before she became aware of the first police siren. Two patrolmen arrived. Rache's wounded screaming had alerted her neighbors, and they called the cops. The first officers on the scene had broken down the garage door. But they'd been unable to cope. Try as they might, they had found it impossible to wrestle Ruth free from Rache's grasp. Rocking back and forward, Rache had held her sister tight against her. The cops had quickly called it in, requesting female officers on the scene. Three female officers had arrived just as Ira Fischer and his wife pulled into their drive. One of the officers had ushered Miriam Fischer into a neighbor's house and sat with her. They told her Ruth was dead and that Rache had found her. Miriam Fischer had simply shut her eyes and had cried for what seemed an eternity.

It took the combined efforts of both female officers and much cajoling from her father to persuade Rache to loosen her grip on Ruth. She had pleaded with them to leave her with her sister. "Don't take her from me, don't take her from me," Rache had begged, her voice breaking. But eventually she had yielded. Ira had gathered her up in his arms, all the time whispering to her, assuring her. Rache had wrapped herself around his strong shoulders, her face resting on one of them. She sobbed incessantly as he carried her into the spacious lounge, easing her gently onto the couch. But Rache was, by that time, inconsolable.

Rache faced Danny and Susan now. Susan was crying, and Danny could feel the tears well up in his own eyes.

"She was my best friend, Susan. She was my best friend, and I miss her so much," Rache said, burying her head in her hands. Rache remained like that for a moment, but within seconds, Susan had moved around the table and held her. Rache found comfort in the embrace, and she began to cry again.

Danny and Susan stayed with her for some time, neither speaking. Eventually Rache had no tears left.

"Thanks," she said. "Thanks for listening."

Susan merely nodded. Danny half smiled, not trusting himself to speak.

Eventually Rache stood up from the table and walked out. Susan watched her close the door behind her. It gave a small click as it shut.

Danny leaned back in his chair. Clasping his hands behind his head, he let out a long breath. "Jesus," he muttered, "no wonder she's been on edge."

CHAPTER 16

RACHE SPENT THE REMAINDER OF the morning reviewing old cases, her eyes scanning photographs and reports in an effort to jog some memory. But she came up with nothing. Whoever this guy was, she hadn't met him before. *Maybe Danny's right*, she thought, *maybe I am overthinking it.* Yet it was there, in his gaze. She took lunch with Danny and Susan, and they all agreed they needed a break on the Mason case.

Back at the precinct, Rache approached the captain's office with a slight sense of guilt. She knocked and found it comforting that the captain was alone. Rache stepped in and quickly apologized. Captain Woods nodded, accepting, but added that there had really been no need, that she had merely brought to the surface a truth—a truth that they'd all been harboring. He thanked Rache for her honesty. She told him she wanted to continue working old cases to see if there was a connection. Somewhere at the back of her brain, she still had this gnawing feeling that the perp somehow knew her. She understood this was highly unlikely, but she'd continue to sift through old cases all the same. The captain told her she was to run the investigation as she saw it. She was in charge, and whatever she needed, she was to ask for.

"You're number one on this, Rache. I only ask one thing," he had said.

"What's that?" she'd asked.

"Bring me a result!"

She had left it like that. She was happier she had talked to the captain—cleared things up, so to speak.

The perp had certainly given her a strange look, she remembered, and perhaps their paths had crossed before, so she spent the remainder of the day going over old cases.

But she discovered nothing. She studied the oldest cases in detail, examining every scrap of evidence. Nothing! Although she hadn't found anything to shed light on her theory, the work in itself had provided her with an opportunity to keep her mind off the earlier events. Today was Ruth's anniversary. Seventeen years ago today, Rache had cut down the limp body of her dead sister. Strange, but she felt a little relieved, having told Danny and Susan.

Closing the last folder on her desk, Rache realized that this was the first time that she had talked about it. It was strange. Although she'd felt a strong connection with Jensen, she'd never been able to discuss Ruth with him...or anyone else for that matter. Sure, she'd told him she'd had a sister who'd died, but when she hadn't elaborated on it, he hadn't pressed her. It was one of the many things she liked about him.

Talking about Ruth today, about her ordeal, the trial, and her sister's suicide had, in some way, eased Rache's sense of loss. She had always kept the pain to herself. But now she felt relieved.

Ruth's death had devastated her family. Her mother had been hospitalized for months. Her father became a shell of his former self. But David, her brother, had stepped up to the plate. He was only nineteen, but he became a rock for the family. He had deferred college by a year and had practically taken over as head of the household. With painfully tiny incremental steps, the Fischer family had returned to some semblance of normality. Ira Fischer had found strength in God. He had immersed himself in his faith, looking for meaning in Ruth's death. But this had held no sway with Rache. Ruth was dead, and if that was God's will, she wanted nothing to do with it. She couldn't understand how something so loving could inflict such pain on a family who had done nothing to deserve it. And somewhere along the way, it slipped from her grasp.

This had resulted in immense problems at home. As Ira Fischer's faith grew, Rache's diminished. The more she thought about it, the less sense it made. They became opposite sides of the one coin,

their nature forged in metal, neither one capable of bending or seeing the other's side. Rache began to grow apart from her father. As
the months turned to years, so the gulf between them widened. Of
course she loved him. She loved him beyond words, but she couldn't
reconcile her beliefs with his. These days, they had very little contact.

Her phone buzzed. Stretching across her littered desk, Rache
picked it up.

"Got your mom on hold, and a Leo Caldwell called," Martha
said.

"Leo who?"

"Caldwell. DNA lab with the results from the Mason case."

"You get a number, Martha?" Rache wrote it down. "Thanks."

She took her mom.

"Hi, Mom."

"I know, you said I shouldn't call you at work."

She wasn't sure if it was just hearing her mother's voice, or the
events with Danny and Susan had sparked it, but Rache now felt
a strong need to see her mother. It was not something she could
explain, nor did she want to try, but there was this longing to make
contact. A void needed filling. Perhaps she had left it too long?

"I'll come, Mom, I promise. When is it again?" Rache said,
knowing her mother had called about David's celebratory dinner.

"You're sure, Rachel?"

"Yes, Mom, I'm sure."

Her spirit was lifted a little by the sound of her mother's voice.
Miriam was genuinely happy that Rache was coming. She could tell
by the tone.

"Best keep Sarah at the other end though," Rache offered.

Her mother laughed. Laughed! Rache couldn't believe it. Her
mother told her it was this coming weekend. That her father would
be happy. Rache didn't comment on this, save to say it would be good
to see everyone again. The image of her dead sister intruded on her
thoughts.

"You know we all miss her, Rachel," Miriam added.

Rache was silent a moment. "I know, Mom. I know."

"I'll see you on Saturday then?"

"Yes, Mom. Bye, Mom."

"I love you, Rachel."

"I know. I love you too, Mom, very much."

Rache hung up. She looked at the phone number she'd scribbled on a scratch pad. *What the hell*, she thought, *we're going nowhere fast*. She dialed the number.

The new forensics lab was located on Manhattan's fashionable Upper West Side. Bordered by Central Park to the east and the Hudson River to the west, north of Sixtieth Street, the Upper West Side was a huge residential sprawl.

Having stopped off briefly at home to shower and change, Rache now drove north on Broadway, passing the famous Time Warner Building.

When two hijacked airliners ploughed into the Twin Towers of the World Trade Center, destroying two of the city's most iconic buildings and ending the lives of over three thousand people, it heralded a much-needed decentralization of key emergency services. In the aftermath of 9/11, key law enforcement agencies were spread throughout Manhattan. The Manhattan Crime Lab was one such agency. It had been moved in its entirety and now occupied a spot three storeys above, as well as several stories below, Manhattan's more salubrious West Seventy-Second Street.

Rache drove on past the celebrated Juilliard School of Music. Beyond this, Broadway snaked northwest. Rache continued along Ninth Avenue, eventually taking a right onto Seventy-Second Street.

Checking her address, Rache pulled up opposite one of the city's most infamous landmarks—the Dakota Apartments. Looking at the impressive neogothic edifice, Rache felt herself shudder. On a cold December night in 1980, Mark David Chapman shot ex-Beatle John Lennon five times with a .38 calibre revolver. Lennon was rushed to hospital in a taxi by the doorman but died en route from massive blood loss.

Rache shivered again. *Another senseless murder*, she thought.

Rache had spoken to Danny only briefly. She had told him she was going to check it out.

"Maybe we can use this, Danny," she'd said. "Who knows, he might turn up in Codas. Could be he was profiled before." Asked if she needed company, Rache had declined.

It wasn't so much that she didn't want Danny with her. It was more Leo Caldwell's cryptic tone. She had spoken to him at length, and he had sounded like one those conspiracy nuts off the *X-Files* TV series. He had whispered down the phone, saying he had come across some unusual results concerning Kell Mason's DNA.

"What kind of results?" she had asked him, eager to examine any snippet of new evidence.

"Findings, Detective Fischer, findings," Leo'd whispered.

"Findings! What the hell does that mean, Leo?" she'd shouted down the phone at him.

"Not saying over the phone, Detective. You know how it is."

"No, I don't know how it is. What does that mean?"

"Can't say. You coming or not?"

There was finality to his tone.

"Okay, Leo, I'm on my way. But this better be good, or someone's going to lose their job."

She had put the phone down and laughed. It was not the emotion that she though would come out. She had a vanishing suspect, and now she'd have to deal with a conspiracy nut. Rache had smiled to herself as she'd thought about the *X-Files* and the conspiracy theorists on the TV show. What was it they called themselves? *The Lone Gunmen*, yeah, that was it. Sure it was great TV, but she needed something more tangible. She needed scientific evidence if she was going to track down this guy—this killer.

On the phone, she had been annoyed at his secrecy, but this was by far the weirdest case she had ever investigated, so one more crackpot in the mix was to be expected. She thought back to a case she had investigated only two years ago, how a seemingly unrelated piece of evidence had come to light, and they had not only put a killer away, but had also prevented him committing another murder. A man was alive today because of an unpaid parking ticket. *Strange how random this work could be*, she thought. So she would see what Leo Caldwell had to say.

The twenty-block drive found Rache deep in thought. Maybe if she could put this guy away, she could, in some way, atone for what had happened to Ruth. She knew it was a crazy idea, but couldn't help the way she felt. Today had reopened old wounds, her own perceived cowardice among them. Rache glanced at the little digital clock on her dash. It was already eight thirty. The day had gone.

Leo Caldwell greeted her with a bright smile. An intern had walked her to Leo's office, telling Rache that everyone aspired to be like Leo. Looking at him now, she couldn't understand why. Leo Caldwell stood about five-foot-six with long brown hair held in a ponytail. He had pasty skin, skin that never saw much daylight. Heavy rock music played as Rache entered the room. Rache glanced about as Leo walked over to turn down the music. There was nothing unusual about his office. Only, it wasn't exactly an office. It was a lab with an office, or more correctly, a cluttered desk.

"Hi, I'm Leo," he said, offering his hand.

"Detective Fischer," Rache replied, thinking it wiser not to be on a first-name basis. *Keep it professional, Rache,* she told herself. She sized up Leo as she shook his hand. It seemed he hadn't shaved in a week. Looking at his clothes, if you met him on the street, you'd give him your loose change. But Leo Caldwell's attributes lay not in his physical appearance. Leo's were of a more cerebral nature. If there was a base pair coded with information, Leo could find it. If a suspect left as much as a single fiber at the crime scene, Leo would nail him with it. No matter how hopeless a case seemed, Leo would never give up on it. He was a bloodhound, capable of putting in sixteen-hour days, overextended time periods. Leo's services had been asked for back in September 2001, and he hadn't balked at the enormity of the task. Leo had spent months helping to identify victims of the atrocity through DNA analysis of grieving relatives.

"Detective Fischer," he said, letting go of Rache's hand. "Well, as you can see, they keep me down here, out of sight. Not exactly the poster boy for law enforcement now, am I, Detective?"

"You said you had startling information, Leo."

"I said I had unusual findings, if I recall."

"Unusual, startling, why are we arguing?"

"Yeah, like I said, got some weird shit for you, Detective."

"Why am I not surprised," Rache muttered, beginning to wonder why she'd bothered.

"What?"

"Nothing. You were saying?"

"Yes, the Houdini case."

"Who?"

"Houdini. Your escapee, we called him Houdini, after Harry Houdini, you know, the famous escape—"

Rache cut him off. "Leo, it's eight thirty. Why am I here?"

"You'd best take a seat."

"No, I'll stand, thank you."

"Okay, but take a look at this." Leo sat at his desk, scattered with folders and printouts. He typed at the computer. "What do you know about DNA profiling?" he asked Rache.

"We use it like fingerprinting. It's unique to us. It's how we often convict felons. What has this to do with Kell?"

Leo ignored her question. "The development of DNA profiling has been the single biggest breakthrough in law enforcement since the discovery of fingerprinting. DNA profiling is genetic fingerprinting," Leo began. "No two are alike. In the nucleus of every cell are these things that we call chromosomes. If we unravel a chromosome, we would have a long string of DNA. On each chromosome are found our genes. Genes are made up of what we call base pairs. Each base pair code for some particular function. Do you know why the mapping of the human genome took so long?"

Rache shook her head. "But I got a feeling you're going to tell me."

"It's because the human body has billions of base pairs. All of us have these base pairs. It's the sequencing that differentiates us. The gene sequencing."

"Why the biology lesson, Leo? I'm getting a sinking feeling, here," Rache said, wondering where all this was leading.

"I want you to understand that this is an exact science. This country executes people on the strength of DNA evidence."

"Okay, okay, so the evidence is airtight. No two people have the same DNA," she said, exasperated.

"You would think!"

"What? What are you saying?"

"I cross-referenced your mystery guy's DNA with hairs found at the crime scene."

"And?" Rache asked.

"Perfect match."

"Okay, so it puts him at the scene, so what?"

"Hair's female."

How could that be? thought Rache. "Kell's?" she inquired.

Leo looked at her. "Well, if it is, it's got the same DNA."

That was it, she thought. They had to be related. Her hunch was right. Kell Mason knew her attacker. They were related. That would explain why there had been no forced entry. She had let him in.

"They're related, Leo?"

Leo shook his head. "I didn't say that, Detective."

"But you just said—"

"No!"

Leo's raised voice took her aback.

He smiled, a little embarrassed. "They have the same DNA. It's not similar. It's identical."

"How can this be? Fucking crime scene is contaminated," Rache said.

"Maybe, but that would not explain the fact that the DNA taken from the blood and saliva of Mr. Houdini is a DNA match with Kell Mason."

"The hair, it's female, right?"

"Yeah."

"But we're not sure it's Kell's hair, are we?"

"Well, it is our only reference point," Leo said.

"Leo, I've had a pisser of a day. To tell the truth, it has probably been one of my worst ever. Do whatever you have to. Just sort this mess out." She handed Leo her card. "You can call me on my cell when you have something more definitive." Rache started to walk to the door. "Fucking crime scene's contaminated," she mumbled to herself again.

"I'm gonna need a swab from the kid, Detective," Leo called after her.

But Rache was already gone.

She drove back to her apartment, annoyed. Everywhere she looked, every time there was a small glimmer of hope, it was snuffed out. Sure, Leo was only doing his job, but matching the perp's DNA to that of Kell Mason was impossible! Even she knew that. She needed a break. In every case she'd investigated, something had always turned up, but this…this was different. It had been two days since the perp's disappearing trick, and the odds of catching him were lengthening by the hour.

Leo's call, however cryptic, had excited her. She had hoped to turn up something with the visit. But that had been a complete waste of time. Someone must have messed up at the crime scene. She made a mental note to talk to Office Marks tomorrow.

Arriving home, Rache headed straight to bed. As she made herself comfortable on the pillow, she thought of her sister Ruth, of Kell Mason, and finally of Leo's discovery. Before drifting off, she thought of just how insane the whole case had become.

CHAPTER 17

RACHE SLEPT, DREAMING OF BASE pairs. They had all lined up, taking on some kind of human form, as they swarmed around the perp, shielding him. Try as she might, Rache couldn't find a way through. No matter how she struggled to push past, they always blocked her path. The perp stared back at her. At one point, she had almost broken through when she woke. Her cell phone was ringing. She looked at her clock. It was almost five thirty. Who was calling at this hour?

Leo's voice was shaky when he spoke.

"Eh, I think I've found something definitive," he whispered. "Meet me at the lab, and come alone."

Rache dressed quickly. Driving through the near-empty Manhattan streets, Rache thought she must be mad. But Leo had been insistent. He had evidence, he'd said. Evidence he didn't understand. *How can you gather evidence and not understand it?* she wondered, pulling up to the Dakota Apartments for the second time in just a few short hours.

Leo was waiting for her at the door.

"Leo, this had better be good," she greeted him.

"Come on," he said, taking her by the arm and propelling her down the corridor. The lab was empty, devoid of last night's hustle and bustle. The place was in near total darkness, the only light source coming from subdued blue fluorescent strip lighting running the length of the corridor. Rache got a distinctive spooky feeling as they took the elevator down to Leo's office. They exited left, out of the elevator, and walked the twenty yards or so to Leo's office. He held the door open for her. As Rache stepped into the office, Leo glanced about nervously. He quickly followed her inside, closing the door softly behind him, as if afraid he'd disturb somebody. In this light, Leo looked paler than yesterday.

"Why all the secrecy? And hey, don't you sleep?" she asked.

Leo turned on the lights.

Rache blinked, adjusting her eyes to the sudden brightness. He walked over to a desk, picked up a blue folder, and handed it to her.

"What's this?"

"Results," he whispered.

"Why are we whispering?"

Leo sat at his computer, shaking the mouse on the pad. He keyed in a few commands, bringing up a split screen on the monitor.

"Okay, you're the detective. After you left last night, I had a swab done on Kell Mason. Said you'd ordered it. You know...get a rush on it."

Rache gave him a look, but she let him continue.

"Anyway," he said, ignoring her, "got the results early this morning."

"You've been at this all night?" she asked. She was impressed.

"Hey, Detective..."

"Rache, call me Rache."

Leo nodded. "Rache," he said, pausing. "A case like this comes along once in a fucking millennium."

"What kind of case..."

She didn't finish. Leo had whispered the words *X-File* at her.

She stared blankly at him. *Fuck, he's lost it*, she thought.

But Leo hadn't lost it. The analogy was the only route open to him to express what he had discovered only hours earlier. Leo had been fascinated at matching the perp's DNA to the hairs found at the scene. He'd figured that they belonged to the kid, the young girl in the coma. Detective Fischer—the good-looking one—had had a bee in her pants about someone contaminating the crime scene. Sure, he'd seen it happen before. But this case was different. No one had fucked up here, he was sure of that. He'd called the hospital, dispatching a trainee to take a mouth swab on Kell Mason, at pains to point out that the order had come from the lead detective on the case. Leo had been aware he was stretching it, but he'd needed that swab! He'd processed the swab as soon as the trainee had reported back. The result had shocked him. He'd verified it over and over, experiencing various emotions each time the result came back, even found himself giggling like some demented inmate. That's when he'd decided to call Rache. He needed to share this with someone.

He sat at his computer now, with Rache looking over his shoulder. "The DNA taken from the swab done on Kell Mason is a DNA match to your pal, Mr. Hou-fucking-dini," he told her.

Rache couldn't believe what she was hearing.

Kell has the same DNA as the perp? How can that be?

"What exactly does that mean, Leo?" she inquired, puzzled now.

"It means that Kell Mason and your escapologist are one and the same person. They even have the same blood group. A positive. Ran a test to be sure," he added.

Rache sat down beside Leo. "Break this down for me, Leo, cos I'm lost."

He explained to her that no two people have the same DNA. But Kell and the perp's were a perfect match. It was as though they were one person, split in two. Every base pair matched. One hundred percent!

Kell Mason and the perp were, in his books, the same, not related, not similar, but the same.

"How is this possible?"

"It's not. Detective Fischer, I'd say you have yourself a genuine X-File."

"There's a little kid in a coma fighting for her life, and you're telling me that the guy who put her there is the same person as she is. So she put herself in the coma? This is madness, Leo," she said.

"Do you believe in otherworldly events, Detective?"

"What...no, I do not...no, no, no, I see where this is going. Now, maybe your machine messed up, or there was a short circuit..." Rache trailed off. She looked at Leo, wondering where all this would lead her.

Leo was adamant. There had been no mess up, no contamination of the crime scene. The result was conclusive and beyond doubt. Kell Mason had the identical DNA to the perp!

"Who else knows about this?"

"Just us."

"Let's keep it that way, okay? Least till I figure this bitch out," Rache said, trying to buy herself some time.

Leo nodded. "Look, Det—Rache, I've never seen anything like this. Ever! I'm not about to shout it from the rooftops, okay?"

Rache was satisfied. She needed to look into this some more.

CHAPTER 18

THE NEXT COUPLE OF DAYS passed quickly for Rache. The perp had disappeared, leaving everyone connected to the case feeling deflated. The hospital video had proved fruitless. Every tape had been thoroughly examined, but it had been of no assistance to them. Nobody had ever, in their wildest dreams, factored in an attack on a hospital, its sanctuary virtually guaranteed, and so no cameras had been installed in the stairwell. The videotape had merely shown the perp arriving at the main entrance and had picked him up again entering the intensive care unit. ICU had not been fitted with cameras.

Rache, Danny, and Susan had, between them, painstakingly examined every minute, from a couple of hours leading up to the perp's arrival, through to the end of the day. But it was no help. They had a visual of him entering and had caught the briefest of glimpses as he approached intensive care. At one point they'd broken for lunch, but Rache had decided to stay on. Better to stagger lunch, that way someone was viewing the tapes all the time. But this was only partially true. Rache had decided to keep Leo's DNA analysis to herself. She couldn't quite put her finger on it, but something had urged her to remain silent.

As Rache settled in to check the tapes again, she could feel a weird sensation driving her. She tried to dispel it, but it was there, at the back of her mind, urging her on. *I gotta get help.* She laughed to herself. *Enough of this*, she told herself, pulling her chair forward and pressing the play button on the recorder. She'd look at it one more time.

Rache glanced at her watch. She sat in silence a moment, observing the little red second hand as it glided around the face, ticking off small, almost incomprehensible segments of time. Shit, that was it—the timeframe!

Damn it, how could she have missed it? In their haste to discern anything at all, they'd forgotten to check the timeframe! Rache rewound the tapes to when the perp entered the hospital—14.01. She fast-forwarded it to when he was caught walking into ICU—14.03. Next she checked the corridor to Kell's room. Nothing! No sign of him!

Kell had been moved to the ICU earlier in the day. Rache ruffled through the file, fishing out a photocopy from the hospital. She'd requested all changes in Kell Mason's status to be forwarded to the precinct. Kell had been moved before lunch.

Rache stared at the TV monitor in fascination. She watched herself enter the intensive care unit at 14.07—four minutes after the perp. He had been alone with her over four minutes. He'd ample time to kill her, yet Kell was unharmed. Why? Why had he not killed her? What were the words he'd spoken? Don't shoot! *Words of self-preservation*, thought Rache. Or were they? But it wasn't just that. It had only taken him two minutes to find Kell. Shit, he'd bypassed her room. She just could not fathom it. She rewound the tape again. It was there, staring her in the face. He'd made no attempt to find Kell in her room, electing instead to go straight to ICU. Two minutes between entering the hospital and arriving at intensive care—two minutes. The perp had known exactly where to find Kell!

The DNA match, and now this!

So when Danny and Susan returned after lunch, Rache decide she'd hold off telling them. Leo's analysis had freaked her out, and this only seemed to add to that feeling. No, she'd hold off a while. Better check this out first, to be sure. She'd already told Danny that the crime scene had been contaminated and that lab guys were doing their best. But the evidence was far from contaminated.

Looking at Danny and Susan in the eye, she told them she'd found nothing! Deep inside, she realized that this case was getting stranger by the moment. One thing was certain though—she'd look into it alone. At first she'd told herself it was because she didn't want to come across foolish, but now she wasn't sure.

Pete and Joe were getting nowhere with their investigations, so when Danny told her he was going to see his uncle again, she figured she'd tag along. "Maybe Fr. John left something out, Danny," she offered. "We did leave in a kinda rush, ya know."

Danny threw his eyes skyward. "Okay, but no dipping your fingers in the holy water. Don't want to have to rush you to the emergency room with third-degree burns."

Rache smiled at him. "Come on," she said good-naturedly.

***

Walking through the giant doors of the church, Rache was taken by the smell of burned candles. It hung heavy in the air. Both sight and sound combined to draw her attention to the huge altar where a school choir stood rehearsing. A group of about thirty kids, all aged between twelve and sixteen, sang from small white hymn sheets. What struck Rache was that they all sang from the heart. It wasn't any of this "I want to be famous" bullshit that seemed to obsess most kids now, thought Rache as she approached the altar.

Fr. John greeted them warmly, walking them back down the aisle toward the door as they talked.

"So, where exactly did he sit, Father?" Rache asked as they approached the first few pews.

Fr. John walked her to the first Station of the Cross. Rache stood under it. The painting was magnificent. It was the Annunciation.

"The Angel of the Lord declared unto Mary, and she was conceived of the Holy Spirit," he said.

"One way to get the bad news, I guess," Rache replied.

Danny threw her a disapproving look.

"I'm sorry, Father. I don't share in your belief."

"You're not a Catholic?"

"Jewish. Well, in theory."

"Jesus was Jewish, so was his mother, Mary," Fr. John said, looking up at the painting.

Rache walked over to the pew and sat in it. "And he just sat here...for hours?" Rache asked, not wanting to get drawn into any deep religious debate.

Fr. John nodded.

"The angel in the picture, he's the..."

"Archangel Gabriel."

"Yeah," she said.

"He's not like a Guardian Angel, is he?" she probed.

Danny looked at her again. What was Rache up to? She had no interest in religion. The crew back at the precinct had always joked about Rache bursting into flames if she stepped into a church. But here she was, in a church, asking a priest about angels. Danny couldn't believe it. What was she up to? If Fr. John had any information, he'd give it voluntarily. He didn't need to have it drawn out of him this way.

But the priest was intrigued. "No. He's not a guardian. The guardians are different."

"Different how?"

"Well, for one, they are assigned to one person. It is their duty or mission to stay with that person to advise and counsel that person as long as he or she remains alive on this earth."

"What then?"

"I'm not sure what you mean," he replied.

"It doesn't matter," Rache said, standing.

"No, you have a genuine interest, I can tell. Most people pay some kind of lip service, but you seem interested."

"Not to burst your bubble, I'm not. I was born into one faith. I don't believe that. I'm not about to take up someone else's hocus-pocus."

"Rache!"

She glanced over at Danny. He looked furious.

"Yeah, Father, we should be going. Thank you for your time," Rache said. "I didn't mean to be rude."

"You weren't." Fr. John smiled at her. "I like a challenge. I discount no possibility. Question is, Detective Fischer, do you?"

He was testing her. He knew more than he was letting on.

"He hasn't been back now, Father, has he?" she asked, holding his stare.

"No, Detective, he has not."

"Well, you seemed taken by him."

"I just don't believe he's capable of—"

"Murder! Believe me, Father, it's always the ones you'd least suspect," Rache said, turning to Danny. "I'll wait for you outside."

Both men watched her disappear out the oak doors. Danny quickly apologized to his uncle. He felt foolish in doing so. He explained that this had been one the hardest cases to date, and with their suspect escaping custody and turning up at the hospital…well, it had got them all jittery. Danny explained the reason for their visit, feeling that Rache has usurped the time to run her own agenda. Could Fr. John remember anything else about the day he'd talked to the suspect? The priest shook his head, telling Danny he'd given them everything. Danny thanked him and left.

Driving back to the precinct in near silence, it was Rache who spoke first. "Sorry. I suppose I was a little hard on your UNCLE."

"It's okay, Rache."

"No, it's not. I shouldn't have done it. You…you have such faith, Danny. Your uncle has enough for the entire island of Manhattan."

Danny laughed. "He does, doesn't he?"

Rache fell silent a moment. "You see, I don't. I don't believe in any of it. For me, it's bogus. After Ruth died, the trial fell apart. They were acquitted, and Senator Williams was reelected. Not much justice for the Fischers, huh?"

"Rache, I'm sorry."

"You know, I thought about it a long time. It's the one thing that separates us from the animal kingdom. That and language."

"Now, you've completely lost me," he said, turning the wheel.

"The inevitability of death. Animals don't know that they will someday die. They just go about their little lives. We do! From an early age, we know we'll die. So we make up this wonderful afterlife. It's a big comfort blanket, and we gladly wrap ourselves in it. I don't buy it myself, but if it helps you make sense of things, well…"

Danny thought about it. He felt sorry for her. Not in a patronizing way, but genuinely sorry. She had had it tough. She had almost been raped and found her sister dead. In many ways, she reminded him of Kell.

Now it all made sense to him. No wonder she was so pushy on getting the perp. Yeah, they all wanted the scumbag, but Rache had been obsessed. He saw in Rache a mirror image of what had happened to Kell. A young girl, her life torn apart by some random act of unspeakable violence. In both cases, the guilty parties had walked. What had she said to him? They always get away. If not through an unlocked door, then through some fancy lawyer. He knew why she needed a result. She needed to lay the ghost of her dead sister to rest. If she didn't, it would destroy her.

He looked over at her. She smiled back.

CHAPTER 19

Officer Marks walked over to a holding cell. Six hookers sat inside. He watched them all closely. Most had given him a hard time when he'd first arrested them, some even offering sexual favors if he'd let them go. So as he approached he cell door, they started to whistle at him.

He smiled to himself. "Okay, ladies, okay, you're all free to go. Just part of an ongoing investigation."

"Ongoing harassment ya mean, lover," one of the hookers, Doreen, taunted him. "Anytime ya wanna learn a thing or two… well, you give me a call, baby."

"Yeah, yeah, Doreen, I'll bear that in mind," he replied as he held the door to the cell open.

"Wouldn't mind bearing yours anywhere," she taunted him, pushing her tongue against her cheek to simulate oral sex.

Some of the other girls latched onto this little pantomime and started to join in. Cole Marks laughed as the girls began to moan and call out his name.

"Oh, Officer, please take me, I wanna make a statement," one called out. But he wasn't listening now. His concentration was focused on one girl in particular. She hadn't said a single word. He held the door open.

"Come on, girls, you can all go now." He smiled as he watched them file out. Most of the friendly banter had died down now as the girls made their way past him. One or two told him they would sue the precinct for loss of earnings. The last girl to file past him was Jessie Adams. He stopped her.

"Not you."

"Come on, man," Jessie groaned at him.

"Just got a couple more questions, Jessie."

"Yeah, yeah."

It was more than a few questions in store for Jessie. Rache had approached him a few days back. It was just after the news of Joe Mason's death. She had asked for his help in tracking down a young hooker. He was happy to have helped out. He knew Rache Fischer by rep only, but to work for her was an opportunity not to be missed. He had asked her what she'd needed. Rache had briefly told him about the incident in the alley by St. Killian's, leaving out some of the more salient details. Basically, she wanted him to do a missing person's search. She had figured that the kid was from the Midwest and was no older than eighteen or nineteen. Asked if it had anything to do with the ongoing investigation on the murder of Joe Mason, she had told him yes. Personally he couldn't see how, but he was not about to challenge her.

It had taken him a few days, but he had come up trumps. Her name was Jessie Adams, eighteen, from Richmond, Kentucky. Her mother, Julia, had filed a missing person's report three months ago. Richmond police had faxed him a copy of her photo, and he'd shown it to Rache earlier yesterday, with Rache confirming that it was the kid she'd wanted to talk to.

Rache now sat across from Jessie's mother. Julia Adams was a mother of two. Her husband was a nasty drunk, doing a five-year stretch for larceny. Rache looked at Julia. *She can't be much older than me*, Rache thought. In fact, Julia was only thirty-four.

As she shifted uncomfortably in her seat, her surroundings bearing down on her, Julia told Rache she had being fighting with Jessie for over a year and that one morning, a little over three months ago, she had found a note from Jessie, saying she was going to New York to make something of her life. Julia had filed a missing person's report, but with Jessie no longer being a minor, there was not much Richmond police could do.

When she'd taken the call from Rache the previous day, asking her to come up to New York, Julia couldn't believe her ears. At first, she'd thought her daughter was dead and had begun to sob. Rache had quickly assured her that Jessie was very much alive and that Julia should come up as soon as possible. She had asked a neighbor to look after Patrick, her youngest, and had used what little savings she had to fly up the next morning. Now she sat directly opposite Rache, still thinking the worst.

Rache had been impressed with the way Cole Marks had handled everything. He had come up with a result in no time. When he told her that they had Jessie in custody, Rache had got him to keep her overnight, to be sure. She'd told him her plan, and he'd agreed. He had rounded up several hookers to make it look like it was a bust. In fact, they had wanted Jessie to suspect nothing.

"Can...can I see her?" Julia asked, her thick Southern accent pronounced.

"Not just yet. In a little while, okay?" Rache said. "I'll have to ask you to remain here until then. We just need to ask her one or two more questions. Then you can see her."

"She's alright, Detective, isn't she?"

Rache looked at Julia, nodding, as she touched her lightly on the shoulder, reassuring her. "She's fine, Julia. She's just fine."

Rache left Julia sitting in her office. She knocked on Susan's door, and they both headed to the room.

Jessie sat at table as Susan and Rache looked on through the two-way mirror. Both Theo and Joe had positioned themselves opposite Jessie, neither saying a word. Both cops stared her down, Theo drumming his fingers repeatedly on the table. Joe was an imposing figure who would frighten his own mother. It was something Rache was banking on.

Jessie's body language said it all. She was frightened but cocky. It was cockiness born out of fear. It was not seasoned bravado, the type they were used to seeing. The longer they stared, the more unsure Jessie became.

"What about the mother?" Susan asked as they looked on.

"Got her back in my office. No way I want her seeing this."

In the room, Joe stood up slowly from the desk, his movement carefully choreographed. Jessie's eyes followed him as he began to move about. He stretched as he walked over to a table by the door. A couple of files lay strewn on it. Picking up a folder off the table, he began to leaf through it, glancing up occasionally to look at Jessie.

Jessie's eyes were riveted on him. *Why had they kept her?* she wondered. She was scared now—scared of what Mr. Jakes might do.

Joe strolled back over and sat down opposite her. He frightened her. He had mad eyes. Joe had discussed the routine with Rache and had agreed. Rache knew what she was doing. Let the kid talk first. If that happened, you had her.

"Can I go now?" Jessie asked, her eyes thrown to heaven in an effort to sound nonchalant.

"Go where?" inquired Theo softly.

"I've got places to be," Jessie said, turning her attention to Theo.

Theo held her eyes. Jessie blinked, looking down. "How long do you think you'll last? You're, what, eighteen now? There's an expiry date on your forehead, honey," Theo snarled, his tone changing.

"Look, man, you can't keep me here for no reason."

Joe completely ignored her, continuing to sort through the folder, all the time keeping it angled back toward him, denying Jessie's eyes access to the material within. Theo continued to challenge Jessie as Joe remained silent.

Joe had truly begun to frighten her now. What did they want with her? Theo's questions were coming thick and fast now, not allowing Jessie any opportunity to answer before he'd jump in with another.

Suddenly, Joe placed a photo in front of her. Theo shut up immediately. Jessie stared at the high-resolution, full-color photograph. Her heart almost stopped beating. The image of a dead girl jumped off the table at her—the photograph revealing a young girl, no more than seventeen, taken shortly after her life had been snuffed out. She lay alone on what looked to Jessie like a mortuary slab. She was naked, and her stomach had been horribly burnt with a cigar. Twenty or thirty deep circles, each about an inch in diameter, covered an area from her belly button up to her breasts. Her neck had been snapped, and her dead eyes glared off the page. Jessie found herself drawn to the picture. She could actually see into the dead girl's mouth. Most of her teeth had been knocked out, and part of her top lip was missing. Jessie gasped.

Theo and Joe caught it. They had her attention. There would be no holding back now. It was time to jack it up.

In the adjoining room, Rache watched with mixed emotions. Part of her wanted to go in and put a stop to it. But she knew that if her plan was to work, she had to let the guys do their job. In a way, she was glad it wasn't her grilling the kid. Of course, she'd have no problem putting the screws on a suspect. This was different. Jessie Adams was no suspect—she was a victim whose mother now sat in Rache's office. Rache recalled the beating she'd witnessed back in the alley. Shit, the poor kid has been through hell. Yeah, she was glad it was Theo and Joe working her. Rache didn't think she'd hold up herself. All she wanted was to see the kid back with her mother.

Subconsciously, Rache realized that at some level, it reflected her own relationship with her mother. Damn, she'd let it go too long. It had been over three months since she'd actually seen her mom.

Looking through the two-way as Joe turned up the heat on Jessie and Jessie's bravado began to wilt, Rache could almost see herself all those years ago—a young kid, her youthful dreams shattered, bravado her only mechanism of coping.

Pull it together, Rache. This is not the time, she urged herself.

Rache forced herself to concentrate on what Joe was saying.

Joe placed another photo in front of a now terrified Jessie. "Had the same conversation with her last month," Joe said. "Not pretty, is it?"

Jessie's eyes brimmed with tears.

"And her last week." Joe placed two more photos in front of her.

Jessie looked at them. She began to sob.

"Where do you see yourself next week, Jessie?" Theo asked her as he leaned in close, his face almost touching hers.

Jessie's eyes were drawn to the last photo.

Joe picked it up. "This girl was a year younger than you are now. See the way the acid burnt down to the bone? Took her a week to die." Joe put the photo back in front of Jessie. A young girl, her features horribly disfigured, looked off the page, her face frozen for eternity.

Jessie began to cry now.

Theo and Joe glanced at each other.

"Take a good look, missy. She died screaming. All the morphine in the world can't alleviate the pain caused by sulfuric acid," Joe said as he and Theo stood up and walked out, leaving Jessie staring at the picture of the dead girl. The faces of dead kids were silently screaming off the table now. Jessie couldn't take anymore. She began to wretch.

In the adjoining room, Rache and Susan looked on.

"Jesus, they're good," remarked Susan.

"Come on," Rache said.

Jessie wiped her mouth as Susan and Rache walked in. She was crying nonstop.

"Why…why are you doing this? I hate you, I fucking hate you!" she shouted between sobs.

Susan handed Jessie a glass of water. "Here, drink this."

Jessie took small sips. Rache gathered up the photographs.

"I don't want this…I don't…" Jessie began to cry some more.

Sitting next to her, Rache put a comforting arm around Jessie's slender shoulders. "Come on, it's okay, it's okay. Someone else wants to see you," Rache whispered as she stroked Jessie's hair. Rache nodded to Susan, who walked over to the door. Susan opened the door and beckoned Julia in.

As she walked in, Julia Adams tried to hide her shock on seeing her daughter. Rache stood up and walked past her. Julia stood in the middle of the room as Susan and Rache closed the door behind them.

Julia moved over to her daughter and sat beside her.

"I'm so sorry, Momma, I'm so sorry," was all Jessie could say over and over again.

Julia held her as they both cried together.

"Hush, baby, hush. I'm here to take you home. I'm here to take you home."

Rache, Susan, Joe, and Theo watched through the mirror as Julia rocked her daughter back and forth.

"Thanks, guys," Rache said. "I couldn't have done it without you."

Joe put his hand on her shoulder. He nodded as he looked into her eyes. "You did a good thing here, Rache." He walked out with Theo, leaving Susan and Rache looking on.

Rache watched as Julia helped her daughter to her feet. Jessie stood. Reaching over, she sipped some of the water Susan had left. Putting the water down, she tried to steady herself. But the last few months had exacted a heavy toll on her young body, and the events of the last few hours overwhelmed her. Jessie slumped back into the chair. "I'm okay, Momma, really. I'm okay," Jessie whispered as Julia wiped the tears from Jessie's soft cheeks.

Rache gave them a few minutes alone before walking in. She carried some clean towels. "There's a washroom just down the hall, and you've brought her some fresh clothes, right?" Rache asked.

Julia nodded, remembering the small bag she'd left in Rache's office. "Thank you," was all Julia could say.

Rache looked at Jessie. "There are no charges against you, Jessie. You're free to go home. I'll let you get cleaned up, okay?"

Julia reached over and hugged Rache. "Thank you," she said again.

Rache nodded and walked to the door. Yeah, she'd see her mother this weekend, she thought as she opened the door.

CHAPTER 20

ACHE LEFT EARLY THAT DAY. She had gotten nowhere on the Mason case, and while she felt a sense of achievement at reuniting Jessie with her mother, she still felt helpless when it came to Kell Mason. She had toyed with the idea of telling Danny about Leo's discovery and the hospital video timeline, but for some strange reason had decided to hold back. She had genuinely believed that the crime scene had been contaminated. But the swab from Kell had proved conclusively that not only did the perp share the same DNA as Kell Mason, but it was the same DNA. Her theory that they may somehow be related had been blown out of the water by incontrovertible proof that Kell Mason and the perp were one and the same person. The whole thing sounded crazy. But the scientific evidence was there.

Rache had always held science in the highest regard. For her, scientists were the real heroes. They were the ones who could help convict serial killers and other murderers. Yet now, as she started to draw on her whiteboard in her little apartment office, she realized that she was now faced with something that no scientist could explain.

Who was the perp?

She had written it down, drawing a box around the sentence. Rache stood back and looked at the simple question. She thought back to the bullet Dion had found in the ceiling. Dion had explained that the only possible way for it to have ended up there was for someone to have leapt off the bed and pushed the shooter's arm upward. They still had no weapon. So there must have been two of them. It was the only explanation. Again, the question pushed itself to the front of her mind. *Okay, clever bitch, who is he?*

If he were not in fact the perp, then he must have been the one who prevented the shooter. But why? The more she thought about it, the madder it made her. She would almost have an answer, and then four or five more questions would jump into her head. She needed answers. Maybe she could get Leo to… No, best not involve him. Yet Leo was involved. He had discovered the relationship between Kell and the perp.

Have to stop calling him that, Rache made a mental note to herself. But if he wasn't the perp, then who was he? Well, they were the same person. It was simple. She'd just tell the captain that she'd cracked the case wide open. Kell Mason was the perp. She put herself in a coma, killed her dad, and then escaped police custody. Rache laughed at her own cynicism. Perhaps Leo was wrong? Nothing made sense.

She looked at the whiteboard. A multitude of mostly unanswered questions stared out at her. *The hell with it*, she thought. Rache went to wipe it clean. No, she'd leave it overnight. Things might seem different in the morning. Yeah, what the hell, she'd sleep on it.

As Rache placed the eraser back, she smudged one of the questions. *Damn it*, she thought. She wiped the ink off her thumb on the board. Walking into her bathroom, she ran some water over her hands in an effort to wash the ink off, the ink quickly blackening the water. Pulling up the chain and watching the discolored water disappear down the plughole, Rache figured she'd better check to see if it were an important question. Walking back into the office, she grabbed her pen and was about to write over her question when she saw it.

Her thumbprint!

It was very clear. Black ink against a white background. The little swirls meandering in different directions, forming a unique pattern. Rache's next thought frightened her to death. Not the thought itself. That was bad enough. But it was the process that led to the thought. Her breath caught in her chest.

No fucking way! she figured. It was not possible. This was indeed the weirdest case she had ever investigated, but as Rache Fischer stared at her thumbprint on her whiteboard, she knew instinctively that her life had altered. What would have been impossible just a few days ago was now not only possible, it was probable. She'd have to talk to that old priest again. This time without Danny. But there was something she needed to do first.

She had to print Kell Mason!

Rache drove straight to the hospital. She had kept a fingerprint kit at home. And although she had never used it, she always figured it might be useful one day. She hoped that most of the doctors would be gone home. She didn't want to start explaining herself to them. Rache knew she could not get a copy of Kell's prints from the precinct without raising the flag of suspicion.

The hospital seemed quiet enough as she took the elevator to the fourth floor. The journey over had scared Rache. Why had she decided to print Kell was the question foremost in her thoughts. No doubt, it needed to be done. But why? This was the big question. Some part of her subconscious had already accepted the possibility. But Rache was a skeptic. Deep down, she had no belief. But this was in itself a belief, and now that was being challenged.

Rache knew she would not sleep until she had the answer. But before she pulled her car into the dimly lit hospital parking lot, she had an inkling that she already knew the answer. It was an answer that scared her to death. Never before in her life had she been this frightened. Well, not since she'd dived overboard all those years ago. Yes, she had been scared then, but this was a completely different sensation of fear. Oddly enough, this was coupled with a twang of excitement, of discovery. She began to feel alive. She couldn't explain it. It was as though a voice was urging her. So as she pushed the door to Kell's room, her hand trembled.

The printing took just a few moments. Rache took Kell's right hand and printed it first. She spoke softly to Kell as she proceeded. "I'm sorry, baby, I'm really sorry." Rache quickly wiped Kell's hand and printed the other. She looked at Kell's peaceful face.

As she began to wipe the ink from Kell's other hand, all hell broke loose. The door was pushed open, and a woman rushed in.

Rache knew instinctively that it was Kell's mother, the likeness startling.

Liz Mason rushed over to her daughter. "What...what are you doing? Why are you printing her?" she demanded of Rache.

Rache was taken by complete surprise. "I'm Detective Fischer... I'm investigating this—"

She didn't finish. Danny had walked in, throwing her a weird look and nodding for her to follow him outside. Liz sat beside Kell now, weeping softly as she held Kell's hand. Liz stared at her own hand. Some of the ink had rubbed off onto it.

"Who did this to you, my little angel? Who did this to you, baby?" Liz sobbed.

Rache remained rooted to the spot.

"This is Liz Mason, Kell's mother," Danny told her.

"Why are you printing her?" Liz demanded tearfully, looking up at Rache.

Rache was shocked. It was all happening too fast. She needed time to think. "I...I just needed to...count out certain prints. It's standard..." she stammered. She knew she sounded less than convincing.

Danny walked over to her and took Rache by the arm. He nodded his head toward the door. Let's get out of here, he was saying. He put his hand on Liz's shoulder in a gesture of comfort. "We'll be right outside, and Agent Franks is on her way," he told her.

At the mention of the word *agent*, Rache's head whipped about. Her face gave Danny that quizzical look.

"Come on, Rache." Danny escorted Rache to the door.

She was lost for words. She looked back over her shoulder at Liz Mason as Danny closed the door.

"Want to tell me what's going on?" he demanded.

Rache just stared back at him. Her mind had been rocketed into overload. She was barely treading water, barely keeping abreast of what was happening. Had Danny really said *agent*? What had the Feds to do with this? Where had Kell's mother been all this time? Too many questions. To compound matters, she had her own unanswered questions—questions that had forced her to drive over to the hospital to print Kell Mason.

"Rache?"

"I'm trying to get some results here," she said. She knew it was lame, but she couldn't tell him why she was there. They'd lock her up.

"We don't need to print the kid, Rache. You're stalling. Now tell me."

Could she? she wondered. Could she tell him? She didn't even believe it herself, so how could she tell Danny?

She looked at the fingerprint kit. "I don't know, Danny. I just don't know."

She had to stall him, had to stop him asking questions.

"Rache, I'm sorry about your sister, but it's affecting your judgment on this case."

Rache was taken aback. She immediately became defensive. "It's not affecting anything. I was just trying—"

Danny held up a hand. "It doesn't matter now. Looks like we're off this case anyway."

"What?"

"The Feds are all over this. Liz Mason was…is Maxine Marsh. Kell Mason is Sarah-Jane Marsh. Maxine testified…" He didn't finish. He was looking over her shoulder now.

Three men and a woman were striding purposely down the corridor. Rache turned around. *Feds*, she thought. Danny watched as they walked up to him.

"She's in there," he said, waiting, as the four disappeared into the room.

Danny began to walk Rache down the corridor away from Kell's room. "Maxine or Liz testified against Lorenzo Caruso—"

"The PAPA!" exclaimed Rache. "Shit, so it was a mob hit?"

Danny nodded. "Sure looks that way. That was Special Agent Franks, a real charmer," he said wryly. "We've to meet with her tomorrow. Woods wants everyone there. Go home and get some sleep."

Rache turned to him. "Danny, there's more to this than you think."

"Rache, no more, not tonight. Go home. It's not our case anymore."

But Rache knew she couldn't go home. She nodded at Danny and told him she'd catch him at the precinct in the morning. As she climbed into her car, she knew she had to have answers, and she'd have to have them tonight.

She phoned Leo at the lab. Sure enough, he was still working. Leo had been intrigued by the case, and when Rache informed him that she uncovered startling new evidence that needed to be processed right away, he had quickly agreed to stay on and meet her.

Driving north from the hospital to the forensics lab, Rache tried to recall all she could about the Lorenzo Caruso case and the Caruso crime family. Like many of the families, they were based in Chicago, but had tentacles that stretched from Staten Island to the San Francisco Bay.

Drugs and murder. Those were the two words that Rache remembered from the trial. Lorenzo Caruso had been the head of a Chicago family, but had been convicted of murder sometime back. Rache couldn't recall the details. But she knew he was serving life. Lorenzo Caruso would never see the light of day again.

Pulling up outside the forensics lab, Rache sat in silence a moment, collecting herself. It was time to put all thoughts of the Carusos out of her head. *Concentrate*, she told herself as she reached over to the passenger's seat, lifting up the small fingerprint kit. A cold chill ran down her back. Rache glanced out the window at the forensics building. She took a deep breath.

She already knew the answer she'd get inside.

Looking at Leo's computer screen, she half wished she'd taken Danny's advice. She half wished she'd gone straight to bed. Rache glanced over at Leo. His pallid color seemed tinged with gray now.

"Check it again. To be sure," she urged him.

"Enough already, Rache. I've checked it four times. They're a perfect match."

Rache leaned back in her seat, her eyes fixed on the computer monitor in front of her. A split screen showed the prints of Kell Mason alongside those of the perp, the one Leo called Houdini. But this was no conjuring trick. There was a 100 percent match on all ten digits. Rache felt a knot in her stomach.

"It's a match. The prints taken from your pal, Houdini, match Kell Mason's—are Kell Mason's," Leo said.

Rache shook her head. "How can this be?"

"It can't. It's not possible. Want to tell me what's going on here, Detective?"

"Leo, I swear I don't know myself." But she did know—deep down she knew before she'd printed Kell. Rache's problem was she couldn't accept it.

Leo stared at her, lost in thought a moment. "The actions of the living reside in the ashes and the dust of the dead."

"What the fuck does that mean?" she asked. Rache thought she was going mad. She had just been presented with evidence she didn't even want to consider, and now Leo was blabbering on like some nutcase.

"Got it up on a plaque in Cornell!"

"Cornell?" she inquired, completely lost now.

"Yeah, they got this Paranormal Research Unit up there. Very hush-hush. Personally, I think it's funded out of Langley. Had an interview for a post up there once." Leo pointed at the computer screen. "Anyway, they investigate this sort of thing. Maybe you should give them a call," he suggested.

Leo jumped off his stool as if it were red-hot. He crossed over and pulled a small shoebox off a shelf. Sitting back down beside Rache, he began to rifle through it. He pulled an old card from the box. "Here's their number. Maybe you should give them a call."

"Think they can help?" she said, taking the card and putting it in her purse.

"What else can you do?" He shrugged.

"Leo, not a word of this to anyone, ya hear?"

"No way I'm sharing this with anyone."

Okay, thought Rache. She needed to work this bitch out. Leo was cool. He'd keep shtum. She thanked him, warning him again about the sensitivity of the case. She had to let him in on the Feds' involvement. This tweaked his interest even more. She left him, his head swimming with wild theories.

CHAPTER 21

ACHE ROSE EARLY THE FOLLOWING morning. It had been her first night free of dreams. Well, none that she remembered. She had arrived home a little after midnight, exhausted. She had taken the file with the print results with her. She didn't want them lying about. What tomorrow held in store for her, she did not know. But this she did know: the perp or whoever he was… Rache caught herself. She knew she had to say it. But she couldn't. For to say it was to admit that she had been wrong. Not something Rache Fischer could easily do. But something was gnawing away at her. Little by little, it was breaking her down. Was it possible? Could he be…?

She glanced at the whiteboard again. Among the jumble of words and arrows and smudged fingerprints, the truth was in there. Shit, she even sounded like Mulder off *The X-Files*. Only she was the skeptic! She laughed. If the guys in the precinct could hear her now.

Rache had been removing the last of her makeup when it had hit home. "What am I looking at?" she had asked herself as she had washed off her mascara. A mirror image. That's what it was—a mirror image! The perp was some kind of mirror image of Kell Mason. A living, breathing, walking image. He had protected Kell. He was not the perp, but rather her protector—her guardian. Somehow Kell Mason, or Sarah-Jane Marsh, had manifested this being, this creation, at her time of need. What had Dion said? It would have to have been someone lying on the bed! The gunshot residue on his hand. It all made sense now. Kell had somehow brought this person into being to protect her.

Brought into being, Rache thought. *Get a grip, Fischer. Listen to yourself. What are you talking about? They're going to lock you up,*

143

and you'll never get out. But Rache knew she was right. It was the only illogical logical answer. He was her guardian. The fingerprints, the DNA, the explosion! Her clothes had been shredded. It was the perp—well, not as the perp in the normal sense of the word; it was her guardian who had shredded them. It was why the room was trashed. He had fought the attacker, saving Kell in the process. The bullet in the ceiling, the smashed furniture, the bleeding—it all made sense now. *It must have been traumatic for Kell,* she thought. Somehow, he had forced himself into this world, recreating himself in human form, using Kell's DNA to become this being. It had to be. Rache figured she was reaching a little, but she had no other explanation.

Before falling asleep, she had reached a decision. Well, two decisions. One, she would tell no one, and two, she'd talk to the priest tomorrow.

As she dressed now, she felt an odd sense of liberation. Last night had thrown up just as many questions as answers. Being thrown off, removed from the case by this FBI agent, didn't sit too well with Rache. But if Liz was in witness relocation and her cover was blown, then she was in real trouble. Danny had only sketched over the details.

Liz Mason, aka Maxine Marsh, had been in LA at a medical conference. The family had been in the program five years and had had to relocate twice. Liz was a doctor, so when she traveled, she kept contact with her husband to a minimum. Joe had called her to see if it would be okay for Kell to stay an extra day. Liz had told him that the conference had been extended and that Kell should stay an extra week. They had decided that there be no contact till Liz returned from California. That's why they had not been able to locate her. The FBI had somehow picked up on Kell's hospital admission form, and they had found Liz.

The strain of the witness protection program had taken its toll on Liz and Joe. They had gone for a trial separation seven months ago. This had caused the FBI untold headaches. It meant keeping tabs on two families. Liz and Joe had agreed to keep Kell at the same school, and the Feds had found a house for Liz only a few blocks away.

Rache figured she'd get the lowdown on the rest of it at the precinct. She knew she could say nothing about her own findings until she had conclusive proof. Conclusive proof. Rache smiled to herself. *How much more proof do you need, Fischer?* she asked herself. Another thought popped into her head. *Okay, say you get this proof, what then? Are you going to tell the Feds that Kell Mason's Guardian Angel appeared out of nowhere and attacked the real perp?* The real perp? Just who was he? If she bought into her own theory, this being—this guardian— had helped Kell. Then who was the real attacker? He had to be tied into the Caruso family. *Damn it*, she thought. The gun, the Glock nine millimeter, it's why they'd failed to find it. The perp, the one who'd attacked Kell, he'd taken it with him. Fuck it. But how could she suggest this to anyone? Who'd believe her? Rache Fischer, skeptic supreme! Could she confide in anyone? *No*, she thought. Most decidedly not.

Rache found the whole experience surreal. She was talking about guardians as though it were the normal order of things, as if this was everyday life for her. But Rache Fischer did not believe in the comfort blanket theory, until now at least. Even now, as she pieced the evidence together, the concept seemed alien to her. But she had seen him, met him, even talked to him. Shit, she had almost shot him! There was another question. What if she had shot him? Would he die? She had seen him bleed. Joe had hit him, and he had bled all over the handkerchief. Could he die? Would he die? She had to find him. The priest would help her. He would know what to do. He could give her the information she needed. But would he? Too many questions.

Okay, Rache, she told herself. *Take it one step at a time. Go to work...* Shit, it was Saturday. She had agreed to have dinner with her parents. *Okay, I'll have dinner and then scoot over to the church.* If her father thought she was on her way to a church after dinner on the Shabbat, he would have heart failure.

Concentrate, Rache, she urged herself. *Go to work, find out what the Feds know, and take it from there.* She hoped they wouldn't be removed from the case. If it was a mob hit—and it looked that way—Kell was still in grave danger. Kell had seen her attacker, and that put her life in danger.

The Mafia never forgets. Rache remembered reading about the case. Lorenzo Caruso was the *capa di tuti capi*—the boss of bosses! He had been indicted on several counts of racketeering, fraud, money laundering, and murder. It was the murder rap that had put him away. The trial had taken place behind closed doors and had lasted almost a year. Lorenzo Caruso was in his sixth year of a life sentence. Caruso would die in prison.

The station house was a buzz of excitement. News of the FBI's involvement in the case had spread quickly. Coupled with the fact that Kell Mason's mother had been located, the whole question of motive had been answered. It was a mob hit! The fact that Kell's mother had testified against Lorenzo Caruso had buoyed many at the precinct, giving them a new belief that they may now catch the perpetrator. The photos taken of Kell shortly after her ordeal had sickened everyone. But the perp's escape had led an almost resigned air of pessimism in the department. The news that it was mob related had served to lift this and had, in some way, kick-started the investigation. Everybody wanted this bastard—everybody but Rache.

She arrived shortly before the scheduled meeting at eight. Rache hadn't been surprised when the captain had called her the previous evening, requesting she attend, given the conversation she'd had with Danny at the hospital. Woods had apologized for the short notice. He knew it was a Saturday and was aware they'd all worked the previous one. She had told him it was no problem—she was glad to help in any way.

She met Susan coming in. "Suppose you heard about the Feds?" Susan inquired.

"Yeah, what's the deal, d'ya know?"

"Not sure, Theo called me last night."

"You talk to Danny yet?"

"No," replied Susan.

Good, thought Rache. She hoped Danny wouldn't say anything about the fingerprinting. Rache told Susan she'd catch up with her at the briefing. She needed a few moments alone. But Danny was already in the office.

"Morning," she offered, smiling at him.

Danny stood and quickly closed the door. "Christ, Rache, what were you up to last night?" he whispered, trying to keep the emotion out of his voice.

"Yeah, Danny, sorry about that."

"Liz was distraught, and you printing the kid freaked her even more."

"You didn't say anything…?"

"No, Rache, I didn't."

"Thanks. I know it was stupid, I just wanted to try something… well…I don't really know."

"It's okay, Rache. I won't say anything."

"Thanks, Danny." Rache hated having to lie to him. But what could she tell him?

"You want a coffee?"

"Yeah, thanks."

Danny poured them both a coffee. He handed one to Rache and sat down.

"What do you think will happen?" she asked him, sipping the coffee.

"Not sure. But I'd say the Feds will take over everything now."

"They can't do that, can they?"

"They're the Feds, Rache. They can do pretty much anything."

"Shit."

"Shit is right. They've put some arch-bitch in charge. Special Agent Franks. A real fucking charmer."

"Danny O'Connor, language in front of a lady," Rache said, feigning indignation.

"Well, you didn't get to spend four hours with her yesterday." He sighed.

"So she gave you a hard time, huh?"

"Let's just say I needed something a little stronger than hot chocolate to get to sleep last night."

Rache sipped some of her coffee. "Come on, give me half an hour with her, and she—"

"Jesus, don't do anything mad, Rache," Danny butted in.

"Don't worry, I'll be an example of police-bureau cooperation," Rache assured him.

Four minutes into the briefing now, and Rache could see where Danny was coming from. Never in her professional career had Rache encountered anyone so condescending as Agent Renee Franks. Rache and Danny were the last to take their seats. Rache sipped from her mug as she listened to Captain Woods introduce Agent Franks and outline the events leading up to locating Liz Mason.

"We don't have time for refreshments, Detective. If you want to drink coffee, I suggest you do it on your own time, not on mine," were the first words shot at Rache.

Rache had responded by sipping the mug of coffee, standing as if to leave. "Fine by me."

Captain Woods stared her down. "We're all on board here," he said, addressing the room, his gaze directed at Rache.

Rache took the hint. Better not cause a scene, she figured. Besides, she'd enough problems cluttering her own mind. Why add to them?

"As you are all aware, this is now a federal matter," Woods continued. "And we will do everything in our power to help the FBI apprehend the criminal or criminals in this case." He nodded to Agent Franks.

Franks addressed the officers, never once even glancing in Rache's direction. She spoke in a slow, almost hushed monotone, as if she were talking to first graders. Rache was disgusted at the captain for prostituting himself in the manner she had just witnessed. What was happening? *Somebody shoot me*, she thought.

Rache looked at Franks now. About five foot eight, 120 pounds, with light brown hair, Agent Franks had passed forty some time back. Oh, was that a hint of gray at the roots? Rache thought to herself. She didn't like her at all.

Rache glanced around the room. Susan, Theo, and Danny were giving nothing away. *Always the professionals*, she thought. Franks was talking. Better keep an eye on what she was saying, Rache figured.

"Lorenzo Caruso is serving life for the murder of Donovan Smith, a millionaire casino owner. It was Maxine Marsh's, aka Liz Mason's, testimony that put him away. We placed the family in witness protection."

Maybe I should tell her, Rache thought. Yeah. Tell her that the perp was really the kid's guardian who had somehow ended up in the kid's bedroom and saved her life. It was FBI incompetence that had contributed to the murder of Joe Mason after all. Rache found herself smiling.

"And perhaps you care to inform us what you find so funny about this case, Detective Fischer?"

Oh shit, thought Danny. He glanced over at the captain. Woods had already closed his eyes and was rubbing them with his fingers.

Rache looked at Franks. "I was just wondering what the letter I stood for in FBI!" she said. "I'm pretty sure it's incompetence, but hey, maybe you could help me out on that one, Agent Franks."

"The Federal Bureau of Investigation will handle this case from here in. Captain Woods has assured me of your full cooperation and that as primaries on the case, Detectives Fischer and O'Connor will spend today briefing me," she said without even cracking a smile.

Oh shit, thought Rache. *Ah well, let's get this bitch over with.*

"When I'm up to speed, you will be kept on in an advisory capacity only. This is a federal matter now. We have the entire Caruso clan—Tony, Bruno, Tulip, and Chazz—under surveillance. Detectives, let's hear what you have to say." Franks walked over to the door. Holding it open, she looked at the room full of officers.

Everybody took the hint. Shuffling feet accompanied a low mumbling noise as chairs and desks were moved. The remaining cops filed out past Franks.

Rache spent until lunch filling Agent Franks in. Franks kept asking her if she were stalling. But Rache couldn't tell Franks—or Danny, for that matter—her suspicions. Their initial hostility had cooled a little, and Rache told Franks everything that had happened, feeling particularly foolish when trying to explain the forensics team's findings. She couldn't tell Franks that the cause of the bleeding was due to Kell's Guardian literally manifesting himself from her body. That was the reason Rache had decided on. It was the only explanation possible. The energy, or force, generated by this Guardian appearing must have pushed Kell into some sort of coma, causing her eyes and ears to bleed. It must have been like some kind of explosion.

Rache desperately needed to talk to Fr. John. She couldn't share any of this with Franks. She'd be fired for insubordination, or worse, locked up.

Rache kept her answers as brief as possible. She did not expand on anything. Just before lunch, she knew she was in trouble when Franks leaned across the desk, her hands placed firmly on the multitude of files and photographs that lay scattered about, and told her that by and large, it had been one of the worst displays of obstruction by any officer she had ever worked with and that she'd be reporting Rache to Captain Woods. Franks made a point of telling Rache it was her duty to inform Rache that she may possibly seek to have her suspended if Rache did not improve her cooperation in the afternoon session. She dismissed them, urging Danny to have words with Rache.

Rache was on her way out the precinct door when Danny caught up to her.

"Jesus, Rache, what are you playing at?"

"What, you going to let that bitch walk all over you?"

"No, I'm not. Look, she's a pain in the ass, but let's use her. We all want to find this guy."

He had said it. The fundamental difference between Rache and the other officers was that she now believed that the perp hadn't done it. But she couldn't tell them that. The perp, as they all called him, had saved Kell. Rache had a hard enough time believing this herself; she knew she had no chance of persuading anyone else. She'd talk to the priest tonight, and if she got the answers she needed, she'd tell Danny. But no one else! Better still, she'd get Fr. John to tell him. That would convince him.

"Danny, I'm sorry if I come across as obstructive. I don't mean to be. I'll be a good girl this afternoon, I promise. I'll cooperate with Franks, okay?"

He smiled at her. "I don't want a good girl, as you put it. I want my partner to be herself."

"Best behavior, I promise," Rache said, turning and running down the steps.

CHAPTER 22

KELL MASON LAY SILENT IN her hospital bed. On account of her condition, the medical staff had refused to even contemplate moving her. Liz was under twenty-four-hour protection at a safe house ten blocks away. She was allowed two daily visits, but only under stringent security. Franks had placed an agent inside Kell's room, under orders to sit with her at all times.

As Liz Mason sat beside her daughter, she held her child's hand and wept. Joe was gone. Dead! Murdered! *Joe*, she thought. It wasn't even his name. She looked at Kell, and she saw her daughter. She thought back to baptizing her, the image of the water running off her tiny forehead into the front clear to Liz now. Sarah-Jane Marsh. But that name seemed alien to her now. They had all received intensive training and instruction by the Bureau when they had entered witness relocation. Her old life was over, they had told her. Liz had her new name and those of her husband and daughter drummed into her head 24-7. They had been taught to forget—to forget one identity and to assume another one. It had been vital that they not only became familiar with their new personae but to actually begin to live them. She had taught herself to forget her own child's name. It could never be said again. Sarah-Jane Marsh was gone. It was now Kell Mason. Never, ever forget that, the Bureau had told her.

The FBI had wanted to take them out of the country after the trial, but Liz would have none of it. She was an American, and she was staying in the States. Liz was an orthopedic surgeon and had witnessed the murder of her patient, Donovan Smith, by Lorenzo Caruso. She had given evidence, believing it was the only way to save herself. Liz had simply been in the wrong place at the wrong time. When told about Lorenzo's mafia connections, she had agreed to testify. Lorenzo was convicted on her evidence, and the family had been taken from the courthouse and placed in witness relocation.

They had first moved from Chicago to Nevada and, in the last two years, over to New York. They had become assimilated in a city of nine million, and Kell had settled in at her new school. She had taken up tennis and in two short years had become a star. Liz had experienced mixed emotions about Kell's success. Part of her was overjoyed for her daughter. The sport had helped her to return to some sense of normality. She had gone through so much. She had severed all contact with all her friends. But Kell had always remained positive. It was Kell's outlook on life that had sustained Liz through her darkest moments. But Kell's success raised a problem. What if someone recognized her? Yes, she was almost six years older and looked nothing like the ten-year-old girl at the trial. No photos of Kell had been taken, and nobody knew what she looked like. The problem was that Kell had grown into a beautiful young girl who bore a striking resemblance to her mother. When Kell and Liz Mason walked into a room, you knew they were mother and daughter.

Kell had begun to beat all around her on the courts. In fact, the Nick Botticelli School in Florida had offered her a scholarship. The whole family had discussed it, with Kell eventually turning it down. Two months later, Joe and Liz had separated. Liz loved Joe, but the strain had become too much. Kell refusing the scholarship and agreeing to play less tennis had been the last straw. She and Joe had argued over it. Kell had made the decision to stop playing, and it had broken her mother's heart. Liz and Joe had decided to have a trial separation. Even the separation had not fazed her. She told Liz that she'd get back together with Joe.

"Look, Mom, you and Dad are going through a tough time right now. But everything will work out, I know it," she had said just a few short weeks ago. Liz had hugged her. Kell was so positive.

Looking at her daughter now, lying in a coma, made Liz weep. She wished she could gently shake her awake. She longed to talk to her. She needed to hear her baby's voice. Liz recognized that this was due in part to selfish reasons. She needed reassurance. She felt guilty, and the feeling caused her great pain.

As a medical doctor, Liz was puzzled by Kell's condition. All the usual scans had shown nothing. Agent Franks had shown her the police report of the attack. Joe had never stood a chance. His right ventricle had been ruptured. The bullet had splintered on hitting his rib cage. Part of the bullet had shot through the soft intercostal muscle, puncturing the ventricle, causing Joe's aorta to tear and slightly separate from the atrium. The hospital had done their best, but reading the hospital report, Liz knew her husband's fate had been sealed the moment the bullet had left the chamber.

Try as she might, she could not come to grips with Kell's condition. She had suffered no trauma as such, save a few minor cuts and abrasions. Kell's body had simply shut down!

So Liz Mason held her daughter's hand, worried by the latest news. Kell was growing weaker. It wasn't any massive change, but she was slowly deteriorating. Her blood pressure had fallen, and her pulse had dropped. There was no medical explanation, and Liz Mason's heart was breaking. As she sat in silence, she realized her little girl was slowly dying.

CHAPTER 23

HEADING SOUTH PAST HELL'S KITCHEN toward the Circle Line Ferry, another person was close to death. In a small nondescript warehouse close to the Lincoln Tunnel, Tommy "the Trigger" Crespo sat bound to a chair, oblivious to the world around him. He cut a pathetic figure, slumped forward, his face battered almost beyond recognition. Tony Caruso, Lorenzo's thirty-eight-year-old nephew, had been questioning Tommy for hours, angered beyond words at the responses Tommy had given him. But Tommy had not deviated from his story.

Tony looked at the unconscious figure in front of him, surveying his handiwork. Tony was mad as hell. He had tried everything from reason to unadulterated brutality in an effort to prize the truth out of Tommy. Tommy had just this moment lapsed into unconsciousness—the ten-inch nail driven through his right foot, splintering two metatarsal bones, had seen to that. Tony glanced over at his cousin, Bruno Caruso, a huge brute of a man, who willfully did Tony's bidding. Bruno had happily fulfilled Tony's orders, driving the steel nail into Tommy's bare foot, pounding the head until it was buried in the floorboard. Tommy had passed out screaming with pain.

Tony nodded to Bruno now. Bruno walked over and threw a can of water on Tommy. Tommy spluttered. The agony in his foot was excruciating, but Tommy forced himself not to look at the cause of his torment.

"You want me to get Bruno to douse you in gas, huh, Tommy," Tony said calmly, walking over to Tommy. Another goon from Tony's gang quickly placed a chair for the boss. Tony swivelled the chair about, straddling it as he lit a cigarette.

"Ya know, Tommy, if Bruno pours gas on ya, ya couldn't have a smoke." He placed the cigarette in between Tommy's broken lips.

Tommy took a long and deep drag on the smoke. He coughed. "Please, please Tony, I'll do her, I swear," he sobbed. "I won't let you down, Tony, I promise."

Tony shook his head. "You had one simple job to do, Tommy. Off her old man and her kid. That bitch was supposed to suffer for what she did to my uncle."

"I'm sorry, Tony. I'll do her, I swear."

"How? How ya going to do her? She's in a hospital under guard. The Feds are swarming all over us like bees on honey. How ya going to do her, huh?" Tony demanded.

"Now, I'm gonna ask ya one more time, nice like, and ya better spill, Tommy…"

"Tony, I swear, I told ya everything—"

"Don't interrupt me when I'm talking."

Bruno looked at the other goon, Chazz. He knew what was coming next. Tony had been crazy ever since the hit went sideways. When Tony had found out about the Marshes' new identity, he had planned their deaths for months. He had been like a child waiting for Christmas. But Tommy had fucked up, and now Tony was pissed. Chazz winced as Tony stubbed his cigarette out in Tommy's ear. Tommy screamed.

Tony turned to Bruno. "Burn him Bruno."

Somehow Tommy managed to put the pain out of his mind. He drew in shallow breaths. "Tony…I swear…I'll do her…I swear. Gimme one more chance…please."

Bruno begun to unscrew the top off the gas container, the rising gasoline fumes stinging his eyes.

Tony held up a hand. Bruno put the container down.

"Tell me everything…and no fucking fairy stories. Ya hear?"

"I swear, Tony, he came outta nowhere."

"Outta nowhere. I told ya, no fairy stories." Tony took out a gun and pressed it to Tommy's head.

"Please, Tony, please!" Tommy cried. "I'll make it up to you, I swear."

"You're a fuckup, Tommy. You got one simple job to do, plug her old man and do her kid. But no, you have to have your fun. Now the kid's in hospital, and she got a good look at you. That makes you a liability, Tommy."

"Tony, I swear, he came out of nowhere. One second it's just me and the kid…then he's all over me! He was crazed."

"Just you and the girl, huh! But you wanted to have your fun, huh, Tommy?" Tony screamed at him. Tony paced back and forth, the movement itself the only thing preventing him from shooting Tommy. The plan had been simple. He had wanted exact his revenge on Maxine Marsh. He had wanted Maxine—or Liz as she now called herself—to suffer the way he had suffered when he had lost his uncle. Tony had decided that the best way would be to take away everything she held dear. Lorenzo had been like a father to him. The bitch would suffer. He'd take away her family. She'd suffer too.

Tony had sent Tommy with orders to "take out Joe Mason and his fucking kid." Tony's mistake had been in sending Tommy.

Tommy Crespo was a repeat sex offender who had managed to stay below the radar of the sex offenders' register and, to some extent, control his predatory urges. Tony had only just been made aware of Tommy's condition. This made him look bad. His men would lose respect for him. Sending Tommy had made his decision-making look suspect. Maxine's bitch was a real looker—musta got Tommy all fired up. Yeah, Tommy musta lost it trying to fuck the kid. Shit, Tommy had fucked up big time, he thought. Maxine Marsh's kid was not only alive, but she'd gotten a good look at Tommy.

Tony's answer now was to lash out. Tommy was bullshitting him. He had to act. Aware all eyes were on him, Tony walked over and shot Tommy through the kneecap. Tommy screamed in agony. Tony looked at Chazz. "Shut him the fuck up!" he ordered Chazz.

Tearing off a strip of duct tape, Chazz gagged Tommy. Tommy's eyes pleaded for mercy. Looking into the dilated pupils, Chazz knew Tommy was beyond help. This was only the start. Chazz was happy it wasn't him strapped to the chair. Tommy had fought some guy at the house. This had got the boss all crazed. That and the fact that

Tommy had failed to kill the kid. Chazz continued to tighten the gag on Tommy. Jesus, was the boss really gonna burn him?

A huge steel door opened, and as Chazz looked up, he saw two more of Tony's crew push a terrified Mr. Jakes inside.

The pimp was in a state of shock. Out of nowhere, two hard asses had arrived at his crib, smacked a couple of his bitches about, and stuck a gun to his head, asking if he'd ever hear of Antonio Caruso. Everybody had heard of Tony Caruso. Mr. Jakes had never met him, the name itself enough to terrify him. Mr. Jakes had wondered what Tony Caruso would want with him. He couldn't figure it out. So he had simply nodded. The two goons had smiled and told him Tony wanted to see him.

Now he stood in some run-down warehouse looking at Tony Caruso torturing some poor bastard. Judging by the look of the guy, they'd been at it for hours. Mr. Jakes shivered. *Keep it together, man,* he told himself. *These guys can smell fear.*

Tony lit another cigarette, staring at Mr. Jakes, his eyes wild and crazed. "My associate here tells me you're a man who can get things done, Mr. Jakes. Is that so?" Tony asked, his polite manner confusing the pimp.

Mr. Jakes looked at Tony. He simply nodded, not knowing how he should reply. "Yeah."

"Do you know who I am?"

"Yeah."

Tony was about to bring the smoke to his lips. He stopped abruptly. He stared at Mr. Jakes.

Mr. Jakes saw it. Pure viciousness. "Yes, Mr. Caruso," he added swiftly.

Tony smiled. "There's one hundred large in that envelope and another hundred when what's inside the second envelope is…no longer with us," he said as Bruno handed him an envelope. "Go ahead, open it." Tony smiled at him.

Mr. Jakes opened the second envelope. He pulled out a photograph of Kell Mason. Mr. Jakes swallowed hard. Did the mad bastard want him to kill this kid? He wasn't sure.

"You got a problem with that, Mr. Jakes?"

"No, sir, no problem at all." This guy was a nut job.

Tony nodded at Bruno. Unscrewing the cap, Bruno walked over to Tommy and doused him in gasoline. Tommy tried to scream, but the gag held. Tony drew in deeply on his cigarette and tossed it on Tommy, igniting him in a plume of smoke and fire. Tommy was instantly turned into a human fireball as a massive flame engulfed his body, incinerating his clothes and melting flesh from his bones. Tommy threw himself forward in a pitiful attempt to extinguish the searing heat. He wriggled about, his nailed foot and the chair making movement almost impossible.

Mr. Jakes thought he would throw up. Tommy's agony was too much to bear. The smell of burning flesh filled the room, invading his nostrils, causing his stomach contents to flow back up his gullet. Mr. Jakes was sure he was going to throw up.

Tony calmly walked over and emptied his entire clip into Tommy, killing him. Tommy lay still, his body burning.

Tony's action was in some way an act of mercy. But Tony had wanted to make a point.

"I'm glad we understand each other cos I hate failure. My associate here," he said, patting Bruno on the shoulder, "will fill you in." Tony turned and walked out. Chazz and Tulip followed, leaving Bruno grinning at Mr. Jakes.

"Okay, your turn," Bruno said.

"My turn?" Mr. Jakes was frantic.

Bruno laughed. "Your turn to kill the kid." Bruno looked over at what was left of Tommy. The two goons in Tony's crew had extinguished the burning remains of what had once been a human being and were wrapping it in some kind of fire blanket. Bruno put his large arm around Mr. Jakes's shoulder, dwarfing him. "Ya see, the last guy was a fuckup. Really annoyed the boss. You don't want to do that now, do you, Mr. Jakes?"

Mr. Jakes shook his head.

"Okay, good," said Bruno, walking Mr. Jakes to the door.

CHAPTER 24

I RA AND MIRIAM FISCHER LIVED in a spacious two-bedroom apartment on the corner of Eighty-Sixth and Madison in close proximity to the Guggenheim Museum. They had inherited it eight years ago when Ira's only brother, Eli, had died suddenly. Eight years Ira's senior, Eli had carved out a lucrative niche for himself in the electronics industry. He had never married and had willed everything to Ira. At first, Ira thought of selling, but David had persuaded both his parents to move, pointing out that they had lived all their lives upstate, and it would be good for them to live closer to him. They had agreed, and for the past seven years, they had been residents on New York's fashionable and expensive Upper East Side.

The property had only appreciated, and as Rache arrived for dinner, she thought of her brother's wife, Sarah. Sarah had her eyes on her parents' apartment. She would have said nothing to David, of course, but watching Sarah checking out the apartment had always annoyed Rache.

Sarah was like a circling buzzard, just waiting for its prey to become too weak to fight back. Thinking about it now made Rache realize that she hadn't seen Sarah or her nephew, Ben, in over a year. Ben was a polite kid, and Rache liked him. She wished she could say the same about his mother. Lawyers and Feds. She grinned to herself.

Heading north on Madison, Rache thought about dinner with her family. She felt bad she would probably have to cut it short, but she needed to talk to the priest.

She was slightly annoyed at events earlier in the day. Annoyed at her own foolishness. Her interrogation with Franks hadn't gone too well, and she had allowed Franks to get under her skin, prompting her to do something she now regretted. She'd called Leo's pals at Cornell.

During her lunch break, she had ordered a turkey salad sandwich from the small deli around the corner, and as she was putting the loose change back in her purse, she'd discovered Leo's card. Should she call them? Should she talk to the priest? She had pretty much made up her mind she'd chat to the priest. But what if they could help? What if there was some scientific explanation? She'd look foolish—no, insane—if she went to her captain with her present theory.

Rache had dialed the number.

"Para-psychic research, how may I direct your call?" The words had echoed out of the earpiece.

Rache had immediately hung up. What was she doing? She didn't know what to say. It was then she'd made up her mind. She'd talk to Fr. John. But what the hell was she going to say to him? she'd wondered.

She'd simply finished her sandwich and headed back into her briefing with Danny and Franks.

Now drawing her car alongside the curb, Rache tried to put this out of her mind. She thought of her mother and how good it would be to talk to her.

Rache walked up the steps to her parents' apartment. She rang the bell. Ira Fischer answered. Rache was dumbstruck. He ushered her in and hugged her. She hugged him back. "It's good to see you, Rachel."

"And you too, Papa."

Sarah, Ben, and David were already there. Sarah and Rache exchanged pleasantries.

Rache walked over and hugged her brother. "Congratulations, I believe."

Took me long enough," David said.

"Hey, what did I tell you? Wait long enough, and the cream will always rise to the top."

David smiled. "Thank you," he said. He poured her a glass of wine, and Rache sought out her mother. She told Miriam that her father had hugged her at the door.

"He's mellowed, Rachel."

I hope so, Mom."

"He has, you'll see."

Dinner passed without incident, but as David rose to pour Rache some more wine, she stopped him.

"No, thanks. I got to go soon," Rache said, placing her hand over her glass.

Her mother looked hurt. Ira said nothing.

Rache rubbed her mother's hand. "It's a case, ya know, Mom."

"Rachel, it was good to see you."

It was her father. He had mellowed. Well, a little anyway.

"Yeah, two years goes so quickly, doesn't it. I mean, it was two years ago that we all had our last meal together?" Sarah piped up.

David shot her a look, but Sarah ignored him.

It had been over a year, sure, but Rache knew she couldn't use that in her defense. You can't justify not seeing family in over a year. Sarah was such a calculating bitch.

"I'm not sure, but if you say so, Sarah. You're the one who keeps tabs on these things."

"Don't get defensive, Rachel. I was just saying—"

"Well don't!"

"Enough already," David interjected.

"Sorry, I didn't mean to upset you, Rachel," Sarah said.

"I'm not upset."

"More wine anyone?" said Ira.

Sarah held out her glass first, to make the point. She was rubbing Rache's nose in it. "Look at me, I'm staying. I'm not running off" was what she was really saying.

"Thank you. So, Rachel, what's this urgent case you're on?" Sarah asked, determined not to let it go.

"It's nothing really. Just some poor kid watched her father get shot, was almost raped, and now she's in a coma. Oh yeah, her father died. But hey, let's have some more wine."

"Rachel!" Ira looked at her. He nodded to Ben, who had been sitting quiet as a mouse.

Shit, thought Rache. She hadn't intended to bring him into this.

"I don't think that was called for," Sarah said.

Why does she dislike me so much? wondered Rache. *Who cares.* Rache glanced over at her mother. Her mother looked so sad. But Sarah was impossible. God, she wanted to smack her. "What is it with lawyers? They all want to have the last word."

"Oh, and cops are different how?" Sarah retorted.

That was just it, thought Rache. In her mind, cops were different. Sure, there were good lawyers, but most of the fuckers were in it for one thing. Money!

"Police officers fight, every day, on the front line. Friends of mine have died in the line of duty. How many of your friends have been shot in the line of duty? Cops can make a difference before the fact. Lawyers just fuck up afterward!"

"Rachel, I will not tolerate such language in my house!" Ira Fischer shouted.

Rache looked at Ben. He was crying now. Her mother was fighting back tears. But Rache couldn't stop herself. She stood up and walked to the piano. She picked up a photo of Ruth. Calmly she placed it in front of her father.

"Look at her, Papa. It's your daughter. Lawyers failed her." Rache walked over to her mother and kissed her. "I'm sorry, Mom, I should go."

David stood. "This is my celebration. Rachel, sit down and behave. Sarah, not a word from you, understand! Now, Rachel, you'll have another glass of wine. I'll call you a cab."

Rache said nothing. She looked at her father. She wasn't angry at him. *Shouldn't have let Sarah get to me like that,* she thought. "I'm sorry, Papa," she said.

Ira nodded, accepting the apology. Rache's mother squeezed her daughter's hand. Rache smiled at her mother. *Better stay. I can see the priest tomorrow,* she figured. Damn, she should have known better than to let Sarah bait her.

Rache ended up having more than one glass. She had been wound tight the past week, so she used the opportunity to unwind, the alcohol having its desired effect. For the first time in weeks, Rache actually relaxed. Sarah kept quiet, and the remainder of the evening passed peacefully. Rache was glad she'd stayed. She had a great chat with her mom, and later, as she stood on the terrace with David, watching as he inhaled deeply on a cigarette, she felt better. It was probably the wine, but she felt better.

David closed the door inside. He turned to Rache. "They miss you, you know."

"I know," she said. Rache looked at her brother a moment. "David, do you think it would have made a difference had I taken the stand?"

David didn't answer. He sucked cigarette smoke into his lungs. As he exhaled, Rache continued.

"In Ruth's—"

"I know what you mean. Why this persecution, Rachel? Ruth is dead seventeen years, and God, we all miss her, but you have to stop blaming yourself. You didn't kill her."

"No, but I—"

"Rachel," he said, stamping out his cigarette.

"Why did she do it? If I had taken the stand—"

"It's a mystery you cannot solve. No one can. You've got to start looking forward, or you'll miss your whole life. You didn't kill her, Rache. You didn't kill her."

Rache fell silent. It was too hard. Being here, with the family, it was too hard. Ruth's death was a wound she knew she'd never close.

"It's just that...I'm investigating this case, and it's got similarities, and..." She trailed off.

"I'm sorry, I didn't know." David walked over and put his arm around his sister. "You may be a smart-ass, but you're still my baby sister," he said. "So believe me when I tell you, I know what's best for you."

"Oh, and what's that, counselor?"

"A good Jewish boyfriend."

He had caught her unawares. Rache began to laugh. "Really. Well, okay then. Who do you suggest? And don't say Sarah's brother."

They both laughed.

"Come on, I need another glass of wine," David suggested as he opened the terrace door for her.

CHAPTER 25

RACHE WOKE, HER HEAD HEAVY. It was almost noon as she rubbed the remnants of the previous night's sleep from her eyes. Shit, too much wine last night. She hadn't slept that late in years.

Rache forced herself up off the bed. She was glad David had persuaded her to stay. Her father had hugged her as she was leaving. Twice in the one night. Her mom had looked good. All in all, it wasn't the disaster it could have been.

Rache jumped in the shower. She figured she'd clear her head and collect her car. Yes, a walk in Central Park before picking up the sedan would be good. Dressing now in a pair of blue jeans and a blouse, she picked up the black cashmere sweater she'd worn the previous evening. She half remembered tossing it on the floor at the foot of the bed when she'd arrived home. *Untidy bitch*, she scolded herself as she walked back into her adjoining bathroom.

Lifting the lid to her wickerwork wash basket, she was about to throw her sweater in when she smelt it. Lalique! Her mother still used the same perfume. Rache brought her sweater to her face, sniffing the soft scent that still clung to the wool. She remembered the smell from when she was a kid. For over thirty years, Miriam Fischer had used the same fragrance.

Allowing herself to rest on the side of her bathtub, Rache slowly closed her eyes, content to let the scent once again fill her nostrils. Rache suddenly had an image of when she was eleven years old and had just made a dramatic breakthrough on to the A Squad in her swimming club. Time spent training in the pool had doubled, and as Rache was almost a year younger than most of the kids, she'd struggled to keep up with the other members of the squad. Nearly all were faster, which only encouraged Rache to work harder. But Rache had failed to qualify for the finals in a series of galas, and disillusionment quickly overtook her.

Perched on the edge of her bath now, she recalled her mother tucking her in one night after a particular disastrous competition. Rache had become so upset at her performance, she'd been unable to eat. The smell of her mother's perfume was the same then as it was now, she thought, as she recalled with total clarity her mother pulling the blankets up around her shoulders. "Just remember, Rachel, all you need to succeed is for one person to have faith in you. And I have faith in you," her mother had said softly as she'd swept some of Rache's blonde hair from her eyes.

Rache opened her eyes, and lifting the top of her wash basket, she dropped the sweater inside. She longed for her mother's embrace again—to once more feel that closeness.

***

Officially opened in 1876, Manhattan's Central Park is many things to many people, both New Yorkers and visitors alike. It's a beach, a theater, and an environmental haven. The park has also seen its share of dark days, falling victim to an undiluted crime wave in the eighties. But today, due to major renovations and the actions of one man, former New York mayor Rudy Giuliani, the park is a clean, safe, tranquil sanctuary in the midst of concrete high-rises.

As Rache walked past the Shakespeare Garden toward Turtle Pond and on to the Seventy-Ninth Street entrance, she thought about last night. She was happy she'd remained on, her overindulgence in the wine not withstanding. The one-hour walk in the park had given her time to reflect, not only on the previous night, but also on the task at hand—her meeting with Fr. John.

She left the park, stopping off at Jerry's on Madison Avenue. They made a superb breakfast, and she was starving. Thumbing through the Sunday papers, Rache took her time to enjoy her breakfast. Folding one particularly difficult broadsheet, Rache found her eyes drifting to a young couple who were more than amorous with each other. She smiled at David's suggestion that she ought to find a good Jewish boy. *Face it, Fischer, you're a loner,* a voice told her.

Rache called her mother to say she would drop by before picking up her car. Miriam was happy to see her daughter. They chatted and drank coffee. Ira had left earlier, and Miriam was grateful for the company. Rache told her mother she regretted many things, but not becoming a cop. Miriam agreed with her. She told her that deep down, her father was proud of her, but his belief in nonviolence conflicted with the fact that his daughter was a homicide detective. Rache had never killed anyone but had shot four people, all of whom had survived.

Collecting the silver tray off the small coffee table, Miriam asked her daughter if she'd like another cup. Rache smiled, saying she'd love one. As Miriam brewed fresh coffee in the kitchen, Rache sat back in the soft leather armchair, allowing her eyes to drift about the room. They always came back to the same thing. A framed photograph of her sister.

Placing the tray back down on the table, Miriam followed her daughter's gaze. She touched Rache softly on the knee. "About last night..." she began.

"I'm sorry, Mom, I shouldn't have shot off like that."

"It's okay, love."

"No, Mom, it's not. I was rude, and you and Papa deserve better."

Miriam was silent a moment, her own thoughts focused on Ruth now. She looked over at Rache as she sipped her coffee. "This case you spoke about, it reminds you of what happened to Ruth, doesn't it?"

Rache turned to her mother and nodded. "Yes," she whispered.

"And the little girl?"

"She's in a coma, Mom."

Miriam said nothing, allowing Rache to continue.

"It's not exactly the same, Mom. It's similar, but not the same."

"You said she'd been attacked?"

Rache turned to face her mother. But it was Ruth, not Kell Mason, who occupied her mind now. "I see her, Mom. In my dreams

I see her. I can hear her voice, and sometimes I can see what they did to her. And when I wake, all I can think is that I ran away."

"You stop that right now, do you hear me!" Her mother's raised voice startled Rache. But Miriam wasn't finished. "Rachel, you jumped overboard to get help, not to save yourself—never forget that. You were not responsible, do you hear me?" Miriam told her sternly, holding Rache's gaze.

"Yes, Mom," she whispered, her voice barely audible.

"Good."

Rache smiled at her mother.

"Now drink your coffee and tell me about this case."

Rache briefly sketched over the details, leaving out any reference she felt her mother didn't need to hear. Just being able to talk about it felt liberating.

Rache checked the time. It was already after six, and in a few short hours, it would be dark. She decided to call in on Kell before going to see the priest. Discussing Kell's case with her mom had once again focused Rache's attention at what lay ahead. She badly needed answers—answers she knew only the priest could supply. She was certain that Fr. John had been holding back on something. It was there in his tone of voice. What was it he'd said? "I discount no possibility." Yeah, that was it. What the hell had that meant?

Pulling away from the curb, she wondered exactly what it was she would say to him. *Hey, Father, guess what? I think Kell Mason's Guardian has somehow jumped into our world. Think I'm nuts?*

It sounded crazy. But now that she had said it, Rache needed to ask herself the million-dollar question. Did she believe it? She wasn't sure. A week ago she'd have scoffed at the suggestion. But the evidence all pointed in that direction now.

Rache decided to swing by the hospital and look in on Kell. Although she wanted to see her, there was another reason lurking in the shadows. It delayed seeing the priest and asking him the questions she knew she had to ask.

Arriving at the hospital shortly before seven, she found one of Franks's crew standing outside Kell's room. Feds, thought Rache showing him her badge as she went to push the door.

"I'm sorry, Detective Fischer, no visitors. You need clearance from Special Agent Franks," he told her, aggressively blocking her way through.

Rache couldn't believe it. "I'm not visiting. I'm working the case," she replied, surprised at his attitude.

"This is a federal matter, ma'am," he said dryly. "You'll need to see Special Agent Franks."

"Where is she?"

"I'm sorry, I'm not at liberty to say."

"Not at..." Rache was dumbfounded. "Are you guys insane? I just want to check in on the kid."

This argument continued for two of three minutes, with Rache becoming more and more annoyed. She failed to notice Agent Franks sneak up behind her with Liz Mason. Liz had been briefing Franks on the last few weeks. Franks thought the police were a joke, letting the suspect escape not once but twice. Detective Fischer had been nothing but uncooperative if not positively obstructive. So when she saw Rache arguing, a wry smile crept over her lips.

"Frustrating, isn't it, Detective?"

Rache spun around. *Shit*, she thought. *Liz looks bad.* "What?"

"When you can't get the help you require," Franks said, folding her arms, her mouth set in a smirky grin.

Bitch, thought Rache. She grabbed Franks by the arm, leading her down the corridor. Before Franks or anyone could react, Rache had pushed her up against the wall. "A little child is in there, fighting for her life, and you're scoring points with me. You sad bitch," Rache whispered to her, letting go of her arm. Rache stared at her with contempt, turned, and began to walk away.

"Don't go, please!" It was Liz Mason. "I...I'd like you to stay."

The request caught Franks by surprise. Liz had been difficult to work with. Well, she'd lost her husband, and her kid was in a coma, so Franks couldn't really blame her. But she needed answers from Liz. Franks smiled to herself. She nodded to the agent on the door. "Let her in. Whenever she wants, let her in." She needed Liz to trust her. As for Detective Fischer, well, her days were numbered, she'd see to that.

Franks turned to Liz. "I got some calls to make. I'll see you back here in twenty." She nodded to Rache. "Detective," she said, giving Rache a plastic smile, walking away, her cell phone already to her ear. Jesus, she had a grip like a vise, Franks thought as she rounded the corner, cradling the phone between her ear and shoulder while she massaged her arm.

Rache sat with Liz. Liz was exhausted, and it showed. She had spent the morning with Franks being debriefed, as Franks put it. The FBI believed it was a hit, but had no conclusive proof it was the Caruso family. Lorenzo had been questioned but had given no indication that he was behind it. In fact, he had seemed genuinely shocked by the whole affair. Franks was wary of him, but even she had to admit if he was acting, he was damn good.

Liz looked at Kell as she held her daughter's hand. "I keep thinking she's going to wake up," Liz said.

"She's a fighter."

"When we…when we went into witness protection, it was Kell who kept me from cracking up. We couldn't even say goodbye to our friends. I have a sister and two nephews I haven't seen in years."

"I'm sorry," said Rache, putting her hand on Liz's shoulder.

Liz turned to her. She looked at Rache a moment. "Danny… Detective O'Connor…he told me that you saved her, that he…he came back to kill her. Thank you!" Liz said, her voice low.

Rache didn't know what to say. But Liz's words had suddenly sparked off a bunch of new questions. Why had he come back? How had he found her? Rache recalled studying the hospital footage back at the precinct and drawing the conclusion that he had gone straight to the ICU, bypassing Kell's room. He had known exactly where to find Kell. Rache had figured that there must have been some link between them. If he didn't come back to kill her, a fact Rache now believed, then why had he risked coming back at all? She'd ask the priest.

Rache found her mind drifting back to the incident in the ICU. She had held the gun on him. What had he said? "Don't shoot." Why had he come back? She could make no sense of it. Was it to protect her? If he was her Guardian…had he come back to protect her? But from what? She was safe in the hospital.

Rache pushed the thoughts aside. She was driving herself mad. She'd have to talk to Fr. John. "You're welcome," she said, squeezing Liz's hand. "The guy who did this, I promise I won't rest till I find him, Liz." She took a card from her purse and handed it to Liz. "Keep this safe. Don't tell anyone, okay! If you need me, you call."

Liz thanked her. She felt better, more secure, knowing she could call Rache. Franks was self-obsessed, and she never felt a connection with her. She liked this detective, even if she came across as a little strange.

Rache leaned over and kissed Kell on the forehead. As she withdrew her head, she noticed a small anomaly just above Kell's left eyebrow. Rache pulled her head back abruptly, startling Liz.

"What is it? What's wrong?" Liz cried, frightened now.

"Nothing. This scar on her eye, what happened?" Rache asked, pointing to a small two-inch scar that ran just above Kell's left eyebrow.

"Oh, that," Liz said, relaxing now. "Bad tennis partner." She proceeded to explain about Kell being struck in the face by her doubles partner, but Rache's mind was elsewhere. She was back in the Intensive Care Unit, staring at the perp as she held her gun on him. She could see every inch of his face. She had tried to memorize it when he had escaped. Back then, she had figured he might try to disguise himself. But right now, listening to Liz Mason explain about Kell's little accident, she saw his face again. Just above his left eyebrow, he had a similar scar. She knew now who she was dealing with. *If ever you wanted proof, Fischer*, she told herself, *well, you got it now.*

The perp was Kell Mason's Guardian, no doubt.

Rache said goodbye to Liz, reminding her to call if she needed anything. She left the room, smiling at the agent outside. As she took the elevator to the first floor, she wondered what exactly she would say to the priest. Would he throw her out? No, no way. He had to listen.

CHAPTER 26

Mr. Jakes pulled into Washington Memorial's parking lot just as Rache exited the hospital doors. He was a hundred grand richer, but if he didn't kill this kid, he was a dead man. The image of Tommy being set alight was fresh in his mind, the stench of burning flesh still prevalent in his nostrils. Mr. Jakes liked to think he was hard. Compared to Tony Caruso, he knew he didn't measure up. The big goon, Bruno, had given him the lowdown on the kid. She was pretty, that was for sure. He could have used her in his stable. She was young and had that exotic look going for her. Yeah, he could have used her. But Tony Caruso wanted her dead. So she would have to die. Pity.

Mr. Jakes had no problem killing Kell. It was the logistics of the operation, as he saw it, that presented him with a difficulty. Tony had only given him a week. *Look on the plus side*, he had told himself. *Kill the kid, you get another hundred Gs. Not too bad.*

But Mr. Jakes was not too bright. Whatever providence had granted him his street smarts had come up way short in the brains department. The Benjamin Franklins in the envelope had only served to diminish his primitive thought process. The dollar signs were flashing before his eyes now. Mr. Jakes couldn't see he was being set up.

There would be no additional envelope for Mr. Jakes—no second delivery of Benjamins, as Mr. Jakes like to call his hundred dollar bills. Bruno had been instructed that as soon as the kid was dead, Mr. Jakes was to be taken care of. Tony wanted no traces left. He had thought that one hundred grand was a small price to pay for severing all connections back to the Caruso family. He had even told Bruno that once he'd taken care of Mr. Jakes, he'd probably find the hundred grand back at the pimp's crib.

"The guy's not gonna put it in a safety deposit box," he'd explained to Bruno. Tony had been acutely aware of the serious error he'd made in using Tommy for the Mason hit, and this pimp was none too bright either. But he figured he'd scared him enough with the stunt in the warehouse to force him into action. Nobody refused Tony Caruso!

Mr. Jakes studied the picture of Kell now, his eyes wandering over the photograph as he held it in his hand. *Yeah, wouldn't mind breaking this bitch in*, he thought as he began to think about exactly how he was going to get to Kell. Bruno had explained that the kid had been in some kind of accident and was unconscious. This fact had buoyed Mr. Jakes, making him believe his task would be that much easier. Reaching over, he stuffed the photo in his glove box and stared out a greasy window. His car, like his life, was ugly. He couldn't see out properly, so he started to roll down the window.

Then he saw *HER*!

It was her; he was sure. She was walking toward him. Mr. Jakes almost pissed himself as he slinked down in the seat as far as he could.

Rache walked straight past without even glancing in his direction.

Shit! That was close, he thought, his heart racing. He watched as Rache walked farther into the parking lot. *Bitch*, he though, the anger welling up inside him now. She had cost him one of his girls, not to mention making a fool of him. That little southern slut, Jessie, had upped and left. He knew this cop bitch was involved. Jessie had told everyone that some cop had made him crawl on all fours and beg like a bitch. Now all he heard were stupid little comments from his bitches. He'd had to smack a couple around only yesterday. He was losing their respect, and it was all her fault. He'd show her, this cop. But not here. No, too many people. Too close to the hospital.

As Rache pulled out of the parking lot and headed across town toward St. Killian's, Mr. Jakes gunned his engine and slipped into her wake.

Driving toward Eighth Avenue, Rache was completely unaware that only four cars back, Mr. Jakes was hot on her tail, a snub-nose .38 stashed in his glove box. The sight of Rache had maddened him, forcing him to abandon all reason and pursue her. Where she was headed he didn't care. All he knew was he needed to have a conversation with this bitch.

On any other day, she'd have spotted him. But it had begun to rain, and her mind was racing. She forced herself to stop preempting what Fr. John's response might be.

Even if it were true and he was her Guardian, what then?

The FBI had him on their most wanted list. His picture had been splashed across most of North America. He was a fugitive, wanted for murder. What could she possibly tell her Captain? Shit, this was insane. Who would accept the word of a confirmed atheist like Rache Fischer?

Rache eased her sedan up to the curbside. Late evening Sunday mass had just finished, and most of the congregation were now hurrying to their cars. Rache decided to wait. Better let them all go.

What is the bitch doing? Mr. Jakes wondered as he continued on past Rache's car. She had stopped suddenly, pulling up in front of him. He had kept on driving so as not to attract attention, discovering a space ten or so car lengths ahead of her.

The rain had turned into a downpour. It was as though someone had turned on a fire hydrant. Misty drops had become sheets. Mr. Jakes cursed as he climbed into his rear seat to get a better view. He had pulled the gun from the glove box, checked it, and was now looking out through a smudged rear window. Small drops of water dripped down on his head. "Fuck," he exclaimed aloud. Damn roof was leaking again. He'd finish his business here, do the kid, and then he'd buy himself a new car. Not someone else's piece of shit but a new one. He fancied one of those Humvees. All the celebrities were driving them now. He'd have it properly pimped too. Hook himself up real good with those forty-two-inch Giovanni rims and some low-profile Pirelli tyres. Yeah, that would be bitchin'. He'd get more respect from his stable too. Mr. Jakes rubbed the dirty window, making it worse. Damn!

Rache sat, watching the last of the congregation leave the church. It was still raining, but it was no longer a torrent. She jumped out of her car and walked quickly up the steps.

The large oak door was slightly open. Rache stretched her right hand out and touched it gently. It was cold and wet. She could feel her heart skip a beat. Was she nervous? One hundred percent! As her hand came into contact with the wooden panelling, the symbolism was thick in her mind. She was about to open another door—a door into a world that up to now she believed existed in the minds of those who needed a comfort blanket.

Standing on the sodden steps, the enormity of what lay ahead really hit home for Rache. Her life, her outlook had fundamentally shifted. She had, with the help of forensics science, uncovered the exact nature of the perp. DNA analysis, coupled with fingerprint evidence, had led her down a path from which she could only draw one conclusion. The perp—Mr. Houdini, as Leo liked to call him—was Kell Mason's Guardian.

Normally, such incontrovertible scientific evidence would lead to the arrest and subsequent conviction of a felon. But this was so far removed from all she held to be true. They had all believed him guilty. His escape had merely cemented that belief. Shit, she'd even made up her mind to shoot him on one occasion. But she'd been so wrong. They had all been so wrong.

Rache took a deep breath, closed her eyes momentarily, and steadied herself. She felt as though she were standing on the edge of a precipice, looking into a deep cavern. What was not required was not a leap of faith. Rache knew she'd already taken that leap. What frightened her now was that she was about to confide her belief in another human being. Blinking her eyes, Rache pushed the door open fully and stepped inside.

She could feel her heart pounding in her ears, the repetitive beat growing louder as she ventured farther into the church. She'd seen the inside of the church before, and although it had impressed her by its sheer magnitude, it had never frightened or intimidated her. This time round was different. This time round, the church seemed alive. The painting on the walls—the Stations—all appeared to conspire against her, whispering in silence as the eyes of the figures in them followed her, throwing accusatory glances after her. She passed the First Station, recalling what Fr. John had said. She stopped and stared up at it again. Looking at the picture of the Archangel with the would-be Mother of Christ, Rache felt a chill run down her spine. She remembered the priest's words: "Jesus was Jewish, so was his mother." It was something she'd never really thought about. She also remembered Fr. John telling her that the perp—*gotta stop calling him that*—had sat here for hours. Why? When they had him in custody, he was disoriented, subdued, and nonresponsive. Maybe he was trying to orient himself. She had to be truthful. She had no clue.

Fr. John had changed out of his vestments and now wore a simple black shirt over black pants, the white dog collar the only thing breaking the uniform color. He had walked out onto the vast altar when he spotted her. He thought it unusual. So he remained motionless a moment, watching her as she slinked sideways down the side aisle, her movement slow as she seemed to be examining the paintings. Detective Rache Fischer had begun to intrigue the priest, and although he found her presence unusual at this hour, he nonetheless welcomed it.

Fr. John smiled to himself as he approached her. "The mass is over, Detective," he said, unable to resist teasing her.

It's not a mass I need, Father. It's absolution."

"Really." He looked at her but could tell straight away she wasn't kidding.

"You got a moment?"

"Sure," the priest replied, intrigued now.

CHAPTER 27

"WHAT DO YOU THINK, FATHER?" Rache blurted, unable to contain herself any longer. They had moved from the church to a small house on the church grounds. Although he lived in a parish house about two blocks south of St. Killian's, there was a small house and housekeeper on the grounds that he frequently used. It was modest, being more functional that homely. The housekeeper lived in, but had Sundays free, which Rache thought weird. Fr. John had told her he'd wanted total privacy.

The revelation had rocked him. He now sat in a small kitchen sipping tepid coffee, eying Rache as she piled more and more analysis of the events on his already overburdened shoulders.

Rache had talked nonstop since she'd arrived, both in the church and now here, in the small house, barely pausing to catch her breath. Fr. John had remained silent the whole time, occasionally looking at her over the rim of his coffee cup as he'd sipped. She had told him everything, from start to finish.

She had believed him when he'd told her he'd wanted them away from the church. But that was only partly true. Sure, discussing it here in the house afforded them the solitude they needed, but the real reason behind moving to the house was to buy himself some time. He had needed time to think. Fr. John was worried. Something didn't add up. No, he wasn't so much worried as scared.

Rache finished with the scar on Kell's eye—how the suspect had the exact same scar. She looked at her coffee. She hadn't touched it. *Must be a first*, she thought, looking at the cold coffee. Worst still, the priest hadn't said a word. *He thinks I'm insane—a nut job. I knew I shouldn't have come here*, she said to herself. *I knew he'd think I was foolish.*

Fr. John looked at her. He stood up. "I think I need another coffee." He walked over and picked up her cold cup. "I'm sure you could do with one."

Rache watched as he poured two fresh cups. He walked over to a cabinet. Taking a whiskey bottle out, he unscrewed it, pouring a generous amount into his coffee. He offered one to Rache. She nodded. Fr. John poured and, putting down the whiskey bottle, handed her the coffee. He took a large gulp.

Well, he hadn't thrown her out. That was one small mercy.

"What do you think, Father?" she asked again, more urgency in her voice this time.

"Question is, Rache, what do you think?"

"I'm not sure what to think. I'm not sure what's real anymore," she said. "When we processed him, he had GSR on his hands—"

"GSR?" he interrupted her, his head tilted slightly, a quizzical look on his face.

"Gunshot residue! I was sure...we were all sure...it was from shooting Joe Mason, but it was from preventing someone shooting Kell."

She briefly sketched out Dion's theory.

"So he really is..." Rache couldn't finish the sentence. Sure, she had thought it possible. She had even convinced herself it was probable. But she had never said it to another living soul.

"Her guardian," Fr. John finished.

Rache looked at him.

"You're having trouble saying it, admitting it to yourself because a part of you refuses to believe it possible."

"I don't...I'm not sure."

The priest said nothing. He had put his cup down and was staring at Rache—waiting.

"Okay, enough already with the third degree. So I think he's her guardian. Happy now?" Rache said.

"Yeah, but you're not."

Rache sat a moment, lost in her own thoughts. "How can this be possible, Father?" She was looking for reassurance. For the first time in her adult life, Rache Fischer was unsure, unsure of all she held to be true. Everything she believed in had been turned upside down.

Fr. John recognized her struggle. He had had his own faith questioned on more than one occasion. Rache Fischer was no longer the cocky detective he'd first met at Kell's bedside. She would never be the same again. Fr. John recognized this. But Rache was struggling.

"Have you ever heard of this before?" she asked, sipping some more coffee, the combination of whiskey and coffee warming her.

"A number of years ago, a young woman was murdered close to here. The murderer was identified by another woman whom he had approached earlier, but at the last second, he took off."

"Took off? Whatta ya mean took off?"

Fr. John nodded. "When questioned later, he said the seven-foot giant walking beside her had scared him."

"It's not the same."

"There have been—"

"It's not the same," she said, standing. "This guy is a living, breathing...I don't know what. But you saw him, talked to him, and we had him in custody."

Fr. John nodded in agreement. Rache was right. This was different. This guy...this guardian...was flesh and blood.

"Rache, you need to say it," Fr. John said, meeting her eyes.

"Guardian. He's a living, breathing guardian."

"The evidence seems to point that way. But there's something missing. Something doesn't add up," he said, troubled now.

"Add up? I'm lost, Father."

"Why?"

"Why? To help her, of course," she said, as though the priest were stupid.

"No, there has to be a trigger. Something must have triggered this. His desire to help Kell, yes, but something must have triggered it."

"I'm still not with you on this."

"It is our belief that at the moment of conception, you are a human being, and at that moment you have a guardian. The guardian is part of who you are. For the guardian, it is like an assignment.

He must advise and protect. Some people call this intuition when somehow, instinctively, you know something is wrong. I think cops call it a hunch."

"Go on," she said, eager to hear more.

"The guardian's role is advisory," he began. "He assists his charge in everyday decisions. It is a relationship. Many people travel through life and never get to know their guardian. It is not like meeting and striking up a relationship with a person. The guardian is an essence. They are, in some ways, the conscience or sixth sense that dwells in every living being. The sense that we detect danger before it occurs, that we intuitively know something is wrong, is, in fact, our inter-action with the guardian. This intuitive force that can spur someone into action is essentially a communication with the guardian."

"Okay, so I believe you. What's your point?"

"The guardians do not live in our world...until now, it would appear. Somehow, he's crossed that divide. But for him to do this, there must be a trigger," he said.

"So he shouldn't have helped her. Is that what you're saying?"

"No, Rache, I'm not saying that. What I'm saying is that it is not in the guardian's remit to exist in this world. They have no place in the physical realm. The guardian is part of who you are—"

"You keep saying that, but I don't understand it. I'm trying, but I don't get it."

Without warning, Fr. John began to laugh, rocking back and forth as he giggled to himself. He couldn't stop. The irony was too much. Many of his congregation didn't believe a word of what was said at Mass. But here he was, after Sunday Mass, talking to a Jewish skeptic, who was hanging on his every word.

He explained his little outburst to Rache.

"Okay, so I'm not so skeptical anymore," she said, smiling over at him.

"So you believe it?"

"Yes."

Rache thought about it a moment. She had finally accepted it. But then something else occurred to her. It stopped her dead in her tracks. "Do I have one, a guardian? It's not just a Catholic thing?" she said, looking Fr. John in the eye. "Do I have one?"

"Yes," he replied. "We all have them. They are part of who we are."

"Jewish people, they have them?"

"The guardian exists regardless of belief."

Rache sat back. Her mind was working overtime just to keep up. She began to feel overpowered by the enormity of it all. "So what do think then?" she asked.

Fr. John was unsure of what she meant. He gave her a quizzical look.

"Did Kell create him, or did he create himself?"

Fr. John considered it a moment. "I think somehow he has produced himself in our world—as flesh and blood. Kell was being attacked, and he forged a body for himself."

"Using her DNA as a template?" she suggested.

"Maybe the DNA is a by-product?"

"What?"

"The guardian is part of who we are. Maybe he didn't use her DNA intentionally. Maybe he created himself through desire, the force so great that he actually forged a physical body from hers. That could explain why they share the same DNA profile. This is most certainly not my area of expertise," the priest added.

Yeah, could be, Rache thought.

"Rache, this is not an exact science," Fr. John added. "Everything here is pure speculation, based to some extent on a smattering of knowledge."

Rache looked at the priest. She had so many questions. He had been a great help, but even Fr. John had thrown in some curveballs.

"Yeah, you're right, Father," she said. "We really are in the dark here, huh?" Then another thought occurred to her. "Why is he male and not female?" she asked.

"Good question. Honestly, I don't know," he replied. Fr. John brought his cup to his lips, stopping abruptly.

"What is it?" Rache asked, catching the change in his expression.

"Again speculation, but maybe he needed a strong male body to fight off Kell's attacker. He would have known this."

"Would make sense," she offered.

"Rache, the guardian is not a gender, not a person, as you and I understand it. Rather, it is an essence. But to function here on this plane, we need a physical body. He sees Kell's attacker is strong and powerful, and don't forget he had a gun—"

Rache suddenly jumped up, cutting him off. "That's it!" she exclaimed. "Shit, it was staring at me all the time."

"What, Rache, what is it?" asked the priest.

"He must know. If he's her guardian, he must know."

"Know what?"

"Who did it. Who attacked her! It's why he crossed, as you put it. It has to be. Kell was being attacked, and he crossed. He came into our world to save her. He must know her attacker. He knows who the real attacker is!"

"No, no, that's not the way I see it. Anyway, when I spoke to him, he didn't know who he was or why he was here. He has human form now, and it must be confusing for him." Fr. John was certainly not as convinced as Rache.

"Okay. But if Kell is his charge, he must protect her. That's why he went back to the hospital," Rache added.

Fr. John knew they were on dangerous ground now.

"Be careful, Rache, this is different. His desire to help Kell has forced him to cross over. He has human form now and is subject to the physical laws of this world as well as human emotions and human constraints. You must remember he is not human."

Rache was taken aback. What was the priest holding back? He wasn't telling her everything. Why?

"So you're saying he may not be 100 percent? He could be what? Damaged?"

That was just it! Damaged! It was what had been tugging at him. The guardian was spiritual, ethereal—it did not process human form. For a guardian to take this form would be detrimental to the growth of that guardian. He was a spirit guide, an advisor, but he operated on a separate plane to human beings. To have human form could spell disaster because as with all human beings, that form could become corrupted!

Fr. John knew he had to tread cautiously here. This was totally unprecedented, and he was totally unprepared. But he also knew he didn't want to scare Rache.

He chose his words carefully. "I don't know. This I do know. The guardian's world is different. Temporal bodies do not bind them. They do not have our desires. To have human form would be a step back. He would have known this. Yet he took human form."

Rache felt somewhat deflated. Her sense of excitement and discovery had been tempered by the priest's forthright pragmatism. Fr. John had just poured quite a bit of cold water on the fire. But the priest had a point. Rache had to admit that. Back at the station, everyone had thought he was strung out. He had downed water like there was no tomorrow and couldn't answer basic questions. *Of course he couldn't*, she told herself. Everything was new to him. Sure, he had to have been confused. But if he was this kid's guardian—a fact Rache had now unequivocally accepted—then he had to know her attacker. All she had to do was find him. Easier said than done.

Rache spent the next hour batting questions back and forth with Fr. John. At the end of it, she was still no closer to finding him. Fr. John had fielded her queries as best he could. He was no expert. But he had come to the same conclusion as Rache. This guardian now lived in the physical world. He warned Rache not to get too carried away.

"Carried away! Are you mad? Who am I going to tell?" she countered.

"I didn't mean it like that."

"Oh."

"What I mean is that we need to be careful. We don't know how this transformation could have affected him. Life is so different for him now. He has a physical body, but he is not human."

"Father, I'll bear it in mind," she said, checking the time. Handing him a card, she headed for the door. "You see him, you call me, night or day," she said as Fr. John turned the card over in his hand.

"I will. And, Rache—"

"I know, be careful." Rache smiled as she pulled the door behind her.

It was close to midnight, and the rain had started again. The earlier downpour had once again become a torrent. Rache thought of how Hollywood always dramatized these moments on celluloid. There was always thunder and lightning and torrential downpours where church scenes were concerned. But Rache Fischer was in no movie.

As she opened the gate to the street, she fumbled for her keys. Shit, she could hardly make out her car. She ran the few yards, her jacket held above her head.

A searing pain shot across the back of her head, its severity causing her to momentarily black out.

As she came to, she could feel rough hands fumble about on her stomach. Rache tried to get her bearings. She was lying face-down in a puddle of cold water. She could taste muddy water in her mouth. What had happened? Suddenly, she felt her gun being wrenched from her holster, the violence of it ripping her blouse. She still couldn't move, the pain in her head so intense. Then she heard him. The voice sounded familiar. Where had she heard it before? Before she had time to think, she was being pulled by her hair along the ground. She tried to scream. Nothing. Her throat was bone dry. She tried to scramble to her knees. A ferocious kick caught her in the ribs, causing excruciating pain in her kidney. Two more blows followed in quick succession, collapsing her to the ground. Rache was almost paralyzed with the pain.

"See how you like it, bitch!" Mr. Jakes screamed in her ear as he leant into her face. She could smell the alcohol on his breath.

Rache vomited. He had her by the hair again, pulling her to her feet. She looked around. She couldn't see her car. Walls rose up in either side of her. Everything was out of focus, the world blurring.

Mr. Jakes slapped her playfully now. He had the bitch, and he'd have a good time before he'd off this one. He had thought about shooting her there and then, but as he'd dragged her down the alley to the back of St. Killian's, he had felt the warmth of her soft body, and he had become aroused. He felt his erection growing, and he'd have some sport.

To add to this, the pimp was somewhat intoxicated. The wait in the car had driven him crazy. At one point he'd thought about going into the church, but had found a half bottle of vodka and had greedily swallowed it. The liquor had warmed his body as he'd sat, waiting for her to come out. This cop would pay for making him look foolish in front of his bitches. He had planned to knock her out, drag her down the alley, and pop a cap in her. But the struggle to find her gun, combined with the alcohol, had sexually aroused him.

He held her against the wall. Rain poured down, but it didn't faze him. He was becoming more and more frantic. He licked her face and groped her breasts as he pushed his hard cock against her inside leg.

"Feel that, bitch? You soon gonna have it in your ass!" he shouted, slapping her across the face. He began to pull at his belt buckle. "I'm gonna fuck you proper, bitch!" He panted between breaths.

Some of her faculties had returned, but Rache was incapable of movement. She was aware of where she was. She recognized Mr. Jakes. *Think, Rache, think*, she urged herself.

"You're...you're making a mistake...I'm a cop." It was all she could muster. Her legs still felt weak, her head pounding.

"I know, lady. Ain't never fucked a cop before. Least not one as pretty as you." He laughed at her. He threw her to the ground, kicking her again.

She couldn't breathe. *Come on, Rache, come on!* her mind screamed. But she was weak. She felt her eyes close as she began to drift toward unconsciousness. If she allowed that to happen, it was over. But her lids grew heavier now, the world around her starting to fade. She was sure she could hear Mr. Jakes talking. Rache bit down hard on her lip, cutting into the flesh. The sudden pain focused her mind. She could taste her own blood, but it had the desired effect. She had avoided slipping into unconsciousness. Her eyes were wide open now, her senses more alert.

Mr. Jakes was talking again, but it wasn't directed at her. Rache turned over on her side now and, through numbing pain, somehow managed to sit up. Mr. Jakes had his back to her now, but she was still too weak to make a move. The throbbing in her head had lessened somewhat, but the ribs where the pimp had kicked her were too painful even to touch.

Focus, Rache, focus. Who was he talking to?

In the rain, she couldn't make him out.

Was it the priest?

"Hey, I got no beef with you, man. Just a little too much to drink. My wife, she's…" she could hear the pimp say. "Best be on your way, buddy."

But the figure was advancing toward him now. Rache saw him for the first time. It was him! The guardian!

Rache guessed he was a good twenty feet away, each forward step closing the distance between them.

"Fuck off!" Mr. Jakes shouted as he pulled his gun, pointing it at the guardian. "Walk away, buddy… Do it, I swear, I'll fucking end you."

The guardian stopped abruptly. He looked at Rache. She had recovered more of her strength. If she needed to, she could get to her feet. Mr. Jakes had all but forgotten her, his attention being singularly focused on the guardian.

"That's right, buddy. You turn around and be on your way," he said. Mr. Jakes turned his head slightly to face Rache, who had begun to struggle to her feet.

Rache heard the shot. But it took a moment for the events to sink in. In the blink of an eye, the guardian had covered the ground that had stood between him and Mr. Jakes, lifting the pimp off his feet and crashing him hard against the brick wall of the church grounds. It seemed like slow motion, but Mr. Jakes and the guardian had hit the wall at least ten feet off the ground, the force of the impact shattering the pimp's pelvis, crushing his spine, and breaking most of his ribs. Mr Jakes had had no time to see the attack. The guardian had moved with lightning speed, gathered the pimp, gun and all, as Mr. Jakes had fired into his side. Rache had felt a sudden blast of hot air as the guardian had moved past her in a blur.

Mr. Jakes dropped in a crumpled heap, his body shattered.

The guardian struggled to stand. Staggering backward, he held his hand to his side. Blood poured from the wound. Rache stumbled over to the two of them, her movement uneven, as though she'd drunk too much. She saw him hold his hand in front of him, the heavy rain washing the blood from his palm. Rache was in shock. The vicious attack had all but finished her. She was operating on pure adrenaline now, some part of her brain forcing her to keep moving. She looked at the guardian. She saw the wound in his side. *Got to get him out of here.*

She bent down by Mr. Jakes. He was still alive. She pulled her gun from his pocket, quickly holstering it.

"You have to come with me, do you understand?" she panted, her head buzzing.

The guardian nodded.

"Come on."

They moved down the alley and out onto the street. Rache unlocked her car. She ushered the guardian in. The blood flow was not as bad as moments ago. Removing her jacket, she pressed it against the wound, expecting him to wince. He didn't.

"Hold that tight. Do you understand me?"

"Yes."

Thank God, she thought. *Maybe I can get through this.* Rache limped around the car and slowly eased herself into the driver's seat.

CHAPTER 28

RACHE WAS GRATEFUL THAT SHE lived just a few short blocks from the church; otherwise, she didn't think she'd make it. As she drove east on Fifty-Sixth Street toward the Broadway intersection, she slowed, conscious of not wanting to attract any undue attention. As for her passenger…well, she didn't know what to think.

Driving on through the rain, despite the throbbing pain in her head, she found her eyes being drawn to him. But he never once looked at her. He just sat there, staring out the windshield, her bloodstained jacket pressed against his wound.

From somewhere in the far recesses of her mind, she heard Fr. John's voice urging her to exercise caution, that this being, this guardian, could somehow be…broken! She quickly dispelled these thoughts. Staring at him now while trying to keep an eye on the road, she could see the resemblance to Kell—the high cheekbones covered by olive skin was the same, no doubt. Jet-black hair fell to his shoulders. Was it the same length as Kell's?

Rache was unsure why mundane questions like this were popping into her head. Maybe it was because of the intensity of the last few minutes. Minutes ago, she'd been certain she was going to die. She briefly thought of her attack by Mr. Jakes. Much of it was a blur, but one thing was certain—he would have killed her! Maybe this was why she was asking herself silly questions about the length of his hair. She didn't know…

Concentrate on the road, Rache, she urged herself.

Rache drove on, but the temptation to steal a glance was overwhelming. Looking at him, she had mixed emotions. Only days ago, she'd have shot him without hesitation. She'd have pulled the trigger, no problem. But she'd been so wrong. They all had. But how could anyone have known? Now all she wanted to do was help him. He was the key. But what exactly was he? Again, more questions.

"We're almost there. Hang on," she said as she slowed the sedan. She had said it more for her own benefit than his. As Rache pulled up to her apartment, her mind raced. Did he need a doctor? Did she need a doctor? Her ribs ached, and there was a numb thudding at the back of her skull. Through rain-soaked hair, Rache involuntarily felt her scalp. There was a lump, sure enough, but the skin hadn't been broken. She moved her weight to her left buttock, easing the pain in her side only slightly. She was certain one of her ribs was cracked. Only a couple more minutes, and she'd be home. But what then? What if she got him inside, and he died? What then? Could he die? She was going mad.

Concentrate, Rache, she told herself. *Focus on the task in hand. Get inside, unseen. You can deal with everything else later.* It spurred her into action.

Rache parked as close as possible. She sat a brief moment. The rain was still heavy and the street deserted. She winced as she struggled out of the car. The tinted blue glow emanating from the wet street seemed to add an eerie dimension to the unfolding events. Rache felt herself shudder. She needed to get inside—fast! She opened the passenger door and helped him out.

"You okay?" she asked. "We've got to get inside. Can you move?"

The guardian nodded. He seemed to need little help getting out of the car, which surprised Rache as he'd only been shot minutes earlier.

Rache lived on the first floor to the rear of the old four-story building. Everything was quiet. Opening the outer door to the building, Rache became aware of the noise of the rain as it lashed against the concrete steps. Every sound now seemed magnified. The door creaked open, her shoes making a squeaking sound on the hardwood floor. Rache had to steady herself at her apartment door. Glancing about, she quickly slid the key into the lock. They both slipped quietly inside, undetected by the sleeping world around them.

She made him sit on a kitchen stool. "Try not to move. I gotta look at your wound," she told him. Walking straight into her bathroom, she grabbed the nearest towel and pressed it against her face. She held it there a moment as she tried to gather herself. She knew she needed to act fast.

Slowly, she lowered the towel, catching a glimpse of her reflection in the bathroom mirror as she did. She had a small cut on her forehead and a couple of scrapes on her cheek, but otherwise she didn't look too bad, all things considered. Rache stripped quickly, dumping her wet clothes, shoes, and all in the bathtub. She realized she'd have to get rid of them. They were covered in blood.

Standing in her bra and panties, Rache examined her left side, softly pressing her ribs. She winced in pain. "Shit!" she exclaimed. That pimp must have broken a rib. Where had he come from? What was he doing there? Again, too many questions.

Lifting her bathrobe off the back of the door, she pulled it on, taking care to put her left arm in first and then drawing it over her right shoulder. Gathering several towels, she walked into the kitchen.

"You'll have to take off all your clothes, okay?"

He nodded.

At least he understands, she thought. Rache grabbed a garbage bag from under the sink and stuffed his blood-soaked clothes in it. Turning back, she looked at him as he stood naked in the low kitchen light. Well, the question of him being male had certainly been answered. *Get it together, Fischer,* she urged herself. Wrapping a large bath towel around his waist, she checked his wound. With extreme care, she gently pushed the soft red skin on either side of the entry wound. The bullet had travelled straight through, leaving a small almost oval entry wound. The slug had exited out his back, creating an identical exit wound. Blood oozed out and ran onto the towel, staining it a deep purple color. She pushed it again, expecting him to jump.

"Doesn't it hurt?" she whispered softly as she made him sit back on the stool.

"No. I don't experience pain like you."

Rache was completely stunned. It was the first complete sentence he'd spoken. It had shocked her. It was not just the fact that he had strung a coherent sentence together, but it was the content. Like you—he was telling her he was different. They were different. If Rache had had any doubts as to his identity, that one sentence had dispelled them. He felt no pain. What was the significance of that? she wondered. If he felt no pain, did that mean he was incapable of feeling pity, anger, or even remorse?

"Hold this against the wound," she instructed him, placing a small towel to the bullet hole. "We still have to stop the bleeding." Rache headed back into her bathroom. She had always kept a first-aid box in a cabinet above the sink. She pulled it out, quickly checking the contents. They were basic, but they'd have to do.

Taking the box, she walked back into the kitchen. For a moment, all she could do was look at him, overwhelmed by what was happening. Placing the box on the kitchen countertop, she quickly raided its contents.

Rache asked him to move over to the kitchen table. "Try not to move about," she told him, holding some wadding against the wound, front and back.

"Here, hold this," she said as she placed his hand on the wadding. His hand felt warm and strong. She wrapped a gauze bandage around his back and stomach, pulling it tight.

Rache had applied disinfectant and had gone through three rolls of bandages in securing the dressing.

"Can you stay there and not move?" she asked.

"Yes."

She had a bunch of questions, but she needed to wash, and she needed to disinfect her own wounds. She remembered the pimp's tongue on her cheek, remembered him forcing it into her mouth. The memory repulsed her. She felt an overwhelming need to wash.

Rache showered quickly, letting the hot water run down her back. It helped. As she dried, she looked at the bruise in the mirror. She pressed it with her fingers. It hurt like hell. The bruise was beginning to spread up under her armpit. She glanced at her face. A little makeup would conceal the cut on her forehead and the scrapes on her cheek. Luckily the bruise would be covered, and no one could detect the lump behind her left ear. She picked up her wet clothes and bundled them into the sack holding his clothes.

She was thinking like a criminal. Covering her tracks, destroying the evidence.

The irony of the situation was not lost on her. But she needed to do this. He had the answers. He knew the true identity of Kell's attacker—the one who had murdered her father. She had to get that information. Could she trust him? Would he trust her?

Rache remembered she'd bought David a tracksuit for his birthday. She'd been at him to do some physical exercise for months. It had become a pet subject of hers. It would be his birthday next month, so she'd bought the tracksuit. The store had even gift-wrapped it for her, and Rache had written a silly little note that she'd taped to the package.

She pulled it from her closet, ripping the paper off. He was almost the same size as David. It would have to do. She couldn't have him walking about naked in her apartment. Rache walked into the kitchen, holding the tracksuit. He just sat on the table. He smiled at her. *God, he is handsome*, she thought. Dark unblemished skin covered an immensely muscular frame. It was not the body builder look, more one of a well-toned athlete or gymnast. But this was not the body of someone who worked out and watched their diet. He had fashioned it from someone else. A fact that now enthralled her!

Wonder what the pro-cloning lobby would make on this one?

She was nervous now, and silly questions were jumping into her head again. The hot shower had gone some way in easing her pain, and the fact that he could both understand and communicate with her had helped to alleviate some of her worst fears.

"Here, put this on. I'll buy you some shoes tomorrow. Don't suppose you know what size you are?" Rache laughed.

He took the clothes and put them beside him, his huge biceps rippling as he placed the tracksuit on the table.

How insane is this, she thought. *What am I to do with him?*

He looked at her and smiled. It was so disarming. He had Kell's eyes, bright, dark, and alive. She remembered the photos she'd taken from Kell's house. Kell, of course. He'd know. He must know. She could solve this. But she heard the priest's voice in her head, again urging caution, that he may be different—damaged somehow! Best not spook him. Start with the basics.

"You want to put those on," she said, pointing to the tracksuit. Rache helped him up off the table. She felt the heat from his body and, in some way, an attraction toward him. She couldn't explain it. Nor did she want to dwell on it. It was all too weird.

"Easy, don't want to reopen that wound." She helped him pull on the sweat top. "Think you can manage the pants?"

He nodded, dropping the towel as he stepped into the pants. Rache made him sit on the stool. She put on some coffee. She badly needed her caffeine fix. Within a few minutes, she was sitting opposite him, sipping a steaming mug of Columbian mixed bean coffee. Rache knew she needed to question him, but she was also aware she would have to tread carefully.

"What's your name?" It seemed the straightforward thing to ask.

"I don't have one, we don't use them," he said, gazing at her, his deep brown eyes captivating her.

"I see," she said, nodding as though it were the natural order of things. "Well, I have to call you something."

He thought about it a moment. "You can call me Malak!"

"Okay. Malak. I'm Rache."

"I know."

"What else do you know?"

He fascinated her. The physical strength he had displayed a short time ago in the alley was extraordinary. It was inhuman. As she looked at his face, she felt the attraction again. Was it sexual? Absolutely!

Get it together, Fischer, she scolded herself. *You've got to get answers.* To hell with it. She'd ask him out straight.

"So you're Kell Mason's guard...?" she couldn't finish the sentence.

"Guardian. Yes."

"Man, this is too weird," she said, laughing nervously as she did.

What was she going to do? She'd already fled a crime scene with a wanted felon. She hadn't reported the attack. She was destroying evidence, and Kell Mason's guardian angel was sitting in her kitchen with a bullet wound in his side.

I'm screwed, she thought. *I'm positively screwed.*

But she couldn't take her eyes off him. Sure, there was a physical attraction, but it went deeper than that. It was fascination—a fascination born out of being presented with undeniable proof. Rache had, at first, been annoyed with Leo and his analysis, but as she'd begun to piece together the evidence, she'd become more and more intrigued. Only this intrigue had rapidly gathered momentum. The DNA evidence, the blood group, his scar, and the fingerprint analysis had snowballed, pushing her toward the one conclusion Rache had vehemently resisted believing possible. Even the priest's theory had failed to convince her 100 percent.

Looking at Malak now, Rache Fischer realized she'd been wrong.

Her entire adult life she'd always believed that death was it. That there was nothing but a void after. She'd laughed at people who prayed. It had been the root cause of much of the resentment she'd felt toward her father. Ira Fischer had always looked for meaning in Ruth's death. Rache had never shared that particular sentiment, going out of her way to be openly hostile to it. But sitting on her kitchen stool was the walking, talking, living proof that she was the one who'd been wrong. She knew now that there was another world, and she had, in her apartment, someone from that world.

Rache poured herself another coffee. "Do you want one?" *What a dumb question, Rache*, she told herself. But she couldn't help it. Malak overawed her.

"I don't know. I've never tasted coffee."

"First time for everything."

Rache poured him a mug. He took it and sipped it.

As Rache watched him drink the coffee, she tried to force herself to concentrate. It was late, and the headache was getting worse.

The fact that he'd no name had taken her by surprise. She tried to think of the possible answers he'd give her. She had to question him. But she had to be careful. How would he react to her questions?

As a homicide detective, it was her job to preempt a suspect's answers to stay one step ahead. But Malak was no longer a suspect. Someone else had killed Joe Mason and had attacked Kell. Malak—this person, if that was the right word—sitting in front of her, sipping her coffee, knew the identity of that attacker.

Rache knew she couldn't lay siege to him with a barrage of questions. That's why she'd started with more mundane ones. But even the cryptic answers to those had startled her.

She took his mug and placed it on the table. "Malak, I need to ask you some questions. I need you to answer them as best you can. If you're confused or don't understand anything, tell me, okay?"

"Yes," he said.

She began by asking him if he knew where he was. He told her he knew he was in the physical world, that it was different to his world, that when the police had taken him from Kell's house, he had just crossed. His confusion had been great. He told Rache that he was scared, scared for Kell. The physicality of the human form frightened him. He remembered the police questioning him, Joe hitting him, and Rache shouting at him.

She looked away, embarrassed at the mention of this.

He said the journey across required immense energy. Arriving in this world, he had been driven insane with thirst. It had been constant and virtually unquenchable. It was partly what had forced him to flee from the police cell. He told her that he'd opened the cell door but didn't know how.

He feared that he had hurt Kell in some way. He wasn't sure what was wrong with her. But he knew he was inextricably linked to her. He knew he was not supposed to exist in this world. Rache explained that because of the gunshot residue on his hands and the fact that he'd been found at the crime scene, they'd all believed he'd killed Joe and attacked Kell. She told him she'd figured out who he was because of the DNA and fingerprint evidence.

Malak acknowledged this.

"So you used her DNA to create yourself in this world?" Rache still couldn't believe she was asking these kind of questions. But she no longer felt foolish.

Malak looked at her. A strange expression had suddenly crept over his face. But Rache pressed on.

"Kell was being attacked," she continued. "Her father had been shot, and you created yourself —created this body, using her DNA as a sort of blueprint—to stop the attack, to help Kell. Least that's how I see it."

"I created this body to help Kell," he repeated.

It was the way he'd said it that startled her. It was phrased more as a question than a statement of fact. Malak seemed distant now. He was searching, unsure. Rache continued to press him.

"Kell was being raped, and you crossed."

"I crossed?"

Again, the uncertainty was there.

"Yes, to this world! Who did it, Malak? Who attacked Kell?"

He didn't know. He couldn't remember.

"I don't know. I don't know! I can't remember anything," he said, getting up off the stool. As he stood, he collapsed forward.

Rache half caught him, and they both fell to the floor. A hot stabbing pain shot through her ribs and up into the side of her face. Malak was panicked now, his eyes darting in every direction. Rache held him in her arms.

"I can't remember, I can't remember," he kept repeating.

Rache held him. Through her own pain, she held him, assuring him that everything would be alright.

"It's okay. It's okay," she whispered. "It'll come back. It'll come back. You'll remember." It was an effort to soothe his anguish. His body was heavy as it rested against hers, the weight pressing on her ribs hard to bear. But she continued to hold him. She knew she couldn't move him. There was a naked desperation in his eyes. Rache stroked his dark hair, all the time assuring him.

She sat with him on the floor for what seemed an eternity. Only when she felt her leg grow numb from being tucked under her did she attempt to encourage him to sit up.

"Come on. You have to lie down. It must be the blood loss or something. You need to rest." She helped Malak to his feet.

Malak lay on the couch. Rache covered him with some extra blankets she'd taken from her room. What was it Fr. John had said? "He lives in the physical world now, and as such, is subject to its laws and constraints." Maybe this included sleep. She certainly needed it.

"You must stay here until the morning. Do you understand? We'll work this out in the morning."

Malak nodded. He seemed less agitated now as he closed his eyes.

She'd call the precinct tomorrow, take a couple of days. Yeah, let Franks chase her tail. The perp—Malak was no longer a threat to anyone. He could stay with her till she figured it out. Forty-eight hours—that's all she'd need.

CHAPTER 29

THE NATURAL SEDATIVE OF SLEEP left her body, and Rache's eyes blinked open. She had some vague recollection of a siren going off. She turned her head on the pillow, the slight movement sending a sharp stabbing pain down from the base of her skull to her lower back. The siren was ringing now, growing louder. It was her phone!

Reaching over, she answered it. She could hardly speak. Her mouth was dry, her tongue stuck to her palate. She glanced at her bedside clock. It was almost noon. *Shit*, she thought.

Captain Woods sounded anxious as he spoke on the other end. When Rache had failed to show up, he'd let it go. He'd figured she'd come in or at least call any moment. But moments had turned to minutes, minutes to hours. Franks had grown more and more impatient. Woods had been coming under increasing pressure from the chief's office. A suspected felon was at large, a suspected murderer who'd managed to escape police custody, and the precinct had no leads. The captain had been told in no uncertain terms that he was to offer all available assistance to the FBI. So when Franks had begun to flip out, he'd called Rache's cell. When he'd reached her voice mail, reluctantly, he'd decided to call her at home.

Rache sounded like shit, he thought. She told him she needed to take a personal day, explaining that she must have picked up some kind of infection and that she'd try to come in tomorrow. Maybe she'd caught it at the hospital, she wasn't sure, she told him.

She had to stall for time. In her living room was the key—the answer to the case. But last night's wounds hadn't even begun to heal. She felt as though her ribs had been cracked open. She had to stall for time.

Woods desperately needed her. But she sounded like hell. He'd told her to stay in bed and drink lots of water.

"Thanks, Doc," she replied.

"I'm serious, Rache. I gotta deal with Agent Franks today, and she seems pissed at you for some reason."

"Tell Scully I said hi," she added.

He ignored the jibe. "Okay, Rache, Danny can liaise with her for today. Think you can make it in tomorrow?"

"I don't know, Captain. I'm beat."

"Take a couple of days. We'll deal with the Feds here. If anything turns up on the suspect, we'll let you know, but it's practically the Feds' case now. They're just using us to do the spade work."

Rache thanked him and hung up. "If anything turns up on the suspect." The words echoed in her ear. *Their suspect*, she reminded herself. Malak was innocent. But he couldn't shed any light on what had happened.

Malak? If it wasn't his name, why had he chosen it? However, it wasn't just the name, it was the person—the being, if that was the right word—who preyed on her mind now. Rache knew it sounded crazy, but she definitely felt a closeness, a deep sense of affinity toward him. She didn't even want to begin to contemplate the reasoning behind it. If life had been complicated before meeting him, then life after had become insane.

Rache had investigated many crimes, both during her time in vice and now in homicide, but one aspect had always held a fascination for her—the deep sense of attraction a victim often felt toward an officer who had intervened to save them. Was she experiencing this with Malak now? If he had not come to her aid last night, she would be dead now, raped and murdered, her body dumped in a back alley. But she was alive, if not kicking—she was alive. Malak was at the forefront of her thoughts now. There was a strong attraction there. What it would lead to, she didn't know, but it was there.

Rache decided she'd better check on him. Rache tried to get up. Her legs were heavy and ached incessantly. Slowly, she peeled back the bedclothes. She hadn't moved in her sleep, and the pressure of one leg resting on the other made walking difficult. Her head still throbbed, but the pain in her ribs was a little less. She walked slowly into her bathroom, the stiffness in her joints easing slightly with each successive step.

Rache ran the bath. Hot water shot from the faucet. As the bath filled, she eased herself into her bathrobe and walked into her living room.

Malak sat on the couch. He had folded the blankets neatly. For some strange reason, she remembered Dion telling her that Kell was a neat teenager. Kell had folded everything away in her room. Were some of her traits to be found in Malak?

He smiled at her.

"Hi," she said.

"Hi."

"I've got to take a bath, ya know. After, we'll have a look at your dressing, huh?"

"Okay."

"You okay here?"

He nodded.

Rache submerged herself in the hot water, adding some relaxing oils, and she lay there, eyes closed, trying to work out her next move. The near-boiling water helped ease away some of her discomfort. Every now and then, she'd add more hot water. The pain in her side had eased. The rest of her didn't feel too bad. Her head still throbbed.

Rache dried herself slowly, taking care to only pat the area where she'd been kicked. She took some painkillers she'd kept in the first aid kit.

Dressing in a sweat top and pants, as it involved the least amount of effort, Rache headed into her living room.

Malak sat exactly as before, his hands clasped on his knee. He smiled at her as she entered.

"I didn't mean that you couldn't move about in here," she said, walking to the kitchen and filling the coffee machine.

As she waited for the coffee to brew, she asked him to sit on the kitchen stool. Malak removed his sweat top. Rache began to unwind the bandage. *Best not push him too much today*, she thought. He'd had some kind of meltdown last night, and she didn't want him freaking out again. But if he couldn't remember anything, she was in deep shit.

She'd bet the lot on Malak. She'd figured that he could ID Kell's attacker, and that would be that. Technically, she was harboring a fugitive. She could be in serious trouble. And to cap it off, he couldn't remember. Well…best not dwell too long on that one, she figured.

Rache gently unwound the bandage. She remembered him saying he felt no pain, but she still didn't want to reopen the wound. She was running out of towels. She'd used six last night, and they were all in the garbage bag along with their clothes. There was a furnace in the basement; she'd burn it all later.

Rache gently removed the wadding at the entry wound. It was sticky from the dried blood. She eased it away. Rache drew in a sharp breath as she took a couple of steps back, her eyes fixed on Malak's naked torso. "Malak, there's no wound here!"

She was dumbstruck. She quickly removed the padding at his back. The exit wound was healed. Smooth, unbroken skin covered what was, only hours ago, a bullet hole. Had he healed himself? Did he possess the ability to cure himself? Rache stared at where she'd dressed a bullet wound. It was unnatural, she thought. *Unnatural? This whole business is unnatural,* she told herself.

Rache stood a moment, as though the distance between them would somehow make what she had just witnessed easier. It didn't. Slowly she walked back to where he sat, her hand outstretched. She needed to touch it. She couldn't believe it. "Can I?" she asked, moving her hand to where he'd been shot. She placed her hand tentatively on his skin. It felt warm to the touch. She pushed the area, half expecting the wound to reappear. It didn't. She ran her hand all the way around to his back.

Rache was enthralled now. She looked up into his eyes. They held hers. They were almost hypnotic, magnetically drawing her in. Rache could feel herself blush as blood flushed through her cheeks. Looking at him in the daylight with the full realization of exactly who he was, was so overpowering. He was incredibly handsome. A small smile crossed her lips. It was an attribute he'd be totally unaware of. Malak would never use his good looks for personal gain. He would never be found in some bar hitting on a girl, never try to charm his way into someone's affection. This only added to the attraction she felt for him, causing her greater confusion. *Get it together, girl,* she told herself.

Rache blinked, allowing her eyes to once again wander down his muscular trunk to where he'd been shot. Her hand quivered as once again she pushed his flesh.

"How is this possible?"

"I don't know—lots of new things to process. This world, this body, the senses. Everything is new."

"Senses, what senses? What are you talking about?" she asked, her eyes still riveted on where he'd been shot.

He stood up off the stool, startling her.

"You feel better?"

"Yes."

"Malak, there is so much I don't understand. Why you're here. How you're here." She was becoming confused now, questions pouring into her head. For every question she'd ask, ten more would spring up. She could feel the weight of the whole situation bearing down on her now. She took a few deep breaths in an effort to focus her thoughts.

"Last night you were shot," she said. "I dressed the wound. Today, not only are you healed, but there's no trace of the wound. You've recovered fully. My head is pounding, and my ribs ache."

"He would have killed you."

It stopped her in her tracks. Malak was right. The pimp would have raped and murdered her. He'd saved her life. She looked at him now. Malak put back on his sweat top.

"Thank you," she said softly. "I...I never said thank you. You saved my life. Thank you."

He was looking at her in an odd, far-off manner. The way he did when they first met. It was a quizzical look.

"What is it?"

"I...don't know...I can't remember."

"Take it slowly, okay? No freaking out, huh?"

Malak continued to stare at her. It was a little unsettling. Rache walked over and sat on her couch. *Gotta try to make him feel relaxed,* she thought. Rache patted the seat beside her. "Sit down a moment, Malak."

Malak sat beside her.

Taking his hand in hers, she began. "You were saying something about the senses, that they were all new to you."

He nodded, looking down at her hands. He was searching, trying to find a way to explain. His world was so different to hers. His was a world without form. How could he explain this to someone who lived in a world of form? He had been overpowered by the physical world, by the physical form, he now inhabited. The body and its associated senses had been a necessity to protect Kell from her attacker. But the accelerated process by which he'd forged it had all but severed his connection—his memory!

Malak looked at Rache's face now, at her long blonde hair. He knew the color was blonde, but he was analyzing through the sensory organ of sight. He understood the mechanics of this. White light falling on the hair is absorbed. The vibratory rate of yellow being different to the other colors is not absorbed. This image enters the eye through the iris and is carried as a beam of electrons along the optic nerve to the visual cortex, located at the back of the brain. The visual cortex is like an editing suite, transforming this beam into an image. The color blonde is understood. But Malak recognized the limitations of this—of the sensory organs. In his world, it was so different. He could smell and taste color, each one individualized. He could taste a burning fire and see a fragrance.

Malak felt her hair with his hand. It was soft to the touch. In his world, he could touch a color, touch a fragrance, and he could taste and smell thought. He knew all this, but he'd lost his connection. The energy surge had wiped clean that connection. There were vague memories, but the process by which he could access them had fundamentally altered. He depended on the five human senses now. He interacted with the world of the physical through the human senses. Looking at Rache, he realized for the first time since taking human form, he was trapped!

Malak smiled at her, letting go of her hand. "You have five rec-ognized senses," he began. "Sight, smell, hearing, touch, and sound. We have twenty. I cannot explain them. Everything you see in this world is given properties according to your five senses. Everything is understood according to these senses. All scientific analysis is based on your interaction with the world through these five senses. But you have more than five."

"You mean like a sixth sense?" she asked.

"You have more than six," he replied, smiling.

"Wait, wait, wait, what are you saying...?"

"We have twenty. I interact and understand your world accord-ing to these senses. When I crossed—as you put it," he said, pausing as he looked at her, "I lost them. I live in this world now and must negotiate this world with the five senses."

"But you just said we have more than five!"

"The human being is not evolved enough to understand, let alone use all nine senses."

"Nine senses? We have nine senses?"

But Malak pushed on, ignoring the look on Rache's face. "When I took this form, I became subject to the laws of the physical world. It took me time to realize this."

The old priest had been right on the button, she thought. She'd have to talk to him again.

"I need a coffee. This is overload," Rache said, shaking her head in disbelief as she rose and walked back into her kitchen.

Rache poured two mugs of hot coffee. Handing one to Malak, she sat back down beside him. She looked at him. She hadn't even begun to process last night, and now this. She needed a year, never mind two days. She sat watching him.

He sipped the coffee. "Thank you," he said.

Rache just nodded. She didn't trust herself to speak right now. But she had to say something. She needed info on Kell. And he had it. Locked away somewhere.

"It tastes okay?" It was the first thing to come to mind. Damn, she sounded stupid.

"It tastes fine. But I have no reference point."

"Reference point?"

"I have never tasted coffee before. So I cannot measure this against anything."

"I see," she said, not really understanding.

"When I crossed…into this world, it was like being born into a new world. For the first time, I had the use of all the senses that human beings have."

"But Kell must have drank coffee, cried tears, smelled flowers?"

"It doesn't work that way," he said, standing. Malak stood a moment, looking at Rache. His stare was intense. She wondered what was going on in his head. He walked about, pausing now and then, as if searching some memory that was hidden, some intangible fragment—unable to unlock it. He explained that his world was different, that time is not measured in the linear way we measure it. He told Rache it was like being outside a coffee shop. He liked the coffee she had made him, and he got stuck on drawing an analogy. He told her it was like standing outside the coffee shop, looking in.

"You can see the people inside. You can observe them talking, drinking, smoking. But only when you walk inside do all your senses kick in. Only then can you smell the smoke and the aroma of the freshly brewed coffee beans or the smashing of a cup as a waitress drops a tray. Only then can you taste the air and hear the voices. Only when you open that door are your senses bombarded by this."

Rache was nodding now. "So it was like some kind of overload for you?"

"Yes, something like that, but worse." He looked away.

"Malak?" Rache asked softly, looking up at him.

"Yes."

"Last night…last night I asked you what happened with Kell. You said you couldn't remember. Can…can you remember now?"

Malak stared at the ground, shaking his head. "No!"

It couldn't have been plainer than that. But she couldn't let it go. She had to know. She had to find the real perp.

"But you know about your world, your role in it," she countered. "You fought off her attacker. I mean, the room was trashed.

You saved her. Her attack precipitated your entry into this world, into the physical realm…"

Malak sat back down beside her. He placed his cup on the floor. He seemed to be searching again. Rache watched him a moment. She could feel his immense strength as he shifted his weight on the couch. Rache stared into his face. Dark piercing eyes that burnt with intensity captivated her now.

"If you suffer memory loss," he began, "you can still boil water. You can dress yourself, wash your clothes. You don't have to think about it. If you drive down the street in a car, you know you can stop by pressing the brake pedal. You know pressing a switch will turn on the lights. But you cannot remember your name. But you know these things."

Rache could see where he was coming from. It made sense. Well…some kind of sense now.

"So it is with me. I know about my world. But I cannot remember details. I am not part of it now. I have no connection to those memories anymore. I no longer have contact with my world. I don't know who attacked Kell."

"I see what you mean," she said, standing. She looked down at him now. "But, Malak, just because you have no way of accessing your memories doesn't mean they're lost. If you could just stimulate them somehow, maybe…" she trailed off.

He was looking at her again in that strange manner.

Fuck, I'm losing it, she thought.

"What's wrong?" he asked.

"Nothing, you just look at me strangely sometimes."

"Oh, I wasn't aware of it."

"Forget it. It's probably me anyway," she said. She had to talk to the priest. He had to be able to help. He must have some insight into this. "Malak, I need you to stay here. You're not to leave, okay?"

"Okay."

"Good. It's too dangerous for you to be outside."

Then it occurred to her. Outside! He'd been outside the church. In the attack and what followed, she'd never thought about it. Why had he been outside the church? Why had he gone to the hospital to see Kell?

She asked him. Malak was unsure of himself. He told her he'd tried to visit places where Kell had been to help him orient himself. That's why he'd been to the church and back to her house. This revelation shocked Rache. She told him under no circumstances was he to return to Kell's house. Malak said he'd been back to try and get his bearings. He had followed her trail to the hospital.

"Trail, what trail?" she asked him.

"I can't explain it. It's like when you touch something, you not only leave a fingerprint on it. You leave another kind of print. That print is you, your very being."

"Like your...soul?" Rache couldn't believe her own words. But she'd said it.

"In a way, yes," he said. "It's not that straightforward."

Malak was struggling now, struggling to articulate this thought. As Kell's guardian, he could follow her anywhere. He read and understood her thoughts and feeling through his senses. He was able to taste her emotions as she battled hard-won victories on the tennis courts. He could smell and see pain in her defeat. If Kell sat on a seat, he knew a month later that she'd been there, what she wore, and how she'd felt at that precise moment in space and time. But operating on the physical plane through the human body with all its limitations, he had found difficulty in tracking her—the physical form, itself a clumsy interface with which to decipher her movements.

In the first few days of his being, Malak had retained some of his spiritual faculties. He had been able to read Kell's trail and had experienced no difficulty tracking her to the hospital, even knowing her exact location before he'd entered. But the longer he spent using the human body, the quicker the remnants of his spiritual side diminished. Everything he experienced now, he had to process through the human form and its associated senses. This caused him great confusion.

"Malak, you gotta be honest with me," Rache said, his long silence disturbing her.

"I am. At least with what I know. I remember some of before. But it's not clear. It's fuzzy, and even when I receive a clear image, I don't understand it. This I do know. Kell is still in great danger. This is not finished. Someone went there to kill her, and he failed. He will try again!"

"How can you be certain?"

But Malak pressed on, ignoring her question. "Kell is my responsibility, my assignment. I have to look out for her, and I can't do it here."

"No no no, you have to stay here. If the cops see you, they'll shoot you. They don't understand who you are."

He walked over to her. He held her by the arms, moving her effortlessly toward him. *Shit, he's strong*, she thought. But Malak meant her no harm. He had to stop her talking.

He gazed into her eyes. She held his stare. "Don't you understand? I don't know who I am."

That was the crux of it. He was lost. Lost in this world and lost to his own. He straddled two dimensions. Rache reached up and held his hand. It was warm. She looked up into his eyes. Her heart began to race. She felt desperately sorry for him. Touching his face, she felt the stubble on his cheek rub against her hand. She found herself being drawn to him. He was staring at her. Did he feel the same? Could he experience love and attraction, the same as her? But she knew his body had been forged from another's. Everything confused her.

She whispered, "I need you to stay here. Just for today. I have to see someone, and we'll talk tonight, okay?"

He seemed calmer now. Rache stepped away from him. She had almost kissed him, the attraction so intense. *Gotta keep it together. I'll see the priest. He'll know what to do. I'll go and come back as soon as possible*, she thought. Rache gathered up the bandages, pushing them into the garbage. *Gotta burn that*, she told herself.

Her doorbell rang!

Rache froze.

Shit, she thought. She looked about. Lifting the intercom phone, she spoke into it. Both Danny and Susan were outside. They wanted a word. *Not now*, she thought. But to refuse them would only add to their growing suspicion. She had to act natural.

Rache pretended to buzz them in, buying a little time for herself. Gathering up the blankets, she hurried Malak into her bedroom, telling him that some police officers were coming, and he was to stay put. Under no circumstances was he to come out. She left him in the room, closing the door behind her.

The buzzer rang again. She picked up the door phone. "Yeah."

"Rache, we didn't get in," Danny said.

"Sorry, try it now." She pushed the buzzer. She could hear them opening the door. Moments later, Rache opened the door to her apartment.

Susan and Danny walked through.

She doesn't look good, Susan thought as she greeted Rache. *Jesus, looks like she was up all night. Was that a cut on her forehead? Rache's eye seemed all puffed up. Was she in a fight?*

Rache caught Susan staring at her. She knew she was in trouble. Danny had walked in to the center of the room. He just thought she was sick. Rache shook her head from side to side quickly. It was a signal to Susan. *Don't ask, not in front of Danny.* Susan nodded twice to indicate she'd understood.

Danny turned to Rache, impatient now. "Rache, what's up?"

"Nothing. Just woke up feeling like shit!"

Danny shook his head. He didn't like being taken for a fool. "Christ, Rache, the shit has really hit the proverbial fan," he said, glancing over at Susan. "Franks has gone ballistic," he continued. "She's reported you to the captain for being uncooperative. And now she's got hold of some call you made to Langley."

"Langley?"

"That Para-Psychic-what's-it, you called. All numbers are routed through Langley. Franks thinks you're withholding information. You've become distant and hard to talk to—"

"Rache, we're worried, that's all," Susan chipped in, feeling Danny was getting too heavy.

"Guys, I'm fine, really. I just woke up feeling like crap. I'm gonna take a day or so—"

"Rache, like Susan said, we're worried."

"I'm fine, really."

Rache saw it the same time Danny did.

She'd dropped a piece of bloodied bandage.

Danny walked over and picked it up. Holding it up, he stared at her. Strolling back over to Rache, he dropped the bandage in her hand.

"If you say so," he said, walking to the door. "Come on, Susan."

"Danny," Rache called after him.

He turned around.

"Thanks…for coming…ya know."

He nodded.

Susan looked at her a moment. "Get some rest, Rache. I'll call you."

"Yeah."

Rache closed the door after them. Damn! She knew them too well. They knew things weren't adding up, and it would only be a matter of time before they started to figure it out. That's why she had to talk to Fr. John.

She called the parish number listed. Fr. John was away for the day and wouldn't return back until tomorrow. *Great*, she thought. She couldn't keep questioning Malak. They'd both crack up. She told him she'd go and buy him some clothes. He needed shoes.

Rache went to the basement. She lit the furnace. It would take a while to heat. She wanted everything burnt. Rache walked out and bought a few essentials. She had to guess his shoe size. She had a fair idea of his size from the tracksuit. She bought him cheap trainers and jeans, picking up a few T-shirts, before she returned. She was grateful to find Malak still there when she got back.

Rache got him to change. She ordered in pizza, and after, she went to the basement and burnt everything.

She felt like a criminal. She had used cash for all her transactions. But she could have no one tracing her to last night. It occurred to her: the forensics lab! Dion and Raul would have moved on to new cases by now. But all the evidence was logged in with Leo. She'd have to get him to cover. Would he? She called him. He told her that the Feds had already been. Rache felt her heart skip a beat.

"Don't worry, Detective Fischer, our dirty little secret's safe. All I told that condescending woman was that the DNA matched. Didn't tell her to what. She simply dismissed me out of hand."

"Leo, I owe you, big time," she said, feeling more relieved than anything.

"Hey, I would suggest dinner, but I just want to meet this guy if you catch—"

"Dinner it is," she said, interrupting him. She thanked him again before hanging up.

She chatted with Malak some more, but got very little out of him. He had become more withdrawn as the day had progressed. By late evening, Rache decided to call it quits. She made it plain to Malak she would help him. She decided to get to bed early. She still ached from the previous night. Malak told her he knew she wanted to help, but he wasn't sure how.

"Leave it to me. That's my worry now. I need you to stay here. You cannot leave this apartment," she said.

Rache thought about the last twenty-four hours. So much had happened. She was harboring a fugitive. She knew she could be looking at prison time. But he knew, he knew who had attacked Kell. She just had to find a way in, to unlock that memory. Somehow, she had to be able to access it. With his knowledge, she'd blow the case wide open. But first she had to find a way in.

CHAPTER 30

Taking full advantage of the captain's offer to take two sick days, Rache arrived at the church a little after rush hour, waiting for traffic to ease before driving the couple of blocks to St. Killian's. The last two days had been a whirlwind, and she certainly wasn't out of the woods yet. At least Malak seemed a little more settled this morning, she thought as she approached the church. She couldn't risk him going off the deep end. No, he was a little calmer today. He still got agitated over certain things—things Rache couldn't understand. He'd been going on about needing to see Kell, about not being able to read her field or something. Rache hadn't paid too much attention to it. Rather she'd explained to him that she was going to see Fr. John, that the priest knew Kell and perhaps he could help. This seemed to calm him somewhat, and Rache had left.

Rache felt a good bit better herself. True, her head still hurt like hell, but her ribs had improved a lot. She'd taken another hot bath earlier, and it had helped soothe them. She had far more freedom of movement than yesterday. *Mustn't have broken them*, she thought. They were still bruised, but her movement was definitely better now. Malak was safe at her place. She'd told him not to answer the phone or door, explaining that other people, especially the cops, would not understand who he was. Malak had found this difficult to comprehend. He knew he was here to protect Kell, and he struggled with being confined to Rache's apartment.

As Rache approached the scene of her attack, she thought about the pimp. Had he survived? What had happened to him? Fuck him! He'd have killed her. He'd have raped and killed her. But she was still a cop. She knew she needed to find out. But how could she do it without raising suspicion?

Climbing the steps, her thoughts turned again to Malak. It must be so confusing for him, she figured. He didn't belong here. Hell, she did, and most days confused her. Hopefully Fr. John could help.

Rache stopped at the entrance to the church. *If the guys at the precinct could see me now*, she thought. She knew she was putting all her chips on Fr. John, knew he had to come up trumps for her.

But who else could she turn to? He'd know what to do, she was sure of it. He'd find a way to unlock this memory problem.

Rache now believed that what she'd taken as recognition at the start was, in fact, confusion. Malak hadn't recognized her. How the hell could he? No, he'd been confused. It occurred to her suddenly. It would be like putting a newborn baby in the body of a thirty-year-old man and expecting him to function normally. It wasn't possible. Malak had simply been looking to them all for answers. She felt guilty for being so hard on him when they'd first arrested him.

Rache pushed the large oak door. It creaked slightly and glided open. The smell of lingering incense and burning candles assaulted her nose. She thought of what Malak had said, about not using the senses. It was true, Rache thought as she inhaled deeply through her nose. She closed her eyes and really smelled the church for the first time. She wondered what it must have been like for him. To smell and see and feel and taste and hear for the first time, what must it have been like? To undergo this sensory bombardment and have no one to explain it to him must have overwhelmed him.

Smelling the inside of the church now, she recalled him telling her about his senses, about being able to taste color and see cold. This she'd found extraordinary. How could you taste cold? she wondered. As a guardian, could he see the color of the wind? Shit, she'd need years to try and understand half of it.

Rache opened her eyes and walked into the church proper. Suddenly, she wished she'd waited till later. Halfway up the long aisle, Danny stood facing Fr. John. He spotted her immediately.

Shit! she thought.

Danny said something to Fr. John, who turned to see. The priest smiled at her. She had to keep walking. What had the priest told him? As she got closer to them, she could see that Danny looked annoyed.

"And you heard nothing?" he said.

It was there in his voice as he spoke to his uncle. Danny was pissed.

"Nothing," she heard Fr. John reply.

Rache stood beside them now.

"Hi, Danny, Father," she greeted them.

"Hello, Rache," the priest said.

"Can you give us a moment, Father?" Danny asked, taking Rache by the arm and walking down the aisle, out of earshot. "Rache, what are you doing here? You're supposed to be ill. If the captain—"

"Danny...I—"

"Never mind!" he interrupted her.

"We caught a break. Uniform responding to call about a shooting night before last found some guy in the alley out back."

"Some guy?" she said, trying to disguise her shock.

"Yeah, some pimp. He was pretty badly smashed up. Guy looks like he was hit with a wrecking ball," Danny continued.

Rache got a sinking feeling. She just stared at Danny. She didn't trust herself to speak.

Danny took her silence to mean she was interested. "Anyway, he's over at county. We got two cops sitting on him now. He's all busted up, so he's going nowhere. They found a gun at the scene, one shot discharged. Also got lots of blood. So it looks like he shot someone."

Rache continued to stare.

Shit, if they run his blood, she thought, *what then?*

"You're probably wondering how all this ties in, yeah? Well, search of the area turned up his car, and guess what?"

Rache shrugged, shaking her head.

"We found a photo of Kell Mason in his glove box."

"What?" she said involuntarily.

"Yeah, my thoughts exactly," Danny said.

"You think it was a hit? On Kell?" she asked. "You think it was a hit?"

"Has to be. Problem is why was he at the church, and who did he shoot? His prints were all over the photo. Forensics lifted a couple of partials from another set. They're working on it now. Franks is on top of this. Impressed with our police work or some bullshit like that. She's requested you and I be assigned back on the case."

That was it, Rache thought, not really listening to Danny's last sentence. The pimp had followed her from the hospital. *He must have gone to check it out, spotted me, and followed me*, she figured. But why did he want to kill Kell? Was he the attacker? Was he the one Malak had fought? It had to be? No, he had a photo. *Shit*, she thought. But the photo could be there from before—from the first attack. Yes, that's it. Damn!

She'd met him shortly before they were called to the house. The pimp could have done it and gotten away. Could be why he was beating the kid, Jessie. Time frame fits. Malak could have fought him, and he'd fled, leaving Malak behind. But Rache had a bigger problem. This pimp could also identify her. That was a problem. Danny was talking, but she wasn't listening.

"Rache?" he said.

"What?"

"This is great news. We're back on the case. This pimp is tied in somehow." He held up a blue folder. "Here's what we got on him. Goes by the name of Mr. Jakes. A real scumbag." He told her reading the pimp's jacket would take all day: assault, attempted rape, battery, attempted murder (he got off), assault with a weapon, people trafficking. The list was endless. Most of the raps he'd beaten. He'd been arrested in connection with the disappearance and death of two young Hispanic girls, but was released on insufficient evidence.

A real pillar of society, thought Rache as Danny continued to read snippets from the pimp's jacket.

"I get the picture, Danny. He's a bad ass."

"Yeah, Franks wants you to interview him later. I was going to call by this afternoon and give you this," he said, waving the folder. "Saved me the trip."

Rache tried to process it all. What the hell could she do? "Is he…is he conscious?" she asked, trying to sound nonchalant. Her voice sounded shaky, unsure. *Damn it!* she thought.

"Don't know. Either way, it's good news for us."

Danny drew in a deep breath. He looked at Rache.

"Hey, sorry 'bout yesterday, you know. You had us all a little spooked, that's all."

Rache reached up and kissed him on the cheek. "It's nice to know you care!" she said, half smiling.

He nodded. "You'll talk to this pimp, okay?"

"Sure."

"Franks wants to see you tomorrow."

"I'll make it in, don't worry, Danny," she said, tapping the folder. "Just don't tell Franks you gave this to me here, say you called by, huh?"

He looked at her. What was Rache playing at? Sure, she looked sick yesterday. And if he admitted it, she didn't look too hot today. But what the hell was she doing back at the church? Had she discovered some information? He hoped she hadn't come to quiz his uncle again.

"Okay," he said, without sounding too convinced. Danny waved to Fr. John and walked out.

Rache watched him disappear through the great doors. She turned and hurried up the aisle to the priest, her shoes making a *clop-clop* noise on the mosaic floor.

"Rache, are you okay?"

"His name is Malak, he's at my apartment," she whispered. "He gets shot, and hey, presto, next morning he's healed. He's no memory—"

Fr. John had to grab her by the arms to stop her talking.

"Slowly," he said. "Start from the beginning."

"Okay, okay," she said, realizing she'd been babbling. She looked about. The huge church was empty. Rache sat on a pew near her. "There's so much, I don't know where to start," she said, trying to gather herself.

Fr. John sat beside her. "Tell me everything that happened after you left here on Sunday night."

Rache nodded. She was more with it now. She told him. In as much detail as possible, she told him of her struggle, her attack, her beating at the hands of this Mr. Jakes character. How they'd met before. She spoke about Malak, how he'd saved her life, about his extraordinary strength, how he'd been shot and had somehow healed himself, of who he was, how he'd crossed to help Kell, to save Kell! Rache left nothing out.

"So you think this pimp, this guy, is the one who attacked Kell and killed her father?" Fr. John asked when she'd finished.

Rache was silent a moment. She began to nod her head. "Maybe," she said cautiously. "It fits the time frame. Malak smashed him up pretty bad." Rache opened the folder Danny had given her. She read from the hospital report. "He's got a ruptured spleen, a shattered pelvis, a punctured lung, a broken arm, fractured vertebrae, and nearly all his ribs are broken."

"And you say he hit him only once?" the priest asked.

"Yeah, I mean, he...took off...like in a fraction of a second," Rache said, raising her hand and snapping her fingers to help emphasise the speed. "I was on the ground," she said slowly, remembering the incident. "I was on the ground. This pimp was standing over me. I heard him cock his gun...then WHAM! He hit the pimp full force. They flew through the air and hit the wall. I heard the gunshot, and next thing I know, the pimp was out cold, and Malak was bleeding from his side."

"And the next day it was healed?" Fr. John asked, more than intrigued now.

"Yeah. What do you think that means, Father?"

Fr. John didn't reply. Something didn't add up. It was there, but he couldn't put a finger on it. He stood up and walked away. When he turned to face Rache, he shook his head. "I don't like it, Rache. I don't like it."

"What's not to like? He saved my life, no doubt."

"That's just it. The excessive force. If he can do what you say, and I believe you, by the way." He said the last bit just as he caught the change in her expression. Her brow had furrowed, and she was about to challenge him. Fr. John continued. "Nonetheless, the force was excessive. It was like he was some kind of avenging…force."

"Avenging Angel," she whispered, the words themselves almost sounding prophetic. True, Malak was Kell's guardian, but perhaps he was also some kind of retributive force. She caught his stare. No, she thought. No way. The priest was less convinced.

"No, I don't think so. You haven't really met him. He's like a pussycat. You tell him to sit, and he does exactly that. He sits. You tell him to stay, and he won't budge for hours. No way!"

"I'm not happy, Rache, and I certainly don't like this memory loss," Fr. John continued.

Rache jumped up. She looked about. An elderly couple had entered the church and were lighting offertory candles only a few yards away.

Rache whispered to Fr. John as they both walked in the opposite direction. "But that's why he was confused when you met him—when we had him in custody. The world was new to him."

"Maybe, but this attack—"

"You think I care a jot for that scumbag? I found him beating on a kid the day Kell was attacked. That son of a bitch would have killed me. He deserves everything he gets, no question." She was angry now, the memory of the attack still fresh, her wounds still tender.

"I see," Fr. John said.

"Don't presume to know me, Father. I came here for help, not judgment. It you can't offer any—"

"Rache, Rache, Rache," he whispered, trying to get her to calm down. "I want to help. Really I do, but you've dropped a huge bombshell on me just now. I'm only trying to process it."

He was right. She had spent thirty-six hours with Malak, and she still couldn't process it. Perhaps she was being too hard on the priest. But she was impatient. She knew it was only a matter of time before Danny started to put things together, and she didn't even want to have to think about that.

They talked a little more. Fr. John told her he was still coming to terms with the news. The reason he was worried about the memory loss was that the guardians are not meant to exist in the physical world. If Malak couldn't remember his true identity, he might become confused about his reason for being here. Although his reason for being here may initially be for good, Fr. John was worried that with time, that intention may itself become corrupted. By Malak's interaction with this world, his true self may become lost, and a more sinister self could emerge. He told Rache it was imperative that they try and reconnect him with his own world.

She knew Fr. John was right. Well, at least she thought he was right. But she still had to find out who had attacked Kell. She'd have to ask him. She'd have to show him the photo of Mr. Jakes. Would this spark him off? She didn't know. But Danny and Susan had their suspicions. She'd heard it in their tone. And Franks... Well, best not think about her.

Fr. John could understand Rache's predicament and its associated pressures. She had accepted Malak unconditionally. She was the doubting Thomas who'd put her hands in his wounds, literally. But deep down, he was worried. This case was unprecedented. Never before had he heard it even suggested. Unless Rome was hiding something, and that wouldn't surprise him. But he had to deal with Midtown Manhattan, not Rome, and this being, Malak—this angel—was real. He'd met him, spoken to him. Granted, he'd had no clue who Malak was at the time. But he'd seen him in the flesh and blood, so to speak. This was the part that worried him the most. This taking of human form worried him. Sure, there had been sightings of guardians down through history—but nothing like this.

He'd told Rache that the guardian had no reason to exist in this world. They were like mentors or spirit guides, and no way should they exist independently of their charge. Malak being here now was wrong. It was against the natural order of things. Malak? Was it a derivation of the Hebrew Mal'akh, a messenger? Is that what he meant? Was he saying he was a messenger? And if so, what message did he bring? *Perhaps I'm overthinking it.* Rache had told him that according to Malak, the guardians don't use names. Another puzzle!

Fr. John prided himself both on the knowledge he'd acquired over the years and his open-mindedness in employing that knowledge. But this one baffled him. If Malak was indeed Kell's guardian, a fact that seemed more plausible by the moment, then him being here could only spell trouble, no matter how good his intentions.

That was it! His intention!

His intention had been to save Kell. He must have in some way used her genetic code to generate a human body. How this worked, he'd no idea! It was a necessity to fight the attacker. To operate here on this plane, he needed physical form. His intention had been true and honorable. But fundamentally, it had been the intention of a guardian. Malak processed human form now and was no longer a guardian in its purest sense. The form he had taken was human, and that could, like all humans, become corrupted! A corrupted human form may perceive the world in a different light to that of the guardian. That coupled with certain powers he seemed to possess could be a recipe for disaster.

The more the priest thought about it, the more worried he became—that and the memory loss. Did it mean his connection to his world had been severed? Fr. John knew he was walking a tightrope.

Rache had been watching him for some time now as he'd sat in silence, contemplating. She asked him what was troubling him. He explained his concerns.

"No! No way," she said. "I can't accept...I don't believe—"

"He's not human, Rache. It's a mistake to think so."

Suddenly she felt lost. She looked at Fr. John a moment. "Will you come, Father? Will you come and meet him?"

The priest nodded.

CHAPTER 31

RACHE WASN'T SURE HOW FR. John would react to meeting Malak. But she knew she'd better get them together. The priest, for all his doubts—and there were many—could help. No! *Would* help. The fact that he'd doubts had encouraged Rache. She would never in a million years have brought up the type of questions that Fr. John had raised. The whole thing was getting too big. Sooner or later, something had to give. She needed to be able to identify Kell's attacker before that happened, and Malak was the key. Yeah, the priest had his doubts—but she knew the key to solving the case was sitting in her apartment. All she had to do was unlock his memory. Easier said than done. But there had to be a way.

When Rache led Fr. John into her apartment and found Malak was no longer there, she was devastated. She rushed through her apartment, checking each room, calling his name. Nothing! Malak was gone!

Fr. John gently eased himself onto the couch. Rache was frantic. She came back into the living room, flopping onto her couch, deflated.

Fr. John looked at her a moment. "He's not yours, Rache! He's not some puppy dog you get to keep."

She nodded, burying her head in her hands as she sighed. She stayed like that a moment. Looking up, she asked, "You said we have them…Jewish people, I mean?" It was more of a question than statement of fact.

"We all have them. They're part of who we are," he told her.

"So I have one, I have a guardian?" she asked.

"Yes."

"And he looks out for me?"

"Yes."

She thought long and hard before asking the next question—partly because she didn't understand it and partly because she was afraid. "And the one who attacked her and killed her father, he…he has one…a guardian?"

Fr. John nodded. "Yes."

"I don't get it."

He knew she was struggling with the concept. He tried to explain it as best he could, knowing he had to keep it simple. He explained that if she lost the power in her arm, she would no longer be able to move it. It didn't mean that the arm was no longer there and may be used again. People become disconnected from the guardian. They laugh and ridicule the guardian, causing him great harm. The guardian's ability to help and advise us diminishes as the person becomes more and more disconnected, but he never gives up—he never stops trying to connect with us.

Fr. John told her it was like losing an interface. It is the guardian's duty to advise and counsel. Sometimes people slip into depression or other illnesses, and they become harder to reach. When people cross the threshold and become involved in crimes such as premeditated murder and child abuse, they are shunning away from their guardian, and they descend into a spiral from which it is almost impossible to return. Such crimes show the process of evil at work, he told her. These people were not born evil, he said. It was a process, a gradual separation from the guardian.

"They develop a blind spot in their own minds. Whilst deep down they know that what they are doing is wrong, they overcome it. This is, in itself, a separation from the guardian—from the intuitive force that dwells within us all. Evil starts by manifesting itself as a blind spot, and people like Kell's attacker find themselves more and more drawn down this path because of the nature of the arousal patterns that drive them," the priest said.

It made some sense to her.

He told her that even someone as loving as Kell may not have been aware of the fact that she had a guardian.

"Rache, sometimes you know instinctively that a certain thing is right or wrong—and you act upon this instinct. This instinct is your guardian," he told her. "A message or revelation has slipped through the barrier, and you receive it as an impression or gut feeling. Cops call it a hunch, I believe! How you choose to act on this message is what we call free will."

Fr. John was right, she thought. It kind of made sense. But if we are to receive messages or impressions from our guardian, Malak's presence confused her.

"Why is he here?" she asked.

"I don't know. He shouldn't be. It could upset the natural order of things."

That was just it, she thought. "Damn it!" she exclaimed, standing now. Realizing what she'd said, she looked at Fr. John. "Sorry, Father."

"I've heard worse. What exactly do you wish to damn?"

"I...never mind. It's him being here. It's what we've missed. Malak's presence here in our world has left Kell in some nonstate... or coma. It's why the doctors are baffled. They can't work out what's wrong."

"So you think—"

"You said it yourself, Father. It's against the natural order of things, physical or metaphysical," she continued, interrupting the priest before he had a chance to voice his own opinion.

Rache paced back and forth now, her newfound discovery troubling her. Although she spoke to Fr. John, the push behind the thoughts was really for herself.

"He said the energy released...the energy required...was intense. If the guardian is really part of who we are, then that part has been taken from Kell...ripped out, if you will."

"And now she's comatose while he has human form," he said, finishing her thoughts.

"As long as he is here—"

Fr. John quickly shook his head before continuing. "No, I'm not sure...this is purely speculative, Rache," he said.

"Is it? What other explanation do you have for it?" she asked.

"I take your point. But we must be careful with our assumptions."

He told her that telling Malak this could cause him harm—not in the ordinary sense of the word, but at a deeper subconscious level. Malak's journey into this world was extraordinary. It was reminiscent of a hero's journey—sacrificial.

Fr. John thought back to his early years when he'd attended a seminar by the writer Joseph Campbell, whose book, *The Hero with a Thousand Faces*, had intrigued and fascinated him. Campbell believed that the hero's journey was not an abstract theory or quaint belief of ancient peoples, but a practical model for how we live our lives. Campbell had taken the mythological structure of the hero's call to adventure, the refusal of the call, the accepting of the call, and engaging in the adventure and explored the notion of sacrifice in the hero's journey. Studio executives in Hollywood often applied this to movies. But Fr. John realized this was no movie—the characters in this piece were real. The life of a young child hung in the balance, and the hero of this piece, Malak, was indeed flawed.

He explained this to Rache, this concept that we all have our own journey, that we receive a call and follow or refuse that call. He told her he had chosen to be a priest and knew he would encounter tests and trials and obstacles on his journey. He told her to look at herself, at her journey. Something happened to make her take on the mantle of a police officer. He explained that this was her call, and she had answered it. She was now engaged on her journey as a police officer and would encounter tests and trials on her road to discovery.

Malak was the same—well, in some way similar. He had answered his call. But in his answering, he'd upset the natural order of things.

Rache was more than impressed. Had Danny mentioned her sister's death to Fr. John? No, why would he? She developed a very healthy respect for the old priest. He hadn't judged her. Even when she'd been rude to him, he hadn't judged her. Shit, he'd been right on the money. Ruth's ordeal and subsequent death had propelled her into joining the police academy and going on to become a detective.

"How will it end? My journey, I mean," she asked.

"Who can say?"

She sat down again. "This case…it has similarities with what happened to me," she told him.

Fr. John nodded. "I wondered…about your hostility. I wondered."

"It's so unfair, Father, it's so unfair."

She told him. She told him everything about her childhood and Ruth's attack and death. How it spurred her to join the police, to do something of value. She told him how she had wanted to kill Malak when she'd discovered him at Kell's bedside.

Telling him had been a release for her. It was not like telling Danny and Susan. That had been more of a cleansing, an unburdening of survivor's guilt. This was different. She couldn't exactly put her finger on it, but it was different.

"I suppose you think I'm a bad person?"

"For wanting to kill Malak? No, I don't."

She looked at him, perplexed.

"You made a choice. You chose not to pull the trigger."

"Could be because of the oxygen."

"Maybe, but you still didn't fire," he said, smiling at her. "Your sister was Kell's age when she died?"

Rache nodded.

"And if you catch this killer, you think it will in some way atone for what happened to her?"

The question was brutally honest, and she respected him for it. Rache knew the answer was yes. She had spent half her life seeking atonement, seeking forgiveness. She supposed she saw this case as some kind of closure.

"Yes," she said quietly.

CHAPTER 32

ACHE SWUNG BY ST. KILLIAN'S, leaving Fr. John at the gates, and drove the few blocks to the precinct. She had made copies of the Mason file, and she needed them now. The answer lay hidden in there somewhere. Danny's file on Mr. Jakes was too limited. If she were going to prompt Malak's memory, she needed more. She needed her file.

Approaching the precinct, Rache thought back to what she'd discussed with Fr. John. They had differed on some aspects of the priest's take on things. Rache was sure that Malak's presence had, in some way, contributed to Kell's coma, whereas Fr. John was unsure. Either way, they had both agreed not to confront Malak with this news. "The shock may be too much for him," the priest had warned her. Rache had concurred. But she had to do something. If her theory proved to be true, then the longer they waited, the worse it would be for Kell.

And what was she to do with Malak? The FBI had him top of their wanted list. Even if he did remember, and they were able to identify Kell's attacker, what then? She couldn't have him stay with her indefinitely. If she were seen to be helping a felon, she could go to prison. Should she confide in Danny? No, she'd hold off a little longer. Sure, she had concrete proof of just who Malak was, but she needed to be able to ID the real killer. And to do that, she needed her file!

Setting out to retrieve her file had, in some way, taken her mind off the biggest problem she now faced. Where was Malak? She had discussed this at length with Fr. John, recounting the time that Malak had told her he'd returned to Kell's house. This had only worried Fr. John even further. "Rache, it's paramount we reconnect him with

226

his world," were his parting words as he'd stepped from the car at St. Killian's.

Rache had agreed, but she'd no clue where to find Malak. She couldn't involve the precinct. If they got so much as a sniff of his whereabouts, they'd have a dragnet sprung with Franks and the whole weight of the Bureau tucked in behind it.

This posed another problem. Rache wondered, should Malak be faced with overwhelming force, how would he react? She remembered the escape at the precinct. Nobody had been injured. When he'd been cornered at the hospital, he'd chosen to run rather than take on the cops.

Suddenly it occurred to her. Could Malak make a distinction between those who meant him harm from those who wanted to help? The image of Mr. Jakes—his pummelled body—floated before her. It hadn't fazed Malak. Had he attacked the pimp, employing such force as to almost smash the life out of him, because he believed the pimp deserved it? Or had he been merely unaware of his own abilities? The questions were coming thick and fast. Were the concerns of Fr. John—that as human form, Malak could become corrupted— were these concerns bearing fruit?

Malak had all but killed the pimp, she figured. But he could have easily overpowered him. Had he employed this force willingly? What had he said to her? "Lots of new things." That was it, she thought. Malak had been unaware of this fantastic strength. Yeah, he didn't know how he'd healed himself.

The brief examination had helped Rache reaffirm her belief in Malak being a force for good. She'd run this by Fr. John the next time she saw him. But she knew she still had to tread very carefully where Malak was concerned.

Opening the double doors to the precinct, she felt a whole lot better. She'd still needed to find him, but something told her it wouldn't be long before he found her. She decided not to get in any conversations with colleagues at the station. Get in and out.

Rache made her way up to her office on the third floor without incident. The place looked decidedly empty. *Guys must be out*, she figured. She eased the drawer to her filing cabinet open. Her file was still there. Fishing it out slowly, she heard a noise behind her.

"Rache!"

The sound of her name being called caused her to jump.

Danny stood in the open doorway. "Little jumpy…how'd it go at the hospital?"

The blank stare said it all.

Danny quickly closed the office door. He whispered to her as he looked at the file in her hand. "The interview with the pimp, how'd it go?"

Rache recovered quickly. "Oh, he was out cold. Doc said he could be like that for the next twenty-four hours. I'll swing by tomorrow." *Shit*, she thought. She hated lying to Danny.

He nodded but didn't look too convinced. "Thought you were staying home today?"

"I'm feeling much—"

"And what were you doing at the church? You find religion or something?"

Rache threw him a quick smile. "I wish. You know me, Danny."

"I thought I did."

"What the hell does that mean?" She rounded on him. "You got something to say, spit it out."

Her words and their delivery caught him off guard, giving her the upper hand. Danny remained silent, not sure how to respond.

Rache quickly picked up on his hesitation. "Danny, I was feeling a little better, so I thought I'd get the file and look over it tonight. I went to see your uncle because as you know, in these cases, sometimes the smallest thing a person remembers can break a case. Fr. John was the only one to talk to him outside the precinct, and we got no sense out of him when we had him here."

Danny seemed convinced. "I'm sorry, Rache… It's just that you've been acting weird. I don't doubt your commitment, really I don't."

She put the file on her desk. "Danny, if I'm weird, it's because of Ruth. You were right. This case is too close to home for me. It's got my head all spun." Damn, she hated lying to him. But she couldn't tell him the truth.

Danny nodded, more convinced now. *Of course*, he thought. This case had to have messed her up a little, got her all jumpy. "Rache, go home. Look at the file if you wish. But you'd be better off getting some sleep. I'll see you here in the morning, okay?"

She smiled at him again. "Thanks, Danny. Just don't tell Franks, huh?"

"Go home," he said, opening the door for her.

Rache skipped out past him.

***

Walking up the steps to her apartment, Rache's one thought, now she'd figured she was in the clear, was where had Malak gone? He needed to be more careful. If he's spotted, it's over. She needed him to go over the file. She had appeased Danny, but for how long? She knew he'd be pissed when he found out. She'd have to deal with that when it happened.

Rache turned the key in her door and walked in. Malak was standing in the middle of the room. Although this seemed strange, it didn't upset her. She was just relieved to see him.

"How did you get in?"

"I can open locks and things."

Rache thought back to the precinct and to the hospital. He had simply walked out of both. How many other powers did he have? He'd swatted the pimp like he was Superman, plus he'd taken out two cops in the hospital stairwell. Could he ultimately control his abilities? That was the question.

"Where did you go?"

Malak avoided her gaze.

"Malak?" she said in a questioning tone.

"Kell is my responsibility. She needs my protection," he said, his own tone confrontational now.

Rache froze. Her worst fears had just been realized.

"Malak...you...you didn't go to the hospital."

"Kell is still in danger. I can feel it."

"Malak, you can't go there. The police will shoot you or arrest you, and I won't be able to help you. Kell is protected now. We have officers guarding her."

This seem to calm his anxiety. He relaxed a little. "Everything is wrong. I feel helpless."

"I understand, but until we have concrete proof of who attacked Kell, you have to stay here. You cannot leave, understand!"

Malak nodded.

"Malak, I need to ask you some more questions, okay?"

"Okay."

Sitting at the kitchen table, Rache asked him if he was aware of his abilities. He wasn't sure what she meant. She tried to explain, but found herself thinking about his role in this world and the problem it had created for Kell. Best stay off this subject, she figured. Get him to examine the file.

Rache told him that the file contained everything they had on Kell. It could help. It was important that he take his time. If anything stirred, he should tell her. No matter that it made no sense to him. If it was a faint or strong memory, everything was important.

Malak seemed eager to participate, which only encouraged Rache. She had given him a focus, telling him it would help Kell. Rache explained that the FBI had suspected that a Mafia don, Lorenzo Caruso, ordered the attack on Kell and Joe Mason. Malak did not respond to the name. She explained that the family had been taken into witness protection and had to change their identities, that the mafia had tracked them, and that the FBI believed the Caruso family had ordered the hit on them. But all of this was news to Malak. He told Rache that because he'd become separated from his world and from Kell, he'd no memory of this. His first memory in this world was fighting off Kell's attacker, and even that event was hazy. Rache assured him everything would be okay. He was to take his time, and they would both look at the file together.

Rache spent the best part of an hour going over Kell's file. But it had been a waste of time. Malak had recognized nothing. Rache felt deflated. She could tell that he was upset. It had been useless.

"This is of no help," he said.

She couldn't let him see it had upset her too. "Give it time," she replied, trying to be upbeat.

"We don't have time. Kell is in great danger."

"How...how do you know?'

"I can't explain. I just know."

Shit, she was frustrated. She had been sure that seeing Mr. Jakes would rekindle his memory. Rache had convinced herself Mr. Jakes had attacked Kell. But the pimp's mug shot hadn't even raised an eyebrow. Malak had looked at much of the Caruso clan, photos she'd copied from Franks, but he hadn't given them a second glance. But something had him stirred up. Some shattered fragment of a past memory must have surfaced, and it had agitated him. The priest had told her that Malak was subject to not only the physical laws of this world, but to human emotions and constraints. This was the barrier, she thought. His human form constrained him. But what could she do? She needed a break. She needed a way in.

Rache's cell phone ringing broke the spell. She checked the caller ID. It was Danny. Pressing the little green telephone symbol, she held it to her ear.

"Hey, Danny."

Danny seemed excited as he spoke to her. He told her they'd got a break, and she needed to come in immediately. Franks was going to make a big announcement, and the captain needed her in. Was she up to it? It was important.

Excited by his message, she told him she'd be in as soon as possible.

When she'd thought she'd convinced Malak not to leave, she headed out. Danny had sounded positive, and Malak was at her place, albeit reluctantly, but it could only mean one thing. It was to do with the Caruso family. Franks was a pain in the ass, as Danny had succinctly put it, but she was thorough. Rache had to give her that. Must have been why they were all out earlier. It had to be. If it was not connected to Malak, this announcement had to be connected to the Caruso family.

**

Sitting in Captain Woods's office surrounded by coconspirators, Danny felt like Judas. He knew now the price of betrayal. Yeah, he'd felt bad that Rache had lied to him. Well, Rache had a way of being economical with the truth. He knew deep down that what she'd done had come from a good place. But his actions were nothing short of betrayal. For that reason, he dared not look at her.

Rache sat directly opposite Franks now. Perched to Franks's left and right were Danny and Captain Woods. Both Rache and Franks were locked in a game of eye-chicken. Who would blink first? he thought. Danny was embarrassed. Franks had bullied him with an ultimatum—get Rache to come in, in the next hour, or kiss his pension goodbye. She'd arrest him as an accessory.

"To what?" he'd asked.

"Obstructing a federal investigation," was the answer he'd been given.

Danny'd grown accustomed to Franks's hyperbole, so he'd told her he'd better run it by the captain. Woods had ordered him to cooperate with Agent Franks. So he'd called her. He'd felt bad. Neither Franks nor Woods had told him what lay behind the deceit.

So Danny sat, embarrassed, unable to look Rache in the eye, as Franks and Rache stared at each other.

Rache closed her eyes. When she opened them, she didn't look at Franks but rather at the small band of silver that had been the cause of this summons—this trial! Lying on the desk in front of her was an ornate silver bracelet. It was broken. Rache looked at it a moment. She'd wondered where she'd lost it. It had troubled her for days. Her sister had given it to her, all those years ago. It was the last present she'd received from Ruth, and it had meant so much to her.

"I'm waiting, Detective."

Let the cocky bitch wait, thought Rache, but deep down she knew her bravado was only to keep her own spirits up. She was in deep shit.

Her eyes involuntarily moved to the bracelet. She knew where she'd lost it. It had been ripped off her wrist in the alley at the back of the church. In the two days that followed, Rache had been so preoccupied with Malak and other events, she'd thought she'd misplaced it. It was rare that she'd take it off that she'd been unable to think of where she'd put it.

But this small bracelet stared up at her now.

"So it's mine," Rache said finally.

Captain Woods closed his eyes.

She knew it was a blow to the captain. Franks had a smug look on her face. Man, she wanted to punch her.

"Would it surprise you that we recovered this in the alley where we found the pimp, Mr. Jakes? You know, the one you've conveniently forgotten to question!"

Rache shrugged. She'd give this bitch nothing. Let her figure it out for herself. Problem was, Franks was good at putting it together.

Franks took her silence to mean only one thing. Detective Fischer was in this up to her eyes. "It has specks of blood on it. Not his, but from your old friend, Mr. Likes-to-Disappear. We even found his print on the pimp's gun. What I want to know...what we would all like to know, Detective Fischer, is what exactly you were doing there?" Franks said, smiling sardonically.

Rache shrugged. "Hey, maybe I lost it."

Franks nodded as if it were a possibility. She picked up the bracelet, examining it. She turned it over in her hands. "Love, Ruth," she said, reading the inscription. "How touching."

Rache was angry now. One more word from Franks, and she was afraid she'd lose it.

"It's broken," said Franks, tossing it back on the table toward Rache.

Rache's first instinct was to reach over and retrieve it. It was a mistake!

As her fingers touched the bracelet, without warning, Franks grabbed Rache's wrist, pulling back her sleeve and exposing a recent scar. Rache's wrist was marked where the chain had dug into her flesh during her assault by Mr. Jakes.

"You're interfering with a federal investigation!" Franks screamed at her.

"A federal fuck-up, you mean." Rache was mad as hell. "If you'd done your job properly, Joe Mason would be alive today, and his little girl wouldn't be in a fucking coma."

Captain Woods stood up. He had to make some effort to intervene; otherwise, he feared he was about to witness some kind of showdown.

"Enough already!" he shouted, holding up both his hands. He waited a second or so before continuing as Rache and Franks continued to face off, neither prepared to back down, the atmosphere electric.

"Okay," he murmured. "Agent Franks, Danny, can you both give me a moment with Rache?" He looked at Danny, who stood almost immediately. He wanted out of there as fast as possible. He was pissed that Franks had used her muscle as a federal investigator to get him to hoodwink Rache. Danny walked out without a word.

Franks stood. She glared at Rache, snapping her head back at Captain Woods for the briefest of moments before glancing at her watch. "You've got five," she said before storming out.

Captain Woods closed the door after her. He was weary, weary of the whole damn mess. What had Rache gotten into? Was she hiding something? If so, why? What had she to gain? Franks could bring the whole thing crashing down, and Rache was playing some kind of game. It didn't make sense. How could she profit from it? She wanted the perp as badly as anyone. None of it made any sense to him.

He spent the next five minutes arguing with her. He told her he would have no option but to suspend her, pending further investigation. Rache knew she could tell him nothing. How could she? If she told him the truth, he'd see it as an insult.

"I'm sorry, Captain, but if you're going to suspend me, I understand."

"Understand...understand, Rache? I *don't* understand. You're one of the finest officers I have, but you have to give me something. I can't cover for you."

Rache looked at him. She remained silent.

The captain shook his head. He asked for her gun and badge. Rache gave it to him without protest. He told her he was suspending her for two weeks. She'd have to attend a hearing the day after tomorrow, and she should contact her union representative. The Feds would carry out their own investigation, independent of the department, and she'd be on her own on that one. He suggested she get a good lawyer. Franks wanted blood.

Rache half smiled at the mention of a lawyer. "Captain, I know I've no right to ask, but can you give me an extra day on the hearing?"

Woods shook his head. "I can't, Rache, it's out of my hands. But I don't see why you won't come clean with me."

"Believe me, Captain, you don't want to know."

"I'm sorry, Rache."

"Yeah, me too. I'll need the car to get home. I'll drop it back tomorrow."

"Look, keep it until the hearing," he said, feeling bad about not being able to cut her more slack on the hearing.

"Thanks."

CHAPTER 33

DANNY DROVE A VERY IRATE Agent Franks over to County Memorial. So much had happened in such a short space of time that he had difficulty in keeping pace with it. Rache had been suspended. He couldn't believe it. Two weeks suspension, plus she'd have to attend a hearing. The Feds were pissed too. Withholding evidence and deliberate obstruction were federal offenses, both of which carried custodial sentences. Rache had gotten herself in deep, no doubt. The bitch beside him had a real pair of brass ones—she wanted to put Rache away bad. It had all happened too quickly. He'd waited, at the captain's request, outside while he and Rache had their own powwow. Franks had spent the couple of minutes pacing back and forth, glancing at her watch every few seconds, as though she could in some way speed up time.

Before the five minutes had expired, Rache had walked out of the captain's office. Flashing her plastic smile, Franks had brushed past her. Danny had watched as Woods had with resignation closed the door behind Franks. The captain need not have bothered. Rache had only just begun to tell Danny about her suspension when Franks burst out of the room and had almost accosted Danny.

"You're with me," she'd said, addressing Danny. "You're to have nothing more to do with Detective Fischer, or I'll have you suspended too, understand?"

Joe and Theo had been outside, and they'd heard it all.

Danny blinked at Agent Franks. "With you, how?" he'd asked.

She'd told him he was to accompany her to the hospital to question the pimp. She wanted to establish what his relationship was to Rache and the perp. Danny wondered himself what the connection could be. Rache never did anything on a whim. It wasn't in her nature.

Now, as they pulled into the hospital, he began to have his own doubts. She knew where the perp was. She was covering for him. But why? He'd have to talk to Rache. But this bitch had acquisitioned him, as she put it. The chat with Rache would have to wait. He'd keep his thoughts to himself. No way he'd tip Franks to what he was thinking. No way!

Mr. Jakes looked in serious discomfort. Lying on the flat of his back, one arm in a cast, his only view since regaining consciousness was the fluorescent tubing on the ceiling. The motherfuckers had chained his good arm to the rail, and he had to piss through a tube. The nurses had been spoon-feeding him as a precaution. He looked a broken man. The severe injuries had done nothing to tone his temper. He had complained constantly, demanding more and more morphine for the pain. The doctor who'd reset his pelvis with several screws and fixed his arm had told him he'd make a full recovery—he'd be in traction for some time, but he'd recover.

He had two problems, as he saw it—Tony Caruso and his stable. That dumb fuck Carlos would be trying to run his bitches now! But Mr. Jakes was not the sharpest tool in the woodshed. His stable was the least of his worries.

As he lay on his back, he heard voices at the door. "Hey, shut the fuck up, I'm trying to get some rest here."

A moment later, he was staring up at Agent Franks.

"And who might you be, Mother fucking Teresa?"

Franks flashed her badge, the federal insignia silencing him instantly.

"Jason Patrick Summerville, what the fuck are you doing working for the Caruso family and Tony Caruso in particular?"

Mr. Jakes didn't quite know what to say. He didn't know who was a worse devil. Mother Teresa here or that pyromaniac Tony.

"Hey, I'm an innocent victim. I was attacked by some fucking lunatic and his coked-up bitch—" He stopped abruptly. He was now looking at a photo of Kell Mason.

"Recognize her? Found this photo in your car—well, that pigsty you call a car. Got it out of your glove box, and guess what?"

"Tell me."

"It's got your grubby little prints all over it."

"So?"

"Did you know that the kid in the photo is part of a federal investigation?"

Mr. Jakes bit his lip. The psycho ginny had pulled one on him. Fuck Tony Caruso!

"Didn't think so," Franks continued, showing him the photo of Malak. "This the guy?"

"Hey, that's the fruit. Man, he was revved up!"

Franks snapped her fingers. Danny passed her a photo of Rache. She showed it to Mr. Jakes.

"That's the bitch! Broke my fuckin' arm, man. Bitch." Mr. Jakes spat out the words.

Agent Franks smiled. Well, that was put to bed. She figured she could arrest Detective Fischer and get a warrant for her apartment. She leaned in toward Mr. Jakes. She stroked his cheek. He was scared now.

"Mr. Jakes, you will testify against Tony Caruso, or you will do the hardest time known to man. I will personally see to it that everyone knows you're a kiddie rapist, a child killer, and we'll have you in general population, no cozy solitary for you."

Franks leant over and kissed him on the forehead, smiled, and walked out, leaving Mr. Jakes staring back in total shock.

CHAPTER 34

"**M**ALAK, I'VE BEEN FORCED TO take two weeks leave. I'm to have nothing more to do with the Mason case. I'm lucky they left me with the car. I can't call my captain and tell him Kell Mason's guardian angel can solve this," Rache said, pacing back and forth. She needed to think. Two days to the hearing. She was in too deep. Malak had just informed her he needed to see Kell. He had to make physical contact. He thought if he could read her field or something like that. Rache hadn't really been listening. She was too busy just trying to keep her head above water. She needed a plan.

Rache walked about shaking her head. She had removed her shoes and was walking barefoot across the cherrywood floor. Everything was closing in on her. Malak turned the damaged bracelet over in his hands. Rache had dropped it in his palm, as if to emphasize the point that the break she'd thought she'd get had turned out to be an ambush.

At the back of the bracelet, engraved into the silver were the words "LOVE RUTH." Malak looked at it, examining the etching.

Rache stopped pacing. She slumped onto the couch now. The realization had dawned on her. She had to get him out of the city. Sooner or later, Franks would put it all together. But what about Kell? If her theory about Malak's presence were true, then hiding him away would only be counterproductive. Should she try and have Kell moved? If she contacted Liz and explained... It was all useless. She had no clue what her next move would be.

Suddenly, she felt Malak sit beside her. Before she knew it, he'd taken hold of her arm, turning her hand over, and had placed the bracelet on her wrist.

It was good as new!

Rache was shocked. She turned her hand over. It was perfect. Not a trace of damage.

"How...how did you do this?"

"I can manipulate molecular structures."

"Thank you," she said, touching the metal. Then a thought occurred to her. "This manipulation thing...it's new to you, huh?" she asked, sitting upright, previous dark thoughts dispelled in an instant.

"Yes, I think so."

Rache was off the couch, dragging Malak with her. "Don't you see, now...now is the time to look at the files. You did this without thinking—you did it instinctively."

"I don't understand," Malak said, puzzled by Rache's sudden burst of enthusiasm. He had fixed the bracelet to help her. He had felt her distress, and he had realigned the silver to please her. He hadn't expected this response. But Rache was excited now. She was sure that he had worked this at some subconscious level, tapping into who he really was—a guardian, not the physical form that stood before her. Now was the time, she was sure of it.

"What you did was subconsciously done. Now is the time to study Kell's file," Rache urged as she led him to the table.

But Malak was shaking his head. "When I crossed, I lost contact with Kell. I was arrested, and we were separated. I cannot read her field from here."

"Field...what field? No, no, don't answer."

Rache sat him at the table. She opened the file.

"This will not help."

"Please, Malak, just trust me."

They studied the file for hours. But he remembered nothing. Rache was feeling depressed. She'd been so positive at first, thinking if he subconsciously looked at things, it might trigger a memory or even a fragment of a memory. But they'd got nothing.

They had pored over every inch of the file. She knew it backward at this stage. Nothing! Rache had convinced herself that if Malak could instinctively repair her broken bracelet, then that instinct could be used on the file. But the photos of Tony, Bruno, Chazz, and even Mr. Jakes had prompted nothing. She'd even risked a photo of Kell, taken shortly after been admitted to hospital, only too aware that it was Malak who'd caused her injuries. She wasn't sure if he'd remember. She heard Fr. John's voice in her head, urging her to exercise extreme caution when approaching Malak on this subject. Malak had literally shocked the life out of Kell.

Would this set him off?

Rache hadn't been sure. Nonetheless, she showed him the photo.

Nothing! Malak had just stared blankly at it.

Her head began to throb. She poured a glass of water and swallowed a couple of painkillers. Should have had it x-rayed, she thought as she ran her hand over the protruding lump at the back of her head. Her fingers explored the point of impact where Mr. Jakes had brought the butt of his .38 revolver crashing down on her skull. It was still tender, and Rache had been living on painkillers for the past few days. She had upped the dosage only this morning. Their effect had begun to diminish, and she'd increased the amount. If only she could get some rest. The pain in her head had become acute now, and she had difficulty focusing. The pages were becoming blurry.

Rache decided to give them both a break. Looking at the file had only seemed to agitate Malak, exacerbating his deep sense of uselessness even further.

She told Malak she needed to rest, that he should look at the file later. She'd get a few hours, and they'd try again later. Malak said he would continue to look at the file. Closing her bedroom door, she glanced back at him as he sat hunched over the table.

Rache slipped under the covers. She promised herself a few hours. Her head was ready to explode now. *Two days*, she thought as she closed her eyes. *Two days.*

Malak's memory was a total bust. If she could just get him to connect. Rache drifted off in moments. Although she had partially recovered from the attack, it was still only forty-eight hours previously that her body had taken a pounding. That combined with the mental torment she felt at being suspended and Malak's inability to be of any assistance sent Rache into a deep sleep. It was simply the body's way of dealing with the severe trauma. Rache had intended only putting her head down for a few hours, where in fact, the events of the previous few days sent her into a semi-comatose state. She would not wake for another fourteen hours.

Rache dreamt little, at least not until the moments just before waking when dreams are most common and most vivid. In the few moments before she began to wake, Rache found herself once again back in the alley behind St. Killian's Church. Mr. Jakes had her in a stranglehold. He was pulling her backward down the alley, laughing as she struggled to free herself. He threw her forward. Rache hit the ground with a thud, the pain in her body magnified. Everything seemed darker. She struggled to move. Suddenly, a bright light illuminated the alley, reaching into every crack and crevice, banishing the darkness as the alley lit up with a strange yellow glow. The light vanished as suddenly as it appeared. Rache forced herself to keep her eyelids shut tight, hoping they would adjust to the near total darkness. She allowed them open.

Then she saw him. It was Malak! She felt relieved. Despite being in a deep sleep, some part of her recognized that she was simply replaying a past memory. She knew that in moments, Malak would take on the pimp. A sense of calm began to wash over her, warming her. She could almost taste the feeling of relief. Mr. Jakes was talking to him now, as he did before. Rache smiled, knowing what was to come next. But Malak was crying. What was wrong? She could hear Mr. Jakes laugh. Why didn't Malak take him? Rache looked back over her shoulder. Her heart jumped in her mouth, causing her whole body to convulse. Mr. Jakes had *Ruth* in a headlock, his gun pointed at her young head. Her sister looked just as Rache remembered her. Rache felt sick.

"Not so brave now, are you!" Mr. Jakes shouted at Malak.

Malak remained rooted to the spot.

"Help her, Malak, help her!" Rache pleaded.

Mr. Jakes stroked Ruth's cheek. Rache looked at her sister. Ruth smiled back at her just as Mr. Jakes fired twice into her head.

Rache screamed in horror.

She leapt out of bed, her heart pounding. She tried to wipe tears from her eyes. She heard distant banging. Rache was completely disorientated, the sound of gunshots still ringing in her ears. The late September sun streamed into her bedroom, its brightness reminding her of the light in her dream. *Wait*, she thought. Someone was banging on her door. *Oh shit, Malak!* she thought.

Rache threw on her bathrobe and rushed out of the bedroom. Malak was gone, but she could hear voices now. Her head was a little clearer. She could make out the voice. It was Agent Franks! *Great!* she thought.

Struggling, she opened her apartment door. Two federal agents brushed by her, followed by a very irate Agent Franks. Franks pushed a piece of paper into her hand. "That's a federal search warrant."

It took Rache a moment to process what was happening; her brain still hadn't clicked into gear. The dream had really thrown her, and Franks's Gestapo tactics had surprised her.

Both agents began to search her place. Danny walked in sheepishly. Rache threw him a "what the fuck is going on?" stare. Danny said nothing. Rache grabbed Franks by the arm. Franks remembered Rache's strength from the incident at the hospital.

"You want to tell me what's going on here?" she shouted at Franks.

Franks looked at her arm. Rache's grip was growing stronger. "Let go, Detective," Franks said.

Rache relaxed her hold. "You haven't answered my question."

Franks ignored Rache. She told the agents that she wanted a thorough search.

"Agent Franks, you better have a good reason—"

"That pimp gave us a positive ID on you with the perp in the alley—together. Well, what have you got to say now, Detective Fischer?" Franks demanded, folding her arm in a smug gesture.

"What are you talking about?" Rache demanded. But she knew she was in trouble. *Shit, that lowlife had given this bitch an ID*. She couldn't let Franks get the upper hand. She had to fight her corner.

Franks was on a roll. "Well, let me break it down for you. The pimp, the one you so conveniently ignored to question, put you and the suspect in the Mason case…" Franks paused dramatically, milking the moment. "Your escapee, in the alley together two days ago. Your bracelet also puts you at the scene, and the pimp's ID confirms it," she continued, smirking at Rache.

Rache just nodded. She glanced over at Danny. She could hear the Feds searching her bedroom, and it pissed her off, big time. She wanted to smack this bitch in front of her. But Rache held her cool.

"You'd better be sure of your facts here—I mean really sure. I don't know what you're playing at, but you'd better have some proof, not just the word of some bottom-feeding lowlife. That son of a bitch killed two kids last year, and you're going to take his word over mine."

For the first time, Franks felt a little unsure of herself. She hadn't factored that into the equation. Outwardly, she showed no emotion, but she began to have some doubts. Was this true? Yeah, she knew he was a pimp and a scumbag, but if he'd killed two kids… *Shit*, she thought.

Franks turned to Danny. "This true?"

Danny told her it was.

"And you forgot to mention this because…?"

"Well, you just seemed so happy in your little world. Besides, the scum walked on a technicality." He knew he was taking a risk, but he'd trust Rache's judgment, crazy as it seemed, over that of this… this crusader.

Rache was grateful for the backup. She owed Danny. She'd lied to him and would probably have to lie again. But she was grateful for his show of solidarity here.

"What exactly do you think you are going to find?" Rache demanded of Franks. She'd only said the words when she remembered the file. She tried to be casual as she walked over to the kitchen table.

The file was gone!

"Detective Fischer, I don't care that you've been decorated. I know you're involved with this guy, and when I have enough evidence, I'll—"

"You'll what?" Rache shouted at her.

The ferocity startled Franks.

Rache suddenly felt she had her. Franks was on the back foot a little. Rache knew she needed to get to the next level.

"You sad bitch, you fucked up, and Joe Mason is dead. So now you're wasting time over here when you should be looking for the killer. You let the Caruso family back into Kell Mason's life, and they destroyed it. You gonna file that in your report, huh?" Rache roared at her.

Franks didn't know where to turn.

But Rache wasn't finished.

"You should be ashamed. She was your responsibility, and now you're looking for a scapegoat for your incompetence."

The two Bureau agents stood behind Rache now. The cop was right, they felt. Their search had proved fruitless. They had nothing.

Franks needed some way out. She used their presence. "Well?" she demanded, glaring at them.

"Nothing," they replied.

This only added insult to injury. The word itself had meaning. Franks had nothing, nothing on Rache, and nothing to help her on the case.

Rache looked back over her shoulder at the agents, then back at Franks. "Happy now?"

Franks was not about to lose face in front of her men. She squared up to Rache, staring her in the eye. "You're hiding something, girlie, and I'm going to find it." She turned abruptly and walked out, with both Bureau guys following quickly in her wake.

Danny held back a moment. "I gotta go, Rache...been assigned and all...ya know," he said, glancing over his shoulder, making sure Franks was well out of earshot.

"I understand, Danny," she said, placing a hand on his arm.

Danny turned to leave.

Rache called him back. "Sorry about before. Not being truthful, sorry."

Danny nodded. "Rache, I trust you. I just hope you know what you're doing."

Rache hesitated a moment, not knowing what to say. He was her friend and her partner, but she couldn't tell him the truth.

"So do I, Danny. So do I."

Rache sat on the couch a long time, a shroud of gloom begin-ning to envelope her. They had linked her to Malak. The game was nearing its end. She had to do something. It was only a matter of time before they pieced it all together. That lowlife, Mr. Jakes, had fingered her. It was ironic. Scum—at least he wouldn't hurt any more kids, she thought. Injuries aside, he'd been found with a photo of Kell. He was looking at a long stretch.

That was it, she thought. Kell's photo! Who'd given it to him? It had to have been the Caruso family. Rache was certain they'd ordered the hit, the original hit. They'd given Mr. Jakes the photo of Kell. The fool had kept it. The family must have put pressure on him to finish it. Kell must have got a good look at him, Rache thought. Or maybe he went back on his own accord. This last bit frustrated her. If Kell had gotten a good look at him, surely Malak must have seen him also. As Kell's guardian, he'd have to have seen him. Yet Malak had no recollection of this. Alive in this world, he must have fought Mr. Jakes, and Mr. Jakes had fled. It was beginning to make sense to Rache. It had to be Mr. Jakes.

The bullet, she thought, the one that had struck Malak. It would be the same as the one that they'd found in the ceiling, mak-ing Mr. Jakes the shooter. If ballistics could match these, it would put Mr. Jakes at the scene.

Could he have done it? she wondered. She tried to think through the timeline. Rache suddenly felt reinvigorated. She jumped off the couch, showered, and within a few minutes stood, pen in hand, at the whiteboard in her office.

She thought her theory was pretty solid. She worked out the time frame on the whiteboard. Standing back away from the board, she studied it now. Everything was beginning to make sense.

Mr. Jakes had shot Joe – attacked Kell – fought Malak – fled and had beaten the kid, Jessie, in the alley behind St. Killian's. The timeline fitted. Rache was sure of it. She and Danny had responded to a call at 8:20 a.m. The cops, Officer Marks, and his partner had answered a call a little after 8:00 a.m. That meant Mr. Jakes had attacked Joe and Kell just before. Could have been quarter of?

Damn it, she thought. She was right. It gave the pimp ample time to get to the alley. But then a thought struck her. Why stop to beat the kid? He would have needed to put as much distance between himself and the scene as possible. *What am I thinking?* she told to herself. He's stupid. Dangerous but stupid. If he were stupid enough to leave the photo of Kell in his glove box, he'd be stupid enough to stop and beat on Jessie. These guys were all the same.

Rache remembered the beating he'd dished out to the kid. He'd been manic. Perhaps he'd been pumped up after the fight and the shooting—that would explain it. Had to be, she thought. He was hyped after the fight. Another thought struck her. Had Mr. Jakes recognized him in the alley when he'd attacked her. Had Mr. Jakes recognized Malak? Had to be. That's why he'd fired. *Shit*, she thought.

So it *was* Mr. Jakes!

The question bothering her now was how could she prove it? She'd need the bullet, the one that shot Malak. It had to be in the alley. No, wait, she told herself. The Feds had his gun. All they had to do was run ballistics on it. Bet Franks hadn't even thought of that. Rache felt a smug sense of satisfaction creep over her. Franks would look foolish. She had to force herself to concentrate. *This isn't about you, Rache*, she told herself. *This is about finding a killer.* Well, they had the killer. She just needed to prove it. But she was off the case. She'd call Danny on her cell.

Rache looked about. She couldn't remember where she'd left it. Damn it, she'd left it in the bedroom. Had the Feds taken it? They were slippery enough to pull a stunt like that.

Rache rushed into her bedroom. No phone! She looked down beside her bed. It had fallen between her locker and bed. She remembered leaving it on the bedside locker yesterday. Had she slept that long? Yesterday began to come back to her. Malak had remembered nothing. He hadn't given the mug shot of Mr. Jakes a second glance. That part worried her the most. If he'd fought him, how was it he'd no memory of it? The fight had taken place in the physical world, not his. He was not Kell's guardian in the true sense when he'd fought Mr. Jakes, so she wondered why it was he'd no recollection.

Rache turned on her cell phone, punching in her pin code. She walked slowly back into the living room.

Rache almost jumped out of her skin. Standing in the center of her living room was Malak. He held the folder they poured over the previous evening.

"Malak, where have you been? Franks was here looking for you. I've got to get you out of here." She was out of breath. Rache checked her cell for messages. Malak didn't respond. He just stood there looking at her.

"Do you think some crimes are unforgivable?" he asked, his voice breaking slightly.

"What? Where did you go? Hold on, just want to check messages." Rache held the cell to her ear.

Malak did not move. Rache stared at him.

"Do you think some crimes are unforgivable?" he asked again.

He had a strange look to him—distant, removed. Something was up. He was different. She couldn't put her finger on it. But something was wrong. Should she tell him about the timeline? No, better get the ballistics report first. She searched his face. Had he being crying? His eyes were red, and he looked strange.

"Malak, you okay?" she asked. What was it he'd asked her? Something about forgiveness.

Her answering service cut in. "You have one new voice message," a hollow-sounding metallic voice told her.

"Rachel—"

"Hold on," she said, holding up her hand.

Danny's voice was loud and panting as his recorded message was replayed to Rache. "Rache, Rache, it's me. Mr. Jakes is dead...had his neck snapped. The cop guarding him is also dead—same MO, Doc says... Doc says it would take someone of immense strength to kill them. Franks is going mental. She wants you arrested. You'd best come in. Call me as soon as you get this message."

Rache stood frozen to the spot. She couldn't move. All the timelines didn't matter now. The stakes had been raised. She watched Malak as he stood in front of her. She became aware of the increase in the flow of blood in her carotid artery as the adrenaline rush kicked into action, pumping rich oxygenated blood to her brain. She tried to focus her mind. It was impossible. The artery was throbbing now. A voice in her head was screaming at her now. *Get out, get out,* it urged.

But Rache couldn't move. One thought above all immobilized her.

Had Malak killed Mr. Jakes?

Rache was adrift on a vast sea of emotion, tossed about like a bobbing cork on its giant waves of doubt. Had he remembered? He was staring at her now. For the first time, Rache was frightened of him. Had he heard Danny's message? She couldn't ask him out straight. She'd have to be careful. If he'd killed Mr. Jakes…had he killed the officer guarding him as well? Rache now recalled the dangers in Fr. John's warnings. Had Malak embraced this darker side the priest had referred to? Had he become corrupted?

Malak took a step toward her. Rache took two back. This surprised him. He took another step toward her. Rache held her ground. Malak held up the folder.

"This is no use."

She was trying to control herself now. These were unchartered waters she was entering.

Rache suddenly felt very alone.

"Malak, have you been to see Kell?" she asked, her voice barely audible.

"Kell is my responsibility. She is my responsibility—not yours!" he shouted at her. "She needs my protection."

"That is not what I asked you," she said, trying to keep her voice even. She had a pain in the pit of her stomach. It had begun to spread up into her chest, making breathing difficult for her. *He must spot something's wrong*, she thought.

But Malak hadn't. His attention was elsewhere, his mind tormented by what he perceived as failure—his failure to assist Kell! He was aware that he was Kell's guardian, and the separation from her was now causing him great distress. Reading through the file with Rache had only serve to exacerbate that feeling. He was like a tree, uprooted, its purpose forever changed. Malak knew that in his desire to help Kell, he had chosen an action that had ultimately separated him from her, effectively making him useless. He was the tree torn from the soil, its roots now exposed. Without his connection to Kell, Malak had begun to wither.

"I cannot read her field from here. I cannot help here from here." He turned away from Rache, walking over to the window. Malak stood a moment, his own mind in turmoil, trying to reach a decision. Turning back to Rache, he shook his head.

He has *been crying*, she thought. Oh shit, he's killed them! Rache again remembered Fr. John's warning. *He's not human, Rache, it's a mistake to think so*, he'd told her. Fr. John had explained that because Malak now possessed human form, it was also possible that that form could somehow become corrupted. Murder could well be on his agenda now, and if this were true, it could lead to a host of other problems.

Malak was staring at her in that strange manner again, the way he'd looked at her when they'd first met.

Does he see me as a threat? Rache wondered. Now, she was genuinely frightened! She was exhaling slowly now in an effort to remain calm.

Malak stopped in front of her, locking eyes with her. "This is no use! I cannot help her from here," he said, placing the folder in her hand. Then Malak simply walked out.

Rache watched him close the door. What could she do? Was Malak a killer? She couldn't contact Danny now. She'd better get out of the apartment. If Franks arrested her, she'd be no use to anybody. She'd go to the priest. It was all she could do.

Rache tossed the file on the table. It slid across, and some papers flew out. Better hide it, she figured. Just to be safe. No, better still, she'd take it with her.

Rache picked up the couple of papers that had fallen out. She bundled them together. One photo in particular caught her attention. Suddenly, she felt sick. She was staring at a mug shot of Mr. Jakes, a red *X* drawn through it.

Oh no, she thought. *Don't let this be.*

CHAPTER 35

RACHE FELT BITTERLY COLD. THE huge church did nothing to alleviate her somber mood. A dark air of unrelenting pessimism hung in the place now. Moving uneasily in the pew, she recalled her excitement at discovering Malak's true identity, that as she'd walked in to the church to meet the priest, a sense of discovery lay before her. Now, all she felt was cold. A bitter chill had penetrated her being, and she couldn't shut it out. Her close association with Malak these last few days had helped to all but banish her demons, but now they were back I full force. The contemptuous demon of despair was toying with Rache now, goading her, challenging her to face up to him or lie down under his unrelenting attack. Rache knew she had to quell him; she had to shut him out if she were to have any chance of figuring out her present predicament.

She studied Fr. John's face in the low light of the dying candles, watching as one flickered and spat, its life over. A thin plume of smoke rose from its charred remains. Another dark shadow was added to Fr. John's already worried face. *Come on, Rache, snap out of it*, she told herself. Feeling sorry would achieve nothing. Bottom line: what did she believe? That was it—what did she believe?

Fr. John held the photo of Mr. Jakes. The red *X* drawn through the mug shot stared back at him. It was very unsettling. He carefully placed it back in the open folder beside him. Closing the folder on the pew, he slowly turned to Rache. An uneasy quiet hung in the air. Fr. John began to shake his head as he addressed her.

"Rache, this is very serious. If Malak killed Mr. Jakes and that officer, we're in a world of trouble."

"Do you think he did it?"

It was the question that had troubled her the most. If Malak's desire to help Kell was so great it had catapulted him into this world, was he capable of murder? All the evidence pointed to him. The action he had taken to save Kell's life had come from a good place. There was no malice of thought in it. He had merely wanted to prevent a murder. He was her guardian. It had to have been a good reason.

Years of working as a homicide detective had forced Rache to divide people into good and bad. Yeah, she knew there were gray areas, but basically people fell into two categories—good and bad. Malak was a force for good. He had saved Kell. Shit, he had even saved her own life. No, she shouldn't doubt him. He was here for a purpose. That purpose had to be good. But she thought back to the phone message. "Only someone of immense strength," Danny had said. Could it have been Malak? She was driving herself mad.

So she now sat in the front row opposite the impressive marble altar and listened to Fr. John's theory. Sure, the evidence pointed a guilty finger at him, but it was only a few weeks ago that they had arrested him at the scene—all the evidence back then had said guilty.

Rache closed her eyes in an effort to still all thought. She had a choice to make. Her logical mind told her to accept the possibility that Malak had now murdered. It was telling her the same as before. He was guilty. Yet another force was at work, tugging at her, pushing to believe in Malak, to give him a chance—to have faith. That was it!

It hit her like a thunderbolt. She had never really understood the meaning of the word. Faith was a surrender to an infinite possibility. Could she embrace it in a way akin to reckless abandonment? It went against all logical thought. It contravened all her police training. She couldn't explain her decision, but if it came down to it, she'd bet on Malak.

Fr. John was not so sure. He was more buying into the theory that Malak had come under the influence of his human form.

"No. I can't believe he'd do that. I know he's been holding something back, but I don't think he'd do that," she whispered.

"Rache, we have to consider the possibility."

"You said it yourself. He is her guardian."

"Malak isn't human. It's a mistake to think so. He has human form, but he is not human."

"He's an angel, huh?"

"Yes, but he may be corrupted. He is subject to the laws of our world. And if he thinks killing this pimp will help Kell, then that may be okay by him."

"What about the cop? Why would he kill that officer?"

"I don't know. Kell is his charge. He must protect her, and if he's somehow…broken, then that may now include murder."

"I don't understand it. I just can't accept this. I can't believe he'd cross—"

"Look, Malak is here now, and if he's killing people, we are in a world of trouble," Fr. John repeated, interrupting her.

"What should I do? The Feds are after me. They think I'm hiding him. I've got no backup from the department cos I'm suspended, and now they'll have him pegged as a cop killer."

Fr. John could feel her distress. She had placed immeasurable belief in Malak. Was she merely reluctant to let go, or did she really believe? He knew it wasn't just reluctance. She believed totally in Malak. She'd gone "all in," and now her life, career, and future rested on the turn of a card. In all his years as a priest, he'd rarely witnessed such faith. He had to help her. No matter what, he would help her.

He removed the folder that lay between them, edging closer to her. Gently, he placed his hand on hers. When he spoke, he spoke softly. "Okay, Rache, tell me everything he said before he left."

Rache tried to recall what he'd said. None of it made sense, really, but she told the priest as best she could.

"Oh yeah," she said, remembering. "He kept jabbering on about not being able to read her field. He couldn't read her field…whatever that meant."

Fr. John was staring at her now. She saw it in his eyes.

Recognition!

"What is it, Father?" she asked.

"The field…the luminous energy field…of course," he said, snapping his fingers.

"What…what are you talking about?"

"Remember, when we first met here, and you asked me about the light in the painting," Fr. John said, turning around in the pew and pointing at the painting of the Ascension that hung at the far end of the church.

"Yeah, I thought it was a story you'd made up to explain the colors," she said.

Fr. John looked at her. "So you believe in angels but not in the energy field?"

Rache looked away, embarrassed. "You're right, Father. I've seen so much in the last week. But you're right. I do believe. I just don't understand it."

"Rache, I don't fully understand it either."

"But what has it to do with Malak?"

Fr. John explained that in his opinion, Malak needed to reconnect with Kell's energy field. He told her that all humans possess an energy field that surrounds the physical body. This energy field existed since before our birth and will endure long after the physical body has rotted and decayed. The field dwells outside of time but manifests in time by creating new physical bodies lifetime after lifetime.

He told her to imagine she were enveloped in a translucent multicolored orb, pulsating with greens and blues and blinding yellows. Just above the skin run streams of incredible light, along the acupuncture meridians. Between the skin and the membrane of the luminous energy field is held a reservoir of light energy. It is a sea of living energy and is as vital to life and health as the oxygen and nutrients that are carried to our cells by the bloodstream.

He told her that we humans are essentially light bound into matter. Every living thing on this planet is composed of light. Everything is made of light, bound and packaged in different forms and vibrations. Physicists who study subatomic matter know that when you look deep enough into the very heart of matter, you will find that the universe is made up of vibration and light.

He pointed to the painting. "It would be a mistake to think that the accounts of light that surrounds the Christ are merely legends or stories. They depict the luminous energy field—the invisible matrix that informs the body."

"I think I see, but I'm not sure," Rache said. "You're saying we are fundamentally a light form, bound to the body?" She tried to grasp what exactly the priest was saying. It was new to her. "Bet they didn't teach you this in Sunday school, Father?" She was unable to resist the jibe.

"No, Rache, they did not," he replied, smiling at her. "They most certainly did not."

"Where then?"

He told her that when he was a young priest, he'd worked in a mission deep in the heart of the Peruvian Andes. There, he'd witnessed an Inka shaman cure a native child diagnosed with terminal cancer. It was his first contact with the shamanic rites of the Inka. He explained that modern medicine was new to the world and that people had been curing disease for tens of thousands of years, otherwise the human race would have died out long ago.

"I appreciate the story, but how does this help us, and what has it to do with Malak?" she said, interrupting him.

He could sense her impatience, but he needed to cover some background. So he told her. He told her how he'd studied the shamanic rituals. Had the church discovered this, he'd probably have been thrown out—excommunicated. The shamans had taught him about the luminous energy field, the chakras, and the shaman's way of seeing. He told her that the energy field contains an archive of all our personal and ancestral memories, of all our early-life traumas and even painful wounds. These records or imprints are stored in full color and intensity. All imprints contain information that informs the body.

It suddenly hit Rache. Malak had lost contact with her imprint—her field. As a physical being, he needed the physical proximity of Kell to read her imprint. It was why he'd told her he'd been unable to read her field.

She told Fr. John her thoughts.

He concurred.

"That's why he went to the hospital the first time. We…I believed it was to kill her. But we didn't know then he was her guardian," Rache said as the enormity of the priest's revelation began to set in.

"I think you're right, Rache. He needs to make contact with her. All of Kell's memories are stored in her imprint. It makes sense."

Suddenly, a thought occurred to her. If he'd lost the connection with her and her memories, how did he know Mr. Jakes was the attacker?

"Maybe he wasn't," Fr. John suggested after Rache had voiced her thoughts.

"But it fits, Father. The timeline fits."

"Because it fits doesn't make it true. You believed Malak guilty of the attack—but that turned out to be the opposite."

Rache thought about it. He had a point. She'd wanted to kill Malak. When she saw him standing over Kell in the hospital, she'd wanted to shoot him. She'd never jump to conclusions again.

"You think he'll head for the hospital?" she asked.

The priest nodded. "He has to. He needs to make contact with her."

"Jesus Christ, Father, NYPD have him pegged as a cop killer. They'll shoot him on sight," she said, standing up. "I gotta get to him."

Fr. John grabbed her by the arm. "Rache, this FBI agent will have you arrested if you're spotted. Let me go."

Rache shook her head. "No, Father, I need you here, in case he comes back. I'll take my chances. I still got some friends."

This energy field explained a lot. Malak would have been part of that. Of course! When he became human, he could only have human memories. Rache began to feel a new sense of purpose. She had to find Malak.

Father John walked the length of the aisle with her, accompanying her outside to her car. Running down the steps, Rache already had her car keys in her hand.

Rache opened her car door. Fr. John held it open as Rache climbed in. As he leant in, Rache keyed the ignition.

"Can't talk you out of this, Rache, no?"

"Father, I have to do something," she persisted.

The priest nodded. "Okay, but if you—"

Rache's police radio suddenly burst into life, a female voice issuing instructions, the words stinging both Rache and Fr. John.

"All units, all units, we have shots fired at Washington Memorial. Officers down, I repeat, we have shots fired, and we have officers down."

The color drained from Rache's face. "That's Kell's hospital. Shit!"

The voice continued, "Be advised, suspect is armed and is the suspect wanted in connection with the Mason murder. Repeat, suspect is armed."

What the hell was Malak up to?

"Go," Fr. John said, slamming the car door.

Rache spun the car around, heading south on Eighth.

Would she get there in time? she wondered. If she did, what could she do?

CHAPTER 36

THEO AND SUSAN WERE THE first to arrive on the scene. They had been discussing Rache on and off, all day. Danny had filled them in on the sequence of events that had taken place with Franks back at Rache's apartment. But that was before news had filtered through that the perp had killed Mr. Jakes and a young cop. They had both died a brutal death. The cop had had his neck snapped at the third thoracic vertebrae with Mr. Jakes suffering the same fate. Try as they might, neither Theo nor Susan could figure out Rache's connection. Rache was involved, that was certain. She'd all but confirmed this to Danny. Why? Theo had wondered. It was so out of character. But Mr. Jakes was dead, and someone had just attacked the cops guarding Kell Mason. They were grateful that Franks hadn't arrived.

Hurrying along the corridor, they wondered what had happened. Surprisingly, a rather calm scene greeted them. Directly opposite the nurse's station, the door to Kell's room was closed over. A couple of nurses busied themselves, both on the telephone requesting x-rays and trying to aid a very dazed cop. The cop in question sat on a chair, his head tilted back. Sam Weir was shining a pencil light in his eyes, asking him to look left, then right, checking his head movement. Dispatch had reported shots fired.

What the hell was going on? wondered Theo.

Sam continued to examine the officer. Susan watched a moment before tapping him on the shoulder. "He going to be okay, Doc?" she asked. She too had expected some kind of carnage. The scene was surreally calm. Something was wrong here, she thought. Where was the perp?

"Yeah, he's a little shaken, but he'll be fine," Sam replied, clicking off the light and standing up.

"And the kid?"

"Kell is fine," Sam told them.

Theo sat beside the cop. "What do you remember?" he asked. "Take your time, son."

Before he answered, Susan jumped in with another question. "Wasn't there an FBI agent here?"

"He's upstairs," Sam said. "He suffered some blindness, but he'll be okay."

Theo showed the cop a picture of Malak. "This the guy?"

The cop nodded. "I...I think so. Man, he came out of nowhere. He's strong as an ox. Picked me up like a doll. I could feel his strength. He must have used some kind of flare on us."

"Flare...what do you mean flare?" Susan asked, intrigued at this development.

"I didn't see too much. He blinded us somehow. Last thing I remember, he went into the kid's room. I felt terrible, I was sure he was going to kill her, ya know."

"But she's okay?" Susan said, turning to Sam.

"Yeah, she's fine," he added. "In fact, I'd say she's improved a little. Her pulse is stronger, and her pressure is back up. She's still in a coma, but—"

Theo didn't let him finish. He stood up, taking Susan aside, making sure they were well out of earshot before voicing any opinion. "I don't like this. What do you make of it? I mean...why not kill the kid? I know it's terrible to say, but...he had enough time."

"I don't know, Theo. But as you say, he had enough time, and he didn't do it! What does that tell you?" Susan replied, herself puzzled.

Rache was tied in to this, big time, but how? And more importantly, why?

"Tells me I'd like to talk to Rache," Theo said.

Susan agreed. They were both reading off the same page.

What the hell was Rache up to?

The cop was up off the seat now, his legs wobbling under him, making any movement impossible. Sam made him sit back down.

"Detective," he said, addressing Theo as he eased himself back onto the chair.

Theo and Susan walked over to him. "Yeah."

The cop looked up at both of them a moment. "I'm not sure, but after I was blinded, I swear I saw a light. I know it sounds crazy, but as I lay on the floor, I could have sworn I saw a really bright light coming from under the door," he said, looking over at Kell's room.

Theo glanced over at Sam, who shrugged. Before they had a chance to ask him, Franks breezed into the scene, accompanied by an entourage that wouldn't have looked out of place at a rap concert.

Franks was her usual abrasive self. She'd commandeered a car from the precinct and had made Danny her unofficial driver.

She didn't want to hear from the police or the medical team. The suspect had just been spotted in a two-storey building close to the West Side Highway. A SWAT team was en route, and she needed all available personnel. They were all with her now.

***

Driving south on Eighth, Rache listened intently to the police radio for any snippet of information. Silently, she thanked the captain for letting her hold on to the car. She'd never have picked up on Malak's whereabouts otherwise. She thought about him now. Had Malak hurt anyone? Dispatch had reported shots fired and officers down—there had been no reports of fatalities. Rache didn't worry about Kell. She had a gut feeling that she'd be okay. Malak must have gone to the hospital to try to reconnect, she figured.

Damn, she'd been so dismissive of Fr. John when he'd tried to explain the energy field the first time. If only she had listened, she might have been able to help Malak earlier. She gripped the wheel intensely as she thought about it.

Don't beat yourself up, Rache, she told herself. *Concentrate on the here and now!* She had to get to Malak before the cops. If they thought he was a cop killer... *Well best not go there,* she told herself.

She continued down Eighth Avenue, swinging right onto West Forty-Fifth Street, crossing Ninth and Tenth avenues, and headed toward the West Side Highway. She'd discovered that he'd been spotted in the industrial complex close to the United Parcel Service's building. A SWAT team was already in place. The radio had also informed her that the FBI was at the scene, and NYPD were to defer to the Feds.

Shit, thought Rache. Franks would be there.

Rache slowed, as she reached the intersection between Forty-Fifth and Twelfth. A SWAT truck rushed by, punching through the red lights. Rache decided to follow. She pulled the sedan in behind the Special Weapons and Tactics truck, careful to maintain her distance. She didn't want to lose sight of them, nor could she afford to get too close. Franks would have called SWAT, and judging by Danny's tone in the message he'd left on her cell, the mad bitch wanted blood.

As she followed the truck, Rache could see that the Feds had established a very tight perimeter. The place was sealed—she'd never get through!

"Suspect last seen entering United Parcel Service building. Be advised, suspect is still armed," the dispatch voice burst from the radio.

Malak, Malak, why have you got a gun? she wondered. The thought really frightened her. Why would he need a gun? Rache pulled over to work out her next move. She knew she couldn't approach the cordon. If spotted, she'd be arrested, and it would be over.

Rache was certain that Franks would have ordered her arrest. Shit, she'd practically dared her to! She studied the perimeter as best she could, the enforced distance affording her little opportunity to assess anything of real value.

WHAM!

Out of nowhere, Malak landed on the hood of the sedan. The force was so great that it crumpled the metal. Rache screamed with the shock. Malak glared in through the windshield, catching her eye. His stare was wild. Rache was out of the car in a flash. In the briefest of moments, she'd made up her mind.

"Get in, get in," she ordered.

Malak hesitated, unsure of himself. She noticed the gun too. It was pushed into his belt. Malak was drenched in sweat. His hair was soaked, and a fountain of perspiration gushed down his cheeks. He looked as though he'd just run a marathon. But it was his eyes that scared her. They had the same look when they'd first arrested him—wild, untamed, and—dare she say it?—crazed.

Malak panted nonstop as he tried to talk. "Rachel, I…I…"

"Get in!" she shouted again. She could hear a siren now.

Malak heard it too. He jumped off the hood and dived into the back of the sedan. Rache was back in the driver's seat in seconds, turning the car about and heading north, away from the scene. She had to put as much distance behind her as possible.

Malak tried to catch his breath. He was manic.

"Stay down," Rache ordered. "Stay down, or we'll be spotted."

Malak remained crouched behind her seat for the next couple of blocks. The few minutes gave him time to get his wind back.

"Malak, what happened? Why have you got a gun?" she asked, glancing at him over her shoulder as she continued her route north.

"I remember, Rachel. I remember it all!"

"What? No, stay down," she told him as he moved to sit up. She drove on a couple more blocks.

When she thought it safe, she pulled the car over, killing the engine. The Feds thought they had him cornered in the UPS building. It would buy them some time.

"Malak, why have you got a gun?" she demanded.

"Here, take it," he said, handing it to her.

Rache grabbed it, quickly stashing it in the glove box. Malak moved himself into the passenger seat. He was less manic now, his eyes searching her face.

"You've been to see Kell?"

It was more a statement than a question.

Malak nodded. "Yes. I had to. I needed to reconnect—to see this as her guardian. I needed to read her field," he said, his breath still labored.

Fr. John was right.

She told Malak what Fr. John had said. Malak agreed, but added that he'd only taken the gun because the FBI agent had fired on him.

"Were you hit?" she exclaimed worriedly, her hand reaching out and involuntarily touched his chest. She could feel his heart pounding.

"No," he replied, his own hand taking hold of hers. Malak looked at Rache. His brown eyes shone with intensity now. "I remember. I remember it all. I know what happened to Kell."

Malak explained that the police file had been no use as it had referred to and documented everything that happened after he'd crossed. He explained that they'd been looking at it from the wrong side. He'd lost contact with his world when he'd crossed, the energy surge so great it had literally wiped his memory clean. He'd arrived in a state of great confusion and immediately had to confront Kell's rapist.

"Who was it, Malak?" Rache asked, almost tentatively, in some ways afraid of the answer.

But Malak remained silent. He looked at her, his stare intense. "You thought I'd killed that pimp and the cop, didn't you?"

Rache looked down, ashamed.

"It was Bruno Caruso. Tony's cousin. Tony sent a hit man, a guy called Tommy the Trigger, to kill Kell and Joe Mason," Malak told her, his recall crystal clear.

Rache listened intently as Malak explained that both he and Rache had been looking at the file exclusively from a human standpoint. He needed to reach Kell and read her imprint to search the memories that were stored in her energy field. It was here he had to make contact, not as a person, but as her guardian. This enabled him to connect with his world, with his memories. Once he'd read her imprint, he'd remembered everything.

Malak thought back to that fateful morning—the morning when he'd entered the world of the physical. As Kell's guardian, he'd tried to warn her of the imminent danger. Tommy had approached the house, his mind fixed on the assignment ahead. Malak had desperately tried to stop Kell from opening the door, but nothing had worked. After Tommy had shot Joe and chased a screaming Kell upstairs, all thoughts of finishing his task and fleeing had vanished. His mind was now singularly focused on feeding his compulsion.

Kell Mason had become his next fix—the need to rape and torture overriding all reason. Malak explained to Rache that all people experience thought before they act. It is manifested and held in their luminous energy field. So when Tommy had pursued Kell upstairs, Malak knew the nightmare that lay in store for her.

"So you created this body? To help her, you made this body?" she asked. She had been silent, unable to speak, her attention completely given over to Malak as he revealed the events of that morning.

Malak nodded.

"That's why you took human form? To fight him off?"

Malak nodded.

Rache steadied herself before asking the next question. "So how does it work? How do you create a body?"

Malak thought of Kell and what he'd done to her. He had looked at Tommy, gauging his height and weight. Based on that reference, he had generated a physical body capable of tackling Tommy. The whole process had taken a millisecond. The energy required was so immense, it had ruptured Kell's eardrums, bursting blood vessels in her eyes and nose, causing her to lose almost half her body's blood. Kell had suffered a massive internal shock. Her organs were electrified with high voltage, and brain wave patterns were rewired. Kell's body had simply shut down.

Malak explained all this to Rache, his voice breaking as he did. Rache could sense his hurt at what had happened. Malak's journey into the physical realm had almost ended Kell Mason's young life, she thought. *Best steer clear from this*, Rache told herself.

"So you were literally born into this world, all of a sudden having a human body?"

"Yes." He told her that nothing could have prepared him for life in the physical world. He had shot out of Kell's body with such force, it had shredded her clothing and ripped apart her bed linen. He felt as though he had been born into a large vat of molasses. Whereas before he could move freely, now he was restricted by the physical nature of his body. He had knocked Tommy backward off the bed, causing him to shoot, more out of reflex than desire. Tommy had used his gun to threaten Kell as he beat her. It was in his hand as he straddled her, pushed up under her chin in an effort to make her more compliant. In an attempt to frighten her even more, Tommy had stupidly removed the silencer, thinking the gun looked more sinister without it. Tommy had never intended to shoot. He'd meant to choke the life out of her, and the thought had added to his heightened frenzied state.

"So you fought this Tommy guy?"

Malak shifted in his seat. He seemed a little relieved to be off the subject of Kell's injuries, his attention on recounting his fight with Tommy, on how he'd struggled to overpower Tommy.

As he talked, Rache was putting a mental picture together in her head of how the room had looked when the forensics team had worked it. The energy release Malak had talked about must have done most of the damage. Malak's fight with Tommy added to the destruction they'd discovered. Shit, it was a miracle Kell was still alive. *Don't go there, Rache,* she urged herself.

The fight with Tommy had only lasted seconds, but its intensity had completely drained him. He was sure he'd broken Tommy's shoulder as he'd crashed him into Kell's dresser. "The fight was intense. I can't explain it, but operating in the physical world for the first time caused me great difficulty. Everything was new," he said, searching for words now.

"So what happened?" she asked.

Malak told her that the fight had finished before he knew it. He had collapsed beside Kell. Tommy had used the opportunity to escape.

"And when the police arrived, they found you, not Tommy?"

Malak nodded. "That's right. I was exhausted. I couldn't even lift my arms up. The thirst—the thirst was maddening."

It all made sense to her now. No wonder he hadn't recognized Mr. Jakes. He'd fought this Tommy person. She felt so much better. She knew she was in deep shit. But it didn't matter somehow. She'd been right about Malak.

"So it was Tony, not Lorenzo, behind the hit?" she asked.

"Yes. Tony Caruso had become insane with grief when the courts had sentenced Lorenzo to life. Lorenzo was almost sixty and had been Tony's only father figure as well as his mentor. Tony had wanted Liz to suffer as he had suffered."

"So he decided to kill her family," Rache volunteered, disgusted at what she was hearing.

"Yes," Malak said simply. Pausing a moment, he continued. "Lorenzo is dying. He has terminal cancer. He thinks if he repents now, the afterlife will be easier for him."

Rache was shocked at this knowledge.

"And will it?" she inquired, fascinated.

Malak looked at her a moment. "We should go."

"Malak?"

"It doesn't work that way, Rachel. It doesn't work that way!"

Rache started the car. Malak refused to be drawn on the subject. The afterlife. She had always scoffed at the notion, thinking it was just that—a notion. She had so many questions. But Malak had become somewhat withdrawn, like he was keeping something back. Rache was unable to pry anything more out of him.

She had to get out of town!

Thirteen miles long and two miles wide, Manhattan was growing increasingly smaller for Rache Fischer. They knew where she lived, and soon they'd tip to the fact that Malak had evaded them. The hunt would be on. She had no option. She had to leave—and she had to take Malak with her.

She knew immediately where she'd go.

Maine.

After Ruth's death, Rache had suffered a near breakdown. She'd become uncontrollable at home. She fought constantly with her parents. She'd become disruptive at school, even punching out a couple of her friends. Everybody felt for the Fischers, but politely, Ira Fischer had been told that he'd have to sort out his youngest daughter. It was David who'd suggested it to his father. His cousin, Hannah, who as a ten-year-old had come to America, lived north of them in Maine. She'd survived the war in Europe, immigrating with her family to the United States. Both her parents were dead, and Hannah, having never married, lived alone, way up beyond Moosehead Lake, close to the Canadian border.

David had driven up one weekend, laying out the situation at home. Hannah hadn't hesitated. Rache had spent the best part of a year in the company of her second cousin, and little by little, life had returned to some semblance of normality for her.

Looking back, Rache didn't know if she'd have made it without the help. At fifteen, she'd only felt deep guilt and resentment at herself for what she perceived as cowardice. She'd left her sister to face her ordeal alone and fled. Rache had not been able to deal with the guilt, and it had manifested itself in uncontrollable anger. At fifteen, she had processed none of the social skills to cope with her torment. Bottom line, Rache had hated herself.

But Hannah had helped her, encouraged her, and tutored her. It hadn't been easy. Hannah lived an outdoor rustic life. She had a small farm, and she made Rache work. Rising early every morning, Hannah had worked her mercilessly, the physical activity exhausting Rache. But it had also been therapeutic. Rache had spent almost nine months at Hannah's farm. In the beginning, she'd resented Hannah, but she grew to first respect her, and then to admire her. Between the physical labor and the long evening talks, Rache had found some sense of peace. But her hatred of injustice had never diminished. It was the influence of Hannah's philosophy that had persuaded Rache to join the police academy.

"If that is what is truly in your heart, then you should do it," she'd told Rache.

They'd kept in touch. Birthdays and such. No one knew about Hannah. As the years passed, the family had lost contact. But not Rache. She needed Hannah again.

Rache almost smiled to herself. Hannah would shit herself when she found out who Malak was.

But Rache knew she could only stay a couple of days. It was just to give her time to think. She knew she'd have to turn herself in. But before that, she needed a plan.

CHAPTER 37

LOOKING AROUND HER BEDROOM FOR what she figured could be the last time, Rache hastily pulled a light travel case from her closet. She hadn't used it in over a year. Last year, she'd flown down to Florida and spent her vacation on the Keys as a free woman. Now, she was a fugitive running from the law—the law she'd sworn an oath to defend. The sense of irony was bitter in her mouth.

She hurriedly threw in a few items—a sweater, a clean blouse, and a pair of jeans. Life on the farm was rough and ready. She'd only stay a few days. She'd work out what to do. Hannah would help. She was sure of it. Rache had decided to hold off calling her until she was almost there, her mind made up to use a payphone.

Rache zipped her case quickly now. She'd have to move fast. Two days—that should do it. Two days, and she'd contact Danny. Turn herself in. But right now, she had to move.

Malak was dead set against the plan. He'd told her she'd only cause more harm than good. He'd suggested that he should surrender to the police. No way, she'd told him. He was the only one who knew what had happened, and the Feds were not going to believe a word he said. In their minds, he was the killer!

Rache had another problem. She didn't know how long his memory would last. She needed his undivided attention to build a case against Tony. It was her only hope. If she could somehow finger Tony, she'd have a chance. Later, she'd explain how she came by the information.

Malak was calling her from the other room. What was he saying? "We can solve this now, Rachel! You don't need to run!" he shouted.

Malak was sure running was a bad idea. Everything had happened at lightning speed. He had reconnected with Kell, and the

268

memories had followed in milliseconds. A torrent of images had downloaded in the blink of an eye. Past, present, and future had rushed upon him.

He'd evaded capture easily, but he'd pushed the body to the limit of its capabilities. The reconnection had infused Malak with extraordinary sensory perception. His speed and strength had multiplied tenfold. He had easily outrun the chasing cops. Running from the cops had been no problem, but there was something from which there could be no escaping—his past. The torment of which cut him now. Like a thousand stabbing knives!

Rache had been wrong about his memory. It would not be a flash in the pan. His memory had returned, whole and intact. One past incident in particular had pained him to the point that he'd pushed the body he now possessed to near destruction. The past could be dealt with sometime in the future—strange paradox. But right now, he needed to concentrate on matters closer to hand. He needed to help Rachel! He was adamant that running served no purpose. Rachel was in enough trouble. Fleeing now, in this rushed manner, would only worsen her predicament. Rachel needed to turn herself in. He needed to convince her of that. Tony Caruso had ordered the hit on Kell and Joe Mason. Malak was sure he could convince her not to run.

He knew he owed it to her.

Rachel was talking to him now, what was she saying?

He had to convince her not to...

Rache stood in the open doorway, her hand empty, the travel case on the bedroom floor where she'd dropped it. She was crying nonstop, and he couldn't understand why. He asked her what was wrong. But Rache couldn't answer. Her throat had seized, constricting her vocal cords. She was unable to get the words out. Her eyes were fixated on him, her body rocking back and forth. Slowly she articulated the words. "Why...why do you call me Rachel?"

Malak was perplexed. "It's your name," he replied.

Rache shook her head. "Everybody calls me Rache, but you called me Rachel. All the time in the car, you called me Rachel. Only my family call me Rachel. How is that, Malak?"

He stood there, silent.

Rache pushed on. "When we first met, you called me Rachel. You called me Rachel, and Joe hit you," she said, thinking back to the morning in the interview room. "You'd recognized me, hadn't you? How is that? In the precinct, you'd recognized me. I'd never met Sarah-Jane or Kell, as she is now, but you'd recognized me." Her voice had become louder now, the tone accusatory, the questions coming thick and fast.

"I want to know how?"

Malak looked away, unable to meet her eyes. He glanced up at her a moment, his dark lashes fluttering, his nervousness evident.

Rache continued. "At the church, you told Fr. John that you'd failed, failed in your assignment. But you hadn't failed. You'd saved her. You weren't talking about Kell, were you? You were talking about a different assignment?"

"Rachel, please. We need to think about surrendering to the police. Running serves no purpose," Malak said in an effort to distract her. He knew where her questions would lead.

But Rache persisted. "You looked at me from the patrol car... back at Kell's house, when we first arrested you. God damn it, you looked at me and recognized me."

Malak looked as though he too was about to burst into tears. He stared down at the floor, his front teeth gnawing incessantly on his lower lip.

Rache's heart beat loudly in her ears now. Images and sounds danced before her. It all made sense. She'd employed the concept of timelines throughout the investigation, but she'd missed the biggest one of all—Kell Mason's age!

"Little girl's a Kell Mason, sixteen." Susan's voice played in her head now.

"Ruth is dead seventeen years—and we all miss her," her brother David was speaking to her also.

"We believe that at the moment of conception, you are a human being. And at that moment, you have a guardian." Fr. John's was the last voice to call upon her.

As it faded, she turned to Malak.

Malak was crying now. Small salt tears rolled from both eyes, splashing onto his dark cheeks.

"You failed because you'd let another young kid die. Time moves differently for you. Seventeen years could be what—a moment?" Rache was out of breath, her eyes stinging. "Tell me it isn't true, Malak. God damn you, tell me it isn't—"

"I couldn't help her, Rachel...I couldn't help her," he blurted.

His words paralyzed her. Her whole body froze. This was quickly followed by a spasm as every muscle in her body twitched in unison. She seemed to convulse. Rache vomited the contents of her stomach onto the floor as she doubled up. The pain was too great. She started to shake, the action completely involuntary. The tears came again. She couldn't stop them.

It was him...Malak...

Malak was Ruth's guardian!

He moved toward her. He didn't know what to say. He could feel her pain, the intensity of her emotion rolling over him, but he could offer no help.

Rache backed slowly away from him.

He was back in the hospital now. Kell's energy field had liberated his memories—good and bad had washed over him. The memories of his previous assignment, Ruth, were as vivid as those of Kell Mason. He remembered why he'd crossed. His inability to help Ruth had forced him to break the rules—to cross and save Kell from the same fate! Malak knew the price would be high.

He inched forward toward Rache now.

"Don't touch me, don't fucking touch me!" she screamed at him.

"Please, Rachel, you need to know."

"Get out, get out, get out!" she shouted at him. She was sick again.

Malak looked at her. There was so much he needed to explain about Ruth's death. It had all come too quickly. Once he had reconnected with Kell, it was like opening a floodgate. All his memories had come surging back in a blinding torrent. A billion images had struck him at once—memories of not only Kell, but of Ruth and other past assignments had shot through him, lighting up his entire body. It was this glow that the half-conscious cop guarding Kell had witnessed.

Malak knew that for the guardian, like humans, memories are not a contingent of time and space. We can recall childhood memories spent at the beach when we are sitting on a snow-peaked mountain in our sixties. He had been bombarded by images, and he needed to tell Rachel the truth.

But Rachel wouldn't listen. She was screaming hysterically now. If he didn't leave, she'd attract attention.

Malak turned his back on Rache and walked out.

Rache had no idea how long she'd spent on the floor. She had simply collapsed to the ground, shaking violently, as Malak had left. Curled up in the center of the room, she'd cried until she had no more tears.

It was over.

Malak had been Ruth's guardian, and he'd let her kill herself. Part of Rache wanted to die. She didn't care anymore. Franks could arrest her. She'd go to prison for sure—she simply didn't care.

She became vaguely aware of strong arms lifting her off the floor. A familiar voice was whispering in her ear. But Rache was almost catatonic. She rocked back and forth, unaware of the world around her. A bubble of isolation began to envelop her. She was withdrawing more and more into herself. But the voice was louder now, more demanding. She could feel herself being drawn toward it. The comfort of oblivion beckoned. But something pushed her back toward the voice.

"Rache, Rache... What happened? Rache...Rache?" the voice was asking.

Slowly, her eyes began to open. It was Fr. John!

He shook her. He'd no idea what had happened, but it had to have been bad. Rache wasn't even lucid. He had to get her on her feet. He hauled her up, placing one of her arms over his shoulder, supporting her with the other at her waist. He walked her round and round the room, constantly calling her name.

The movement helped orient her a little, and slowly, she was able to focus. In a few minutes, she was able to string some thoughts together.

Fr. John helped her onto the couch. He sat beside her. "Tell me, Rache. Tell me what happened."

Rache was slowly coming back to some semblance of normality. But she still couldn't speak.

Fr. John left her on the couch. He made them both some strong coffee, remembering her visit. Setting the steaming mug in front of Rache, he turned his attention back to the kitchen. He searched under her sink, pulling out some cleaning products. Fr. John quickly set about mopping up her vomit.

Rache sipped the strong coffee as he worked. She was exhausted, but she couldn't help wonder at his thoughtfulness. When she'd finished her coffee, Fr. John made her drink another one. He sat beside her, all the while talking to her, hoping to keep her focused. He held her hand, his eyes soft as he asked her to tell him what had happened.

Rache felt terribly wounded by Malak. She could feel bitter resentment rising at the mere mentioned of his name. But she told the priest—everything.

Fr. John listened intently but never interrupted. "I see," he said when she'd finished. Rache was close to tears again. Picking up her cup, she sipped her coffee.

He nodded, placing his cup on the floor. "You are angry at him?" he asked finally.

"Yes," she said simply.

"Rache..." he began, stopping abruptly. A thought had just struck him. "That's it," he said.

"What?"

"The trigger! I knew there had to have been a trigger. His inability...his failure to help Ruth was what forced him to cross." Fr. John leaned back on the couch. "That must have taken great courage," he remarked.

Rache couldn't believe what she'd just heard the priest say. She repeated it.

"Courage?" It was something she didn't understand. What was he talking about?

"Think about it, Rache. How does he get back? To his world? He has risked all for this child. How does he get back?"

Although the pain she was experiencing continued to unnerve her, Rache had to admit that the priest had a point. Malak was trapped here. She tried to make sense of it. Why had he helped Kell and not Ruth? But Fr. John was right. Malak was not human, but he had assumed the form to rescue Kell. And now he was trapped, belonging to neither world.

"Your sister's death devastated your family, but it would have crushed him. He would carry that torment with him, and now, he's here, and he's trapped," the priest told her.

Slowly, Rache began to see it now. If Malak had risked all, as Fr. John had put it, what was all in this context? It must mean he'd broken some amount of rules or laws or whatever they have there. His actual being here was a step backward. This would have been clear to him before he crossed—but he hadn't hesitated. Yes, the act was indeed courageous. If she'd learnt anything in the past two weeks, it was never rush to judgment.

Rache's silence hadn't gone unnoticed. Fr. John placed a hand on her shoulder. "God's judgment is not our judgment," he told her. "Your sister's death is not for us to judge. But somehow Malak judged himself. He saw it as a failure. That's why he crossed—to atone in some way."

"And now he's trapped?" she said, looking at him.

"Yes."

"And he needs my help?"

"Yes."

"But how can I help?"

"He needs your forgiveness, Rache."

She thought about it. Could she forgive him? Malak hadn't caused her sister's death. He'd merely been unable to help. How strange that they'd met in this manner. Never in her wildest dreams could she have conjured up such a scenario. He'd only begun to call her Rachel after he'd made contact with Kell. Had he recognised her?

No, not until later, yet at every turn he'd come to her. He'd saved her life in the alley when Mr. Jakes had tried to kill her. He'd looked to her at every turn. Perhaps he'd had some fragment of a memory, but he couldn't have known it was her.

Rache turned to the priest. "What can I do, Father?"

CHAPTER 38

S PECIAL AGENT FRANKS WAS A ticking time bomb—at any moment, she'd reach critical mass, setting off an unstoppable chain reaction. The suspect had given her the slip, making her look foolish in front of SWAT and the police. As she'd pursued him all the way to the West Coast Highway, she'd made a point of humiliating the police. They had allowed the suspect to escape not once but twice and had been ordered to defer to the FBI—the professionals would handle it from here on, she'd advised everyone. Most of the people on her team had squirmed at this. They knew the importance of inter-agency cooperation in these cases. One only had to look back to 9/11 to understand that. Detective Fischer could not be located. NYPD and SWAT had pursued him all the way to the UPS building. He'd been spotted entering the building, but a thorough search had proved fruitless—adding insult to injury.

She'd have Detective Fischer arrested and questioned.

Hunched over a file, Franks occupied the front seat of Danny's car as he negotiated traffic on their way back to the precinct. The last few days working in close proximity to Franks had caused him to all but give up on the human race! Franks had bullied, belittled, threatened, insulted, and abused him on a constant basis. He'd made his mind up. He'd get back to the precinct, and that would be that. She could stick it where the sun don't shine! A person could only take so much shit. And Franks was a dung heap. To hell with it. Perp or no perp, he wanted out.

Rache and the perp.

The two names sprang to mind, both inextricably tied together like soldered links in an unbreakable chain. Who was he? And why was she helping him? He'd suspected something was up way back.

Rache had starting acting weird around the time Kell's mom had come on the scene. Liz hated Franks—that he could understand. What he couldn't understand was Rache. She'd changed. Why in the name of God had she printed Kell? It didn't add up. The pimp, the now very dead pimp, had given them a positive ID on Rache with the perp. Much as he loathed the pimp, he'd believed him. But why would Rache help him? Why help the perp? He understood how the death of her sister must have driven Rache to seek justice in whatever form. Her family had been denied it. Jesus, he'd have gone crazy himself. All the more reason to put this guy away, not help him. It made no sense.

Danny glanced over at Franks. She was muttering under her breath again as she flicked through the open file on her lap. It was a habit of hers he'd picked up on. Franks would go through this little routine, this little pantomime just prior to blowing her top. Vesuvius was about to erupt. She gave him that stare again. *Oh shit, here we go*, he thought. Franks was about to give him hell when her cell phone rang. She held it to her ear.

"Speak," she commanded.

Whatever tidings Franks was getting from the other end, they were neither good nor joyous, Danny figured as he watched Franks drop the file. For some strange reason, the song "A Whiter Shade of Pale" by Procol Harum played in his head. Danny smiled inwardly. But his contentment was short-lived.

"What!" exclaimed Franks as she whisked the phone from one ear to the other. "When did this happen? I don't care...no...I don't care. Find her. And I want Detective Fischer arrested. Yes, arrested, you heard me the first time." She hung up.

At the mention of Rache's name, Danny looked over at Franks. She glared at him.

"What?" he said, looking away, focusing back on the road.

Agent Franks kicked the glove box in front of her, denting it.

"Liz Mason is AWOL!" she told him.

"What do you mean AWOL?"

"I mean she's fucking disappeared, gone—kaboom. She's vanished into thin air."

"You lost her, didn't you," Danny said, shaking his head at the stupidity of it.

"Just drive, okay?" she ordered him. She kicked the glove box again.

***

Liz Mason wasn't AWOL. Tony Caruso had snatched her from under the noses of the agents accompanying her to visit her daughter. Mr. Jakes's arrest had propelled Tony to take drastic action. He'd dispatched Bruno with orders to kill the pimp.

As a happy-go-lucky sociopath, Bruno had willingly obliged. Killing Mr. Jakes had been easy. Tony Caruso's criminal tentacles stretched deep. He had been able to ascertain the pimp's exact location and the type of security they'd encounter. Bruno had entered the hospital undetected, killed Mr. Jakes, and slipped out again. Killing the cop assigned to guard him had been a necessity as he'd seen Bruno's face.

Now Tony had one last problem. Tommy had encountered some guy at the Masons' house. Tony figured it had to have been a houseguest. Had to be. He needed to know who. It was the last link back to him. Joe Mason was dead, the kid was a vegetable, and he'd solved the Tommy and Mr. Jakes problem. The only lose end was this guest who Tommy had fought. What had Tommy said? The guy came outta nowhere. Well, for Tony Caruso, guys don't come outta nowhere. This guy had gotten a good look at Tommy, and everybody knew Tommy's connection with the Caruso family—although no one would ever find Tommy. A large vat of concentrated hydrochloric acid had erased the last vestiges of Tommy Crespo from this world.

This mystery guest could, in theory, identify Tommy. He needed to find this guy.

His work with Mr. Jakes complete, Bruno had taken Tulip, Lorenzo's godson, to keep an eye on Washington Memorial. Tulip had always relished working with Bruno. He'd always figured he could learn so much from him. Neither was under the illusion of ever getting near the kid, but you never know—they may just catch a lucky break.

When federal agents descended on Washington Memorial en masse, it was Bruno's cue to hightail it out. They needed to back off fast. But the quick exodus of most of the force shortly after Franks's arrival had found Bruno stalling. Within minutes, most of the cops had gone. The four black Chrysler Escalades hadn't remained long, telling Bruno that the Feds were no longer a problem. With what appeared to be some kind of law enforcement withdrawal, Bruno had become more emboldened. Sneaking into the parking lot, they'd overpowered a couple of hospital laundry workers and had begun to check out the hospital.

Liz Mason had been en route to the hospital when the FBI had received word that the perp had been spotted entering Kell's room. The agent's radio had announced the unfolding drama. The metal-sounding words had sent Liz into a subsequent panic. She had become frantic, convinced something terrible was about to happen to Kell. No words of assurance from her protector could quell her heightened anxiety. Liz jumped out of the agent's car before he'd parked and had run straight into the arms of Bruno Caruso. Recognizing her instantly, Bruno hadn't hesitated. He'd knocked her unconscious, and in the ensuing couple of moments, both Bruno and Tulip were out of sight with an unconscious Liz Mason bundled in their stolen laundry cart. With all the confusion, the federal agent had simply headed for Kell's room, believing he'd find Liz there.

The Caruso family owned properties south of the Circle Line Ferry, and as soon as Tony had received word of this new development, he'd ordered Bruno to meet him there with their catch. Dumping the contents of her purse out on the table, he quickly discovered Rache's card. As Bruno shoved a petrified Liz into a chair, Tony looked on in a maddening rage, his jaw clenched as he ground his teeth. His first thought was to shoot Liz then and there, but he somehow managed to restrain this compulsive urge. The family had a friend in the department who'd informed them that the cops had arrested someone at the scene. He needed information on that person. Shooting Liz—however gratifying—would not lead him to that goal. That fuck-up Tommy had fought some guy at the Masons' house, and he needed to find that person. So instead of shooting Liz, he found solace in mentally torturing her, telling her that she'd never see her kid again, that she'd die knowing her brat would spend the rest of her life as a vegetable if she didn't answer his questions.

Tony screamed at her, demanding to know who else was staying at the house. Liz insisted that she knew nothing about anyone staying with Joe. She told him that they'd separated, and perhaps a friend of Joe's had been there, but she swore she knew nothing. Tony had Bruno punch her a couple of times, just to be sure.

Holding Rache's card in his hand, Tony decided that the cop on the card must—why else would she have given Liz her card? Yeah, she had to know. He'd get her over, and they'd all have a little chinwag.

Liz was out of her mind with fear—fear at what Tony would now do to her. Being surrounded by the Caruso clan, her face stinging from Bruno's fists, and knowing Tony's propensity for violence actually caused Liz to pass out with fright. Her dark eyes rolled back in her head, and she slumped forward, hitting her face off the table in front of her.

"What the fuck!" Tony said, almost jumping back as Liz lay slumped in front of him. "Wake her the fuck up, Bruno," he demanded, fishing a pack of cigarettes out of his inside jacket pocket.

As Bruno began to shake Liz awake, Chazz Caruso had to point out that if Tony upset her too much, she might not be able to make the call to the cop.

Tony nodded, calmer now. Chazz had made some sense. They'd get this cop over. *Yeah*, thought Tony, *this cop, this detective would know*. Once he had her, he could get Bruno to persuade her to spill. He needed to tie up all loose ends before he'd finish off Liz.

"Better to get da skank to make da call Tony. Dat way we don't give notin' away," Chazz urged him.

As Liz came to, Tony sat down beside her, his manner friendly now. He smiled as he caressed her hair. "Okay, you're going to call this cop. Tell her you think I'm after you. You're hiding here, and you need her help. You get her here, and you have my word no harm will come to your kid. You fail, and I'll have Bruno cut both your fuckin' eyes out."

Flipping open Liz's cell phone, Tony dialled Rache's number. He handed the phone to Liz.

CHAPTER 39

Rache sat in her car, figuring her next move. Fr. John had left to go back to the church. She'd made up her mind. She'd contact Danny, try and get him to broker some kind of deal. She'd have to tell him all—everything! She wasn't sure if he'd believe her. She regretted having shouted at Malak now. She needed him. If she could convince Danny...

Her cell phone rang, interrupting her train of thought. She checked the caller display. She didn't recognize the number. Pressing the small green telephone symbol, she held it to her ear.

"Hello."

"Detective...it's Liz...Liz Mason."

Why was Liz Mason calling her now?

"Liz, you need to contact Agent Franks at the Bureau. I'm—"

"No...I don't trust her. It's Tony, he's after Kell. I think he'll kill her."

Rache thought she sounded strange. She couldn't quite put her finger on it, but Liz sounded scared. That was it. Liz sounded genuinely frightened. Rache wondered what had happened. Had Tony gotten to her? Why was she not with Franks or the Bureau people?

Liz told her that she'd gone to the hospital, and some of Tony's guys had chased her.

"Where are you now?" Rache asked.

Liz told her. Rache jotted it down on a scratch pad she kept in her glove box.

"Yes, Liz, I know it. Stay where you are, okay? I'm on my way," she said, hanging up. Rache tore off the address. In her haste to jot down the address, she left the glove box open. A Beretta 9mm stared at her now. Rache looked at the gun Malak had taken from the agent at the hospital. *Malak*, she thought. Where was he now?

She took the gun and pushed it into the small compartment in her door. This changed everything. Liz sounded scared. If Tony found her, he'd kill her, no doubt. She had to reach her first. Malak and Danny would have to wait.

Danny and Franks had actually passed Rache's sedan when it registered with Franks. She threw a fit.

"Stop, stop, stop!" she screamed at a very perplexed Danny.

Danny's first reaction was to hit the brakes. The car screeched to a halt, and Franks was out of the door in moments. Danny couldn't fathom what she'd seen, but he figured he'd better follow.

Rache saw her. She didn't need this. Franks was storming toward her, crowing like a rooster. "Detective Fischer, I'm arresting you—"

She didn't get any further. Rache shot out of the car, grabbing the gun as she opened the door. It was now pointed at Agent Franks.

"On the ground, now," she ordered Franks.

Franks may have been a drama queen, but she was certainly no hero. She dropped to the ground. Danny was a little behind, and by the time he'd realized what was happening, Rache had cuffed Franks and had now trained the gun on him.

"Your gun, Danny, I need it," she said.

Danny was shocked beyond words. Rache had lost it! If he drew it, would she shoot? If she didn't, did he want to shoot her? Whatever had happened to Rache, he knew he couldn't shoot her. But this was madness. Rache had a gun on him. What had happened?

He looked at her. He could tell she was uncomfortable with the situation. Could he talk her down? She looked like shit. Her eyes were puffy and red. Danny remembered the morning she'd told him about her sister's death. Shit, she now looked worse than that. He decided to hand over his gun.

Easing it slowly from his holster, he placed it on the ground, stepping back. The fact that Franks had surrendered without a struggle made his decision to give up his weapon all the more easier.

"Now you. Cuff yourself!"

Danny placed his cuffs around his wrists, tightening them. Rache heard them click.

As she helped her to her feet, Franks, feeling foolish, let loose with a verbal assault. "Your career and your life are over! I mean officially fucking ended!" Franks roared at her. "They'll fry your fuckin' ass—"

"Where is Liz Mason?" Rache demanded, staring her down.

The question had its desired effect! Franks blinked in disbelief. How could she know? Franks wondered. She'd only just found out herself, yet Detective Fischer knew.

"You lost her, didn't you?" Rache's tone was low but accusatory.

Franks didn't reply. What could she say?

Leading her over to Danny's car, Rache made her sit in the back. She looked over at Danny. She owed him one hell of an explanation. Rache closed the door on Franks.

Danny used the opportunity to plead with her. He had to get her to see sense. Rache was fucked, and this insanity didn't help. "Rache, this is madness. What are doing? Franks thinks you helped the perp escape. She's already gunning for you, and now this?"

"I did. I helped him escape."

"What?"

"Danny, he's not the perp. We had the wrong guy. Listen, go to the crime lab. Talk to Leo Caldwell. Get him to show you the fingerprint and DNA analysis done on Kell Mason and the perp. Then talk to your uncle."

"My uncle? What's he got to do with this?"

"I can't explain now. Liz is in big trouble. Will you do what I ask, please?"

He nodded. He didn't understand any of it. But he'd do what she'd asked.

"Now, let's get you in the car. Make it look good for Franks." Rache slipped the gun in her belt. Danny caught a glimpse. She'd taken the clip out. Rache's gun was empty! Danny was glad he hadn't drawn his weapon. He decided never to play poker with Rache.

Rache smiled as she pushed him into the back of the car. "Talk to your uncle, please," she whispered as she held the door open.

"You'd better have a fuckin' good exit strategy, or you're looking at life, Detective!" Franks screamed as Rache closed the door.

Danny turned to Franks. "Shut up!" he said.

***

Rache knew the clock was ticking. She had to get to Liz. If she could find her before Tony, she'd have some leverage. If she could just get there in time. The Feds had lost her. No surprise there. She couldn't use Malak's testimony.

Malak.

Again she was sorry she's shouted at him. Where had he gone? If he had reconnected with Kell, he would know more than before. She could use that knowledge. Would he go after Tony? Painful as it was to think of her sister's death, she'd stopped blaming Malak. The two bastards who'd raped Ruth were responsible, not Malak. She'd have to find him too. She knew she had little time. Leaving wasn't an option now. She'd get Liz and turn herself in. Hopefully, Danny'd talk to his uncle. Would he believe it? He was a Catholic—he'd have to! Fr. John would convince him. She would need at least one ally when the shit hit the fan.

Rache pulled up to the warehouse with a little trepidation. It was certainly off the beaten track, but Liz had sounded frantic. *Come on, Rache, find her, and let's get out of here*, she told herself.

She pushed the door. It opened. It all seemed wrong. Why had Liz not gone straight to the police? She could have stopped any cop, and he'd have taken her to the station. Rache wondered at this hide-and-seek business.

What was Liz up to?

Perhaps she'd information she only wanted Rache to hear. But this warehouse was all wrong. Rache took out the gun. She'd slipped the clip back in after she'd left—it was loaded now. She'd felt bad about Danny, about pulling the gun on him like that. Perhaps when he'd talked to Fr. John, he'd get it. Rache checked the Beretta. She slid the safety off.

Rache had climbed the first flight of stairs when it occurred to her—last call received. She put the safety back on and pushed the gun into her belt. Taking her cell phone from her back pocket, she scrolled down through it, calling the last number received. She could hear it. It was ringing. Why hadn't Liz answered?

"Liz…Liz!" she called out. The ringing was growing louder. Was she hurt? Rache ran up the next flight and straight into Chazz and Tulip.

Both smiled as they held their guns on her. Tony Caruso walked out from behind a door. He held her business card in his hand as he spoke to her.

"Detective Fischer, the pleasure is all mine."

Chazz grabbed her while Tulip took her gun.

***

St. Killian's saw a struggle of a different nature take place. Fr. John had walked into the church to find it empty. He had been trying to come to terms with what Rache had told him. Approaching the altar, he realized that there wasn't a single soul in the church. Turning around, he looked back at the door. *Strange*, he thought. When he turned back, Malak stood in front of him. Fr. John had no idea how he'd gotten there. He looked at Malak, not knowing what to expect.

"Rache and Liz are in trouble. I need your help."

Fr. John was shocked. He didn't know what to say. So he just nodded.

"I need an anchor…in this world, I need an anchor. This must end tonight," Malak had told him.

"Can you help her?"

"Yes, but we must hurry. Kell doesn't have much time."

"Kell? I don't understand," Fr. John said, having regained some of his composure. It was his first time meeting Malak with the full knowledge of who he was, and it had scared the shit out of him. So far, he had only discussed Malak in the abstract with Rache. Fr. John's faith was unshakable, but standing before Malak, knowing who he was, terrified him. Malak did not belong to this world, yet he was here. Flesh and blood stood facing him. It both scared and intrigued him. He realized that Rache was somehow right. Malak's presence had pushed Kell into some kind of non-state. The word *coma* was too simplistic to explain it.

Fr. John caught himself glancing over at the angels in the paintings. He had to stop himself. Being in Malak's presence was overpowering.

Fr. John regained his composure. He asked Malak what he'd meant about Kell.

Malak explained that Kell's present condition could not be solved by medicine. His presence had caused it, and only his return to his world could reverse it. But Liz and Rache were also in danger. He needed to act before any harm could come to them.

"What do you mean harm?"

"The imprint, it contains not only past and present events but also possible futures. As guardians, this is clear to us. When I lived as a person, I couldn't read the imprint, but when I reconnected with my past through Kell, I regained this ability. I have seen Rache's, and she will die today."

The priest was dumbstruck! Malak could read not only Kell's imprint but Rache's too? The imprint in the energy field held not only past wounds, but possibilities that could trigger future events?

The priest remembered the old Inka shaman, who all those years ago had searched his own field for signs of illness. If he could read swirling pools of light that held the imprints, how much in tune would a guardian be?

Fr. John challenged Malak on this.

Malak was agitated as he explained they had little time. But the priest simply couldn't let it go. Malak briefly outlined that just as thoughts are held in the energy field before they become spoken words, so too are possible events. They are expressed as colors, which are visible to the guardian. The more intense the color, the greater the possibility it will be expressed as words or actions. The same held true for events. The events leading to Rache's death had reached such intensity that it was no longer a possibility but had now become a strong probability.

"What?" Fr. John said. He was confused by this revelation. "But Rache has her own guardian, can't he...?"

"It is not within the guardian's remit to interfere."

"You did."

"I broke the rules."

"Because of Ruth?"

"Yes, she...she was my first charge...my first assignment...to...to..." Malak was struggling now, struggling to find human words to describe his feelings.

"To what, Malak, to what?" asked the priest.

"To die before her time."

Fr. John nodded slowly. It was so clear now. "So you took this form to save Kell? What will happen, Malak? What will happen to Rache?" Fr. John asked.

Malak didn't answer. He became silent. He began to walk away.

"What is it?" Fr. John pressed.

"It's not just Rache's life that's at stake here. Kell is also in mortal danger."

"How?"

Malak told him.

CHAPTER 40

DANNY BURST THROUGH THE DOOR of Leo Caldwell's small office. "I want the Mason file, and I want it now," he demanded, striding toward Leo.

Leo had been munching chocolate chip cookies. He loved his chocolate chips, devouring at least a pack a day. Most people's drug of choice was nicotine or alcohol. Leo's was chocolate. He had developed his own little ritual. He'd try and break them into perfect quarters, then dip them in his coffee and suck the liquid out, closing his eyes almost in reverence as it crumbled in his mouth. Now, this cop had made him drop the entire cookie into his coffee. What was it with cops and dramatic entrances? The Feds had been in a few days earlier... Some satanic bitch had screamed at him then. What was it with people and badges? Now, he was staring at some cop in a uniform and some overweight zealot. Leo made a mental note to cut back on the cookies.

"And you are...?"

Danny flashed his badge. Officer Cole Marks stood directly behind Danny. Looking at Danny's badge, Leo remained silent. Danny moved quickly toward Leo, startling him now. Leo jumped up.

"Let me see...I told that other detective that the findings were inconclusive," Leo said, covering as best he could for Rache.

Danny grabbed him, pushing him up against the wall.

"Hey, hey, hey!" Leo shouted. "No roughhousing. I bruise easily."

Danny released him. He told Leo that Rache had specifically wanted him to cross-reference Kell's DNA with that of the perp. He also needed all the fingerprint analysis.

This took Leo aback. No way he'd worked this out on his own. Rache must have sent him. Okay, Leo figured, this guy is on the level. But something was wrong. Where was Rache?

"She okay? Detective Fischer, I mean?" he asked.

"The file, Leo," Danny demanded.

Leo held his ground. He looked over at Officer Marks. *Looks like a nice kid*, Leo thought.

Danny was ready to hit Leo. He would have, he was so mad, but Leo's voice was genuine when he'd asked after Rache. *Rache must have been up to something with this guy. She'd have never sent me on a wild-goose chase. No*, thought Danny, *there's something here.*

"No, Leo, she's not okay. She's in deep shit." His own brutal honesty frightened him. But it was true. Rache was fucked! No matter what they discovered here, it wouldn't help her. She was wanted on a federal arrest warrant. And why did she want him to talk to Fr. John anyway? He thought back.

It had only taken them ten minutes to raise the alarm. Franks had turned into some kind of wriggling eel. She'd scurried out of the back seat into the front, using her mouth to operate the police radio. Danny had just sat there, fascinated. Franks was manic, screaming at him for doing nothing. When he'd tried to explain that he too was cuffed, she'd threatened to have him arrested for aiding and abetting a wanted felon.

Officer Marks had been the first on the scene. He had almost finished his shift when he'd taken the call from dispatch. He'd swung by, more out of fascination than any sense of duty. Everybody hated Franks, and when he'd taken the call telling him that Agent Franks had somehow managed to cuff herself in her own vehicle, he'd decided to swing by out of perverse curiosity.

Arriving on the scene shortly after calling it in that he'd respond to the call, Cole Marks couldn't help but chuckle to himself. Franks had managed to wedge herself between the front seats, her legs sticking back at a forty-five-degree angle as her upper body rested against the car radio. He had quickly assessed the situation. Humorous as it was, Franks was still FBI, and he didn't want any shit! He'd opened the rear door, uncuffing Danny, and between them, they'd freed

Franks from her predicament. Franks hadn't waited for any pleasant-ries. She'd jumped behind the wheel and had taken off, mumbling about reporting people.

God, that girl needed to calm down, Danny had thought.

"Tell me about it," Leo said, bringing him back.

"What did you say?"

"Tell me about it?"

"About what?"

"Deep shit, Detective O'Connor. She's not the only one, we all are."

Danny threw a glance at Officer Marks. What was this toad on about?

"What are you talking about, Leo?"

"Buddy, you don't want to know."

"Leo, do you want to spend the next twenty years in a correc-tional facility as some bull queer's bitch? No. I didn't think so. Now, spill."

"It's your sanity, buddy. It's your sanity," Leo said, opening a cabinet and fishing out a file.

Danny thought this last remark a strange one. Leo began by explaining the reason for cross-referencing the DNA results.

Twenty minutes later, Leo sat back in his chair, watching as both Danny and Cole Marks tried to fathom what they'd just been shown.

"Leo, are you for real?" It was all Danny could think of saying. He'd removed his jacket and tie. Cole Marks sat in total silence beside him, his own mind racing a mile a minute. His usual bright red cheeks were a pallid white now.

Leo, however, was smiling. "Told ya, buddy, didn't I?"

"Leo, there has to be some mistake..." Danny started to say.

"No mistake. See, that's what Rache thought initially. That's why she printed the kid. Prints are a match too."

"What?"

Leo pushed his chair up beside them. Typing on the keyboard, he brought up both Kell's and Malak's prints.

Danny stared at the fingerprints on the screen. The word *MATCH* pulsated over and over, the repetitive blinking of the five letters almost sending him into a trance.

"Most fucked-up case I ever worked on. But the evidence is conclusive. Kell Mason and your perp are the same person."

Danny sat there, staring at Leo. Had Rache passed him a poisoned chalice? Would he too go insane? Had Rache gone insane?

"Leo, who else knows?"

"Just us ducks, Detective O'Connor. Oh, and Detective Fischer, of course," Leo said.

Danny picked up the file. "Not a word, Leo, okay?"

"My lips are sealed."

"Come on," Danny said to Officer Marks.

But Cole Marks couldn't move. He remained stuck to his seat, gazing at the computer screen. He stared at the two sets of fingerprints. He touched the screen, as if touching it would somehow make it real.

"Come on," Danny repeated, eager to get out of there. "Mind if I take this, Leo?" He indicated the file in his hand.

"Be my guest."

Danny and Cole Marks left. As they reached the patrol car, Danny asked the young officer what he thought.

"I wish to God I'd never answered that call," was his shocked reply.

They headed straight to the church. If Rache had dropped this bombshell on him, what was waiting for him at the church? Danny wondered. But he had half an idea. He didn't believe it, but he suspected Fr. John would confirm it. Jesus, no wonder Rache was messed up. What had she said?

It wasn't him. We got the wrong guy.

CHAPTER 41

Tony's open palm struck Rache sharply across the face, the unexpected blow knocking her off the chair she'd being sitting on. A sudden biting pain ran up the side of her head. Rache blinked her eyes a moment, wincing at the severity of the blow. Tony stood above her, glaring down at her.

"I want to know who he is, Detective Fischer?"

"Or what, you'll kill us?" Rache shouted back at him. "That's what you do, Tony. You kill women and children. If your uncle Lorenzo were here, he'd put a bullet in that mash of a brain—"

Tony raised his hand again, this time clenching his fist. Rache flinched, bracing herself for the blow—it never came. That first blow had taken her by surprise. Tony had been asking her questions about Malak. She'd told him that he'd escaped custody, and she'd no idea who he was other than the fact that they'd found him at the house. Rache put her hand to her face. She could feel the heat in her cheek.

Liz sobbed beside her. "I'm sorry, I'm sorry!" she cried.

Although her face stung, she still tried to console Liz. "It's okay," she said to Liz as Bruno stood behind her and lifted her to her feet.

Tony gestured to the chair as he smiled at her. "Have a seat, Detective," he said as Bruno pushed her into the chair. Tony suddenly became the personification of charm. "My apologies, I can be a little...hot tempered. Must be my Italian blood."

Rache said nothing.

"You see, Maxine here—oh, sorry...it's Liz now—has been most unhelpful. She insisted that she didn't know anything."

Tony sat opposite Rache. Lighting a cigarette, he inhaled deeply, allowing the smoke to drift upward before resuming his conversation.

293

"Thing is, I believe her. Let's say we had our own little conversation...before you arrived." He looked over at Liz, a twisted smile on his lips.

He didn't have to say any more. The thought of what he'd done to Liz sickened Rache.

"So I believe her, you see. I do not, however, believe you. Which will make the next few hours interesting."

Tony stood up. He nodded to Bruno.

Without warning, Bruno grabbed Liz by the hair, pulling her across the table. Rache jumped up in a vain effort to help her. Tony merely slapped her back down. Bruno and Chazz dragged Liz, screaming, over to another table by the window. They began to tie her to it, facedown. Bruno held her arms as Chazz quickly bound her hands with a piece of rope he'd been holding.

Tony spoke matter-of-factly to Rache, never once glancing behind him at the ensuing savagery.

"Bruno just loves to hurt people," he said, grabbing Rache by the face, his fingers digging in, distorting her features. "She's no use to me now, so we can kill her. I want you to watch, you little bitch. You watch because you're next."

"Stop it, stop it, stop it! I'll tell you, I swear, I'll tell you! Just don't hurt her," Rache pleaded, unable to bear what was happening to Liz.

Tony held up his hand. It was a command for them to stop.

Chazz and Bruno lifted Liz off the table, dragging her across the dusty floor, pushing her into the chair next to Rache.

She fell into Rache's arms. Rache held her. She didn't think Liz could hold it together much longer. Bruno went to grab her. Rache screamed at him.

"I fucking told you I'd tell you! Now leave her be, okay!"

Bruno stopped a moment. He looked over at Tony, seeking instruction.

Tony nodded as he pulled on his cigarette.

"Liz, you need to be strong. Strong for me and strong for Kell," Rache whispered as she held Liz's hands. Kell's name seemed to ground Liz somehow. "No matter what you hear, you need to be strong." Rache made her sit back on the chair. Rache stood. She walked behind Liz, all the time staring at Tony, who was enjoying this little drama. He'd give this skank exactly one minute, then he'd shoot Liz in the ankles. If that didn't work…well, he'd get Bruno to make her walk round the room on them. Yeah, that ought start the cop blabbering.

Rache put her hand on Liz's shoulder. A gesture of comfort. Tony stood opposite. He blew smoke in her direction. *Smug bastard,* Rache thought. She knew Tony would kill her and Liz. What could she do? She thought about what she'd say.

Tony made a gesture as if to wipe a tear from his eye. "I'm very touched. But my patience is running out, Detective."

"Your time is running out, Tony."

Chazz and Tulip looked at Rache, stunned. Nibbling on the inside of his lip, Tony tried to remain calm. "Really."

"You think you'll get me to tell you what I know?" she said, holding up her hand. "And I will. But your hours are numbered."

Tony'd heard enough. "Enough already! No more Mr. Nice Guy," he said as he nodded to Bruno. "Bruno, have a word with—"

"I don't believe you'd be stupid enough to send an idiot like Tommy the Trigger, a sex offender, to kill Joe Mason!" Rache shouted as Bruno moved his huge frame toward Liz.

Bruno stopped dead. How'd she know that? he wondered. He turned back to Tony, a dumb expression fixed on his face. Tony gestured for Bruno to back down. This revelation needed his attention. Chazz and Tulip shuffled uneasily, the same question running through their minds.

Rache knew she had to shock them again. "You used Tommy, but forgot Tommy likes little girls. So you send that no-good pimp, Mr. Jakes, to finish the job. Only he fucked up, so now you have Bruno kill him at the hospital. Am I right so far?"

Tony remained ice calm. But just below his seemingly controlled façade, there was a boiling volcano just waiting to erupt. How did she know about Tommy? Had to be from the mystery guest. The one the cops lost. But who the fuck was he? Tony quickly weighed the situation. The guys were looking at him now. He had to show leadership.

"I'll give him up," she said before he had a chance to figure his next move.

"What?"

"The guy we lost. The one who escaped, I know where he is. I'll give him to you. But that won't solve your problem. Even if you kill us—and him—that still won't solve your problem."

"What the fuck are you talking about?"

"Tony, you're way in over your head. Mr. Jakes told us everything."

"He's dead. You got nothing."

"Lorenzo's dying."

It was a cutting blow. Tony's sharp intake of breath finally exposed cracks in his outwardly calm exterior. How did she know this? He had to find the source. He wanted to kill her, but he needed to find out where she was getting her information.

"Bet you Tommy told you that his attacker came out of nowhere, huh?" she said, smiling.

Tony and the rest of his crew were genuinely shocked. "There's no way she could know dat, Tony," Bruno blurted, unable to conceal his surprise.

"Shut up, Bruno."

"Suppose you questioned him for hours. Beat him real bad, yeah? Only Tommy was telling you the truth. He came out of nowhere. Do you believe in angels, Tony?"

"Hey, I'm getting nothing here. How'd you know about Tommy?" he shouted.

"Do you believe in angels? Simple question."

Tony drew his gun. He'd off this skank, her and Maxine. The cops had nothing! He cocked the gun.

It was the move Rache had been counting on. Better to die this way than to be tortured for hours. She needed to make him madder. She needed him to shoot. She was close to Liz. If Tony was mad enough, he'd shoot them both. *Shit*, she thought, *what an end*.

Liz gripped Rache's hand now, the understanding of what Rache was trying to do clear.

"No, I don't believe in angels, Detective. But you are about to find out if they exist." He cocked his gun. Bruno had pulled his own gun. *Better back the boss*, he thought.

Chazz and Tulip had walked away from the door, both sensing a climax.

"I'll ask you one more time—"

"I believe in angels, Tony. It was Kell Mason's guardian angel who attacked Tommy. Do you know how I know this? He fucking told me, you stupid, inept motherfucker."

Rache waited for the bullets. None came. She thought she'd done enough to push him over. If he thought she was making a joke of him in front of his crew, he'd lose his temper. Surely she'd done enough.

But Tony only stood there. None of the others would dare fire before Tony.

Suddenly Tony began to laugh. He almost became hysterical, slapping his thigh as he convulsed in spasms of laughter. Bruno joined in, but his was nervous laughter. He didn't understand why Tony was laughing, but he figured he'd show solidarity if he too laughed.

Tony continued to laugh as he spoke. "You're...you're good. I'll give you that much. Angels...yeah, you're good. Almost had me fooled. Kell Mason's in a coma. She's a fucking turnip!" he shouted, directing this comment at Liz.

Rache could feel her pain now. *Damn*, she thought as she watched Tony push his gun into his belt.

"Tell me, Detective. This guardian angel, he just appeared?"

"That's right."

"And he wanted to help the kid, yeah?" Tony was amused now, his thought process happy to flit from one extreme to the next. He was no longer angry. Sure enough, he'd enjoy killing Rache, but for the moment, he'd have some fun.

"So tell me, Detective. This guardian, what's his plan?"

"Tony, you have a chance now. Let us go, and I swear I'll cut you a deal."

"A deal? A deal? Lady, the Feds don't cut deals with murderers."

"Not with the cops—with Him," she said in a hushed tone.

"Why are you whispering?" Tony asked, his own voice lowered now, mocking Rache.

It was the expression on Liz Mason's face that alerted Tony. He whipped his head around.

Malak stood in the open doorway.

Liz had merely thought that Rache had being trying to bait Tony, to end it all before he unleashed any more pain on her. Liz had prayed for her death to come quickly. But then she'd watched with fascination as a metal door had silently buckled and opened. Liz was taken by the fact that the metal in the door had been crushed inward, but as it strained and separated from the frame, it had made no sound whatsoever. The person responsible now stood in the door-way, looking at her—and that person looked remarkably like her lit-tle girl. Liz had let out a gasp!

Tony spun around, looking at Malak and then back to Liz and Rache.

"You wanted to meet him? Well, now's your chance," Rache said.

Chazz and Tulip both held their guns on Malak, who remained motionless. Bruno looked at Tony and then at Malak. He was unsure now. How had this clown gotten in? he wondered.

Tony pulled his gun, aiming it at Rache and Liz. But Liz was looking at Malak. At once she understood. At once she knew who he was. His resemblance to Kell, her sleeping beauty, was uncanny. She locked eyes with him. They could have been Kell's eyes. For the first time since being given the news that her daughter was in a coma, Liz experienced a quiet peace. If asked to explain it, she would not be able to find the words—only that she felt safe.

At first, she'd thought Rache had lost her grip. In the circum-stances, it was understandable—angels and guardians, who'd have thought? But she'd quickly realized Rache's plan for them. As Rache had begun to talk about these angels, she'd thought it was merely part of her strategy. She pressed Rache's hand, indicating her understanding. She knew how vicious Tony was, what he was capable of. When Rache had pressed Tony, she'd prayed. She'd prayed for a quick death. Tony had a short fuse, and Rache had almost ignited it. She'd become paralyzed with fear when Tony had begun to laugh. Liz had closed her eyes, expecting the bullet to rip her apart. But Tony hadn't fired; he'd just laughed. She'd feared the worst.

But not now.

Tony wasn't laughing now. His face was a snarl as he pulled the trigger repeatedly. Liz could actually see the five bullets as they traveled toward her and Rache. In a little over a second, Tony had fired off five rounds—hot arrows of lead shot across the room. Liz felt the strangest sensation. It was like falling. But she was falling sideways, moving away, out of the path of the onrushing darts of death. Liz marveled at how small the bullets looked as they passed her by and exploded into the wall, where only moments before she'd being sitting. She looked to her left. Rache was beside her now. She had the strangest look on her face. Liz looked down. She was still on the chair, but it was no longer on the ground. She could feel herself coming to a stop. Rache and Liz came to an abrupt halt. Only then did they catch the sound of the bullets being discharged.

Tony no longer held his gun. It shot across the room, landing at Rache's feet. She picked it up. Tony was at least fifteen feet off the ground. This guardian had him by the throat, lifting him upward and slamming him into the wall beside them. She could hear Tony's bones break.

Rache felt as though she had been in a dream. Unlike Liz, she hadn't marveled at the bullets. Her attention had been firmly fixed on Malak. She'd been vaguely aware of Tony saying something to Chazz and Tulip—then she too was moving through the air. It had happened in a fraction of a moment, an immeasurable second, but Rache had somehow caught it all. She watched in awe as Malak overpowered first Chazz, wrenching his firing arm from the shoulder socket. Sinews and bone snapped as his entire arm was twisted 180 degrees counterclockwise. Before Chazz had had time to register the searing pain, Malak had knocked him unconscious with a pounding blow to the base of his skull. Tulip fared no better. By the time he'd placed his finger between the trigger and the trigger guard, Malak had pounced, crushing his left hand beyond repair while simultaneously dropping him to the floor with such force that Tulip's head punched through the floorboards. Tulip wouldn't wake for hours.

As Malak reached Bruno, Tony had fired only his third shot. The look on Bruno's dumb face had been priceless. But his look became a grimace of pain as Malak broke his arm and wrist, snapping both the radius and ulna, rendering his right arm useless. As Bruno fell forward screaming, Rache watched as Malak threw him against the far wall, snapping his neck and causing him multiple spinal fractures.

Rache was keenly aware that she was in some sort of suspended state where the rules of the physical world didn't apply. She knew that some unseen force—or forces—had pulled both her and Liz out of the path of the oncoming bullets. Then it occurred to her. Was she experiencing Malak's world? His speed and strength were unreal. What had happened in the alley with Mr. Jakes could not be compared to this. It was as though the entire Caruso clan had become immobilized. Rache marveled at his speed. And just like Liz, she could feel herself coming to a stop. It was not like a jolt, more of a slow down. It was weird because Rache felt she hadn't been moving at all. Only as she slowed, did she become aware of the sound of gunfire.

Tony's gun was beside her now. She reached down to pick it up.

Rache's world came flooding back. It was only at this point did she realize that the world of sound had also been suspended. The sounds and sights of her world rushed into her sensory perception that had, up to now, been suspended.

Had anyone used a stopwatch to time the events, it would all have taken place in under a second. Malak had utilized his abilities as a guardian to their maximum potential. He had shifted and warped their potential and channeled them into his physical body. He had merged both worlds into one. But it came at a price. The human body is not constructed to withstand such extreme forces. Malak had moved through the room at a speed that had generated a force of over 20 Gs on his human body. With the average human losing consciousness at 9 Gs, Malak had counted on this. The excessive force had crushed the air from his lungs, collapsing both of them. His spleen and kidneys had ruptured. The muscles in his arm had become detached from the tendons that held them to his bones. The intercostal muscles in his ribs had turned to a soggy mess. His body was shattered.

Falling back off the wall, releasing Tony, Malak was close to death. He landed on his feet and sank to the floor, gasping for air—air that could not enter his ruined lungs. He tried to stand. His breath was gone, and he felt as though he were drowning.

Malak had fractured four of Tony's ribs, crushing his shoulder blade. Tony had smashed his right shinbone as he'd struck the floor.

Rache was still in a state of shock now she'd returned to the physical reality. Grabbing hold of Tony's gun, she recognized it as a nine millimeter. Tony had fired five, which meant there was ten left in the magazine. She looked at Liz. Liz too was withdrawing from the effects of what had just happened. Although it had only been a few seconds, it now began to feel like a distant memory. It was clear, but it felt as though it had happened weeks ago. The sounds and smells of the everyday world had returned.

Liz screamed as Rache heard the shots. She spun around. Malak was thrown backward as Tony fired six shots into his chest. The last of his strength drained from Malak's body as he dropped to the floor.

Malak knew he was finished.

By engaging his corporal form as a guardian, he had effectively destroyed it. The human body he'd forged from Kell Mason had been unable to withstand the extreme pressures and unnatural force exerted on it. For a split second, Malak had lived once again as a guardian, only in human form.

His body would die in moments.

Malak had known this all along. It was a calculation he'd counted on. It had been the primary reason why he'd become so exhausted when he'd fought Mr. Jakes in the alley and Tommy when he'd first entered the world of form. Living in the physical world as a person was possible—only as long as he acted as a person. Living as a guardian in a human body was not sustainable. Standing at the door before Tony and his goons, Malak had known that the action that he was about to undertake would ultimately end in the destruction of the body. It had to be destroyed. In order for him to return, the body had to die. Kell was growing weaker, and if she died before he returned, he would remain trapped. Kell would die, and without her spirit guide, without her guardian, she would not be able to negotiate the afterlife.

He had sought the help of the priest. He had required an anchor in the physical world as he sought the guardians in his.

He needed to locate both Liz and Rache's guardians. He had interacted with both as Kell and Ruth's guardian. He needed to locate them to pinpoint Liz and Rache's position. It was why he'd returned to the church. The priest had helped anchor him in the physical reality as he sought out his companions.

Malak had explained to Fr. John that just as people come into contact and form relationships, so too do their guardians. Their relationships are interdependent on the relationships of their charges. As Ruth's guardian, he had formed a relationship with Rache's guardian. As the guardian of her daughter, Sarah-Jane—or Kell as she was now called—Malak had formed a special relationship with Liz Mason's guardian. Both guardians had worked tirelessly throughout the Caruso trial and its aftermath in an effort to encourage and guide Liz and Kell.

He'd told Fr. John that because he'd separated from Kell, he had no anchor in the physical world, and there was a danger that he might become lost and unable to return. The time to contact the other guardians would be measured in seconds in the physical world, but time is not counted that way in infinity.

The amount of effort required to return Malak had almost killed Fr. John. Malak had left him unconscious in the church and had gone straight to the warehouse.

As he'd fought the Caruso clan, Malak was aware of the short life span of his body in this undertaking. He had calculated the distances with precision. With the help of their guardians, he knew he would easily move Liz and Rache out of harm's way and subdue Tony and his goons before the destruction of the body was complete.

He had not factored in Tony keeping a small thirty-eight strapped to his ankle.

As Malak fell to his knees, he heard two more shots. Tony Caruso fell forward, grabbing his shoulder. Rache was shouting now. The world was growing darker for Malak. He needed to talk to Rache. He needed to explain—to tell her the truth about Ruth. He hadn't counted on being shot.

Rache had seen Tony shoot Malak. She hadn't hesitated. Firing twice, she caught Tony in the shoulder, spinning him backward. As he fell, Rache rushed over and kicked Tony's gun beyond his reach.

Malak lay beside him. He was barely alive. *God, don't let him die!* she begged. *Please don't let him die.* She had so many questions—so many questions.

Tony groaned, causing her to switch her attention back to him. Rache trained the gun on him. How she hated this piece of shit—this diseased sore. Tony looked up at her as Danny, Fr. John, and Officer Marks burst through the door.

"NO!" Danny screamed as he watched Rache cock the gun. "Rache, don't—"

Danny turned his head away as Rache emptied the entire clip. She continued firing until the hammer struck metal, making a *clip-clip* sound.

"Sonofabitch!" she screamed, kicking Tony hard in the nuts. "Sonofabitch." Tony moaned.

Danny ran across the room, taking in the scene as he did. He looked at Tony. Rache had fired into the floorboards beside him. Tony was deaf in his left ear, the floorboards all chewed up from the impacting rounds.

Tossing the gun aside, Rache rushed over and dropped to Malak's side. She helped ease him up, cradling him in her arms as she did. She couldn't stop crying. Small rivers flowed down both cheeks.

"It's going to be okay, you'll be okay," she whispered to him.

Malak began to close his eyes.

"No!" she cried. "No."

"Rachel," he choked, his voice barely a whisper now.

"You can do it, Malak. You can stop the bleeding. Come on, you did it before—you can do it."

Malak struggled to talk.

"Don't...don't talk."

She could sense Fr. John beside her now. She turned to him. "We have to stop the bleeding, Father! We have to stop it!" she begged frantically.

But Fr. John shook his head. He knelt beside her, resting his hand on her shoulder. "No, Rache, leave him. The body must die. It's his only way back."

The words stung her. As the last of the life ebbed from Malak's crushed body, Rache could see the answers she so desperately craved begin to evaporate. Holding Malak in her arms, she thought back to holding the dead body of her sister. It was as though history was repeating itself. Why had she done it? she wondered back then. Part of her had been so angry with Ruth for taking her own life—her mind had screamed for an explanation. It was as if a jagged spear had penetrated her stomach and was now being pushed all the way into her heart. But Ruth was dead, and all the questions in the world would not give Rache the answers.

Pulling Malak closer, as though the action would itself prevent the life from draining from him, Rache once again begged him to stop the bleeding. He was still alive, but she could feel him fading fast. Tears continued to flow down her face as she pleaded with him. "Please, Malak, please... You can do it, I know you can."

Rache was wracked with pain now. She would never know, she would never know why.

"Oh God, there's no time...there's no time."

Malak suddenly took a fit, coughing up blood. Bright red blood spewed from his mouth, drenching her clothes a deep crimson color. Her hands too were stained in Malak's blood. But Rache didn't care.

"Please, Father, please!" she cried.

Danny watched helplessly now. His uncle had explained some of what had taken place, pointing out Malak's relationship as Ruth's guardian. Looking at Rache weeping now gutted him. He had to do something. He had to act. He moved to crouch beside Rache, but Fr. John held him back. "No, Danny, you can't interfere."

Malak opened his eyes for the last time.

"Kell was so helpless...just like Ruth. I'm sorry, Rachel...I'm sorry I couldn't help her," he whispered.

"It's okay..."

With a supreme effort, Malak pushed himself upright. He grabbed hold of Rache's hand. It was like being held in a vise.

"Ruth didn't kill herself," he whispered. "She was murdered." Malak pressed her hand.

Rache suddenly felt a warm tingling sensation. It was as though she'd submerged her hand in hot water. In seconds it had traveled on up her arm and into her shoulder, quickly enveloping her whole body. Rache knew instantly that the water analogy was wrong. It was more like a soft radiating heat that resided outside her body, but yet warmed her from within. She soon realized there were no words to describe it.

There was a quick flash, and Rache was transported back to the day her sister died. She saw her sister's death—not at her own hand, as she had always believed, but at the hand of two masked strangers.

Although Rache sat on the ground holding Malak, she received a constant stream of past images. They were like flashes. She saw Ruth lying in bed, wiped out by the drugs the doctor had administered. She saw two guys wearing masks take Ruth and inject her with a powerful sedative, rendering her unconscious in seconds. Rache watched as her sister's eyes fluttered one last time.

Rache was in the garage now, watching as the men lifted Ruth onto a chair, a rope pulled tight around the smooth skin on her young neck. One guy fastened it to the crossbeam. Rache felt a deep sense of pain and frustration—pain at not being able to help and frustration at not knowing who the assailants were.

Malak let go.

Rache was back in the warehouse, holding Malak.

"She was so helpless...just like Kell," he said.

"It's okay, Malak...it's okay."

305

He grabbed her hand again, sending another shock through her. This time she was in Senator Williams's office, the senator talking to the killers.

"There's no way this can be traced to me?" he asked.

They both smiled at him, flashing their badges.

"Who's going to investigate a couple of private eyes?" one of them said smugly.

The experience was unsettling for Rache. She knew it had taken place over seventeen years ago, yet she felt as though she were in the room—the names and faces of her sister's killers burnt into her memory.

Rache felt the last of the strength drain from Malak.

"No, no, no!" she cried as Malak died.

She looked up at Fr. John and Danny, her face red from crying.

As suddenly as he had entered the world, Malak was gone.

Both Danny and Fr. John took a step backward.

"Rache, look at your hands!" Fr. John exclaimed.

All the blood had disappeared. Rache looked down to where Malak had been only moments earlier. The pool of blood on the floor had vanished.

Danny helped Rache to her feet. If he hadn't seen it, he'd never had believe it. Up to this, he'd had a hard time believing anything.

Danny thought back to earlier. He'd left the crime lab and had arrived at the church. His uncle lay unconscious on the altar, the church deserted. He'd helped Fr. John up, telling him to take it easy. The priest had dismissed Danny, telling him that Rache was in trouble.

Fr. John had told him everything as they'd raced to the warehouse. Both Danny and Officer Marks were in a state of shock as they'd arrived. Officer Marks had blessed himself four times as he drove his patrol car to Tony's place. Danny had asked him how he knew where to find Rache. Fr. John explained as best he could. But even he didn't really understand. They'd burst into the room as Rache had fired.

Standing beside her now, Danny felt like apologizing. What she'd gone through, he could just imagine. How had she kept her sanity? No wonder she'd been acting strange. But he didn't know what to say. He put his hand on her shoulder and squeezed gently.

Rache nodded, understanding that words could never fully explain what they had just witnessed.

Liz Mason walked over and hugged her. "Thank you, thank you," she whispered. "So he was really Kell's...?"

"Yes," said Rache, returning Liz's embrace.

Suddenly there was a commotion as Franks swept into the room accompanied by several agents. Franks took in the scene with a deep sense of confusion. Tulip, Chazz, and Bruno all lay unconscious, their bodies broken. Tony Caruso was moaning on the ground, holding his wounded shoulder and talking nonsense about devils. *What exactly had transpired here?* she wondered, walking farther into the room.

SWAT and paramedics followed hot behind her, one team securing the room while the other checked the unconscious Caruso clan. Franks ordered Tony be tended to first. She didn't want him dying on her.

Franks stood in front of Rache. She was red with rage, her finger itching to pull her gun. She almost wished Rache were armed.

"I want her arrested," she ordered the two Bureau guys who now flanked her.

Liz Mason stepped in front of Rache. She glared at Franks. "Detective Fischer saved my life. She rescued me after you allowed me to be taken captive by Tony. She's a hero, Agent Franks," Liz said, holding Franks's eye.

Franks had messed up, big time. Joe was dead, and Liz held her accountable. There was no way she'd allow Rache to be arrested. She owed her!

Franks stopped a moment. What was she really saying? Franks wondered. Liz disappeared on her watch—she'd be held ultimately responsible. All the fingers would point at her.

She eyed Danny suspiciously. "This true?"

"NYPD is grateful for the Bureau's cooperation, especially in allowing Liz Mason to act as a decoy in the apprehension of Tony Caruso and the remainder of the Caruso family. Without the FBI's assistance in this matter, I seriously doubt that Detective Fischer or myself would have succeeded in our operation. It was your pivotal role in accepting and allowing Detective's Fischer to operate beyond the parameters set by the Bureau, and you are to be commended for it," Danny said.

Rache almost laughed.

Franks didn't know where to look. She glared at Rache as Liz stood her ground. Franks knew she had to decide. They'd offered her an out. It was decision time. If she arrested Fischer, she'd be held accountable for losing Liz Mason. She'd already allowed Tony Caruso to find and kill her husband. If Liz spilled the beans, she be held accountable, that was for sure.

"Yes, Agent Franks, we're most grateful. It's been an experience and an honor working in close cooperation with you," Rache said. She was enjoying the moment. If nothing else, it helped take her mind off what she'd just witnessed.

Franks nodded.

"Ma'am?" the Bureau guy asked, his cuffs in his hand.

"Thank you, detectives. The pleasure has been mine." Franks forced a smile. "Put those away," she told her underling.

She then turned back to Rache.

"I suppose congratulations are in order, Detective," she said, offering Rache her hand.

Rache smiled back. "Thank you," she replied, shaking it.

Only then did Franks notice Fr. John. He had been standing back out of the way, trying to figure out the mystery that was Malak. If the Holy See got wind of this, there'd be an investigation. They'd never want it to get out. The Church had convinced its followers that it had cornered the market on salvation—something like this would upset the apple cart. Fr. John had more questions than answers. One thought that was foremost in his mind now, as he listened to Danny, Rache, and Liz tie Agent Franks up in knots, was if Malak no longer possessed physical form, if he'd returned to his world, what had happened to Kell?

"Why is he here?" Franks snapped, looking at Fr. John. "No, don't tell me. I don't want to know." Her hand shot up in protest at her own question.

The scene was mopped up quickly. The Caruso family were all taken into federal custody. Tony was the most vocal, screaming that a crazy man had attacked him, and he'd sue the police, the FBI, and the entire city of New York.

"Where have I heard that before?" Franks asked Rache, still feeling hard done by.

Rache just smiled. She told her about Tommy the Trigger and Tony's plan to make Liz suffer. Franks had to ask about Malak. Rache told her that they'd got the wrong guy—that they had to let him go once they'd discovered it.

"Let him go, let him go," Franks interrupted her.

But Rache held her ground, smiling back at Franks. Both Liz and Danny made a point of standing shoulder to shoulder with Rache, neither dropping their stare as they both eyeballed the Bureau agent. No one spoke. Franks quickly got the picture. Either she'd accept the deal, or she'd have a lot of awkward questions to answer. The balance sheet was a little out, but she knew that the credit column far outweighed the debit. On the plus side, she would have the entire Caruso family up on murder and attempted murder. The Bureau had been after them for years. On the minus, Fischer was still as evasive as ever. *What the shit*, she thought. She'd take the win.

"One last question, Detective Fischer?" she asked.

Rache nodded. "Shoot."

"Who was he? I mean, you found him at the scene. Who was he?"

"He was Kell Mason's guardian angel. He—"

Franks held up a hand, cutting her off. "Okay, okay, I get it. You don't want to say, well, okay. So what'll you put in your report?"

Rache smiled over at Danny. She told Franks that her report would read exactly as Detective O'Connor had outlined. NYPD owed the Bureau—and Agent Franks, in particular—a big favor for their cooperation in solving the Mason case.

Franks nodded, content. She left in a flurry, saying she wanted to get the paperwork started on Tony Caruso.

Rache accompanied Liz to the hospital. The paramedics had insisted both girls get checked out. As they arrived, Sam Weir met them. He told them that Kell had woken up. Liz broke down crying. She was immediately shown to Kell's room. Sam took Rache aside. As he tended to her wounds, he told her that they'd thought they were going to lose Kell. Her heart rate had begun to steadily increase. He'd been called when Kell exhibited more than 180 beats per minute. He'd tried to get it down, but it had continued to climb. As it reached over 300, he'd feared that her heart would give out. Kell had gone into a violent spasm at this point, and when he'd touched her, he'd been blown across the room.

But in seconds, Kell's rate had dropped back to just over 60, and the spasms had ceased. As he'd stood up, Kell had opened her eyes.

Rache smiled at Sam. She liked him. There were a lot of good people about. For every Tony Caruso, they were ten Sam Weirs. Only they didn't make the headlines.

Rache decided to go and see Kell.

CHAPTER 42

S ITTING AT A SMALL WINDOW table in Flaherty's, Rache mopped up the last of her Irish stew. Enjoying the flavor, she watched Fr. John heap his fourth spoon of sugar into his coffee.

He caught the look on Rache's face. He smiled, dropping another spoonful into the coffee. "Sugar hype," he said, stirring it now.

"You okay?" she asked.

"I'm still a little weak."

"Malak?" she inquired.

Fr. John told her he'd had trouble sleeping at night. He explained that much of his energy reserves had become depleted helping to keep Malak anchored in the physical world. It had been two days since the events, and everything was still hard for him.

"And the sugar helps?" she asked.

"No, the coffee helps. The sugar just makes it taste a lot better," he replied.

Rache laughed.

"Kell's improving?" he inquired.

"She'll be discharged tomorrow. She'll stay with Liz."

Fr. John was silent. The child had suffered. She'd seen her father murdered. It would be tough on her. "How much does she know?" he asked.

"She remembers nothing, but somehow I get the feeling she knows it all. She talks and acts just like him…" Rache stopped. She had to take a moment.

"You miss him?" Fr. John asked.

311

"Some, yeah. I still got a lot of questions. I wish I'd had more time, ya know. To talk to him about Ruth. Before he died, he showed me something," she said.

She told him. She told him about the vision she'd had holding Malak's hand.

"I know," Fr. John said.

"How?"

"I saw it too. When I anchored him, I saw it all. His world, his life, Kell's life, and Ruth's. I saw it all."

"No wonder you have trouble sleeping," Rache said as she let out a breath.

Neither of them spoke for a few moments, both reflecting on the events of the past few days.

"And your pal at the Bureau, Franks?" he inquired, lifting the cup to his lips.

Rache grinned, telling him that Franks had written up her report and given it to her the next day, so eager was she that they were all singing from the same hymn sheet. "She even insisted I be reinstated. Effective immediately," Rache said.

"So you're in the clear. You don't have to appear before a federal committee and explain the presence of guardian angels?" he asked, laughing.

"No. Plus all the DNA evidence has disappeared, along with all the photos of Malak. It's like he was never here."

"Must be hard on the others. The other cops I mean?"

"They're a little freaked," she said, laughing nervously. Rache recalled herself and Danny outlining the events to Woods, Theo, and Susan—of exactly who Malak was and his part in the whole drama. Woods had looked at her as though she had suddenly grown horns. "Right," he'd said, pausing, his long fingers scratching the back of his head. "Let's go with Danny's version—ya know, the one referring to Bureau-precinct cooperation that Franks is going with. I like that one. Think that works best. Rache, whatcha say?"

Danny and Rache had felt Theo's and Susan's stares.

"Works for me, Captain," Rache had agreed.

And they'd said nothing more on the subject.

Rache thought about it again. "You know, Father, in some ways, I envy them…their ignorance of the events…I envy them that. I can't go back to who I was. They can. I envy them that."

"But the question is, Rache, would you trade places?"

Rache shook her head immediately. "No!" She was a different person now. She was happier now. Well, not happier in the normal sense. But she was content.

"Ya know, Father, back in the warehouse…before you arrived, something happened," she said.

Rache told him everything.

"And you don't think it was just Malak helping you, do you?"

"No, Father, I don't."

"I see," Fr. John said. "And what else does he tell you?"

"He tells me I gotta see me a senator. There's no statute of limitations on murder. But there's something I need do first."

CHAPTER 43

RACHE STOOD ALONE, PERCHED ON the end of a springboard, her toes encroaching slightly over its edge. The fifty-meter pool shimmered in the reflection of the overhead lighting. It was late evening, and the gym would close shortly. Rache had requested, flashing her badge, if she could have some time alone. The instructor had told her to take as long as she liked. Detective Fischer was a strange one, he thought. She had been a member for years, but he'd never once seen her swim. Sure, he'd helped with her workout on occasion. Man, who wouldn't help Fischer? But he'd never seen her use the pool. "I don't swim," she'd snapped at him once. But here she was, asking for private time. What the hell, never know when ya might need a cop, he'd thought. He'd told her to take as long as she needed. Yeah, Detective Fischer was a strange one indeed.

Rache could smell the chlorine, its strong odor filling her nostrils. She'd never been able to swim since the night of the attack. She hadn't worn a swimsuit since that day.

Now, she stood and gazed at the water. It was almost glasslike—not a ripple to be seen. Rache closed her eyes. The familiar smell brought many memories flooding back. Memories of happier times, when she'd cut through the water like a torpedo, and all she had to worry her was her next race.

A small tear trickled down her cheek.

Rache opened her eyes and smiled.

Yes, tomorrow, she'd see her a senator.

Rache dived in, breaking the surface without making a splash.

THE END

CPSIA information can be obtained
at www.ICGtesting.com
Printed in the USA
LVHW081138100422
715818LV00029B/914